Diamondback CAVE

Diamondback CAVE

a novel by

K.L. Fogg

Covenant Communications, Inc.

Cover illustration © Thomas Tolman. For more information please e-mail tomtolman@tolmanbros.com
Cover design © 2008 by Covenant Communications, Inc.

Published by Covenant Communications, Inc.
American Fork, Utah

Printed in Canada
First Printing: February 2008

13 12 11 10 09 08   10 9 8 7 6 5 4 3 2 1

ISBN 10: 1-59811-512-X
ISBN 13: 978-1-59811-512-3

For my mother

Prologue

The red-haired woman sat in the metal chair with her arms folded resolutely across her chest and scowled at her visitor. People of her wealth and stature weren't accustomed to spending time in jail. Her large, penetrating gray eyes looked down her aquiline nose with contempt for her slightly younger and more attractive visitor.

The visitor was also a woman of wealth. Suntanned year round, and meticulously groomed, the forty-something woman with bleached blonde hair flashed the prisoner a disingenuous smile.

"To what misfortune do I owe this unwelcome visit?" the prisoner asked.

"Genie, you look good." The blonde searched for something more to say. "You really do," she added as if her initial statement needed some extra help to make it believable. "You're so lucky they don't have you wearing one of those horrible orange jumpsuits. You know what orange does to your complexion." She produced the fake smile again, to see if it would fare any better the second time.

"Yes, I'm so *lucky*!" the prisoner mimicked sarcastically. "I'm in wardrobe heaven these days."

The blonde pouted when her attempt to be friendly backfired. "It's not what you think, Genie," she responded. "We are doing everything we can to get you out on parole. It's just that this judge is a big fan of *The Snake Stalker* and she's making things very difficult for us."

"Difficult?" The woman scoffed. "I'm so sorry you feel inconvenienced while I'm obviously enjoying my accommodations here immensely. Might I suggest something to help ease your discomfort? Next time you come in here and try to convince me that you're on my side, you might want to brush up on your terminology. It's not *parole* I'm up for—it's *bail*. There is a difference."

The visitor shifted uncomfortably in her chair.

The prisoner continued as though she were speaking to someone of lesser intelligence, which in this case, she was. "Parole is for people who have been convicted of crimes and have already served part of their sentence. Bail is for people who have not yet been tried or convicted of a crime—a crime for which they may be completely innocent. I fall into the latter category."

"Right," the visitor stammered nervously, "bail—that's what I meant."

"Cut the charade, Feenie," the prisoner said. "I know that you turned me in, and you have absolutely no intention of posting my bail if and when the judge allows it."

"What?" The blonde touched a jewelry-clad hand to her chest in a gesture of righteous indignation. "How could you possibly believe that? We're family. It was that doctor on the island who turned you in. We all tried to get you out, but I got to the hospital too late!"

"That's right. A day late and a dollar short, or should I say two hundred *million* dollars short."

The blonde lowered her voice. "Tell us where you hid them, Genie, and we'll use the money to get you out, I promise."

"You *promise?*" The woman laughed heartily. "My darling sister stabs me in the back and then promises to pull the knife out!" she said bitterly and shook her head. "I would rather team up with Jack Mackey before I'd trust you again, Delphina."

"Genie, please. I'm begging you to tell us where they are. Peter is not going to like it if I come back empty-handed."

The prisoner clicked her tongue and shook her head in mock sympathy. "I thought Peter's reward was your empty-*headed* daughter."

Delphina struggled to keep from losing her temper. "You're making a huge mistake, because we're very close to finding them."

"Oh, really? Is that why you came to see me? To let me know how close you're getting? I'll be sure to make a note of it in my journal."

Delphina took a deep breath and forced it out through her nose.

"Don't attempt to sound intelligent, Feenie. It just doesn't work for you. You can take this information back to Peter. Tell him I'll give him a head start. He can get in his plane and start flying as far away from this continent as possible. Because in two weeks—with absolutely no help from you—I'll be out of here. She pushed away from the table and stood up, her large frame towering over her shrinking sister.

"That's a *promise*."

1

Wedding Plans

The cool, Georgia winter breeze rustled through the bare branches of a large weeping willow, making the air sound as chilly as it felt. Tiny ripples of water formed on the pond and the ducks cuddled underneath an evergreen bush, trying to keep warm. Wesley Mackey zipped up his jacket before dunking his paintbrush into the bucket and slopping some white paint on the gazebo in his front yard.

"Who gets married in February anyway?" he complained to his grandparents and his best friend Amanda. "I thought people only got married in the spring."

"They usually do, but my mom and Alex don't want to wait for spring," Amanda explained, blowing on her hands to warm them and adjusting the fleece headband holding back her dark hair. "If they aren't gazing into each other's eyes, they're kissing all the time." She shook her head. "It's disgusting."

"Disgusting?" Wesley's grandmother questioned. Grandma Penny sanded the peeling paint from one of the two-by-fours. "I thought you were the romantic type, Amanda."

"Oh, I'm totally for it, Grandma Penny," Amanda explained, "but romance is for *young* people, not *old* people in their thirties. And I say the sooner they get married, the better. Then they can start acting like married people and ignore each other."

"Hey, we're old married people, and we don't ignore each other," Grandpa Walter chimed in. "I tell Penny to fetch me my slippers at least twice a day."

"And I smack him upside the head at least four," Penny added.

Wesley dripped some paint on his shoe. "And speaking of *romance*, Amanda's boyfriend is driving up right now."

"Boyfriend?" Penny asked as she checked out the brand-new yellow truck with a lift and mag wheels pulling up into the long driveway beside the Mackeys' house.

Amanda looked up and sighed unenthusiastically. "Elliot is definitely *not* my boyfriend."

Wesley laughed. "But he really, really wants to be."

"What's wrong with Elliot?" Penny asked.

"Well, for starters," Amanda said as she counted on her fingers, "he's the lead singer in a *boy band*."

"So why is that bad?" Walter asked. "I thought girls always went for the rock stars."

"Elliot's not exactly a rock star." Wesley laughed. "But he writes songs for Amanda every chance he gets, and I'm pretty sure he has her wedding ring already picked out."

Amanda flicked Wesley's ear with two fingers. "Well maybe he wouldn't bug me so much if you'd stop encouraging him!"

"Ow!" Wesley retaliated by slashing his paintbrush across Amanda's cheek and decorating her with a stripe of war paint. He splattered Grandma Penny in the process.

"All right, y'all are fired!" Penny ripped the paintbrush out of Wesley's hand. "Go tell Romeo or whoever that he needs to get over here and paint the gazebo. He couldn't be any worse than you two. While he's at it, he can sing me a few songs. I wouldn't mind that."

Amanda wiped her painted face on Wesley's sleeve and then sprinted away quickly before he could return the favor. Wesley wasn't going to let her get away that easily and chased after her. Amanda took off across the big expanse of winter-brown front lawn and headed for the truck that was visibly vibrating from the heavy bass sound system. On the way there, she picked up a soggy tennis ball from the lawn to use as a weapon. She turned around and showed it to Wesley with a threatening look on her face and then walked with confidence over to the truck.

A skinny teenager with curly brown hair and caramel-colored skin hopped out of the driver's seat. "Hey Amanda, want to go for a ride?" he asked adoringly.

Wesley caught up to both of them. "Sure do," Wesley answered.

"Now that I got my license," Elliot drawled as he raised his eyebrows at Amanda, "I can take you out whenever I want."

"Elliot, I told you," Amanda explained. "We're just friends, remember? And I can't date until I'm sixteen, anyway."

"I can wait." Elliot smiled.

"That's nice, but that's a really long time from now, because I just barely turned fifteen."

Elliot pulled out his cell phone and pushed some buttons. "347 days, 11 hours, 26 minutes and counting."

Amanda shot Wesley a look that said "Help me now!"

Wesley was pretty good friends with Elliot, but he had known Amanda since he was born, so his allegiance sided with her.

"Elliot," Wesley said, "Amanda is moving this summer, and she might not even go to the same high school as we do next year."

Elliot gave Wesley a perturbed look. "She isn't moving that far away, and even if she was, a few miles isn't going to stop true love. Amanda and I are kindred spirits. Watch this new move," he said as he moved his arm in an undulating motion then straightened his elbow, made a spiral out of his wrist, and spun in a circle. He sang a few lines in perfect pitch, grabbed Amanda's hand, and slammed it to his chest. "Ooh girl, you're breakin' my heart . . ."

Amanda politely retrieved her hand. "Be careful with the pitching arm, please."

Just then the Mackeys' dog, Teddy, an enormous, black Newfoundland mix, bounded onto the scene, zeroing in on the ball in Amanda's hand. She took advantage of the diversion.

"Watch this—he's so fast!" Amanda said as she pulled back and launched the tennis ball. The ball went speeding through the air, but Teddy scrambled and caught it in his mouth right before it touched the ground.

Elliot seemed even more enamored when he saw how far Amanda could throw. "What an arm," he stated with admiration.

Teddy dutifully rushed the ball back to Amanda and dropped it at her feet. She was about to throw it again when her mother's car pulled into the driveway behind Elliot.

Amanda and her mother, Maria, lived in the guest-house on the Mackey property, which had originally been part of the expansive Scott Ranch owned by Wesley's grandparents.

"Oh look!" She pointed to the car. "My mom and Alex are back."

Alex Harris, her mother's fiancé, whom Amanda described as a nerdy James Bond, had rolled down his window and was talking with Elliot while Maria got out of the passenger side.

"Nice wheels, Elliot!" Alex shouted over the loud music.

"Hey thanks, Alex!" Elliot nudged Wesley. "He is like the coolest guy ever, don't you think?"

"Yeah," Wesley agreed. "It's good thing that you like him, since he's going to be your father-in-law someday."

* * *

Amanda took the opportunity to make a quick getaway by pretending her mother needed her for something. With her back to Elliot, she signaled her mother with exaggerated facial expressions that she wanted to be called away.

Maria motioned for her to come inside. "Why aren't you helping Penny and Walter?" Maria said with a Spanish accent. "And you have paint on your nose."

"Because Wesley got us fired." Amanda wiped her face with the back of her hand.

Maria handed a shopping bag to Amanda, and the two walked into their house through the front door, leaving the boys outside to talk trucks. "Well, we picked out the carpet for the new house," Maria said excitedly. She pulled a sample out of the bag and set it on the counter. "What do you think?"

Amanda looked at the carpet sample and scrunched up her nose. "Why are you asking me?" she asked with a hint of rudeness. "Looks like you already made up your mind."

"Well, you could have come along, but you didn't want to. Don't you like it?"

Amanda didn't say anything at first. "I like the carpet in *this* house."

"I know you don't want to move, but it's only a few miles away. We can't live in the Mackeys' guesthouse permanently."

"Why not? It's not like we need any extra bedrooms or anything. Alex can stay here with us. We like living here. They like us living here. Why ruin a good thing?"

"This was never supposed to be our permanent home. You'll still get to see Wesley all the time. It's time for us to be our own family."

"Really?" Amanda challenged. "Maybe I don't want to be our *own* family. I want to stay here with *this* family. Once we move, I won't be able to see Wesley all the time. I'll have to call first and ring the doorbell every time I come for a visit. You think some new carpet in a remodeled house is going to make up for tearing me away from all this and ruining my life?"

"This is not going to ruin your life. You're being overly dramatic. And very ungrateful. Alex has sacrificed a lot with his work just so we could stay in this area, and you're complaining because it's not enough."

"It isn't enough. Why don't you let me stay here, and you and Alex can move without me?"

"Amanda, sometimes change can be good. You have to give it a try."

"I guess I don't have any choice, do I?" Amanda said as she stomped down the hall toward her bedroom. It was the third time this week she had argued with her mother, and it was obvious nothing she said was getting through. To punctuate her last statement, she slammed her door.

* * *

Jack Mackey whistled his own tune as he opened the door to his house. It smelled like lasagna—one of his favorite dinners. In the kitchen, he spied the silhouette of his wife, Maggie, setting the table. He stopped whistling and planned to sneak up on her, but much to his surprise, the person who turned around wasn't Maggie at all.

"Whoa!" Jack recoiled like a spooked cat. "You know, Al, I about planted a kiss on you."

Alex looked at Jack and laughed. "Lucky for both of us you didn't. If you can't tell the difference between me and Maggie, you really should start wearing your glasses."

"Sorry, mate, but I'm holdin' out for an eyeball transplant. I guess things could get ugly if I don't start wearin' these, though." Jack reached into his denim shirt pocket for a pair of eyeglasses that weren't there. "Shoot! I guess I left them in the car."

A dark-haired beauty with a slim figure made her way into the kitchen. She walked over to her husband with a droll smile. "That's better than last time when you left them *under* the car." She gave Jack a quick kiss. "You don't need to set a place for Wesley," she told Alex. "He and Elliot went to get a burger earlier."

"Maria and Amanda went dress shopping," Alex explained to Jack, "and I was politely asked to stay home."

11

"Good call," Jack agreed. "It's best to set the ground rules right up front. No fashion skills, don't do shopping, and avoid the mall under threat of bodily injury. It's made our marriage a perfect heaven. Right, Mag?"

"What he said," Maggie agreed. "Speaking of shopping, wait until you see what I bought for the wedding with no help from my fashion-challenged husband today." She left momentarily and came strutting back into the kitchen wearing a pair of hot pink, spike-heeled shoes with ankle straps studded with rhinestones. She threw her jeans-clad leg up onto a nearby chair to show them off. "What do you think?"

Jack let out a whistle. "Uh—you'll never be accused of being frumpy, Mag," he said. "Those are *some* shoes."

"Well, I admit they may be a little over the top, but just wait until you see what they look like with my dress."

Jack clasped his hands together. "I can hardly wait to see how *fabulous* those shoes look with your dress."

"You're just humoring me. You really don't like them, do you?"

"This is what women do," Jack said to Alex. "It's a trap. But I know how to get out of it. Watch and learn." He turned to Maggie. "Mag, you could wear army boots and a gunny sack and still look beautiful."

"Good try," Maggie said. "Okay, maybe it worked."

"See, I told ya!" Jack slapped Alex on the back. "Ten days until the big one. Gettin' nervous yet, mate?"

"Actually no," Alex assured him. "I've been a bachelor way too long already. I'm pretty excited."

"So is Maria," Maggie added. "You two are so cute together. Here's a pointer, Alex. When your wife asks you nicely to do something, try to do it within three months. Jack, you said you were going to take a look at that hinge on the gun safe. It still slams shut all the time, and someone is going to get hurt."

"Who were you shootin' at today, Mag?" Jack asked.

"No one. Dad came over to borrow some ammo for his hunting rifle. The door swung shut and hit him. It nearly knocked him over."

"In that case, I think I'll leave it be. Keep Walter on his toes."

"You guys are the only people I know with a safe the size of a meat locker," Alex commented.

"Talk to Mag about that," Jack said. "It's all about style. She had to have it even though we only own three guns."

"It's an antique," Maggie said. "And it's not just for guns; I'm planning to put more stuff in there when I get it all sorted out. We also use it to store our legal documents."

"Oh, speaking of *legal*," Alex snapped his fingers, "I just remembered. Imogene's bail hearing is in a couple of days, and I'm going to be out of town, so I won't be able to be there."

"Another one of your Navy SEAL top-secret missions?" Maggie put two hot plates of lasagna on the table.

"No, I told you I'm not on active duty. I just need to do some interpreting for an interrogation. Can you handle this one without me, Jack?"

"I guess so," Jack said as he pulled three butter knives out of the drawer. "Maria is coming, so between the two of us we'll make sure she stays put." He put two of the knives on the table and handed the third to Maggie. "Here. See if you can stab me with this."

"What?" Maggie asked as if he were a lunatic.

"Come at me with the knife," Jack said as if that were a perfectly ordinary request. "I want to show you what Alex taught me."

"Okay, but you better stop me." Maggie took the butter knife and tried to stab him in the chest. He quickly grabbed her wrist and twisted the knife, forcing her to drop it.

"Hey, that's not bad," Maggie commented.

"I can teach you," Jack offered as he picked the knife up from the floor.

"You could, but I already know how to do that," Maggie said.

"Yes, but are you as fast as me?" Jack asked.

"We'll find out later when I'm not wearing four-inch heels."

"Well, if you're out of practice, then—"

Maggie took the bait, stepped forward, and grabbed Jack's wrist just as the phone rang. Startled, Jack dropped the knife before he had a chance to show off his defensive skills. He sighed. "Why do people always call at dinner time?"

Jack picked up the phone and muttered an annoyed greeting. "This is him." He gave Alex and Maggie a perplexed look, walked away, and had a private conversation for several minutes. After he hung up the phone, he shook his head and raised his eyebrows. "Well, speak of the devil."

"Who was that?"

"The devil's attorney."

Alex didn't need to ask for any more specifics on whom he was referring to. "What did he want?"

"To set up a meeting with Imogene."

"Imogene and who?"

"Yours truly."

Alex frowned. "Why?"

"Don't know. For all I know, she wants to marry me."

"Well, tell her you're already involved with a woman in pink shoes," Maggie quipped.

"She wants to meet tomorrow. Her lawyer said it's 'extremely important.'" Jack made quotes with his fingers.

"Are you going to meet with her?" Alex asked. "You don't have to talk to her if you don't want to."

"It's not talkin' to her I have a problem with," Jack said. "It's *listening* to her."

"My guess is," Alex scratched his head, "she probably wants to bribe you into helping her post bail."

"She can try, but I guarantee you that will not happen," Jack said with conviction. "That's about as likely as me and her gettin' married."

"How long has she been in jail now?" Maggie asked.

"Not quite eight months," Jack answered. "Actually, this might not be so bad after all. I don't mind talkin' to her when she's behind bars."

"Why is that?" Alex asked.

"Because," Jack smiled, "I can walk away, and she can't."

2

Deal or No Deal

Sitting at the table in a small, sterile room at the federal detention center, Imogene Vandergrift looked even more haggard than when Jack last saw her. Her hair was a lackluster red, and the skin around her mouth puckered into what could only be construed as frown lines. But her expression still conveyed the air of someone in control and someone ruthless enough to dispose of anyone who dared stand in her way.

As soon as Jack walked into the room, he felt as if every air molecule were threaded on a string and pulled tight. He had allowed the security guard to wait outside, because he knew that was the only way to get the unedited version of why his sworn enemy had called this meeting between them.

Jack locked eyes with Imogene's when he sat down in the chair directly across from her and immediately realized that this was another one of her power plays. Two and a half years of bitter history flashed behind her steely gray eyes. It was clear that she still considered Wesley her son, and she despised Jack for taking him away from her. The discomfort of the moment escalated, and in some unspoken contest they both knew that the first person to feel uncomfortable enough to look away or break the silence would lose.

Jack lost.

"You called me here. I assume it wasn't to get my autograph, so why don't you start talkin'?"

Imogene smiled patronizingly. "I want to make a deal with you, Jack."

Jack displayed his skepticism. "Well, that sounds . . . impossible. No thanks."

"You don't even want to hear what I have to say before you refuse my offer?"

"Nope," Jack said confidently. "There's nothin' you have that I want."

"Oh, really? The safety of your family doesn't interest you?"

"Is that a threat?"

"It might be. But it doesn't come from me. You know Peter Jaworsky is still at large. I would think you'd be interested in seeing him get his just reward."

"And you think you can make that happen?"

"Yes, I can, but I need you to make sure Peter doesn't get his hands on a very large cache of diamonds."

"Wait a minute. I already know that you think I'm stupid, but am I to assume that you want to hire me to get your diamonds back from the crook that tried to murder my two best friends? I'm supposed to believe that you like me now, and this is perfectly safe, and there's no chance that I'll be killed or maimed for life in the process?"

"No, Jack. Listen carefully. I don't like you. In fact, I detest you. You're an arrogant, reckless, second-rate actor who doesn't deserve to raise Wesley."

"Aw c'mon, tell me how you really feel."

"If you would listen to me for one minute, you might learn an important piece of new information. I don't want you to get my diamonds *back,* because the diamonds have never been out of my possession."

"If you have them, then why are you askin' me to get them?"

"I'm not asking you to get them. I just need you to make sure Peter *doesn't* get them. And that is in your best interest, because as long as Peter is looking for those diamonds, Wesley isn't safe."

Jack cocked his head. "So, assuming you do have possession of said diamonds, what I'm not gettin' here is why not send one of your own comrades to pick them up?" Jack slapped his hand on the table. "Oops! I forgot; they're all in jail too." He leaned back on his chair. "I guess this is a new low for you, isn't it? Of all the people you could get to do your dirty work, you come crawling to me."

"Believe it or not, Jack, this is an assignment you are uniquely qualified for. We both have something to gain from this arrangement. Besides the fact that we're both concerned for Wesley's safety, I am smart enough to see that we can work together on this. In this case, the enemy of my enemy is my friend. I am the only person who knows the exact location of the diamonds, and I am the only person who has access to them. And you are the only person standing in the way at my bail hearings."

"Aw shucks, that's very flattering, but I can't take all the credit. There are several people standing in the way at your bail hearings."

Imogene continued as if she were laying out a business plan. "I want you to convince the judge to let me post bail, or better yet, get me released on my own recognizance.

Just make it happen. After you succeed in securing my release, I'll take you—and any law enforcement officer that you choose—to the diamonds. I'll unlock the safe, turn the diamonds over to the authorities, and my good behavior will give me some bargaining power at my trial in three months. It's a win-win situation for both of us."

Jack laughed. "Sure it is. So to sum it up: I bail you out, you lead me to the buried treasure, and then you bribe a judge and skip the country and we all live happily ever after."

"It's a bit more complicated than that, but we'll keep it simple. We wouldn't want things to go over your head. I don't plan to leave the country, because I know I have a solid case in court—a case that I fully intend on winning. Either way, you have my word that I will leave you and your family alone if you agree to help me get released before my trial. So do we have a deal, then?"

"Let's see." Jack scratched his head as if he might seriously consider her request. "You've kidnapped my son four times—or was it five? You stole my baby daughter and threatened to sell her on the black market. You tried to murder me and my wife by burning us alive and then threw Alex and Maria out of a plane without a parachute. And here's an oldie but goody— the time you blinded me with a spitting cobra. A while back I was stupid enough to save you from drowning. You so kindly repaid me by setting me up for your murder when you weren't even dead. But that's all in the past. I can trust you now, because we have a common enemy. I have to admit, I'm a little curious as to what you had planned to do to me this time, but I'm not an absolute moron. I'm thinkin'. . . NO DEAL." Jack slapped his hand on the table to punctuate his answer.

"This isn't a game show, Jack. You have three days to make up your mind. When you realize what I'm offering you, I'm willing to bet my freedom that you'll be back."

"That's a bet you've already lost, mate. You've turned my life into a real-life comic-strip adventure. I like the way it ends right here. Good guy still alive. Bad guy in jail."

"Aren't you even curious where the diamonds are? Two hundred million dollars in the wrong hands could be very dangerous."

"Are we through here?" Jack yawned.

"Not until you agree to my proposal and tell the judge to let me out on bail."

Jack stood up and leaned forward on his fists so that his face was just inches from Imogene.

"Never."

* * *

The blonde, blue-eyed toddler threw her sippy cup full of milk onto the kitchen floor, making it clear to her mother that the current beverage container was unacceptable. Maggie scolded her daughter and picked up the cup.

Jack observed the scene. "I just don't get what she's after, Mag."

"She wants me to give her a bottle, but I'm not giving in. Emily has been drinking from a cup for over a month, and C.J. should be too."

"I wasn't talkin' about C.J.," Jack clarified. "We were discussing Imogene and her groveling. She was beggin' me to help her out. I don't think she even has any diamonds."

"I don't know. The police never found the diamonds, or Peter Jaworsky. Have you talked to Alex about it yet?"

"No, he's gone until after the bail hearing tomorrow."

"Well, you know that Imogene is a charlatan; she lies about everything, and she's out to destroy you. You didn't even entertain her suggestion, so that will make her mad and she'll try some new mind game. Just make sure you show up at the hearing tomorrow, and she doesn't get bail. You can't let her scare you into letting her out."

"I won't. The only thing that scares me is lookin' straight into her face for too long." Jack shuddered and covered his eyes. "I think I may have some permanent damage from that last visit."

"Well, be strong," Maggie said. "At least we have an honest judge who knows what's at stake here."

"Yeah, and I think the judge has a crush on me too. She's a big fan of *The Snake Stalker.* I'm going to bring her some of my DVDs."

"You can't do that. That's bribing a judge," Maggie informed him.

Jack shrugged. "Is that bad?"

"Normally, yes. But I guess not in this case." Maggie handed a cookie to C.J.'s twin sister, Emily, who looked nothing like her sister but was a mini-image of her mother with her dark curls and green-hazel eyes. "Just skip the DVDs and wear that blue shirt that brings out your eyes. Is she pretty?"

"Who? Judge Warner?" Jack shrugged. "About as pretty as Walter, but she trims her mustache better."

"Well, bat your eyelashes at her and do whatever it takes to keep Imogene in custody, because if she gets out, we're in big trouble. It's been a relatively uneventful seven months since she's been in jail. I don't think that's a coincidence."

"Not a coincidence," Jack echoed. He picked up C.J. and she reached for the cup in Maggie's hand. Jack took it from Maggie and handed it to the toddler. "Go on, C.J., give it a good throw—try to hit the wall this time!"

"Jack, stop encouraging her to misbehave!"

"I'm not. It's reverse psychology, Mag. Watch this. Come on, Carly Jane, let's see what you got!"

C.J. promptly threw the cup and hit the wall, breaking the lid off and spilling milk all over the kitchen floor.

Maggie sighed. "That was great. Maybe you need a little brushing up on your parenting skills."

"Are you kiddin'? Did you see that arm? It takes a special parent to bring out a kid's talent like that."

While Maggie handed Jack a rag to wipe up the mess, Bob the fat calico cat waddled into the kitchen with a piece of toilet tissue stuck to his back paw. He made a beeline for the spilled milk.

"What's Bob doing over here?" Jack motioned to the cat that belonged to his in-laws next door. "And when did he start using the bathroom?"

"Bob!" Maggie scolded. "Aren't you in enough trouble already?" She looked at Jack. "He's in the witness protection program, and he's currently hiding out in our house."

"That explains it."

"Dad put a price on his head because he keeps unrolling their toilet paper and then shredding it with his claws. Yesterday Dad told me to either declaw him or decapitate him, so I agreed to declaw him. But I ran into some problems."

"Like what kind of problems?"

Maggie walked over into the laundry room next to the kitchen and returned holding two poster-board signs taped onto wooden stakes and one that was folded down the middle. She held the first sign up.

Jack read the sign out loud. "Stop the torture and humiliation of Bob." Maggie switched signs so Jack could read the second one.

"Give Bob another chance," he read.

"Wesley and Amanda claimed it was cruel and unusual punishment to declaw Bob, so they formed a picket line."

"What does the third sign say?" Jack asked.

"Equal rights for cats and dogs," Maggie answered. "That was Teddy's. I don't think he would have agreed with the politics, but he was just happy to be included in the march."

Jack pushed Bob out of the way so he could finish wiping up the spilled milk. "Sounds like a busy day yesterday. So now Bob shreds our toilet paper instead?" Jack asked.

"Until he gets permission to return home, I guess he does." She set the signs down on the counter.

"Why not just close the doors?"

"Like that could stop the Purrminator."

A miniature Chihuahua about one-fourth the size of Bob scampered into the kitchen and tried to get in on the cleanup committee. Bob swatted at him with his paw.

"So where's Hercules's sign?" Jack asked as the animals started a face-off in the middle of the kitchen. "Let me guess—it was written on a Post-it note."

Just then Amanda came running into their house, like she usually did, without knocking. She was out of breath and looked very upset.

"Jack and Maggie," Amanda said, "we have a really big problem."

"What is it?" Maggie put her hand on Amanda's shoulder.

"I just can't believe it." Amanda shook her head.

"What's the matter?" Jack threw the soiled rag into the sink.

Amanda took a deep breath and looked as though she might burst into tears. "Alex called off the wedding."

3

Conspiracy Theory

Several hours later, Maria sat on the Mackey's family-room couch with a cup of cocoa clenched in her hands. She wasn't drinking it but appeared to be bracing herself against the cup to keep her body from collapsing. Her face was stained with tears, and her eyes were red and swollen.

"Maria, I'm so, so sorry." Maggie touched her arm affectionately. "We're all so shocked by this. I just can't believe that Alex would tell you something like this over the phone—without any warning."

"He sounded so—indifferent." Maria set her cup of cocoa on the coffee table. "Like he was reading lines off a cue card or something. No explanation or trial separation or anything. He just said, 'I can't marry you, Maria. Please don't try to call me, because it'll just make things worse.'"

Jack was pacing the floor. "What a lousy, good-for-nothin'—"

"Jack, please!" Maggie put out her hand. "We don't have all the facts yet! Something is very wrong here.

27

Alex may be having some sort of mental breakdown. This just isn't like him. Maybe he has posttraumatic stress disorder. It could be a number of things. Sometimes people just get nervous, that's all."

"Yeah, like the time you left what's-his-name at the altar?" Jack said.

"That was different." Maggie gave Jack a disapproving look. "Brian Edwards wasn't the right person for me, and it just took me a little longer to figure out. And it wasn't the day of the wedding; it was a week before."

"And that's different than this because this is *eight* days before the wedding?"

"What are you saying, Jack?" Maggie asked. "That I should have married Brian even though I didn't feel good about it?"

"No, I'm just sayin' that things like this happen all the time. And maybe you can explain to us what Alex is thinking, since you've been in a similar situation."

"I have no idea what Alex is thinking right now, but we shouldn't judge him on his motives when he's not even here to defend himself."

Wesley and Amanda had been talking in another room and came in to join the conversation. "Alex would never leave you, Maria," Wesley said resolutely. "Amanda and I agree that something strange is going on here."

"Like what kind of strange?" Maggie asked.

"Maybe he's been drinkin'," Jack said.

"He doesn't drink," Maria defended. "And he didn't sound drunk. You know what a health nut he is—he doesn't even drink soda!"

"Well, maybe somehow his carrot juice got fermented," Jack commented. Maggie shot Jack another punitive glance.

Maria hung her head. "I appreciate what all of you are trying to do here, but I have to face the facts. Alex doesn't want to marry me. For whatever reason, he doesn't love me. I can't blame him for that. I'd rather find out now than after the wedding. I'm so sorry to drag all of you into this. It's not your problem."

"Maria, you aren't dragging us into this," Maggie said. "You're like family. And so is Alex. You can always come to us. I just wish we could do something to help you."

Maria nodded. "Thank you. I'll be okay, really." She didn't appear to be okay as she got up off the couch to leave. "I guess I better call the caterers first thing in the morning. If you hear from Alex, will you let me know?"

"Of course we will," Maggie said. "You can stay here tonight if you want."

Maria shook her head, got up to leave, and shut the door behind her.

"This is absolutely tragic," Maggie said after Maria was gone.

Wesley punched a number on his cell phone and put it up to his ear. "He's not answering calls from me," Wesley said. "I think Alex has been kidnapped."

"Wes," Jack said gently, "I know it's not out of the realm of possibility for people in this family, but just because Alex is having second thoughts about marriage doesn't mean he's been kidnapped."

"Dad, I *know* Alex. He wouldn't do this. He was in love with Maria, and he still is. Someone forced him to break up with her."

"Like who?" Jack asked. "The anti-marriage thugs?"

"I don't know, but we have to find out."

"Show them that picture, Wesley," Amanda said.

Wesley held out his cell phone. "I've been trying to get in touch with Alex all day, even before I found out about this, but he never answered any of my calls."

"That's not unusual when he's at work," Jack stated. "Besides, he's not going to involve you in his personal problems."

"It's really strange that he told me he was going to translate for a court case, because this doesn't look like anywhere near a courthouse." Wesley looked at the screen on his phone. "He wouldn't just randomly send me this picture. Take a look." Wesley handed his phone to Jack and Maggie.

"What are we looking at?" Jack asked.

"A photo that Alex sent me at 4:17 this afternoon."

"A waterfall that's half out of frame?" Maggie asked.

"And it's upside down," Wesley added. "And you can see that this is the entrance to a cave.

"So Alex is leaving Maria to become a cave-dwelling hermit?"

"No, he's not leaving Maria. He's trying to show us where they've taken him. That's why it's upside down. He probably had to take the picture and send it without anyone noticing." Wesley waited for a nod of agreement from his parents. The look on their faces told him he wasn't going to get one.

"He's a secret agent!" Wesley said emphatically. "He's got top security government clearance. There are plenty of people who might want to kidnap him to get information out of him."

"That picture was sent before he called my mom," Amanda added.

"Then why didn't he send it to Maria—or me?" Jack asked. "Or even the police?"

"Probably because he knows I would be the only one who would understand what this means," Wesley said, starting to get frustrated. "I'm on his speed dial. And I always check my messages."

"I know this conspiracy theory of yours is easier to accept than the fact that he and Maria aren't meant to be," Maggie said, "but it's not the most likely scenario."

"Since when does anyone in this family fall into a 'likely scenario'?" Wesley threw up his hands.

"Wes," Jack said, "let's just suppose you're right for the sake of argument, and Alex has been kidnapped. What can we do about it? Take this to the police? Whoever he's workin' with is probably already on it. We have no idea where this is, and to go sticking our nose into other people's business might put us and Alex in even more danger."

"We may not know where it is, but we could ask someone," Wesley said.

"Like who?" Jack asked.

Wesley hesitated. He didn't want to say her name, but he had to. "Like Imogene. I think she has something to do with it."

Jack made the sign a football referee makes when the kick is no good. "Wait a minute. No way. Don't even think about it. I am NOT going to see her again for any reason."

"What kind of friend are you?" Wesley stood up and moved closer to Jack. "Why can't we just talk to her? I'll go myself. I'll bet you a hundred bucks she knows what's going on and where this place is."

"And I'll pay you a hundred bucks to stay out of this, Wes." Jack pointed his finger at Wesley. "If Alex is in trouble, then he has the experience to get out of it. The guy is a Navy SEAL with a black belt in karate.

He's got all kinds of skills. He's not only the smartest guy I know—he jumps out of planes with no parachute and lives. If anyone's dumb enough to try and take him as a hostage, then I feel sorry for *them*. He'll handle it. And I know Alex would be really disappointed if we did anything that might help Imogene post bail and escape. She's not going to talk to us unless we get her out, and if she gets out, none of us are safe!"

"Alex isn't safe!" Wesley threw his hands up and stomped on the floor. "He's counting on us to help him. How can you even *think* that he would do this to Maria?"

"Wes, I've been around a lot longer than you," Jack explained. "All's fair in love and war. Alex will probably call back tomorrow when he comes to his senses. We aren't going to fall for any tricks to get Imogene out of jail."

"You're being a coward!" Wesley shouted at his dad impulsively.

"That's enough, Wes!" Jack shot back.

Wesley bolted from the family room and ran up the stairs. In all the time he had lived with his dad, they had never raised their voices at each other this way. He sat down at the computer at his desk and looked at a screen saver slideshow of family pictures. His face was hot, and he was already regretting he had yelled at his dad. Amanda had slipped quietly out the back door when the argument got heated, and he planned on calling her in a few minutes.

Wesley could hear his dad and Maggie talking downstairs and opened his door a crack to listen. He crept down a few stairs so he could hear more clearly.

"Jack, I think we've underestimated the trauma he's been through in the past three years. It's time to have him see a specialist."

"You think he needs a psychiatrist?"

"Don't you? He's obviously paranoid—and I can't blame him. He doesn't feel safe, and he thinks every time something bad happens, it must be a kidnapping and Imogene has to be behind it. But you didn't help matters by not validating his feelings. He really is worried."

"I know, Mag. I shouldn't have gone off on him, but I'm not mad at him; I'm mad at *her*. Imogene has turned him into a paranoid kid. I'm mad at Alex too. Why can't he get his act together? The invitations have all been sent out . . ."

Wesley's phone vibrated, and he went back into his room and closed the door to answer it."

"That went badly," Amanda said.

"No kidding."

"I thought Jack and Alex were best friends."

"I thought so too. I never expected that reaction. That's probably why Alex sent *me* this picture instead of my dad. Right now they're talking about sending me to a shrink so I can deal with reality. My dad thinks I'm paranoid. How's your mom?"

"She's really bad. She's convinced he's left her, and she's crying in her room. We have to find Alex, Wesley. I can't bear to think what my mom would do without him. And I've been really rotten about not wanting to move. Alex probably thinks I hate him."

"He knows you don't hate him."

"Well, if he really did leave my mom, it would be because of me. I have to talk to him, Wesley, and apologize. Can't we do some research and find out where this place in the picture is?"

"Maybe. This place—it kind of looks familiar to me."

"You think you've been there?"

33

"I don't know. But a lot of the caves are concentrated in the northwest part of the state. That's where Imogene took me last year. We could drive to the general location in two hours maybe, but I don't know how we'd find this exact spot."

Wesley thought for a minute. "Wait a minute! Alex has a GPS on his phone, and he might have sent me the coordinates to this place along with the picture. Let me check." Wesley punched the keys on his phone.

"I can figure out exactly where this picture came from," Wesley said. That's why he sent it to me. Why didn't I think of that?"

"So what good are coordinates?"

"Coordinates can be plotted on a map, and a map can take us there."

"Let's go there then, first thing in the morning."

"Wait a minute. My dad is really not going to go for this. You heard him. He said we needed to stay out of it. Also, he wouldn't miss Imogene's bail hearing tomorrow, even if we were abducted by aliens."

"Then we'll go alone. We'll cut school, and nobody will notice we're gone until 3:30. When we find the place, we can call Jack, and he'll have to believe us."

Wesley hesitated. "I don't know. I can think of about a dozen reasons why that isn't a good idea. First of all, I don't like cutting school."

"You are such a nerd. You were suspended from school for two months last year, and you feel guilty about missing one day?"

Wesley realized that it was a weak argument. "It's just that I've had a clean slate this year, and I don't want to get labeled as a troublemaker."

"Get over it. Sacrifices have to be made."

"Then there's a second problem: transportation. Whose car are we going to steal to get there?"

"I admit, that is a problem."

Wesley's screen saver popped onto the computer again. A photo appeared of Wesley and Elliot standing in front of his new truck. "Maybe not. I can get us a car—driver."

"Really?"

"I have this friend who has a really nice truck . . ."

"Let me guess—is it yellow?"

"Yep."

"Please don't do this to me."

"Sacrifices have to be made. Think about your life if Alex is gone—think of your mom."

"Okay, okay. I'll call Elliot. But he just drives us there and drops us off. He isn't going on any expedition—he'll blow everything."

"I don't think you understand," Wesley said. "This is going to be awfully dangerous. If Alex really has been kidnapped, then this isn't safe at all."

"Of course it isn't safe. That's why we're the only ones who care enough to do anything. Have you noticed that every time someone gets into trouble, I'm always left at home twiddling my thumbs? Everyone else comes back with these big adventure stories, and I just get to smile and nod my head. To be perfectly honest, I'm tired of it! I'm just some loser with no stories and a boring life."

"A boring life is better than no life. It's not going to be fun, Amanda. There is a really big chance that things will go wrong."

"I say *bring it on*."

"Okay, as long as we're clear on that. I'll work on the directions, and you call our driver and tell him to pick us up at the bus stop tomorrow morning at eight."

4

Desperate Measures

Wesley and Amanda waited behind the bushes at the bus stop. They had purposely missed the bus, and now they were trying to keep themselves hidden so that some well-meaning neighbor like Mrs. Porter wouldn't see them and insist on giving them a ride to school. That was an easy enough task for the two of them, but trying to hide an oversized black dog with a hydration backpack strapped around his neck was another story.

"I don't know if you should have brought Teddy along," Amanda said. "What if Maggie notices he's gone? She'll start looking all over for him."

"She isn't going to notice, because he sometimes goes to the stables with Grandpa, and she'll just think he's there."

"But what if Walter starts looking for him?"

"Then that'll keep them busy for a while. But they won't notice. We need Teddy. He's the closest thing we have to a bloodhound. I stole a dirty shirt from Alex's room over at the barracks." Wesley referred to

37

the summer cabin accommodations on his grandparents' property, where Alex had been living for the past ten months. "I'll tell you, that was hard to find. The guy is a clean freak."

"I know. Feel sorry for me now. My mom is too, and I'm going to have to live with both of them."

"Let's hope you get to live with both of them," Wesley reminded her. "Now, let's check out the arsenal. What did you bring?"

Amanda rummaged through the pocket of her hooded sweatshirt. "Slingshot." She pulled it out for display.

"What else?"

She pulled out a small canister on a string. "Pepper spray." She put it around her neck. "It's also a flashlight."

"Is that all?"

"Yeah, that's all, besides licorice and gummy bears. I don't exactly have firearms just sitting around. What did you bring?"

Wesley produced a black revolver from Teddy's backpack.

Amanda gasped. "Where did you get that?"

"At the toy store. Calm down. It's only a paintball gun. Looks real though, doesn't it?" He put it back when he saw the yellow truck pull up. "I got some beef jerky and this. He pulled out a flat, metal six-pointed star with a hole in the center that fit into the palm of his hand."

"What's that?"

"A hira-shuriken. It's a Japanese weapon."

"What do you do with it?"

"Are you kidding? You throw it. If you have the skill to throw it right, it can slice a finger off."

"Do you have the skill to throw it right?"

"No. But they don't know that."

"So, basically you brought bluff stuff."

"Yes, but bluff stuff can be very effective. Anyway, we aren't planning on engaging the enemy, just gathering information so we can prove Alex has been kidnapped."

The yellow truck pulled up to them, and Elliot jumped out so that he could help Amanda climb in the truck first and make sure she would be sitting next to him. "You know I'm missing band practice for you guys today," he said grumpily.

"Elliot, we'll make it up to you by coming to see your band play every night." Amanda said cheerfully. "We wouldn't ask you for this huge favor unless it was a life or death situation."

"Yeah well, it would be nice if you told me what the situation was."

"Elliot," Wesley said. "We really appreciate this, and we'll pay for your gas. But you're on a need-to-know basis. You'll have to trust us for now, and we'll explain everything after it's all over. You can just drop us off, and you'll be back in plenty of time for practice. Is it okay if Teddy sits up front with us?"

"Sure." Elliot waved him in. "Any dog that weighs two hundred pounds can pretty much sit where he wants. And why is he wearing a Camelbak?"

Wesley pulled out a computer-printed map. "It's full of Gatorade, in case we get thirsty. Do you want some?"

"No, thanks. I'll pass."

* * *

He was back in the high-rise building again. When the last attempt to use the stairs failed, he made his way out onto a floor where dozens of people were working behind their gray cubicles.

"Could someone please tell me how to get out of this building?" Inside he was frantic, but his voice was calm.

"Certainly, sir. Just take the elevator to the first floor."

"I've already tried that, and for some reason the elevator doesn't open on the first floor."

The woman looked at him passively. "Hmmm, that's strange. You'll have to try the stairs then." She went back to her paperwork.

"I tried dozens of stairways." He tried to make her understand. "But they only lead to other rooms. None of them open to the outside of the building."

The woman shrugged as if it weren't her problem to deal with.

He left and ran down two more floors of stairs. On every floor he would ask an uninterested person where the exit was, and they either gave him similar instructions, or ignored him completely. He wanted to scream. There was no way to get to the first floor. The stairway door was locked on the first floor, and the windows wouldn't open. It was an impossible situation. There was no way to get out of this building.

At some point he became vaguely aware that he was dreaming again, but as frustrating as it was, he didn't want to wake up. He needed to know the answer. He ran up more flights of stairs until he opened the last door that led to the roof. He must have gone up thirty stories before he found a door to the outside. But now there was no way down but to jump.

A man with a nearly shaved head and a three-day beard growth appeared and started to laugh. "You can't leave this place unless I say so," the man said. "As you can see, there is no way out."

Alex opened his eyes to total darkness. He became aware of the hard, rock surface beneath him. He was lying prone with his hands tied together at the wrists. Another heavy rope was wrapped multiple times around his ankles. It was too late to go back to his dream; he was fully awake now. It was pitch-black all around, except for the tiny speck of light so far above him that it didn't do him any good.

Alex reached up with his bound hands and touched a sticky wound on his forehead. He would have wondered if that had caused his blindness if he didn't already know that he was in a dead-end section of a cave. His recurrent nightmare was coming true. It wasn't the first time he had dreamt he was trapped inside a building with no exit. He had experienced the same dream at least five times, and he kept wondering what it meant. Now he knew. There would be no exiting this cave without encountering Peter first.

Alex's body ached all over from Peter working him over, but his heart ached even more. Yesterday Peter had held a gun to his head and forced him to tell Maria he didn't want to marry her. One slip to her that he was being held captive and Alex knew Peter would have killed him immediately. When he said the words, they came out monotone, but they hurt him like someone had stuck him with a hot poker. He could only imagine that Maria felt the same way.

The skin on his wrists was raw, and he was bruised all over. But by now he was pretty much numb to the physical pain. He couldn't die here, letting her think that he'd left her. He hadn't consumed a morsel of food or drop of water since yesterday, and he was tired, weak, and thirsty. If he'd been through worse situations as a Navy SEAL in training or in combat, he couldn't remember them.

The sound of footsteps and the reflection of light alerted him that Peter was coming back and that his time on this earth was about to end. He prayed that after his death, Maria would eventually find out the truth about what happened. Peter walked in and shoved a bright fluorescent lantern into Alex's face. Alex could feel his pupils constricting to the size of pinheads as he squinted against the light.

As his eyes adjusted, he observed the high ceiling. He already knew that the room was fairly large from the distant light and echo, but it still appeared that there was no passage out other than the tunnel that led him here. If only his dream could have continued for another minute, he might have gotten an answer.

A sickly, clear-brown, scorpion-like creature scurried up the limestone wall by Alex's head. Peter picked up the insect and waved it in Alex's face. "You know what this is?"

Alex didn't answer.

"It's only a cave cricket." Peter sounded impressed with himself. "One of the many really ugly insects that call this place home. Peter put the insect down on Alex's body. "Sort of makes me wish we would have brought your fiancée along so she could appreciate the wildlife." Peter laughed. "Oh wait, I forgot. She's not your fiancée anymore. She's completely unattached. If I remember correctly, she's pretty good-looking too, if you're into the saucy-little-latina types."

Alex wanted nothing more than to get free from the ropes that bound him and do whatever was necessary to stop Peter from uttering another word. With his nearly shaved head and sinister smile, Peter was much uglier than the cave cricket.

"You know, Alex, I'm beginning to think you don't have a clue where those diamonds are. And as you know, I'm not a very patient man."

Alex needed a stall tactic. He looked up for some sort of inspiration. After thirty feet, the ceiling faded into blackness. He looked down at the pasty white ground. "It's pretty easy to get disoriented in here, but I know where I am now. I can take you there."

"I don't think so. You're becoming a liability to us now."

"If you find the safe, you'll need me to break the code."

"*Break* the code?" Peter laughed. "Good job, Harris. You just blew your cover. If you had any idea how to get your hands on the diamonds, you would know that I didn't bring you here for your code-breaking skills. You think Imogene has some combination lock on a safe somewhere? Or maybe a chain and padlock for your bicycle? It's just a bit more technical that that. The safe is voice activated with an iris scan. Imogene has to be there in person to open it. But we know there is one other person who was programmed to open it too. You used to work for her when you were pretending to be me, so I thought maybe it was you. But now I'm sure it's not."

"If you're so sure it's not me," Alex said, "then how do you plan to open the safe if you do find it?"

"Good old-fashioned dynamite. Messy, but effective. I've got a couple of pounds of PETN with some TNT. We shouldn't have any problem."

"You'll blow up the diamonds along with the safe."

"That is a possibility. That's the only reason why we brought you here alive, Alex—to exhaust all our other options before moving on to more desperate measures. I'd keep you around a little longer and give you the job of lighting the fuse, but I don't think that would be prudent." Peter pulled out a gun and cocked the trigger.

"Before you shoot me, you might want to move to another location," Alex said as he pointed to the ceiling of the cave.

Peter kept his gun aimed at Alex and looked up to see what Alex was referring to.

In a split second, Alex rolled onto his side and kicked the lantern over with both feet. The bulb shattered, extinguishing the only source of light inside the cave.

Peter fired his gun, and Alex felt the bullet rip through the top of his shoulder and kick up pieces of debris around him. Peter cursed and took another shot, this time missing Alex completely.

The sound of multiple gunshots in an echoing cave didn't sit too well with the occupants high above them. In seconds, the ringing sound in Alex's ears turned into an earsplitting screeching noise, accompanied by a thousand drums of featherless wings. The furious animals swooped down from the ceiling in a frenzy, their sonic hearing set off by the reverberating sound waves. In their fear and frenzy, they bombarded without mercy, inadvertently hitting both Peter and Alex in the face and head and screaming in their ears.

Alex lay facedown on the ground, his tied hands at his face, thankful that the bats had been hibernating up there and that the gunshot had set them off.

Peter shrieked and thrashed around, trying to keep the bats off him. The bats forced him back toward the tunnel entrance. A portion of the swarm continued to pursue him into the tunnel as Peter managed to turn on his backup flashlight. The illumination of his situation only made things worse. The bats were so thick that he had no choice but to retreat down into the cave passage.

Alex was plunged back into the darkness, but at least he was still alive for the time being. He felt a sharp pain in his shoulder. It definitely stung where the bullet went through the top of the skin, but it felt like a fairly superficial wound. Even so, he was bleeding, and he was already dehydrated. He rolled onto his back to catch his breath. He didn't want to be facedown if he lost consciousness.

A shard of glass from the lantern bulb dug into his elbow. He scooted over so he could reach it. After trying to sit up and discovering that took too much energy, he decided to stay horizontal. With the tips of his fingers, he worked the shard and tried to cut the ropes that bound his hands. It was fragile and broke after several tries. He felt around and picked up another piece and repeated the procedure with the same result. This was going to take a lot of time, but giving up wasn't an option. If he succeeded in freeing himself, he could at least crawl to another section of the cave so Peter wouldn't be able to find him. He didn't know what he would do after that. It was impossible to find his way out of there without any light. *One thing at a time, Alex,* he told himself.

He listened to the screeching bats and occasionally felt one hit him. He didn't really mind—after all, they had saved his life, even if it was only temporarily.

Blind as a bat, he said to himself. *My kingdom for a flashlight.*

5

♦

The Trap

Even in the winter, the barren trees and rocky outcrop-
pings in northeast Georgia were beautiful. Wesley and
Amanda stood in front of a scene that clearly matched
the picture Alex had sent on his phone. A massive rock,
layered in sandstone wedges in various hues of tan, gray,
and peach loomed ahead. From where they stood, the
waterfall looked as though it was running directly out of
a spigot that was turned on inside the stone structure.
Narrow at the top, the water cascaded down the rock
and widened at the bottom, where the water fanned out
and ran into a stream winding deep into the forest.
Behind the waterfall, just like the picture had shown,
there was an alcove that appeared to be the entrance to
a cave.

Wesley opened his phone, turned it upside down,
and matched the picture Alex sent him with the landscape in front of him. He set his phone to camera and
took several pictures. "Are we good, or are we good?"
he said to Amanda.

"We are *so* good," Amanda concurred. "Less than two hours to drive here and fifteen minutes to hike in."

"And all you had to do was promise to go to your first prom with Elliot in order to make him leave us here," Wesley said.

"Yeah, well, sacrifices had to be made. But now I'm not so sure we should have sent him home. The cave is pretty on the outside, but it looks a little creepy to go in."

"You're not going to wimp out on me now, are you? We know Alex is here—or he *was* here—so we aren't going to leave until we at least take a look around."

Teddy was busy lapping up water from the stream, and Wesley called the dog over and wrapped the leash around his hand. He pulled Alex's shirt out of Teddy's backpack and let Teddy smell it.

Amanda checked the pepper-spray flashlight around her neck and zipped up her hooded sweatshirt.

Teddy pulled against the leash wrapped around Wesley's hand. "Easy, boy. Stay," Wesley ordered.

"Look at the trail leading into the cave." Amanda motioned to the worn-hard piece of ground. "If this is some secret place, why does it look like a bunch of people come here all the time?"

"It's probably a tourist attraction. Look at the sign over here." Wesley hiked over to a freestanding, wooden sign that was partially buried in a tangle of dead vines. He pulled off the vines and read the faded letters. *Diamondback Cave.* Wesley pulled his phone up again and took a picture. "I'm sending this to my dad."

"Good idea. I'm sending Alex another text."

"Wait a minute! You're sending text messages to Alex?" Wesley said.

"Yeah," Amanda said as if Wesley were stupid. "It's not like he's sending any back, but if he can get to a spot where his phone works, he'll know we're out here looking for him."

"You idiot!" Wesley grabbed her phone away. "You told him that we were here now?"

"Why not?"

Wesley sighed and rolled his eyes. "If Alex has been captured, he probably doesn't have his phone anymore. They've taken it from him. You just let the bad guys know we're here!"

Amanda looked at the ground. "Oops. I guess I'm pretty new at this."

"I should have sent you back with Elliot," Wesley said in exasperation. He looked up just in time to see two people coming out of the cave. "Oh great! Someone's over there. Get behind those trees." Wesley shoved Amanda into a thicket.

They were partially obscured by the sign and the brush, but they had to crouch down to stay hidden. Teddy wasn't as quick and stood out in plain sight as two men came walking out of the cave entrance. One of them lit a cigarette. Wesley and Amanda were too far away to identify either of them with any certainty. Wesley didn't dare issue a command for Teddy to come for fear of calling attention to their location.

"I think that's Alex," Amanda whispered. "I recognize his brown leather jacket."

Wesley squinted and nodded. "It looks like him from here. But his back is to us. It doesn't look like he's being held against his will. Who is he talking to?"

Amanda shrugged.

"I'm going to see if I can get a closer look," Wesley said. "Stay here with Teddy."

Wesley stealthily crawled through the brush, staying hidden from the clearing in front of the cave. The rushing waterfall made enough noise to block out the sound of crunching dry leaves, so the two men wouldn't be able to hear him. But at the same time, he couldn't hear them either. The man who appeared to be Alex still had his back to him, but Wesley could see the smoker was a hard-looking man with three days of beard stubble that was about as long as the hair on his head. Wesley shivered. His guess was that this person wasn't a friend to Alex or anyone else he knew.

Suddenly, Teddy barked, and the man he thought was Alex turned around. It definitely wasn't Alex.

Teddy went running at a full sprint toward the two men and took a bounding leap toward the one in the leather jacket. The man with beard stubble dropped his cigarette and pulled out a gun, aiming it directly at Teddy. Wesley stood up and screamed, "No!" He realized in horror what he had just done.

Teddy growled and ripped into the sleeve of the man in the leather coat.

There was nothing Wesley could do. The man had a clear shot at Teddy and now Wesley. It looked like Teddy was going to take a bullet, but before the man could fire his weapon, a projectile from Amanda's location came sailing through the air and hit him in the arm. The gun flew out of his hand and onto the ground several yards away from where Wesley was hiding. Wesley's only thought was if the man got to his gun, he would shoot Teddy and maybe him, too. He ran as fast as he could and dove for the gun. But he didn't get very far. The man was much faster than he was. And stronger, too. In a few seconds, the man had picked up his weapon with one hand and grabbed Wesley by the arm with the other.

"Call off your dog, kid!" the man ordered.

Wesley looked at the man and weighed the odds of kicking him and running away. They weren't good at all. He ordered Teddy to stop, and Teddy complied. Wesley braced himself for the inevitable flogging to come, but instead of manhandling him, the man stowed his gun back in his coat pocket, looked at Wesley's face, and laughed heartily. It was a sinister laugh, the kind of laugh where you don't want to know what the other person thinks is so funny.

"This is just too good to be true, Harlan." The man shook his head in disbelief. He appeared to know Wesley, but Wesley had never seen this man before in his life.

"Who are you?" Wesley demanded.

"A friend of the family," he said without an ounce of sincerity. "Hey, Harlan," he said to the man in Alex's coat. "Looks like our little fishing expedition paid off. We caught ourselves a big one!" He held Wesley up like a he was showing off a trophy. "See this boy here? He's our winning lottery ticket."

* * *

Maggie pulled her car into the drive-through at the bank. C.J. and Emily were strapped into their car seats in the back of her Lexus SUV. Her phone rang, and she shuffled through her purse to find it. The call was from Wesley's phone, and he wasn't supposed to use his phone during school hours, so she thought he might be calling home sick.

"Hello?" she answered apprehensively.

"Maggie." Wesley sounded like he wasn't feeling well at all. "Um, something bad has happened."

"What is it, Wesley?" Maggie picked up on the panic in Wesley's voice. Hopefully he wasn't getting suspended again.

"Amanda and I are in a lot of trouble."

"What kind of trouble? Do you need me to come to school and get you?"

"No. We didn't exactly go to school today. We went to look for Alex."

"You *what*?" Maggie's apprehension turned to fear.

"There's a man who wants to talk to you," Wesley said. It was silent, and then a man's voice came on the line.

"You really should teach your son not to ditch school, Mrs. Mackey."

"I'm sorry—who am I speaking with?"

"Someone who has your child's life in his hands."

Maggie didn't like the tone of his voice. What kind of people were they hiring at school anyway?

"What are you talking about? Cutting school isn't a capital offense!"

"Well, it doesn't have to end that way if you coop-erate."

"Cooperate?" Maggie suddenly realized she wasn't talking to a school official.

"Yes, cooperate. You see, a certain mutual friend of ours has taken something that belongs to me. I want it back. If you get it back for me, I'll make sure that Wesley and his pretty, brown-eyed friend get home safely. To be perfectly blunt, if I don't get it, I'll kill them both."

Maggie's senses seemed to leave her, and she felt her heart pound erratically. This couldn't be happen-ing. Not again. "Don't hurt them!" Maggie cried. "I'll cooperate. But I don't know what you want—I don't have anything."

"No, *you* don't, Maggie, but Imogene Vandergrift does. You and your husband have the ability to get her released from prison until her trial. I happen to know that she's at a bail hearing right now. If you want your children back, you'll have to bring her to me in person. When she returns the item in question, you can have the kiddies back, and I'll even make sure Imogene never bothers you again. Is that clear?"

"But we don't have any control over whether she gets bail," Maggie said.. "That's the judge's decision."

"I disagree with that. You can be very persuasive."

"This is Peter Jaworsky, isn't it?" Maggie demanded. "I can't believe it. Wesley was right—you kidnapped Alex."

"Well, believe this. You bring Imogene to me, or your son, like Alex Harris, will be the victim of a very unfortunate accident."

Maggie gasped at the implication that Alex was dead. She refused to let herself process that information right now. "Let me talk to Wesley again."

"No, I don't think so. We're wasting time now. You have until six tonight—that's about seven hours—to comply with my request. If you decide to delay or call the police, I'm not going to show any lenience. I have some very powerful explosives in my possession, and I won't hesitate to use them. Oh, and I really don't like cops. I have a short fuse with them, if you know what I mean."

Maggie was in shock and could barely speak. "Why are you involving us? Your fight is with Imogene. She isn't going to do what we ask."

"She will. Just tell her I've got her long-lost son— that will give you some leverage. She knows where to find me. We're down to six hours and fifty-seven minutes. Have a nice day." He hung up.

K.L. Fogg

"Wait!" Maggie dialed Wesley's phone again, but there was no answer. She called Jack and Maria, but she knew they wouldn't answer because they were at the bail hearing. *The bail hearing.* She called information and asked to be connected to the courthouse.

When the receptionist answered, Maggie calmly said, "I need to speak to Jack Mackey immediately. This is an emergency. Yes, I know that he's in a closed hearing. Like I said, this is an EMERGENCY. Please send someone in to get him to come out right away." She sighed and waited for a response.

"I don't know what room it's in—it's Imogene Vandergrift's bail hearing!" Maggie checked the girls in the backseat. She didn't want them to pick up on her distress, but she was too upset to calm her voice. "No, I will not hold!" Maggie answered. "Look, if you can't find the room, then find someone who can—just do it now!"

Maggie held the phone away from her ear as the woman proceeded to give her the riot act about being polite.

"I'm not being rude—I need to stop this hearing because I have some very important information. Please, I'm begging you!"

The woman hung up on her.

Emily started to cry, which was exactly what Maggie felt like doing. Instead she pushed the gas pedal to the floor and drove over the median, clipped a stop sign, and sped into the intersection.

* * *

Imogene stood silently in front of the judge with her recently dyed hair coiffed, in full makeup, and wearing an expensive navy blue pantsuit. She appeared as though she were in a boardroom, not a courthouse, and that at any minute she might fire the judge and all the various underlings in the room for not carrying out her orders.

The judge cleared her throat and addressed the defense attorney. "Based on the information presented to me by the people and on the information I've received from you, Mr. Carlisle, I still believe that Imogene Vandergrift poses a significant flight risk based on her past history."

"But Your Honor," Imogene's attorney stated, "my client has the right to be granted a speedy trial and has not been found guilty of any offense and has agreed to cooperate fully with the authorities in apprehending a far more dangerous criminal."

The judge looked at Jack Mackey, who was sitting on one of the benches looking dashing in dress khakis and a crisply pressed blue shirt and tie. She looked back at the defendant. "Although Ms. Vandergrift is presumed innocent, I cannot ignore the serious nature of the charges of multiple kidnappings and attempted murder. In this case, it is my first responsibility to consider the safety of the entire Mackey family."

The defense attorney consulted the notes on his desk. "Your Honor, if you'll allow me one moment . . ."

* * *

Maggie jammed her foot on the accelerator and turned sharply off the freeway. She sped up through the yellow light at the intersection and cut off a city bus, ignoring the honks of angry motorists. The commotion had put C.J. to sleep, but Emily was wide-eyed and sucking on her fingers nervously. Maggie's grip on the steering wheel was so tight, her hands were white.

Her thoughts were in a whirl. She couldn't imagine how Wesley and Amanda had ended up in the clutches of a hardened killer with ties to Imogene. It had to be Peter Jaworsky—and he may have already killed Alex. She shuddered but wouldn't allow herself to cry. That would mean believing that it was true, and she kept telling herself that it wasn't. She didn't know how she was going to break the news to Maria. She decided she would leave that part of the conversation out. Maria would be hysterical enough just to find out about Amanda. Peter might just be trying to scare her. And he was doing a good job of it.

She had to concentrate on her driving and get to the courthouse fast. So far she hadn't attracted the attention of the police, but she was sure several people were probably calling the cops to report her reckless driving. The traffic was mild downtown and she spotted the court building up ahead. She quickly weaved in and out of cars and illegally parked in front of the building. With the keys still in the ignition, she ripped both girls out of their car seats and tried to soothe them with her voice.

"We're going to see Daddy!" she said in a falsely excited voice.

"Wessy!" Emily clapped her hands.

"No, Daddy first, then Wesley." Maggie ran up the steps two at a time, holding a toddler on each hip. "I hope we're not too late."

* * *

The judge adjusted her glasses and picked up her gavel. "Therefore, until the trial date, I am denying bail for—"

The judge was interrupted by a frantic woman bursting through the doors, packing two small children.

"No! Wait a minute!" Maggie was flushed and out of breath, her hair blown all over her face.

Jack stood up from his seat. "What's going on, Mag?"

"I will have order in this courtroom!" The judge pounded her gavel.

"Please," Maggie implored the judge. "I have some new information, and I need a few minutes to talk with my husband and Maria Perry."

"I'm sorry, but I'm going to have to ask you to leave," the judge said sternly.

"Ten minutes!" Maggie pleaded. "Please, ten minutes—that's all I need. This is extremely important, Your Honor."

"Is that okay with you, Mr. Carlisle?"

The defense attorney studied Maggie and nodded his head.

"We'll reconvene at 11:45." The judge tapped her gavel and set it down.

"What's this all about, Mag?" Jack rushed over to Maggie, and Maria was already by her side. "Why did you bring the kids?"

"Jack, we have to get Imogene out. She has to get the diamonds for us or he'll kill them both."

"Who is going to kill who?" Jack asked.

Maggie swallowed hard. She looked at Jack and then Maria. "I don't know for sure that it's him, but I'm pretty sure Peter Jaworsky has Wesley and Amanda." She turned to Maria and couldn't hold the words in. "And Alex, too."

6

Bailing Out

Wesley and Amanda sat on the cave floor with their backs against a crate full of explosives. They were in a small room with four walls formed naturally by the cave and sealed by a heavy metal door. The room had a glass window in it just like at old movie theaters, and above the window outside a sign read *Ticket Office*. The room was electronically lit and devoid of furnishings except for a rusty metal desk with a broken drawer and one metal stool that looked even less comfortable than the floor.

The man who was wearing Alex's jacket was standing in front of the only exit with a grenade in one hand. So far he had been pretty congenial for a thug. He didn't look like a bad guy, either. He had an athletic build, a boyish face with light brown eyes, and dimples that punctuated both cheeks. A person could only look so tough with dimples. And he couldn't be more than twenty-five. He looked more like the type who would be into computer software than demolition projects. Wesley and Amanda had been talking to the guy, trying to get some information out of him ever since they had been dumped in here.

"So Harlan," Wesley said, "is that your first name or your last name?"

"Either or both." He shrugged.

"Where'd you get that jacket?" Amanda asked.

"Santa Claus gave it to me," he answered.

"Are you holding anyone here besides us?" Wesley questioned.

"Will you stop with the questions?" Harlan was getting impatient with them. "I'm not supposed to be talking with you. So keep quiet and we'll both stay out of trouble, okay?" He tossed the hand grenade up in the air and caught it, like it was a visual aid.

"Okay," Wesley agreed. "But can we talk to each other?" He pointed to Amanda and then to himself.

"As long as I don't have to listen." Harlan turned his back to them.

Wesley took the opportunity to motion to his sock, reminding Amanda that he had stowed the shuriken in there. Amanda nodded and fingered the pepper-spray necklace under her sweatshirt. The rest of their arsenal, along with their cell phones, had been confiscated.

"Thanks for saving Teddy," Wesley said to Amanda. "But I'm sorry you got caught."

"I wasn't going to let him shoot Teddy. Especially since it's my fault they found us."

"I'm glad he got away." Wesley directed his voice toward Harlan and turned up the volume.

"Yeah," Amanda said just as loudly. "Teddy could rip a person to shreds if we give him the command," she said.

"But it's not too safe for anyone else," Wesley said. "You know he hasn't had his rabies shot for quite awhile."

"Your dog doesn't have rabies." Harlan examined the tear on his jacket sleeve. "And he didn't bite me anyway. That is some big dog. Looks like a Newfoundland."

"Hey, I thought you weren't listening!" Amanda said.

"I'm not." Harlan turned away again and started making some sort of sculpture out of miscellaneous pieces of wire.

"I like Harlan," Wesley said. "He seems like a pretty good guy, don't you think?"

"Yeah," Amanda said. "I wonder how he got mixed up with a criminal like Peter Jaworsky."

Harlan whirled around.

"Oh sorry, were we talking too loud again?" Amanda said. She had Harlan's attention now. "Peter is pretty well-known in my family after he tried to murder my mom and Alex," Amanda said. "And we can assume Alex is here somewhere, because that's his coat you're wearing." She motioned to Harlan's jacket.

"This isn't exactly a one-of-a-kind leather jacket. And I just borrowed it from my brother."

"Then you don't need to worry that Alex is a Navy SEAL and can kill a man with his bare hands," Wesley said.

"I can take care of myself," Harlan assured them.

"Well, that's good to know," Wesley said. "You won't need our help then."

"Oh, like I need help from a couple of kids." Harlan laughed.

"We're *teenagers*," Amanda corrected. "And we have more skills than you think."

"Amanda knocked a gun out of Peter's hand with her slingshot once," Wesley bragged. "I bet she could throw that grenade farther than you and with better accuracy."

"Well, whoop-de-do." Harlan swirled his finger in the air. "Those skills are what got you into trouble to begin with. If you would have kept that slingshot in your pocket, and your dog on his leash, you two wouldn't be a couple of worms on a hook right now. All you are is fish bait." Harlan put the wire sculpture in the pocket of Alex's coat and paced back and forth. Wesley noticed he had a limp.

"What happened to your leg?" Wesley asked.

"Nothing," Harlan said.

"Then why are you limping?"

Harlan made a fist and knocked on his thigh. It sounded hard and solid. "Sounds good to me."

"You have a fake leg?" Amanda ventured.

Harlan nodded.

"Wow. How'd you lose your leg?"

"Didn't anyone ever tell you it's not polite to ask that?" Harlan snapped.

"Did anyone ever tell you it's not polite to kidnap people, steal their coats, and threaten them with grenades?" Wesley retorted. "I'm just curious. Did you blow it off with dynamite or something?"

Harlan looked through the ticket-office window and then walked uncomfortably close to Amanda and Wesley. For a moment Wesley thought he might slap him for being so impertinent. He was getting ready to apologize.

"Wasn't an accident that took my leg," Harlan confided as if there were something sinister behind his missing limb. He rolled up the leg on his jeans and showed them his prosthesis. "It was my brother."

Amanda gasped and then cleared her throat to cover up the noise she had just made. She and Wesley looked at each other. Maybe it was time to stop asking questions. They were quiet for a moment, and then Harlan sat down on the stool.

"You know," Harlan seemed to be warming up to them after he got that out of his system, "this used to be the best place in the world when we were kids."

Wesley got the impression Harlan really didn't belong here, and that he wanted to tell them something. Now that he and Amanda had passed some sort of test by not overreacting to his leg, they were worthy of his confidence.

"You used to play here when you were little?" Wesley asked.

"All the time. This cave is basically my backyard. There's even a swimming hole about a half mile underground. You could play there all day, and your parents would never find you. Of course, sometimes they didn't want to find you." Harlan smiled as if remembering something very vivid. Then his expression turned cloudy. "That was before they ruined it all."

Wesley hoped his question didn't get Harlan upset again. But he had to ask. "Who ruined it all?"

"Some kid who was where he shouldn't have been. It was a fluke accident."

"What happened?" Wesley asked.

"Some kid about your age was playing in the swimming hole when he drowned. He had no business being here. He didn't respect the cave and had no idea what he was getting into. Five other kids were with him at the time, but the water's so deep, they couldn't get to him. Stupid kid. Thought he was going to find some treasure down there, but there wasn't anything to find. After he drowned, his family forced the county to come in and close the place down. They gated the south tunnel and sealed it off so nobody could get through anymore. Then they took the bridge down and barricaded the front entrance just to make sure." Harlan shook his head. "What they didn't understand is that other things besides people live in here. They messed up the whole ecosystem of the cave." He motioned through the glass window to where the front entrance had been boarded up but then taken down again. "All on account of somebody who made a bad decision."

"That's a sad story," Amanda said. "Did you know the kid who drowned?"

Harlan furrowed his brow. "Yeah, I knew him."

* * *

In the room outside the judges' chambers, Jack walked around with clenched fists while Maggie talked on her cell phone and Maria stared vacantly at the wall. The air was thick with fear and raw emotion. Emily and C.J. had each gained possession of a permanent marker. Emily was scribbling on her arm with hers, and C.J. was doodling on the front of her shirt, but no one cared. Everyone in the room had more important things to worry about.

Jack shook his head and slammed his fist into his palm. "I can't believe we just did that," he said with regret.

"We had to, Jack," Maggie said. "We didn't have any other choice. If we didn't convince the judge to let her out on bail, we'd have no chance of bargaining with Peter. If we had just listened to Wesley and Amanda. They were right."

"They were right, but they're still in trouble!" Jack emphasized. "Why would they take off and go looking for Alex by themselves? They should know better than that!"

"They should know better," Maggie repeated. "But now we know that Alex didn't leave Maria."

"But we don't know if he's still alive," Maria said, coming out of her trance. "I keep wondering if I missed something when I talked to him yesterday. Maybe he was trying to send me a coded message over the phone without making it obvious. I just don't know. But I do know that Peter Jaworsky is a horrible person, and he's definitely capable of murder." She stopped to wipe a torrent of tears from her face.

"Maria." Maggie put her arm around her. "We can only pray for all three of them now. Penny and Walter are coming out to pick up you and the girls."

"No, I'm going with you!" Maria protested.

"You can't," Jack told her. "We only have permission for me and Maggie to bring Imogene."

"But Imogene doesn't care about Amanda—she might give up her diamonds for Wesley, but she won't bargain for Amanda. There's no reason for Peter to let Amanda go."

"We won't come back without both of our kids," Maggie assured her. "I promise you. You take care of the girls, and we'll call you as soon as we know anything."

"And don't call the caterer yet," Jack said. "We'll bring Alex back in time for the wedding."

"It's going to be all right," Maggie assured her. "You better go before they bring her out."

Maria nodded wordlessly, but the tears kept pouring out of her eyes. She took C.J. by the hand, picked up Emily with her other arm, and walked out of the room to meet Penny and Walter in the hallway.

* * *

The bailiff led Imogene into the room with Jack and Maggie. Imogene's expression flaunted the fact that she had been the winner of this round. She smiled smugly at Jack. "You put up your house for collateral, Jack. Very interesting, I must admit. This takes crawling back to a new level."

Maggie touched Jack's arm as a warning not to respond to her comment.

Jack looked at the bailiff. "Thank you. We'll take it from here."

The bailiff exited the room, leaving the three of them alone. Jack stared at Imogene. He could hardly refrain from striking her. "Do you have any idea why we got you out?"

"Because you know my offer makes sense," Imogene said.

"No, that's not it," Jack said sternly. "You're coming with us in the car right now, and on the way there we'll brief you on what's going to take place."

"I didn't agree to that, Imogene said.

"Yes, you did, and so did your lawyer," Jack reminded her. "You said you would cooperate fully in finding a more dangerous criminal. Now start walkin'. We don't have a lot of time."

Imogene walked briskly out in front of Jack. "And just where are you taking me?"

"That's what you're going to tell us," Jack said.

Harlan vs. Harlan

Alex came in and out of his dream. Or maybe it was a hallucination—it was hard to tell. Every once in a while he would hear a bat fluttering by, but by now they had either left the cave through the small exit at the top or had gone back to their upside-down perch on the ceiling. He was beginning to get a crawling sensation and wondered if the cave cricket had returned with its friends and family or if it was some other form of vermin. He sensed some other being in the cave near him but then chalked it up to being severely dehydrated and in shock. He had tried to leave the cave, but he couldn't find the exit, so he just lay on the ground, trying to find his bearings so he wouldn't waste any more precious energy running into the walls.

His shoulder was drenched in blood, but he didn't feel the pain anymore. The biggest discomfort was the cold, and his muscles were spent from shivering. It became increasingly difficult to stay conscious. There was nothing to see, and it was hard to convince his eyes they needed to stay open. Darkness enveloped him, and the feeling that something or someone was nearby grew stronger. He was sure that he could hear it breathing—maybe even detect a heartbeat in the dead silence. Anything that breathed that slowly had to be a large mammal. Humans, bears, and mountain lions were the only things he could imagine fitting the bill.

Alex tried to tell himself he was hallucinating and that the animal was just a stray bat that had refused to resume its perch. Maybe a rat. Perhaps the sound was magnified by the cave acoustics. Something furry brushed against his skin and with quick reflexes he rolled away from whatever it was. He crossed "human" off the list of possible suspects. He was thankful he had been able to cut the ropes from his hands and feet earlier, but he was still as helpless as a newborn kitten against whatever was stalking him. For sure the creature wasn't a bat or a rat. It felt much larger. Alex's heart raced as he sensed a looming presence only inches away. And then his worst fear materialized.

It licked his face.

Alex reached up to protect himself although at the same time realizing that whatever this creature was, it didn't want to eat him. In fact, without his sight, he noticed that his other senses were much more acute, and the animal had the familiar smell of a dog. His fear turned to relief as the animal brushed against him again. What would a dog this friendly be doing wandering around in a dark cave like this? Alex felt for a collar and was amazed at the thickness of the dog's neck. This was not an average-sized dog.

"Teddy?" he asked. The dog answered by licking him again.

"Teddy, it *is* you. You are the best dog in the world!" He patted him and felt the Camelbak he was wearing. With a sigh of gratitude, he found it was full of liquid. He felt around for the hose and took a long drink. He could feel the liquid refilling his shriveled veins.

Lime Gatorade. Wesley must have filled this. He must have gotten the picture I sent. "Who did you come with, Teddy?" he asked as if the dog could answer him. He felt around in the zippered pocket and found a small flashlight. He turned it on.

Alex searched the rest of the zippers and found a pocketknife with a compass attached, a granola bar, and some beef jerky. "When we get home, Teddy, I guess you can inherit my kingdom—for what it's worth."

Alex tried to stand, but he was weak and wobbly. Teddy's leash was dangling, so he picked it up and wound it around one hand. "Now I'm putting you in charge, big guy. I'm assuming if you found the way in, you can get us out."

* * *

Harlan had returned after a short absence from the room where Wesley and Amanda were locked in and began working on a wiring device. For the past hour he had been talking to himself—even calling himself by name—and scolding himself for not doing things right. He no longer talked with Wesley and Amanda but kept snapping at them if they uttered a word. He had refused them drinks of water or a trip to the restroom, which was across the cave, near the entrance.

"Harlan," he said to himself, "these kids are not your friends, and you're not here to entertain them. Quit telling them stories and get the job done."

"Harlan," Amanda said. "We like your stories. Especially about how your family used to own this cave and give tours all the time."

"Well, story time is over!" Harlan snapped. "And quit calling me Harlan."

"That's your name, isn't it?" Wesley was trying to understand this sudden change in temperament.

"I hate it when people call me that," Harlan answered. "Call me Eddie. My name is Eddie."

"Okay, Eddie," Amanda said slowly. "We're sorry if we made you angry."

"Then quit asking Harlan so many questions."

"I thought you just told us to call you Eddie," Amanda said with a look of confusion.

"That's right. You two are getting way too cozy with Harlan. Just stay out of this."

"Wait, there are two of you, then?" Wesley asked.

"Are you stupid?" Eddie said angrily. "Of course there are two of us!"

"And you're identical twins," Wesley noted. "Wow! You two are hard to tell apart. That's interesting because my mother is an identical twin too. My sisters are fraternal twins."

Eddie sneered at Wesley's attempt to find common ground. "That's really interesting," he said sarcastically. "But we aren't like them. We're even closer than twins."

Amanda started to ask another question, but Eddie interrupted her.

"He probably told you it's my fault he doesn't have a leg." He moved closer to Amanda and waved an accusing finger at her. "Didn't he!"

Amanda scrunched down to appear as small as possible. "Yes," she said weakly.

"And you believed him?"

"I don't know." Amanda put her hands up. "We were just wondering why he had a limp."

"Well, it wasn't my fault," Eddie said angrily. "I had nothing to do with it. I'll tell you what you need to know. I'm the boss around here. Not my idiot brother. Got that? He doesn't know how to wire the fuse—I do. He's thinks he's the demolition man, but I'm the one with the brains. He does *what* I tell him to do and *when* I tell him to do it. And so do you." Eddie paced nervously and pulled out the grenade from Alex's coat pocket. He held it up to show them. "See how careless he is?"

Wesley and Amanda were too dumbstruck to say anything.

"I'll be back. Don't you go anywhere near that door. You understand me?"

Amanda and Wesley nodded assuredly.

He closed the door behind him and locked it from the outside with a key.

Wesley waited for several seconds to make sure he wasn't coming back before he spoke. "That guy is psycho."

"No kidding." Amanda nodded. "And now there are two of them. I hope Harlan comes back instead of Eddie."

Wesley shook his head. "Don't you get it? There aren't two of them. Harlan is Eddie. Eddie is Harlan. He's schizophrenic—with a multiple personality disorder. It's like two different people living in one body."

"I don't know," Amanda said. "They could be twins."

"Yes, they *could* be, but they're not. Didn't you notice? Eddie said they were *closer* than twins. How can you be closer than identical twins? They are the same person. And if they're not, why are they both

71

wearing the exact same clothes? Both of their green shirts say *Diamondback Cave Tours* on the front, they both have on Alex's jacket with a rip on the sleeve, and they both have a limp."

"Maybe they like to dress alike," Amanda countered, "and Eddie didn't seem to have the same kind of limp."

"But he still had one. Maybe the limp is a little different, but that's what people with split personalities do when they turn into their alter egos. Maybe Harlan used to have a brother named Eddie who died. Maybe he was the kid who drowned in the underground pool. Harlan probably never got over it, and now he's deranged. You even said Harlan seemed too nice to be working for a guy like Peter. Now we know why."

"Maybe you're right. But what difference does it make? Regardless of whether there's one or two of them, we're still locked in here."

"This could work in our favor if we play it right. We know that Harlan is the good guy and probably doesn't want to hurt us. We need to try to get his personality to come out. Maybe we can persuade him to let us go."

"How? It's not like we're psychologists or anything. It might backfire. And he could turn back into Eddie at any time."

"Well, we'll have to be careful about what we say. He seems pretty sensitive about his leg—maybe that's what triggered Eddie to come out. Eddie also said Harlan didn't know how to set the timer, so maybe that's why Eddie took over—he has to do things Harlan doesn't understand."

"Does each personality know about the other one?" Amanda wondered. "Can they talk to each other?"

"I don't know exactly how it works. We know Eddie knows who Harlan is, but we haven't heard Harlan refer to Eddie other than to say his 'brother' took his leg."

"That's a little creepy. Probably the accident that cut off their leg was Eddie's fault—even though he said it wasn't. This is starting to make sense now."

"I know," Wesley said. "And Eddie always wants to be in control too. So he must be the dominant one."

"Or maybe Harlan is dominant and Eddie is trying to take over."

The noise on the lock caused them to put an end to further speculation. Eddie or Harlan was back. It appeared to be Harlan, just because he wasn't scowling. He wasn't wearing Alex's jacket anymore, and when he spoke, there was no trace of Eddie in his tone. "Okay boys and girls, I say you can have a bathroom break."

"Thank you, Harlan!" Amanda said.

Harlan grunted a response. Wesley was careful not to sound too pleased, just in case Eddie would think Harlan was being too soft and decide to resurface.

Wesley noted the layout of the cave as they headed to the bathroom. This place must have been a thriving tourist attraction before they shut it down. There were several rooms and a small alcove with iron bars on it that looked like an elevator. The bathrooms had been cleaned and were in working order. That meant that people had been working on the cave premises for some time.

After they returned to the ticket office, Harlan even handed them each a piece of red licorice. It looked like the same licorice Amanda had put in her sweatshirt pocket. Wesley and Amanda hesitated before taking a bite.

"Where did this come from?" Wesley asked.

"Where do you think?" Harlan answered. "I stole it from Eddie."

Wesley looked at Amanda, nonverbally telling her he was about to try something. "Harlan, do you know that Eddie is trying to control you?" Wesley ventured.

Harlan blanched. "He doesn't control me—he only thinks he does. It's been this way since we were little. He's always trying to get into my head."

"So he talks to you?" Amanda asked. "Just like I'm talking to you now?"

Harlan made a face that showed he thought Amanda's comment was absurd.

"Is he the one telling you to keep us here against our will?" Amanda continued. "You don't really want to do this, do you, Harlan?"

Harlan sighed. "You don't really know what's going on here, do you?" He looked at Wesley and Amanda intently, as if he wanted to share something but was waiting for an invitation.

"I guess we don't," Wesley admitted. "But you can tell us, Harlan."

Harlan nodded and pulled up the stool and sat down like he was preparing them for another long story. Amanda and Wesley sat cross-legged on top of the old metal desk and leaned forward to show they were a captive audience.

"What's going on here is a lot bigger than you or me," Harlan began, "or some buried treasure." Harlan paused for effect and used generous hand gestures to make his point. "People don't understand. They never have. This cave—it's teeming with life. There are fascinating insects, reptiles, and mammals in here. But they don't just live in the cave, they *are* the cave. People come here and they try to tame the cave—think they can control it by sealing it off or destroying it." Harlan shook his head, drawing Wesley and Amanda into each word by speaking slowly. "But this cave knows how to protect itself. I've seen it time and time again. If it feels threatened, it's going to fight back. This cave can swallow all of us whole. So it doesn't matter a hill of beans what you or me or anyone else does. The cave is going to win."

8

Off the Cuff

The red, 1969 Camaro with a white convertible top sped down the back country road. Jack was intentionally jerking the steering wheel at each turn in order to make the passenger in the backseat as uncomfortable as possible. Imogene tottered in the back of the car; her hands were handcuffed together, the left one attached to the door handle. She wasn't fastened in her seat belt, and every time Jack lurched around the bend, she was thrown from side to side.

Maggie was sitting in the front passenger seat, massaging her temples. Every few seconds she turned around to make sure Imogene hadn't worked loose from the door handle.

Maggie had told Imogene about the phone call from Peter. After Imogene soundly reprimanded them as unfit parents, she tacitly agreed that she would cooperate to save Wesley's life. Jack didn't trust her and had used his tie to bind her hands. Later, Maggie found a pair of handcuffs in the glove box, and they decided that those were even better.

For the past hour, Imogene had been hurling insults at Jack, blaming him for getting Wesley into this situation and whining that she was being treated unfairly.

"Do I go right or left here?" Jack asked as the country road forked ahead.

"I'm not going to give you any further instructions until you release me from these handcuffs."

"Hey," Jack said, "We just put our house on the line to get you out of jail, and you've done nothing but complain about the accommodations. You don't like it? I can open the door right now." Jack took the left fork, assuming that Imogene would correct him if it was wrong.

"You won't do that," Imogene sneered. "Because right now you need me, and we both know it. What kind of people are you, anyway? Why would someone who makes a decent living drive this piece of junk? And who keeps a set of handcuffs in their car?"

"First of all, you obviously don't know squat about classic cars. This piece of junk will give your Maserati a run for its money any day. And second—that's personal," Jack commented.

"The handcuffs are Wesley's," Maggie quickly explained.

"But don't worry—they're the real deal, not the fake kind," Jack said.

Imogene yanked on her handcuffs, trying to see if she could pull out the door handle. "Wesley wouldn't be in this mess if you would have listened to me in the first place," Imogene said bitterly.

"No, *you* put Wesley in danger when *you* teamed up with a terrorist to get rich," Maggie sharply retorted.

"Peter is *not* a terrorist," Imogene said flatly. "He's an entrepreneur who got out of control."

"An entrepreneur who in his spare time likes to throw people out of airplanes just for the fun of it," Jack added.

"As I recall," Imogene said snidely, "I tried to warn you about this very situation, Jack. And you disregarded me."

"Well, you can file a complaint with your congressman when we get back."

"When we stop, we'll take the handcuffs off," Maggie said to Imogene. "Just tell us how to get there."

"Right at the next fork," Imogene said.

Jack drove for several minutes until the road ended in a parking lot in a forested area.

"We have to park and walk in," Imogene said. "You'll have to uncuff me, because I can't walk connected to this door, and Peter is expecting me to be with you."

Jack and Maggie stepped out of the vehicle, and Jack opened the door Imogene was attached to. She stumbled out of the car. He took the handcuff key out of his pocket and unlocked the cuff that attached her to the door without taking his eyes off Imogene. The loose handcuff still dangled from her right hand, and Imogene rubbed her wrist. At the same time, Jack's phone buzzed, and he pulled it out of his pocket. The caller ID was from Wesley's phone.

"Hello?" Jack answered.

With Jack on the phone and Maggie on the other side of the car, Imogene took the opportunity to kick the door into Jack's stomach and make a break for it. Jack buckled over from the blow and took a few seconds to catch his breath. He dropped his open phone on the gravel parking lot and took off in a sprint toward Imogene.

K.L. Fogg

Imogene had a several-seconds' head start but wasn't nearly as fast as Jack. Jack ran to the spot where he had seen Imogene duck into a thicket. Even though the winter trees were mostly bare, the evergreens and low-lying shrubs were dense enough to offer her some cover. Jack darted behind a large tree trunk, expecting her to be hiding there.

Maggie screamed, "Jack, behind you!"

Jack whirled around and saw her running further into the woods. He headed straight for Imogene, even though she was brandishing a large rock in one hand. When she saw that Jack was coming at her, she released her weapon with full force. Jack dodged it, and Imogene took off running again. If she made it into the dense brush, it would be almost impossible to find her. Jack wasn't going to let that happen. He took a few running leaps and then threw his entire body onto her, slamming her to the ground. She squirmed and tried to break free while Jack scrambled for the open handcuff dangling from her right hand. He grabbed the open cuff and slapped it around his own wrist, securing it tightly, and then he yanked Imogene to her feet.

Imogene was covered in dust, her hair completely ruined.

"Give me the key!" she ordered.

Jack shook his head. "Not a chance."

"I said give me the key right now, or I'm not cooperating!"

Jack pulled the handcuff key out of his back pocket and held it up. "You mean this key?"

Imogene lunged for it with her free hand, but Jack kept it out of her reach. She kicked him in the shin and ordered him to comply.

"Ouch!" Jack looked at Imogene and then at the key. Without any warning, he threw it as hard as he could into some heavy brush.

"What are you doing?" Imogene screeched. "Are you out of your mind?!"

Maggie came running up to them looking every bit as shocked as Imogene. Her gaze went directly to Imogene's and Jack's cuffed hands.

"Jack, please tell me that wasn't the key you just threw away."

Jack started to walk forward, but because Imogene didn't budge, it left his arm trailing behind. "Yes, as a matter of fact, that was the key. I'm not takin' any more chances she'll get away before she does the job."

"Are you crazy?" Maggie threw her hands up in the air. "You just permanently attached yourself to her!"

"See, your wife thinks you're crazy too!" Imogene agreed. "You're endangering Wesley's life! We can't get through the cave passageway like this!"

Jack stopped walking and put his hands on his hips. "Now *this* is awkward. You two are gangin' up on me."

"I just don't understand why you didn't think this through," Maggie reprimanded. "Now you've hindered yourself. You could have just given me the key." She handed the phone to Jack. "But we don't have time to look for it. Peter is asking to speak with you."

Jack pressed his phone to his ear and listened to the gravelly, unpleasant voice on the other end. "It sounds to me like you're having some problems, Jack. Is Imogene still with you?"

"Don't worry," Jack said, pulling up his manacled left hand, "she's definitely with me. I want to talk with Wesley and Amanda—right now."

"No, no, no, that's not possible. Cell phones don't work inside the cave, and I'm not about to bring the kids outside until you give me what I asked for."

"I'm not workin' for free here," Jack said sternly. "That was the deal. I brought you Imogene, and I want to see Wesley and Amanda before I turn her over."

"You're jumping ahead, Jack. You may have brought me the wicked witch, but we still need her broomstick. We'll meet you at the cave entrance. When we get to a certain point, I'll let you see them. If you try anything at all, you're going to hear a very loud noise. Am I making myself clear?"

"Yes."

The connection was severed, and Jack pushed Imogene in front of him so she could lead the way to the cave.

"Mag," Jack said as he trudged through the leaves and grass, "I think you should wait at the car. This is an underground cave we're dealin' with here, and you have claustrophobia."

"So, who doesn't?" she said. "I'll handle it." She walked ahead of Imogene and Jack on a trail that seemed clearly marked. "Obviously, you didn't think of that when you threw away the key."

"So I was a little impulsive maybe." Jack sprinted ahead and yanked Imogene like a dog on a leash to keep up with him. "But if she escapes, she won't be any use to us."

"Admit it," Imogene said. "That was an incredibly stupid thing to do, Jack. Just like the bad judgment you used by refusing to take my first offer. If you would have been smart enough to understand what was at stake, Wesley's life wouldn't be in danger now, and we wouldn't be taking orders from Peter like some—"

Jack stopped walking, and Imogene ran into him. He turned and faced her. "That's it. You knew about this all along, didn't you? You planned it. This is all a scheme to get you out of jail—the great escape. You and Peter aren't even enemies, are you?"

Imogene pondered the accusation. "Once again, Jack, you're wrong. Unfortunately for me, right now you and I are on the same team, and we're going to have to cooperate if we want to save Wesley."

"And don't forget Amanda," Maggie added. "If you want to show us some cooperation, tell us something, will you? What does Peter want with Alex?"

"I don't know anything about Alex," Imogene said.

Jack started walking again. "If you expect us to believe that you're with us and not against us, then tell us the truth. Where is Alex?"

"I wasn't aware that he was missing." Imogene ran a few steps to keep up with Jack.

"Well he is," Jack stated. "Since yesterday."

"In that case, I would assume he's running away from something—possibly his fiancée, but then that's only a guess."

"Guess again," Jack said as he twisted her arm behind her back.

"Stop it!" Imogene screeched. "All I know is there is one person who can open the safe other than myself. Peter and my sister Delphina both thought I told one of them the code. Obviously I didn't. If either of them could find it and open it, then they would have the diamonds already, and this little escapade would be entirely unnecessary. If that doesn't prove to you that I'm not working with Peter, then nothing I say will."

"So you and the sis are havin' a little family feud. That's interesting. Is Alex the other person who can open the safe?"

"No. But Peter probably thinks he is."

"Who is this person?" Jack demanded.

"If I told you that, I'd be a bigger idiot than you. The only other person who is authorized to open the safe doesn't know where it is."

"That's using your head," Jack said. "So if you died, no one would ever find two-hundred million dollars in diamonds."

"That is correct, Jack. So if you want to save Wesley—and if Peter wants the diamonds—you both better make sure I stay alive."

* * *

The door to the ticket office opened and Harlan stepped inside. He closed the door behind him and looked at Wesley as though he'd just discovered some important news.

"So your dad is the Snake Stalker?" Harlan asked Wesley.

"Yeah. Do you watch his show?" Wesley asked.

"Once in a while," Harlan said. "It's an okay show, but sometimes he gets his facts wrong."

Wesley wondered if Harlan was trying to tell them something once again, without making it look obvious. Wesley played along. "Really? Like what?" he prodded.

"Like he thinks he's the expert when it comes to rattlesnakes. He doesn't know the first thing about the eastern diamondback. He said on one of his shows that they're an endangered species in these parts of the land."

84

"And you think they're not?" Amanda asked.

Harlan chuckled. "The largest and most venomous snake in North America," he said, not addressing the question. "And probably the smartest too. There are a lot more of them than you think. Maybe your dad just doesn't know where to look."

Wesley and Amanda exchanged glances.

"Are there rattlesnakes in this cave?" Wesley asked.

"There might be a few." Harlan raised his eyebrows. "The caves have been closed for a long time, and I haven't really had much time to explore."

Harlan's two-way radio buzzed. "Harlan, get down to the canyon passage. I have an assignment for you."

"What about the kids?" Harlan said into the receiver. "Someone should guard them, don't you think?"

"Set the timer—that's what you made it for."

Harlan paused a moment before answering. "Okay." He pulled the wire mechanism that he had been working on earlier out of his pocket.

"What is that?" Wesley pointed to the device in Harlan's hand.

Harlan was suspiciously quiet.

"Is it a bomb?" Amanda asked.

"Yes, it's a *bomb*," Harlan said as if that shouldn't be any concern to them. "It's programmed to go off if it's moved or touched. I'm going to hook it up to the door now."

"Harlan, you don't have to do what Peter tells you," Wesley said. "If you let us go now, nobody will get hurt. You'll be a hero, and I promise you, we'll help you protect your cave."

Harlan sighed. "It's too late for that now."

Amanda tried to plead with him. "It's not too late, Harlan. Please don't do this."

Harlan ignored her as he stripped one of the copper wires and twisted it onto another one.

"Eddie does that—" Wesley interjected, "you don't even know how it works!"

"Maybe I *am* Eddie!" Harlan shot back.

"But you know you don't want to blow us up," Amanda said.

"Just trust me." Harlan wiped a trickle of sweat from his brow. "And stay away from the door. You'll be fine."

He connected several wires to the doorknob and then to the timer. He opened the door and stepped outside. Harlan spoke through the open crack. "Once this door shuts, the bomb is armed. You understand that, don't you? If anyone opens the door—it's kaboom!"

"Eddie, wait. Can I talk to Harlan—please?" Wesley pleaded.

"No. He's gone," came the stiff response as the door closed, and a red light indicated the bomb was armed.

Wesley stepped away from the door, and Amanda looked like she might cry. This was a bad time to lose Harlan.

* * *

The entrance to the cave looked like someone had recently torn down a barricade from it. Maggie stepped over boards and nails as she entered the cave with her hands in the air. Jack and Imogene walked in tandem behind her. The narrow entrance opened up into a wide corridor with restrooms on one side, several other shops, and a ticket office up ahead. Electric lights illuminated the tourist area.

Maggie scanned the surroundings. Outside it appeared that they were walking into a small dungeon, but this looked more like a ride at Disney World. Not that it looked like any fun, only that it seemed much more civilized than she imagined. She also thought it was possible that Peter Jaworsky would shoot her and Jack on the spot, but she hoped that they could just trade Imogene for Wesley and Amanda and get out of here. Somehow she knew it wasn't going to be that simple. She was afraid but calm at the same time, as if her mind had become detached from her body, keeping her emotions from taking over.

Maggie had heard Maria describe Peter Jaworsky as a man of pure evil. The image she had created in her mind wasn't the boyish young man who came walking up to them with a slight limp. When he half smiled at her, she knew there must be some mistake. He didn't look like a killer at all.

"Please, let us see Wesley and Amanda," she pleaded.

"Don't worry. The kids are fine. Nothing's going to happen to them," the man said to reassure her.

Maggie wanted to believe him.

Another man with a gun in one hand and a shaved head stepped out from one of the tunnels. His presence seemed to snuff out all the light around him. He gave Maggie a look that made her skin crawl.

"What have we here?" he said in a voice Maggie immediately recognized. He reached over and grabbed Imogene's cuffed arm and pulled it up, dragging Jack's along with it. He let them go and let out a laugh. "You know, Jack, if I had my pick of these two women," he pointed to Maggie with his gun, "I would have hitched myself to the brunette." Peter patted Maggie down to check her for weapons.

"Get your hands off my wife. Here's Imogene. Now let the rest of us go."

"But our adventure has just begun," Peter said as he circled them carefully. "Imogene is useless to me unless I can convince her to hand over the goods. When I have the prize in my possession, you and the kids can go." He pushed his face up to Imogene's and pulled a black device out of his pocket. "This is called a detonator. All I have to do is press this button, and a bomb will go off. See that little window in the wall over there?" He waved his gun toward the ticket office. "That bomb is inside a very small room—and Wesley and the girl are in there too."

"Her name is Amanda," Maggie said.

"Amanda—what a sweet name," Peter said. "It would be a shame to see it carved on a tombstone."

"Let us see them!" Jack commanded.

"The kids are worth the contents of one briefcase," Peter said to Imogene. *"Comprendes?"*

"I'll get the diamonds for you, Peter," Imogene said. "But you have to release me from these handcuffs first."

"No. I rather like this arrangement. Me and Harlan can keep track of all three of you this way. I figure you're the only one I really need to worry about, Jack. And you can't do anything with that old barn horse shackled to you."

As Peter forced the three of them to walk into a sloping tunnel, Maggie sized up the situation. She didn't have a weapon, but she did have a black belt in karate, and she knew how to disarm someone with a gun. Of course that was assuming that the person with the gun could be distracted momentarily. From the stories Alex had told her, she knew Peter was even more skilled than she was, so she didn't want to risk it—at least not yet. This Harlan guy didn't seem too intimidating, but anyone who was working with Peter was her enemy right now.

As they traveled through the lit tunnel, Maggie became very aware of the enclosed space. If she had felt detached earlier, now her pulse was speeding up, her breathing was shallow, and panic welled up inside her. The walls seemed to shrink in on either side of her, even though an average-sized person could fit through without any problem. She was leading the way, and Harlan was following close behind her. When she slowed her step, he nudged her forward.

"It gets a little narrow here, but it widens up later," Harlan said as if he could read her mind. "Lots of folks get hung up in this spot, but you'll be fine."

I'm not fine, and I'm not going to be fine. Maggie tried to push the negative thoughts out of her head. But the tunnel seemed to be squeezing out all the optimism she was trying to create, and it gave her a feeling of dread. She started to tremble but forced herself to move forward. If she gave in to her panic, Peter would shoot her. She had no doubt she was expendable. Jack would go nuts if Peter harmed her in any way, and then Wesley and Amanda wouldn't have a chance. She could hear Jack and Imogene behind her, scuffling over how to get through the tight space. She couldn't worry about that now. She closed her eyes, took a deep breath, and tried to picture herself in a place with wide-open space and lots of air.

9

Countdown

Jack's wrist hurt from twisting and pulling Imogene through the tunnels. The knuckles on his left hand were scraped raw, and he was bleeding onto Imogene's hand. He wouldn't have noticed it, though if she hadn't said something to him—as if she expected him to be able to do something about it. The tunnel ended abruptly, and suddenly there was a breeze and the feeling of having moved into a very large area. As the group stood at the brink of the canyon passage, Jack looked around in awe.

The electric lighting that had followed them through their journey could barely illuminate the majestic view because of the immense space. Beautiful calcite formations hung from the ceiling high above their heads. Some were a smooth, milky white; others ranged from yellow to rusty orange. Below them, the ground fell out into a deep canyon cut by millions of years of mineral-rich running water. The limestone bedrock had formed a narrow rock bridge that crossed the canyon and joined one side of the cave to the

K.L. Fogg

other. Ropes that previously formed the sides of the bridge hung down in disrepair from years of neglect.

"In any other circumstance," Jack said wistfully, "and with any other company, this sight would be magnificent."

"It's incredible, isn't it?" Harlan said. "Just wait until you see the underground pool. That stream there," he pointed to a trickle of water off to one side that disappeared into the rock, "runs for miles underground. Some people think it joins up with Ellison's Cave, the longest—"

"Harlan!" Peter snapped. "Stop with the tour already!"

"What difference does it make?" Harlan argued. "We're going to get there in the same amount of time. Some people appreciate this kind of thing."

"I'll appreciate it if you keep your mouth shut," Peter excoriated then turned to Jack. "You want to check on the kiddies?" He pulled out a two-way radio and handed it to Jack. "Remember, Harlan rigged the bomb so that if they try to get out, it will explode."

"Eddie did it," Harlan interjected.

"Don't start that name thing with me again!" Peter said. "You're both Harlan, understand?"

Harlan nodded.

Jack had no idea what they were talking about. He pressed the button on the transistor. "Are you there, Wes?"

In a few seconds, Wesley came on the line. "Dad? Where are you?"

"We're here inside the cave. Maggie and I brought Imogene. We're going to get you and Amanda out of there. Are you okay?"

"We're fine," Wesley said hesitantly. "I'm sorry, Dad."

"Yeah. So am I."

Imogene grabbed the transistor from Jack. "Wesley, this is your mother. Don't worry—I'm here to save you. I'm going to cooperate fully."

The line was silent for a moment, and Jack imagined that Wesley was trying to come up with an appropriate response to that self-aggrandizing comment.

"We appreciate that," Wesley responded diplomatically. "*Amanda* and I."

"Yes, of course. Amanda, too!" Imogene said after a pause.

Peter yanked the transistor away from Imogene and turned it off. "That's enough. How far away are we?"

"We're very close," Imogene said caustically. "But you can't expect me to walk across that bridge when I'm handcuffed to him. He'll throw us off balance, and need I remind you that if he falls, we both fall. And you won't be able to open the safe without me."

Peter considered it for a moment and then shoved Maggie out in front of him. "You go first," he said.

Maggie stepped out onto the two-foot strip of rock and slowly walked forward. "It gets narrower in the middle," she warned as she put her hands out to the side.

Jack tried to encourage Maggie. "She has an incredible sense of balance, my wife," he said. "That's a lot harder than it looks."

"Get going." Peter pushed Jack and Imogene forward. "And don't fall. I don't want either of you dead—yet."

Jack took a deep breath as he and Imogene edged out onto the narrow rock bridge. The crevasse below them stretched into infinity.

"You hear that?" Jack said to Imogene. "He said not to fall. Hey Harlan! How deep would you say this canyon is, mate?"

"It looks deeper than it really is because of the light reflection," Harlan answered. "It's only about a hundred-and-fifty-foot drop."

"Oh." Jack's voice was shaky. "Is that all? Piece of cake then."

"Don't look down, Jack," Maggie encouraged him after she had crossed the ten yards to the other side. "You could easily walk this if you were two feet off the ground."

"This is classic." Peter laughed. "The Snake Stalker is afraid of heights!"

Jack took several more small steps, making sure not to throw Imogene off balance. "Wouldn't it have been a lot easier to just bury the diamonds in a coffin or something?" he said to Imogene.

"He's going to make us fall," Imogene complained to Peter. "I refuse to go any farther until you take these handcuffs off."

"Request denied," Peter said. "Harlan, hand me the detonator."

"She was just kiddin'—" Jack said, starting to walk again.

Imogene took several unsteady steps but kept up with Jack. When they were just a few feet from the end, Imogene snagged the heel of her shoe on one of the ropes. When she pulled her heel up, she jerked back and knocked Jack off balance. Jack swirled his free arm in circles trying to correct himself, and his right leg came completely off the rock bridge. Imogene screamed and grabbed for Jack, which only made it more sure they would both fall. Maggie lunged for Jack and tried to grab his shirt, but she was too far away to reach him. She thought fast and pushed Imogene to the left, causing them both to fall at the same time— but on opposite sides of the bridge.

Both of them scraped their sides on the way down but stopped with a jerk when their handcuffed hands hooked over the bridge in the middle, with both their bodies dangling on either side.

Jack winced in pain, and Imogene screeched at the top of her lungs. Because Jack weighed more and had fallen first, he ended up pulling Imogene more to his side. She hung there helplessly, kicking like she was pedaling a bike.

As Jack tried to wrap his legs in one of the loose bridge ropes, Imogene came sliding over the top, causing him to fall even farther. He wouldn't be able to pull himself up without both of them falling off completely.

Maggie grabbed onto Imogene's leg.

"Help us!" she called out to Peter and Harlan as she crouched on her knees and held on with all her strength.

Harlan shuffled over the bridge without hesitation and knelt down on the other side of the slipping duo. "Don't grab onto me," he said to Imogene," or all three of us will go over." He held onto Imogene and kept her from tumbling over while Maggie helped Jack by pulling his free arm up until he could kick his leg up onto the rock bridge.

After Jack was all the way back onto solid rock, he took a minute to catch his breath and then backed up on his knees, while Imogene faced him and crawled forward until they were on the other side.

"That was entertaining," Peter commented as he crossed the bridge like a tightrope walker. He shoved Imogene into the opening of the next tunnel.

"My wrist is broken!" Imogene wailed.

"Boo hoo," Peter said. "Be glad it wasn't your neck. Now hurry up and get there already. I'm not in the mood for any dead ends or wild goose chases. If you start going nowhere, Harlan here knows this cave like the back of his hand, and he'll let me know. The first expendable person will be your lovely wife, Jack, and the second will be Amanda. If that doesn't motivate cooperation—it'll be Wesley."

"Stop threatening me!" Imogene said through clenched teeth. "I'm going to do what you want, but if you harm Wesley in any way, all bets are off."

Jack looked at Imogene and muttered under his breath, "I never thought I'd say this, mate, but for the first time in our lives, we're on the same side."

* * *

The ticket office had become a time bomb, and Wesley and Amanda could do nothing but wait and hope that neither Peter nor Harlan's alter ego, Eddie, would get impatient and set it off. If Wesley was a little confident knowing that his dad was there, it was cancelled out by Imogene being there too. He was certain his dad would never get Imogene out of prison unless he was desperate. And he didn't trust Imogene to give in to Peter's demands without a fight.

He walked over to the circuits connected to the doorknob and examined them. "This doesn't look all that complicated, you know."

"Wesley, don't you dare touch that!" Amanda warned.

"Don't freak out on me. I'm not touching it, okay!"

"Seriously," Amanda said sternly. "I'm very stressed out here."

"You think I'm calm? I told you this wasn't going to be fun."

"Great. The last words from my best friend are 'I told you so.'"

"Those aren't my last words," Wesley said with irritation. "We aren't dead yet."

Amanda gave him a pained look.

"I mean, we aren't going to die, so I'm not planning on saying something that would make you think I think that we are going to—"

Suddenly a face appeared in the glass window. Amanda screamed and backed into the wall. Wesley jumped when he saw a man with a bloody face peering inside to observe them.

Amanda buried her face in Wesley's shoulder. He instinctively put his arm around her to protect her.

"Wesley," the man spoke through the vent in a hoarse voice. "Amanda—it's me, Alex." A big dog jumped up and whimpered next to him. "And Teddy too," he added. "Don't worry, I'm going to get you out of there."

"No!" Wesley shrieked, as Alex's face disappeared from the window. "Don't touch the door! There's a bomb!"

Alex reappeared in the window, and Amanda was already there ready to brief him. She put her hand up to the window. "Alex, I'm so glad to see you! We were so afraid you might be dead. You can't get us out because Peter rigged a bomb to the door so that it'll blow up if anyone touches it."

"And there are explosives in here," Wesley added. "I don't think it's just for show."

"I don't either," Alex stated. "How did you get here?"

"Elliot brought us," Wesley explained. "But we sent him home. Teddy attacked Harlan, blowing our cover. Then Peter took us hostage."

"What does he want from you?" Alex asked.

"He used us to force my dad and Maggie to get Imogene out of jail," Wesley said. "All three of them are somewhere down inside the cave now. Imogene told me she's going to cooperate and do what Peter says, and then he'll let us go."

Alex nodded. It wasn't a nod of agreement, but it showed that he understood what Wesley said. "Are there any wires around the window?"

"No, just on the doorknob," Wesley stated. "But I don't think we could fit through this window even if we broke it, and the glass is really thick."

"Wesley, Amanda, listen to me. I'm not telling you this to scare you. We have to assume that Peter isn't planning to let you go even if he does get the diamonds."

"But he made a deal!" Wesley protested.

"His word means nothing," Alex stressed. "We have to find another way to get you out. And then we have to find Jack and Maggie."

"But how did *you* escape?" Amanda asked.

"He shot me in one of the caves, and he thinks I'm dead. But he missed." Alex looked at his blood-soaked shoulder. "Almost missed, anyway. Teddy rescued me."

"Good boy, Teddy!" Wesley put his hand under the change container, and Teddy licked his fingers. "Can't we do something to short out the wires or something?"

Alex shook his head. "If those wires are live, we can't touch anything without setting it off. I'm not really an explosives guy, and I don't want to try anything that risky. I'd rather try some blunt force on the window. Are there any heavy objects in the room?"

Wesley scouted around the small room. The only thing that was wasn't dynamite and was larger than his fist was Harlan's metal stool. He picked it up and heaved it against the window. It bent one of the legs but did nothing to the window.

"I'm going to have to get some sharp rocks outside," Alex said. "I'll be right back."

"No, wait!" Wesley reached into his sock and pulled out his shuriken. He passed it underneath the ticket window to Alex.

Alex pulled out the weapon and examined it. "This is good," he said and backed up several yards. "Get away from the window!" he yelled. He pulled back his right arm and threw the sharp metal star with all the force of a quarterback with an injured shoulder. He hit the window off to one side and put a small windshield crack in it. He ran up to the window and karate kicked it, breaking it further. One more kick and the glass shattered in toward the ticket office.

Alex had started to pick the broken glass away from the edge of the window when Amanda pointed to a piece of glass that had landed on the timer. The red light was still on, but now instead of a solid 15:00, the timer read 14:56. In another second it read 14:55.

"We tripped the timer!" she screamed. "We only have fourteen minutes and fifty seconds until it explodes!"

"We'll get you out," Alex assured them, but even as he said it, he looked like he might pass out himself. Neither the top nor the bottom half of the glass was big enough for either of them to crawl through without removing the metal piece in the middle. And that was securely cemented into the walls of the rock cave. "Stay calm, both of you. I'm going to see what I can find to use for leverage to jimmy that metal bar."

Alex ran off toward the cave entrance, leaving Amanda and Wesley counting off seconds on the clock.

* * *

After hiking through a tight maze of cave passages, Maggie sighed with relief when the tunnel opened up into another huge cavern in the shape of a half-moon. It was the size of a dome-shaped supermarket. The entire cavern was lit with colorful artificial lights, and the reflection on the beautiful polished stone turned the area into a magnificent natural ballroom. Half of the "dance floor" was smooth sandstone with another section of pure ebony. The black section was so smooth that Maggie's first impression was that the ebony stone must be onyx, but she soon realized it was water. This was the underground pool Harlan had been so excited about earlier. It was a little larger than a crescent-shaped, Olympic-sized swimming pool, but it appeared to be fathoms deeper. Behind the pool was a magnificent backdrop of rock formations.

"I've never seen anything like this," Maggie said in awe as she entered this section of the cave. She was sweating profusely, even though the temperature inside the cave was cool.

"We call this the palace," Harlan said excitedly. "I think you'll agree that it is one of the most beautiful places on earth. Too bad no one gets to see it anymore. If you think this is amazing, wait until you see what's under—"

"Keep going!" Peter shouted as he shoved Jack and Imogene forward and motioned for them to hurry up. "Harlan!" Peter barked. "Get over here now!"

Harlan reluctantly walked over to Peter and stood there waiting for his command. Peter pulled the detonator out of his pocket, showed it to Harlan, and mumbled something under his breath that no one else could hear.

"They must have tripped it up somehow," Harlan said loud enough for everyone to hear. "I can try to get back there, but I'll never be able to disable it in time. You'll need to press the abort button."

Peter looked as though he might slap Harlan in the face. "Well, thank you for announcing that to everyone. Now I obviously can't do that, can I?" Peter waved his arms. "Attention everyone. Your children have tried to escape, and because of this, you now have a new deadline. You now have exactly eleven minutes and forty-six seconds to open that safe or the bomb will explode."

"I need more time than that!" Imogene protested. "The safe is underwater, and it takes some time to change the water level before I can access it."

"Then you'd better hurry," Peter said.

Imogene pulled Jack over to a machine a few feet from the ebony pool. It looked exactly like the type of machine used for sightseers. It was a metal device that looked like an extra-large parking meter with a set of binoculars that allowed a person to examine the beautiful rock formations on the ceiling from below.

Imogene pressed a button on the side and stuck her face up to the eyepiece. "Imogene Vandergrift," she said slowly and clearly. She pronounced a series of nonsense syllables into the microphone. "Ichi-ni-san-shi-go-roku-shichi-hachi-kyu-ju."

Underneath the water came a loud click and then a grinding noise that engaged some machinery. It sounded like a garage door opening underwater. The slick ebony pool started to move, and a large whirlpool formed and started to drain. It appeared that Imogene had lifted a barrier under the pool, and the water was draining out somehow into an underground river.

Peter was astonished. "Did you know about this rig, Harlan?" Peter turned around to find him, but Harlan was gone. "Harlan!" he yelled angrily. "I did not give you permission to leave!"

Jack looked at his manacled hand and sighed. "Looks like some sort of water table regulator. Do we have to wait for that to empty?"

"I told Peter that I need more time," Imogene said. "We have to wait until the vault is uncovered, because the door won't open from here until the water goes down. If Peter tries to swim over there any sooner, he'll be sucked under.

"*I'll* be sucked under?" Peter laughed. "You think *I'm* going to swim over there and open the safe?"

"Well I certainly can't swim in this situation!" Imogene reminded him.

Peter grabbed Maggie's arm. "I'm sending her over to set off whatever booby trap you have planned for me."

Maggie wrenched her arm free and was ready to fight but then realized Peter still held the detonator in his hand.

"How much longer?" Jack asked Imogene.

"It's only a few more minutes," Imogene answered impatiently. "There's a ledge over to the side where the water might be shallow enough to walk across."

"Why don't you get a head start?" Peter pushed Maggie toward the side of the pool where Imogene said the ledge was. You've got about nine minutes. Let's see if you can do it."

Maggie took off her shoes and threw them on the ground. There was no use arguing with Peter, because she would only be shot for insubordination. She started to make her way across the ledge. The water came up to her knees, and the suction was pulling on her like an undertow. After about twenty feet, she was halfway across, the water mid-thigh. The water was cold, making her shiver. It was starting to throw her off balance. At that point, she decided it would be easier just to swim. With adrenaline giving her an extra boost, she dove into the deep water and fought the current to get to the other side.

Maggie swallowed some water with a strange mineral taste to it, She could see there were steps carved into the rock now that the water had gone down about four feet. She stepped onto the slippery rock, dripping wet, and inched over to an edge that jutted out a few inches. The door was built right into the rock wall, and it looked like it belonged on a submarine, still partially submerged in the underground pool. It had a wheel on it that turned, which Maggie tugged on with both arms.

"Tell me how to open the door!" she yelled to Imogene. "It won't budge."

"I'll open it from here," Imogene answered. "When I'm ready."

Maggie was suddenly very afraid. She was afraid that if Imogene didn't open the safe, Wesley and Amanda would die. And she was afraid that if Imogene did open it, there would be no reason for Peter to let any of them live. She could hear Jack pleading with Imogene.

"Open it already! Wes and Amanda only have a few minutes!"

"Don't you think I'm aware of that!" Imogene retorted. "I want to make sure that Wesley is safe, and then I'll open it. Not before."

* * *

"What's taking Alex so long?" Amanda asked. "I don't think he's coming back, and we're down to five minutes."

Wesley didn't know what to say. He had no idea what had happened to Alex, but from the way Alex looked, he wouldn't be surprised if he had passed out somewhere. As the clock ticked every second down, Wesley started to think there wasn't a very good chance of getting out in half an hour, let alone five minutes.

"Wesley," Amanda said, "I'm really sorry I pulled you into this. I didn't expect it to be like this."

"I know. I don't ever expect it to be like this, but it keeps happening to me over and over. It's not you, Amanda—it's me. I'm the curse. I'm the person who gets everyone around me into life-threatening situations."

"Do you think there's any chance we'll live?" Amanda asked.

"Of course there is," Wesley said.

"I don't want to die," she said soberly. "I'm only fifteen, and I have a lot more things I want to do."

"I'm not even fifteen, and I definitely don't want to die yet."

Amanda looked at the timer. "You want to hear something strange? When we were little, I always thought we would get married when we grew up. Isn't that funny?"

"Not really. I sort of thought that too, because you've always been my best friend, and I always thought that we would stay that way. Forever."

"Really? You thought that?"

Wesley shrugged. "Yeah. Pretty dumb, huh? When we were kids."

Amanda turned and faced Wesley. She picked up one of his hands—it was very tender gesture and not something she would usually do. "I know what my last words are going to be."

"We still have four minutes left. Alex is going to get us out." Wesley looked around for some reason to believe what he just said.

"This is what I want to say." Amanda took a step toward Wesley and kissed him on the lips.

Wesley had never kissed a girl before, but thought it was a pretty good way to spend the last few minutes of his life. He thought that for an amateur he did a decent job of kissing her back. For a second he almost forgot that Alex was coming back to get them out. He might have lost track of time if he hadn't heard a metal-on-metal pounding noise.

Wesley turned to see Alex hacking at the metal bar with what looked like a crowbar, but it was puny compared to the metal they had to bend. They needed a hacksaw or a blowtorch to cut through a metal bar that thick.

"Amanda, I think you can squeeze through the opening," Wesley said. "There isn't going to be enough time to bend the metal. If I push and Alex pulls, maybe you can fit through."

"I'm too big to fit through. You go first."

"No, you're smaller than me. I'll be right behind you. Go now!" He grabbed Amanda's hand and pushed her out in front of him.

"Wait." Amanda took off her bulky, hooded sweat-shirt and threw it through the opening. She had a T-shirt on underneath. She stuck her arms out and tried to wiggle her hands and head through the bottom half of the window opening.

"No, go through the top!" Wesley stood on the desk, hoisted her up on his back, and shoved her head through the window.

"Position your shoulders diagonally," Alex instructed. "Be careful with this edge. There's some glass here."

"Don't worry about the glass!" Amanda said. "You can stitch me up later—just hurry."

Wesley could see that it was going to be a really tight fit. He was going to have to do most of the work on his end, because he was higher up than Alex was. He could also tell Alex was really fatigued. His shoulder had started bleeding again through his shirt. The clock said 1:11. Wesley believed that he wasn't going to make it this time.

"Amanda," Wesley said. "Don't wait for me. As soon as Alex gets you out, run as fast as you can."

10

Volatile Situation

While Maggie stood by the vault door waiting for Imogene to open it, Jack was trying to figure out how to get the detonator away from Peter. Imogene refused to open the door until he either handed it over to them or produced Wesley. It was clear to Jack that Peter wasn't going to give in to any of Imogene's demands.

"Listen," Jack said to Imogene under his breath when his back was to Peter. "Open the vault—I can take him." He really didn't know how he was going to do that, but he needed to save Wesley first and then worry about how to handle Peter later.

"Fifty-nine seconds," Peter announced.

Imogene looked at Jack skeptically then pushed her face up to the iris scanner and said, "Open the vault." There was a loud click, then the wheel on the door turned by itself, and the door opened. "There you go. It's open."

"We're not done yet," Peter said. "Maggie goes inside and brings them out."

"Push the abort switch, Peter," Imogene demanded.

Peter motioned for Maggie to follow his order. Jack saw her take a deep breath before she ducked inside the vault, which was about the size of a deep refrigerator. Maggie was pretty tough in about every situation, but an enclosed space like this was her greatest fear. Jack wished he could trade places with her.

Seconds later, Maggie dragged out an aluminum briefcase. It seemed to be pretty heavy for her, but she hoisted it up and turned around so that she was standing on the very edge of the vault opening. She held the metal case up in front of her chest and showed it to Peter.

"Here it is!" Maggie shouted. "Now turn off the bomb, or I throw this in the water!"

"No!" Imogene yelled at Maggie frantically. "That's all we have to bargain with!" She turned around. "Peter, you said you'd press the abort switch—do it now!"

Peter's soulless eyes bored into Imogene. "I lied," he said without an ounce of conscience. "There is no abort switch."

* * *

The timer on the bomb was counting down. Ten, nine, eight. Wesley was in the process of climbing through the ticket window, but it was much more difficult for him because there was no one to push him from behind. Alex and Amanda were both pulling on his arms, practically dislocating his shoulder to pull him out, but he was really stuck. He kicked his legs, but it was futile.

"I can't fit through," Wesley said, as he backed himself out of the window and stood on the desk. "You both have to run!" Wesley ran over to the door and grabbed the handle. The timer said two seconds. Maybe if he opened the door the blast would be delayed and he'd have a second to get a little farther away.

He turned the handle as the timer went to zero. He had been wrong about the time delay. The bomb detonated immediately. Wesley, Alex, and Amanda all heard the explosion and felt the tremors. There was no searing heat. No blinding light. No deafening sound.

It took Wesley several seconds to realize that it wasn't the ticket office that had blown up. The bomb had detonated somewhere deeper inside the cave, somewhere beneath them.

Alex and Amanda weren't far from where Wesley stood. Alex had thrown Amanda to the ground and covered her with his own body to shield her from the blast. Teddy bounded up to Wesley.

Alex stood up and helped Amanda to her feet. Everyone looked around in shock and dusted themselves off.

"What do you suppose happened?" Amanda asked.

"I don't know, but it was an answer to a prayer," Alex answered.

"It was Harlan," Wesley announced. "He didn't want to kill us after all. Maybe he turned back into himself again."

"Who is Harlan?" Alex asked.

"You never met the guy with one leg who stole your jacket?"

"No." Alex shook his head. "He has my jacket?"

"Yes, but I'll explain later," Wesley said. "My dad and Maggie are in trouble. We have to help them."

"No, Wesley," Alex said. "The best way to help them is to get you both out of this cave right now. We don't know what just happened here. Maybe Peter thinks he killed you, or maybe Imogene refused to cooperate and Peter needed to make an example out of someone. Or maybe the fuse just shorted out for some reason. Whatever it is, going back into the cave is the last thing we should do."

Wesley rubbed his elbow. "You can't order me not to go down there. You and Amanda can leave and try to bring back help, but I got my parents into this mess and I'm not leaving until I know they're safe. I have to go down there."

"You can't do that!" Alex shook his shoulders. "Peter is running around here with guns and explosives. I know you want to help, but you don't know where they are, and neither do I! I've been down inside this cave for a day and a half and couldn't find my way around. You'll only get lost."

"No, I won't—I have a plan. Harlan told us about a freight elevator he used to take that goes directly into the center of the cave. I saw an elevator over by the bathrooms." Wesley pointed down the wide entrance, where they could just make out an indentation with bars across it. It looked like a metal cage that could have been for some live-animal cave exhibit.

"He did tell us about an elevator," Amanda piped in.

"If it was a shortcut to where they were going, then why wouldn't Imogene have used it?" Alex countered. "For that matter, why wouldn't Harlan still use it?"

"Maybe he does," Wesley said as he picked up the crowbar and ran over to the rusted old elevator that looked like it hadn't been used since World War I.

The decaying cardboard sign wired through the door read *Out of Order*. Wesley shrugged and ripped it off. "That's why Imogene didn't use it. It's probably just a decoy."

"I doubt it," Alex said. "This elevator hasn't been in working order for decades, and it's not electric—it looks like it works on a pulley system."

"I'm going to try it. Look, there's a lever inside." Wesley started to pry the doors open with the crowbar. The doors resisted at first, but with a scraping noise worse than fingernails on a chalkboard, they gave in to Wesley's coaxing. Teddy hopped inside and wagged his tail, as if he wanted to be the first to try out a new ride.

"See," Wesley said, "if it can hold Teddy, it can definitely hold us."

He stepped inside. Suddenly the cage lurched and threw Wesley off balance. A sound like a freight train applying its brakes echoed in the cave.

Alex frowned. "Wesley, I'm sorry to have to pull rank on you, but I can't let you do this. I'm ordering you to stay up here with Amanda and stay out of sight." He jumped inside and quickly pushed Wesley out. Alex closed the doors before they could protest.

"Wish me luck," Alex said as he pulled the lever.

* * *

The four people in the underground pool heard the unmistakable sound of a detonating bomb. The echo reverberated through the hollow tunnels, and it was difficult to tell which direction the blast came from. The cave rumbled and quaked, chunks of stone rolling off the ledges and water rippling in the pool.

Maggie steadied herself to keep from losing her balance in the threshold of the open doorway. "You detonated the bomb?" she screamed as she raised the diamond case over her head and prepared to hurl it into the water.

"You killed Wesley!" Imogene sobbed hysterically and then called Peter a few choice names. "You'll never get the diamonds!" She gave a command and the vault door started to close automatically.

Maggie didn't have a chance to react as the heavy door swung back quickly, hitting her in the shoulder and knocking her down along with the aluminum case into the vault.

When the door shut, Jack watched in horror as the wheel-like handle on the vault door automatically turned and closed. Peter shot at the door, the bullet ricocheting off.

"Open it back up!" Peter ordered as he moved his gun to Imogene.

"Open it!" Jack begged Imogene. "Let her out or she'll suffocate in there."

"He'll kill us all anyway, Jack," Imogene cried. "Just like Wesley. There's no reason for me to let him have the diamonds now. Go ahead. Shoot me," she goaded Peter. "At least I'll die knowing you won't be able to get into that safe without blowing up this cave and everything in it."

"I'll shoot you right now!" Peter said, aiming his gun at Imogene's head.

"Nothing you can say will make me open that vault now," Imogene said, her whole body stiffening in defiance of Peter.

"Harlan may have gotten them out," Jack said. "Wesley might still be alive. I'm beggin' you to open that door."

The water started filling back into the pool, and it was lapping at the edges of the rock ledge.

Imogene looked stoically at Jack and Peter. "The only other person who can open it is dead now. At least I'll go to my grave knowing I never let you have those diamonds. You weren't going to let any of us go anyway, were you, Peter?"

Peter cocked his head and reflected. "Now that I think of it, probably not. But now that I know exactly where to find them, there's no reason for me to wait to kill the rest of you." He shook his head and addressed Imogene. "All this over some stupid kid. We could have made off with almost a billion in the beginning, but no, you had to come back and get *Wesley*. You are a weak woman, Imogene Vandergrift." He backed into the tunnel that brought them into the cave, about thirty yards away from Imogene and Jack.

Just then Harlan came running up behind Peter, dragging his right leg. "He blew the south tunnel!" he yelled, out of breath. "Not the ticket office!"

"What?" Peter asked. "Get back and take care of it!"

Harlan didn't move from where he was.

"Harlan!" Jack yelled. "My wife is inside that vault. Please help us or she'll die!" The water was slowly filling back up. It was already starting to cover the bottom of the vault.

"I can't open it, Jack," Harlan said. "*She* has to do it." He pointed to Imogene.

Jack turned to Imogene. "Wesley and Amanda were in the ticket office, and that's not what blew up. That means they probably survived. Please, open the vault, and I'll do anything you ask. Anything!"

"Not until I see with my own eyes that Wesley is okay," Imogene insisted.

"There's no time for that!" Jack lugged Imogene with him to the edge of the pool and, ignoring her protests, jumped in. Imogene flipped over him and, like a block of cement, immediately pulled Jack underwater.

He struggled to swim toward the vault while Imogene thrashed to the surface to get some air.

Imogene kicked and thrashed, preventing Jack from moving his left arm to swim. The two fought and struggled against each other to stay above water. Jack surfaced and gasped for air. He realized he had truly made the worst decision of his life when he threw away the handcuff key. His wife was going to die, and he wasn't going to be able to save her with this human anchor attached to his wrist. Wesley and Amanda could still be alive or even injured, and Imogene now had all of their lives in her hands. He had to keep fighting, but he couldn't do anything without her cooperation. He spent all the energy he had left just to make it back to the spot where he had jumped in. He dragged himself out, coughing and spitting out water, leaving Imogene dangling in the water to fend for herself.

It was taking longer for the water to fill up the pool than it had to drain, but that didn't give Jack much comfort. He was nearly hysterical. Maggie was suffocating at this very moment. There would be very little oxygen inside a sealed vault that small.

"Why?" Jack asked Imogene as she tried to pull herself up on the slippery rocks. "Why are you doing this to me?"

Peter and Harlan were watching and waiting. Harlan seemed completely under Peter's control, as if he were some sort of puppet. He had resigned himself to the situation. Like a fickle sports fan, Harlan had decided to hitch up with the winning team, who at the moment appeared to be Peter.

"Why can't you be a little more persuasive, Jack?" Peter said. "The love of your life is going to die any minute, and you can't force Imogene to open the vault for you? What kind of man are you?"

Suddenly a blood-soaked figure appeared in the cavern from a formerly hidden tunnel exit on the opposite side of the cave from Peter. His voice wasn't loud, but everyone heard him clearly.

"The kind of man you could never hope to be."

* * *

Peter's face turned white.

"Alex," he said with bitter astonishment. "I thought the bats finished you off."

Alex saw that Jack was about half-drowned with Imogene handcuffed to him.

"Al," Jack said. "Maggie's locked in that vault."

"Let them go, Peter." Alex tried to sound firm, but he knew he was pretty shaky.

Peter laughed. "Or what? You'll come over here and punch me? You don't have a weapon, and you don't look so good, Harris. You've died so many times that there's not too much of you left. Anyway, it seems like everyone in this room wants that vault open except for Imogene. And she's the only one who can do it."

Alex stood about ten yards away from Jack and Imogene to his right, and about twenty yards from Peter on his left—the three of them forming a triangle. Alex looked at Imogene, and then Peter, and then at the person next to Peter who was wearing his coat. He did have a weapon, but he couldn't take out two people with it. He quickly flicked his wrist, and Wesley's shuriken went spinning across the cave, heading right for Peter's heart. Even though his aim was good, Peter had good enough reflexes to dodge it, but not before it barely sliced his left arm."

Peter wiped at the blood on his sleeve. He started to laugh. "Is that it? That's all you got?"

Alex didn't want to admit that it was. He was out of weapons and out of options. Teddy suddenly appeared in the entrance behind Alex and barked, sending echoes through the cave. The large canine ran past Alex and over to where Jack was lying on the ground. Teddy licked Jack's face and whimpered.

"Even your dog won't stand by you, Alex," Peter said. "Don't worry, it will all be over soon. I can take out everyone and their dog with one shot." He pulled a hand grenade out of his pocket and yanked the pin out with his teeth. "Remember our old football days? Let's see if you can catch this. Peter pulled back and launched the live grenade right in between the spot where Alex and Jack were.

Alex had less than a second to make a decision. If he ran as fast as he could, he might be able to catch it or throw himself on the grenade so that he could save Jack. Otherwise it was pretty certain that the grenade would take out all three of them. He looked at Jack briefly. He was a combat-trained Navy SEAL, and he would do whatever the situation required.

I'm so sorry, Maria, he thought as he lunged forward and prepared to make the last catch of his life.

* * *

Jack watched the grenade come sailing through the air. Like in a slow-motion video, time somehow became stretched and distorted. He wanted only to turn back time and make a different decision. How could he have so foolishly handcuffed himself to Imogene and thrown away the key? He tried to tell himself that he did it to save Wesley, but now his rash decision meant they would all die. Because he was shackled to Imogene, he couldn't even get out of the way to save himself. Out of the corner of his eye, he could see Alex running toward the grenade instead of away from it. But it didn't matter—there was no way he could make it in time. The grenade was only a fraction of a second away from landing right next to both of them.

A vision of black jetted past him and blocked his view. It was Teddy doing what he had done hundreds of times in the front yard. He leaped into the air, catching the grenade in his mouth before it touched the ground. With speed and agility, Teddy took several huge leaps back toward the person who threw it.

Peter had no time to retreat before the grenade exploded in a ball of fire and smoke, filling the cave with an earsplitting boom and spraying everyone with rock and debris.

Jack threw his free arm over his head and used Imogene as a shield. Dust particles and rock chips rained down on them. The blast was big enough to fill the entire cave with smoke. He waited several seconds for the air to clear. Jack coughed and looked through the smoke in the direction Teddy had taken the grenade. He could just barely see that Peter, Harlan, and Teddy were lying motionless on the ground. He looked over at Alex and could see he was still moving.

"Peter is dead," Jack said as he shook Imogene, even though he didn't know that for sure. He hit her on the back. "You can have your stupid diamonds. Just open the door now. OPEN IT!" He slapped her face to knock some sense into her.

"Jack." Alex had picked himself up off the ground and was running toward them. "She's been hit." Jack rolled Imogene over and saw that she had been hit with a chunk of shrapnel in the head and appeared to be dead.

"No, this can't be. Wake up, I tell you!" Jack pounded on Imogene and shook her furiously. "You have to open it—she's going to die!" He searched for something sharp on the ground.

"Alex," Jack said. "Get me a knife, anything. I have to get out of these handcuffs."

"A knife won't cut through handcuffs, Jack."

"But it will cut through a hand," Jack responded, not relishing the gruesome task.

He heard more people talking, and suddenly Wesley was kneeling down at his side. "Dad, tell us what to do—we'll get Maggie out."

"Wes—you're alive!" Jack pointed to the half-submerged vault door. "Only Imogene can open it. It's a voice-activated computer."

"We have to find a way to force it open, then!" Wesley said in a panic.

"I know," Jack said. "But the door is bulletproof."

"Is there some other person who can open it?" Alex asked.

"Yes, but she wouldn't tell us who it was." Jack slapped Imogene's face again. "She said they were dead." Jack looked up at Wesley. "Wait a minute. Imogene thought you were dead." Jack yanked on his manacled hand. "She wouldn't open it because she thought Peter killed you. It has to be you, Wes. You're the one who can open it!"

11

Emergency Exit

Wesley examined the machine Imogene had used to open the vault. He didn't have the slightest idea what he was supposed to do.

"I don't know how to open it," Wesley stammered. "I've never seen this before in my life, and Imogene never told me a code."

"It's okay, Wes. Just try it." Jack pushed himself up on his knees with renewed energy and pantomimed the action of pressing the button. "It scans your eyes. Look in there and say your name."

Wesley looked into the binoculars and said, "Wesley Mackey." Nothing happened. He shook his head. "It's not working."

Amanda stepped up next to him. "Try your other name."

"Wesley Vandergrift," he said. In a few seconds, he said, "It worked! Now it's asking me for the code!"

Jack put his free hand to his head. "Okay, okay. It was a bunch of nonsense syllables. Something like itchy knee, son of a Hitachi . . . there was Q in there. It didn't make sense."

Wesley shook his head to show that he didn't understand.

"Wesley, count to ten in Japanese!" Alex said.

Wesley nodded. That made sense. He had taken Japanese in his private school for years. He remembered teaching Imogene how to count to ten. "Ichi, ni, san, shi, go, roku, shichi, hachi, kyu, ju."

"Now say 'open the vault'!" Jack yelled.

As soon as Wesley gave the command, everyone heard the click and sound of grinding gears. The water immediately stopped filling and started going down again.

"I think it worked," Wesley said with some relief. "But why isn't the door opening?"

"The water has to go down first," Jack told him. "But you unlocked it. Someone will have to swim over there and try to open it."

Alex rushed over to the side of the pool and got ready to jump in.

"Stop!" Harlan warned. "The suction will pull you under!"

Everyone looked and saw Harlan running with his slight limp toward them. He came from the opposite side of the cave where the grenade had supposedly taken him out, but he was untouched by the explosion. Even his shirt was clean. "Let me do it," he said to the stunned group. "I can open the door."

"Harlan?" Wesley was aghast. "But you were just . . ."

The group collectively rechecked the two bodies lying prone in the cave rubble.

"Eddie is dead," Harlan said.

"There really *are* two of them," Amanda said. "I told you."

"I'm so sorry, Harlan," Wesley said. "We didn't do it. Peter threw the grenade. Can you open the door? Maggie is inside."

Harlan nodded as he ran to the edge of the pool and sat down. He rolled up his pant leg, quickly twisted off his artificial leg, and set it down on the edge. Without a word, he dove into the black water and started swimming to the other side with strong arms and his one leg.

Jack, Alex, Wesley, and Amanda could scarcely breathe as they watched Harlan skillfully avoid the whirlpool and maneuver to the other side. The door was still half submerged as Harlan pulled himself up on the wheel-shaped handle with his strong upper body and turned it in a half circle. It clicked, and Harlan forced the door open. The water rushed inside.

"Is she alive?" Jack shouted.

Harlan didn't answer.

Wesley watched his dad put his head in his hands and start to pray.

* * *

Harlan pulled open the door, pushed the briefcase aside, and pulled Maggie's lifeless body out of the vault. Her skin was the color of death, her eyes closed. If Jack had been hopeful before, the sight of her was enough to extinguish that quickly. Of all the people inside the cave, Harlan seemed the least capable of pulling off a dangerous rescue, but Jack could do nothing to assist him. The force of the water would certainly pull him into the whirlpool, then swallow him down and spit him out into some underground waterway with no air for miles. But in spite of his limitations, Harlan seemed to be doing very well. Like a seasoned lifeguard, Harlan linked his arm under Maggie's chin and put her on his back. He paddled furiously around the draining water and back toward the rock ledge.

Alex picked up Harlan's prosthetic limb and pushed it out over the water for Harlan to grab onto. Harlan reached for it but slipped.

"You can get it, Harlan. Grab your foot!" Wesley yelled.

Harlan fought toward the outstretched limb and hooked his hand over the foot. Alex pulled them both to the side where Wesley and Amanda were ready to help them out of the water.

Alex quickly laid Maggie on the ground, and everyone could see that her face was blue. He put his face up to Maggie's nose and immediately started CPR, while Jack looked on helplessly.

"Is she breathing?" Jack asked, as he tried to scoot himself closer to where Maggie was.

Alex pumped on Maggie's chest four times. "Not yet."

"That vault is airtight," Harlan told them between labored breaths. "It was dry inside when I opened it."

"How long was she in there, Dad?" Wesley asked as he helped Harlan with his leg.

"I don't know." Jack shook his head. "It felt like an hour, but it was maybe twenty minutes."

Alex continued mouth-to-mouth resuscitation. After a minute, he paused to put two fingers on Maggie's neck. "I have a weak pulse. She's breathing again."

Jack felt a surge of hope. He pulled himself and Imogene over to where Maggie lay, leaving his attached left arm straggling behind him. Maggie's eyes fluttered open.

"You're still with us, Mag," Jack said. "Can you hear me?"

Maggie murmured something audible but unintelligible.

"Wesley and Amanda are fine," Jack said, knowing if she could speak, that would be the first question she would ask.

Maggie looked around disoriented for a moment then closed her eyes.

"Don't move her yet," Alex told everyone. "She needs some time to recover." He went over to check on the bodies of Peter and Eddie.

"Where's Harlan?" Jack looked around.

Harlan had reattached his leg and was heading straight for Jack with a crowbar. Without saying a word, he raised it high over his head and brought the end down just inches from Jack's outstretched hand. The handcuff chain snapped, and Jack pulled his hand away from Imogene. He looked up at Harlan. "Thanks, mate. For that and for saving my whole family. I owe you big time."

"Peter *is* dead," Alex called out to everyone. "And so is . . ." he stopped and looked at Harlan.

"I know my brother's gone," Harlan said. "You don't have to tell me."

Imogene started to stir. She sat up groggily. Her face was covered in dust that had turned to mud from her wet clothes and skin. She noticed that her handcuffed hand was unattached, but it took a moment to register where she was. She rubbed the gash on her head and then saw the vault door was ajar and nearly underwater again.

"What happened?" she asked, although she didn't sound too threatening anymore.

"You died," Jack said. "But unfortunately for us, they sent you back."

"Where are my diamonds?" she demanded.

"You mean the ones in the case we just dumped into the pool?" Jack asked. "Why don't you go dive for them?"

"I can see the case right there," Imogene said as she tried to stand but immediately collapsed on her ankle. "Ouch! I think my ankle is broken."

"That's nice," Jack said. "With your broken wrist, now you have a matching set."

Imogene only then realized Wesley and Amanda were standing several feet away. "Wesley! My darling—you're here!" She reached her arms out to him, and Wesley backed up a few feet.

Jack smoothed Maggie's hair and kissed her cheek. "She needs a doctor. Harlan, what's the fastest way out of here?"

"The way we came in—over there." Harlan pointed to where the bodies were strewn. "We have to go that way. But it won't be easy to carry someone over the narrow canyon pass."

"Been there, done that," Jack said as he scooped Maggie up into his arms and stood up like she weighed nothing at all. "Let's go."

"Wait!" Alex held up his hand. "We can't just leave Imogene here."

"Sure we can." Jack started walking toward the exit. "Just lock her in the vault. We'll send someone back for her—in a few days."

"There's no way I'm going to leave the diamond case and Imogene here alone," Alex reasoned.

"I don't care one bit about the diamond case. She can't walk, and we can't carry her; she's too heavy!" Jack protested.

Imogene cleared her throat. "*Excuse* me?"

"Oh, sorry. What I meant to say was, we can't carry her because *SHE'S TOO FAT.*"

Imogene looked appalled.

"Leave her!" Jack said. "Come on, everyone. We need to go."

"Those people are dead!" Imogene pointed to the bodies. "Don't leave me in here with dead people!" she begged as she hobbled to her feet.

"You'll have to hook up with some other unfortunate bloke," Jack said snidely. "In case you didn't notice, I'm not really your biggest fan." He ignored her as he walked over to the tunnel passage and carefully past the bodies strewn near the tunnel exit. He lingered a brief moment at the scene.

"Thank you, Teddy. You're a true hero," Jack said solemnly.

Amanda and Wesley followed Jack and choked back sobs as they tried not to look at what might be left of Teddy's body.

Alex nodded his head in agreement. "Teddy, we owe you our lives. That goes twice for me."

"By the way, Al," Jack said. "I'm really glad you're alive, mate. I get to keep my promise to Maria and bring you back for your wedding."

"Me too. Thanks for coming for me. How was Maria when you left?"

"Not good," Jack said. "But she looked a lot better than you, mate. You look like roadkill."

Alex nodded. "I feel about the same."

Harlan stopped and stared at Eddie. He was still wearing Alex's coat.

Jack took the opportunity to lay Maggie down on the ground and check her vital signs. Her cheeks were starting to pink up a bit, but her breathing was still shallow.

"I'm really sorry about your brother, Harlan," Amanda said.

"He was only twenty-six." Harlan made the sign of the cross and closed Eddie's eyes with his fingers. "I guess we all have to make our own choices. At least he's free now. He doesn't need to feel guilty anymore."

"Feel guilty about what?" Wesley asked.

"That he got our leg."

Jack turned around when he heard what Harlan said. "*Our* leg?"

"We were conjoined twins," Harlan explained.

"Joined at the hip. My left and his right leg were fused into one. They decided to separate us when we were eight months old, and the doctors thought that one of us should keep our shared leg. They gave it to Eddie."

"That was too bad for you," Amanda said.

"Not really." Harlan shrugged. "Everyone thought he had the better deal, so my parents sort of favored me. You know how that goes." Harlan wiped a tear from his face. "Well, it turned out that Eddie's leg wasn't so great after all. It was kind of deformed and never grew quite right. He had to have a bunch of surgeries, and it caused him a lot of pain. He was angry a lot. Took it out on me because my fake leg was easier to deal with. I could hike just as fast as the other kids, and I could even swim without it."

"You're an amazing swimmer," Wesley noted. "But why did Peter call you both Harlan?"

"That's our last name. Like a lot of people, Peter didn't want to go to the trouble to try and tell us apart. So he called us both Harlan. Some of our friends used to do that too. I never minded it as much as Eddie, so I just answered to Harlan. And then Eddie started calling me Harlan sometimes, because no one knew who he was talking about when he called me Emmett."

"So why didn't the bomb go off in the ticket office like it was supposed to?" Wesley asked.

"Eddie wired the original fuse, but then I rewired it to a remote detonator that would blast through the wall in the south tunnel in case Peter decided to set it off. I never wanted anyone to get hurt, but I had to make Peter think I was carrying out his orders." Harlan left Eddie's body alone and headed toward the exit. "The sooner we get out of here, the better. We're just lucky the explosion didn't take the lights out." He took the lead and motioned for everyone to follow him out through the exit and into the tunnel.

Maggie mumbled a few words, and Jack tenderly pushed the wet hair out of her face and followed Harlan.

Harlan spoke up as they moved along. "When we took this job with Peter," he said, "he told us he was a businessman who was going to fix up the caves and reopen them to the public. He told us his name was Peter Jacobs and he wanted us to help him get it done. He promised to pay us well and give us part ownership. By the time I figured out he wasn't who he said he was, Eddie already had big plans for the money he was going to pay us. I tried to convince him that Peter was bad news, but he wouldn't listen. He kept telling me that this was our dream. I wanted to protect Eddie, and I wanted to protect the cave." Harlan sighed and hung his head. "I did a pretty lousy job of both."

"Well, you saved my wife, and you saved Wesley and Amanda. I appreciate that, mate."

Harlan seemed embarrassed. "I didn't know until today how bad Peter really was. When I found out he was taking hostages and planning to kill people, I had to play along so he wouldn't suspect anything." Harlan stopped, backed up, and turned around. "We can't go this way anymore. The blast shifted a boulder loose, and the way is completely blocked."

"Are you sure?" Alex asked.

Jack looked over Harlan's shoulder to assess the situation. "He's as sure as Imogene is ugly. We can't get through there anymore."

* * *

"There is another way out of here, isn't there, Harlan?" Jack asked.

Harlan sighed. "This is going to get very complicated."

"Why?" Jack asked.

"There are only three ways out of this section of the cave," Harlan stated. "And two of them I would not recommend."

"Which one do you recommend?" Jack asked.

"This was it," Harlan said.

The group turned around and covered the short distance back into the underground pool section.

Jack pointed to the opposite side of the cave. "Why can't we go out that way, the way you and Alex and the kids came in?"

Harlan shook his head. "We took an elevator that isn't in the best working condition. The cable is very weak, and it was a huge risk to try it. I don't know how many trips it can make before it snaps. We'll have to go up no more than two at a time. But I guess we'll have to try." He led the group across the room and into the passageway that Alex had come through earlier.

"Shouldn't we get the diamonds?" Imogene asked. "The vault is open, and anyone could come in and take them."

"Yes, they could," Jack said with mock concern. "You better go over and get them—now that your ankle is miraculously healed."

Alex eyed the open safe. "You know, Jack, the water is down now. I think with the large sum of money we're talking about, it would be a good idea to collect the briefcase. He clambered down on the ledge and hiked through the shallow part of the water over to the safe. He picked up the heavy aluminum brief-case, carried it back to the group, and set it down.

"What's the combination?" Alex looked at Imogene.

"I'm not giving it to you," Imogene said.

"I think you are." Alex grabbed Imogene's injured wrist and twisted it behind her back.

Imogene screeched in pain. "5-1-1-9-3!" she blurted out.

"Good move, Al."

Alex tried the combination, and the case clicked open. Inside the case were black velvet pouches and, as expected, they were each filled with thousands of dia-monds in varying sizes. Most of them were extremely large, and a few were exotic colors. Imogene gazed at the diamonds like a starving castaway tempted with a steak dinner.

Alex seemed satisfied with what he saw. "I just wanted to make sure there was something in here worth dragging out. It's not exactly light."

"Aw, cheer up," Jack said to Imogene. "Peter doesn't have your diamonds. We do."

Imogene gave Jack a disgusted look and followed Harlan and the group to the other side of the cave while

Alex shut the case and carried it over to the entrance he had come through earlier. The passageway was larger and also lighted, but the lights were flickering. However, the more obvious problem was the gaping hole where the elevator was supposed to be.

"Where's the elevator?" Amanda asked.

"Hopefully it's back up at the top," Harlan said as he leaned over the abyss and shined his flashlight up. He clicked his tongue and pointed his flashlight down. "Boy, are we lucky."

"What do you mean?" Wesley asked.

"The elevator isn't up there. It's down *there*. The cable probably broke with one of the explosions."

"So why is that lucky?" Amanda asked.

"Because," Harlan said, as if the point were obvious, "no one was in there when it broke. I'm surprised the four of us made it down safely."

"Wait a minute!" Jack said. "So you were the last person to use the elevator?"

"Yes, when I saw that the elevator had been used, I came down that way too," Harlan explained. "But that doesn't mean I broke it."

"What about the elevator shaft?" Wesley asked. "Can we climb it?"

"Let's see. Harlan has one leg, Alex has been beaten to a pulp, Imogene's really out of shape, and Maggie's unconscious. How about that third way out?"

Harlan shook his head. "The south passage really isn't an option. It's been completely sealed off for years. It's unlit and would be the most dangerous."

"More dangerous than scaling a vertical elevator shaft with this group?" Jack asked. "What exactly do you mean by *dangerous*?"

Harlan pointed to the DIAMONDBACK CAVE TOURS logo on his soggy green shirt. "Read this. Can anyone take a guess why it's called *Diamondback* Cave?"

"Diamondback rattlesnakes," Wesley said.

"Snakes?" Jack heaved a sigh of relief. "Why didn't you say so? I don't know if you know this, mate, but I do have some experience with snakes."

"He knows who you are, Dad. Don't the snakes hibernate in the winter?"

Jack and Harlan answered at the same time. "Yes."

"But," Harlan continued, "they become very aggressive when threatened. And we've just set off two explosions right in the middle of their habitat."

"I'll go first," Jack offered. "Unless we step on one, they'll try to avoid us. It's highly unlikely we'll even run into one."

Harlan put up his hand. "The south passage has been sealed up for nearly fifteen years. They not only gated it but also cemented over the gate. I came in from the other side and set the dynamite to blow a hole through it, but I don't know how well it worked—or even if the passage is clear or not. So we might hike for a few hours just to find out we have to turn around and come back. We won't know until we get there."

"Can't we just send one of us to hike out and bring back help?" Wesley asked.

"That's another possibility. Since I'm the only one who knows how to get out, it would have to be me." Harlan looked at the group. "I might be able to get out through the south tunnel in two or three hours if I don't run into any problems."

"What kind of problems—other than snakes?" Jack asked.

"Well, some debris may have fallen and sealed off any number of the tunnels. It's pretty narrow in some spots. Also, this particular tunnel connects with several other tunnels and winds deeper into the cave before heading out. It's very easy to get lost. With no light—if you lose your flashlight it's all over."

"Okay, now tell us the good news," Jack said.

"On the other hand, even if I do make it out, it'll be several hours before the rescue team can send someone in. It would be dark by then, so they wouldn't start until morning. They need to get maps, professional spelunkers, rappelling equipment, and all the accessories that go along with a major rescue. It could be a day or more before they get the rest of you out."

"And that's assuming you don't run into problems," Jack said. "All in favor of moving out together right now say 'aye.'"

Alex, Wesley, and Amanda said "aye."

"Okay, that settles it," Harlan interjected. "The longer we wait, the weaker and hungrier we'll be. How many flashlights do we have?"

Alex checked his pocket. "The battery went out on this one a while ago."

"I have this one." Harlan pointed to his belt with a high-powered flashlight hooked to it.

Amanda reached for the mini flashlight on the pepper spray container around her neck. "I have a little one," she offered, "but it's not very powerful."

"Eddie always carries a flashlight," Harlan said. "I'll go get it and see if it still works." He headed back to the bodies one more time.

"This is ridiculous," Imogene muttered. "We need to wait for the rescue team."

"Hey, Attila the Hun," Jack said, "that's a great idea. Did you happen to register your travel plans with anyone before you came down here today?"

Imogene lost her temper. "I've had enough of your insults!"

"Then find your own way out of here!" Jack retorted.

Wesley positioned himself between Jack and Imogene. "Stop fighting, okay? Listen, Harlan knows what he's talking about, and I trust him to get us out of here. But we have to cooperate. Harlan's family used to own these caves, and they gave tours here. If he hadn't survived, I don't think we could have found our way out on our own."

"She started it," Jack said.

"Wesley's right," Alex said. "Let's get out of here first and deal with Imogene later."

Harlan came running back, wearing Alex's dusty and ripped leather coat and sporting another working flashlight.

"I'll go first. The Snake Stalker should be right behind me, doubling our line of defense. Oh, I guess this is your coat," he said to Alex. He started to take off the jacket.

"You keep it, Harlan," Alex said. "It's yours now. But I would like my cell phone if it's in there."

Harlan pulled a phone out of the jacket pocket and gave it to Alex, while Amanda ran over and picked up Maggie's shoes. She put them on Maggie's feet to keep them warm. Wesley took off his sweatshirt and draped it over Maggie's wet shirt. Jack shifted Maggie in his arms.

"Why don't you take the case and let me carry her for a while, Jack?" Alex offered.

"No thanks, mate. You can carry your own wife next week."

12

Tunnel Vision

After Maria had stayed with Penny and Walter for several hours, she had gone back to her house under the guise that she needed to take something for her headache. The truth was that she needed to collect her thoughts and figure out how to do something constructive. She couldn't just sit home and do nothing when the five people who meant everything in the world to her were in mortal danger. To lose any one of them would completely devastate her.

What if Peter had been successful in killing Alex this time? What would she do? This really couldn't be happening to her right now. She was supposed to be getting married in a few days. She should be worrying about whether her flowers were going to be the right shade of pink, not whether those flowers would be used for a funeral instead. She thought she'd had enough near-death experiences to last her entire life after what happened last summer. Surely the angels keeping track of her life would say she'd filled her challenge quota and it was time to let someone else take the big ones for a change.

The doorbell startled her. Her heart started to race. Maybe the police had come to tell her that everyone had been killed. They usually came in person to give you that kind of news. It rang again, and she almost didn't answer it, but then she leaped up and quickly opened the door.

Elliot Skinner, the cute boy who had a major crush on Amanda, was at the door. She let out a sigh of relief. "I'm sorry, Elliot," Maria said. "Amanda isn't home."

"You mean she and Wesley aren't back yet?"

"No." Maria tried to think of a cover story so he wouldn't ask any more questions. "They aren't back from school yet. I'll have them call you when they get back—bye." She started to close the door.

"Wait." Elliot stopped the door with his foot. "Do you know where they are?"

Maria was a bad liar, so instead of answering, she asked him a question. "Do *you* know where they are, Elliot?" She didn't expect him to know the answer.

Elliot looked at the ground. "I really didn't think it was a good idea, but they talked me into it."

Maria stopped and opened the door wider. "They talked you into what?"

"Into taking them out there—they said it was really important. Life and death, even. They said they would get a ride home, but neither one of them is answering my calls. I'm kind of worried."

Maria grabbed Elliot by the arm, ushered him inside the house, and sat him on a chair in the kitchen. "Elliot, this is very important. Did you drive Amanda and Wesley someplace this morning?"

Elliot nodded. "I'm in a lot of trouble, aren't I?"

"No, Elliott, you are not in trouble. But Wesley and Amanda are. I really need you to tell me where you took them today."

"I don't know where we were. It's just some place out in the middle of nowhere—like about an hour and forty-five minutes from here."

"Can you draw me a map?"

"Wesley gave me a map so I could drive back home on my own. It's still in my truck." Elliot was starting to look scared. "What's going on? This is a big deal, isn't it?"

Maria bit her lip and couldn't stop the tears that once again filled her eyes. She nodded. "This is a very big deal."

* * *

Jack's arms were getting tired from carrying Maggie, but her being alive gave him the extra strength he needed to press on. He wasn't about to let someone else carry her, in case she woke up. She kept coming in and out of a semiconscious state but hadn't said anything coherent yet. Jack was wondering if she might have been without oxygen long enough to cause brain damage, but he kept his thoughts to himself as they traveled down the south passage with Harlan leading the way and the rest of the group following behind him.

Suddenly Maggie opened her eyes. She looked up at Jack in bewilderment.

"Jack?" She appeared startled. "Why are you carrying me?"

"Mag. You're awake!"

"Where am I?" Maggie pushed away from Jack and tried to stand up on her own. Even though he wasn't sure if she was strong enough yet, Jack put Maggie down on her feet and prepared to catch her if she fell. The rest of the group stopped and waited for them.

"We're still in the cave. You really scared me there, Mag." Jack was elated to see that not only could she talk, but she could also stand without assistance. He wrapped his arms around her tightly and kissed her.

Maggie shoved Jack away, swung her arm back, and with considerable force slapped him in the face.

Jack was so startled, he nearly fell over. He stumbled back, his hand shooting up to his cheek. "What did you do that for?"

"That was completely inappropriate!" Maggie said with indignation.

Jack rubbed his cheek with his hand.

"Inappropriate for me to kiss my wife after she nearly died?"

The group of stunned onlookers waited for Maggie to respond to Jack.

"*You* are *not* my husband!"

Jack narrowed his eyes and looked at Maggie with bewilderment. He started to correct her, but Alex stepped in between them.

"Jack, she's not herself yet. She may be suffering from some temporary disorientation after the trauma." Alex turned his attention to Maggie. She looked at him like he might bite her. "Do you know what your name is?"

"Yes, my name is Maggie Scott. Who are you?"

"I'm Alex, and I'm also your friend. Do you know who the rest of these people are?" Alex illuminated Wesley and Amanda with his flashlight.

"No." Maggie furrowed her brow. "Should I?" Maggie looked around and put her hands up to her head. "What's going on here? Why am I in a cave? I don't feel so good."

"It's a long story, Mag," Jack explained. "Do you know who I am?"

"Of course. You're Jack Mackey." She thought for a minute. "You're my brother-in-law . . ."

"And that's *all* you remember?" Jack asked.

"No, I don't know. Everything's all blurry. I know my sister died—and her baby."

Alex held up his hand, warning everyone not to say anything. "I'm not a doctor, but I've seen this before. It looks like the trauma she experienced has caused some retrograde amnesia. She knows who she is and who you are, Jack, but not Wesley or Amanda, so a chunk of her memory is missing—but fortunately not all of it."

"But it's just temporary, right?" Jack looked at Alex.

"I don't really know. It depends on a lot of different things." Alex aimed his flashlight at Maggie's eyes, and she flinched. "She doesn't appear to have a concussion—her pupils are the same size."

"How did I get here?" Maggie asked again.

"You've had a traumatic event," Alex explained. "You were without air for a while, and you nearly died, but we revived you. You walked into this cave to help save the lives of Wesley and Amanda," he said, pointing to them. "And they are very special people to you. Thanks to your efforts, they're still with us."

Maggie shook her head. "I'm sorry. I don't recognize either one of you." She looked down at her left hand and screamed.

"What?" Jack instinctively ran to comfort her, but she pushed him away.

"I have a wedding ring on!"

Jack nodded. "I told you we were married."

"This is impossible!" Maggie ranted as she pulled on her damp and tangled hair. "I must be dreaming. I remember now. I live alone—just me and my dog, Teddy. I have a great job. I'm a vet. Why would I marry you, Jack? You live in Australia. We never really got along, did we? This is a really crazy dream, isn't it? I just need to figure out how to wake myself up."

"If you were dreamin', would you feel this?" Jack pinched her arm.

"Ouch!" Maggie jumped. She slapped Jack on the arm. "Stop that! See what I mean? You're so annoying!"

"That's true." Jack looked into her eyes. "But you love me anyway. We have twin girls. You don't remember them either?"

"I'm a mother?" Maggie started to hyperventilate. She dropped her hands and started pacing around. It was clear she couldn't process what was going on.

Alex took Jack by the arm and pulled him aside. He spoke very quietly. "Jack, hold off on the information overload. We don't want to get her heart racing any faster, or she'll go into shock again." He turned his attention back to Maggie.

"It's okay, Maggie," Alex reassured her. "I'm sure this is confusing to you, so we'll talk more later when you've had a chance to recover and remember things on your own. Right now we need to focus on getting ourselves out of this cave. Do you feel strong enough to walk by yourself now?"

Maggie wrung her hands and nodded.

"This is Harlan." Alex pulled him over. "We've all just met Harlan today, but he saved your life. He knows where he's going, and he's going to lead us out of here, okay?"

Maggie looked at Imogene, the only person who had yet to be introduced. "Who is she?"

"Nobody," Jack chimed in.

Imogene kept quiet while Maggie studied her dirt-stained face. "I think I know you," Maggie said. "You look familiar to me."

Jack grabbed Maggie by the shoulders and turned her around so her back was facing Imogene. "You don't want to remember her."

Harlan urged the group to keep moving, because they didn't have a lot of time with the flashlights. Maggie took one last look at Imogene before she turned around. "I'm sure I know her."

* * *

The group of seven hiked through the myriad of intersecting tunnels without speaking. Harlan led the group with a high-powered flashlight. Jack, Maggie, Imogene, Wesley, and Amanda followed with the second flashlight. Alex brought up the rear, carrying the diamond case. Wesley was feeling better now that Maggie was walking and talking, but she seemed like an emotional wreck. He also knew that Alex had placed himself and Maggie on either side of Imogene to serve as a buffer between Imogene and Jack.

Wesley had a bunch of questions he wanted to ask Alex about what had happened, but he didn't want to bring up anything that might distress Maggie further. Besides, Harlan had just lost his twin brother and was either recovering quickly from his death or was still in shock. But either way, that was a subject no one wanted to bring up.

Harlan seemed to enjoy being the tour guide and did enough talking for the entire group. When he wasn't pointing out specific cave formations and telling them historical and geological facts, he talked about his dog. When he ran out of stories, he started singing instead. He had a decent voice and ran through a playlist of songs from the top forty.

In the middle of Harlan's rendition of a popular rap tune, complete with sound effects, Imogene clenched her fists and shouted rudely, "Stop that incessant noise!"

Harlan immediately stopped his performance and stood still. He turned around slowly. "Excuse me, would you like to take a shot at being the leader for a while?"

"No. But can't you keep your mouth shut for five seconds?"

Wesley was afraid that if Imogene made Harlan too angry, it would cause an all-out brawl, but Harlan seemed to be taking her outburst in stride.

"This is a big part of cave safety," Harlan said evenly.

"What does driving us all crazy have to do with cave safety?" Imogene demanded.

Harlan turned around and resumed walking. "If you haven't noticed, it's dark in here. The sound of my voice helps people to follow along and not get lost."

"But you said there are snakes in here," Imogene countered. "You're going to wake them up."

"Actually, snakes are deaf. But now that you've brought it up, that's the real reason I'm singing. Snakes can sense sound vibrations, and I'm sending out a warning that we're coming so they can get out of the way before we accidentally step on them."

"Is that true?" she asked Jack.

"Are you askin' me?"

"Yes, I'm asking you."

Jack shrugged. "I don't know. Actually, I'm just an actor—I have a stunt double who does all that snake stuff for me."

Imogene huffed and slackened her stride.

Wesley turned back to Amanda and snickered. Imogene had claimed for years that Jack's show was all a fake.

Harlan resumed the chorus of his song, and Jack joined him, making Imogene even more annoyed. They walked for a few more minutes until Harlan put up his hand and abruptly stopped singing. He slapped the back of his neck and kicked his leg. Jack brushed something off his shirt, and Maggie swiped at her face. Then Maggie screamed, and Imogene screamed louder. Imogene's scream was shrill and high, punctuated with convulsive movements.

Wesley's ears filled with an irritating chirping sound, and the air suddenly became thick with some sort of juicy insect.

"Spiders!" Imogene cried. "Jumping spiders are all over me!" She slapped at the nasty-looking bugs that landed all over her body.

Imogene launched into a full-blown panic attack, running and gyrating, hitting herself and screaming at the top of her lungs. From the back, Amanda's flashlight illuminated the clear, brownish-red invaders.

Jack caught one and held it up to the light. "These aren't spiders. They only have six legs. And some really, really long antennae."

"Don't panic," Harlan said. "They're cave crickets. They look a little scary, but they won't hurt you."

"Get them off of me!" Imogene shrieked. "They're biting me!"

K.L. Fogg

"They don't bite," Amanda said to Wesley. Imogene waved her arms around and swatted the bugs. "They just have pointy legs, and she is freaking out."

Harlan tried to move the agitated group forward. "Keep moving, everyone! Hopefully we'll get out of the swarm if we push forward."

Wesley gave Imogene a swift kick in the rear to get her moving, since she was holding everyone up. She barely noticed as she bounced off the walls, trying to scrape off the bugs. She didn't stop screaming and convulsing until several minutes after the air cleared and the crickets had all disappeared.

Five minutes after the last cricket was spotted, Imogene was still having spasms. "Is there one on me still?" Imogene asked the group. "I can feel it. There's one on me, isn't there?"

"No, you're good." Jack turned around and smiled. "Other than that one in your hair."

Imogene shuddered and slapped herself on the head, wiping the nonexistent cave cricket away.

Jack turned around and started to follow Harlan again, chuckling to himself. "How much farther, Harlan?"

"I think we're about halfway."

"Too bad," Jack said. "This is startin' to get fun."

"Other people's misery is entertainment for you, Jack?" Maggie said scornfully.

"No, just *her* misery," Jack explained. "It's one of life's simple pleasures. Tormenting the person you hate most."

In the darkness Wesley couldn't read Maggie's expression, but he got the impression she wasn't laughing at Jack's comment.

"Are you doin' all right, Mag?" Jack asked. "Do you feel okay?"

"I'm fine," Maggie said coolly.

"But if you're not okay, you'll let me know, right?"

"You'll be the first to know."

* * *

They walked along in silence for a time. Some sections of the tunnels were narrow enough that they had to walk single file. Jack was drained mentally and physically from the day's activities.

Harlan pointed out the red rock formations on one side. "Kind of reminds you of Mars in here, doesn't it?"

"Yeah. Feels like we're on another planet," Jack said.

"I remember when Eddie and I came down here as kids," Harlan reminisced. "We used to pretend that we were astronauts stranded on Mars. We even had our own Martian theme song."

"Isn't that lovely," Imogene said sarcastically. "I suppose we'll be hearing that from you now."

Harlan shrugged. "I reckon you suppose wrong."

Jack chuckled. This Harlan guy was odd, that was for sure, but Jack liked him. He had to give Harlan credit; he didn't let anyone push him around, including Imogene.

Some time later, Harlan turned a corner and stopped the group again. "I was afraid of that."

"Afraid of what?" Jack asked.

"The blast from the tunnel above caused a rock slide down here and closed off this passage. We're going to have to do some excavating."

"How bad is it?" Alex asked from the back.

Harlan shined his flashlight around an area the size of a school classroom, with an exit the size of a doorway.

There were rocks and debris strewn on the floor. The tunnel passage was almost completely blocked by fresh-ly broken, loose rocks, ranging in size from golf balls to basketballs.

"We can move those, can't we?" Jack said.

"That's not the problem," Harlan said. "We can move them, but we have to move fast. Our flashlights won't stay charged indefinitely. This bulb is already starting to dim."

"Okay, let's start movin' then."

Everyone in the group, including Maggie, started picking up rocks and depositing them against the far wall in the cave."

Imogene took the opportunity to sit down on a large boulder and massage her ankle.

Jack tapped her on the shoulder. "Excuse me, your highness, but we need *everyone* to help here."

"I can't. I'm too tired, my ankle hurts, my wrist is broken, and I can barely walk."

"Oh, no problem then." Jack patted her on the back, then walked away and started lifting the heavier rocks. "There's a cave cricket on you."

"Very funny. Like I would fall for that a second time."

No sooner had she said that when a cave cricket jumped directly from her shoulder to her face.

Imogene sprang up and ran toward the group screaming, flailing her arms and slapping herself in the face.

When she calmed down, Jack handed her a rock. "Kept a few extra critters in my pocket for just such an occasion," he said.

Imogene took the rock with an attitude of pure revulsion and set it down on the other side of the cave wall. "I don't believe it would be possible to detest any person more than I detest you, Jack."

"Oh, it's possible," Jack assured her.

Alex, who everyone knew hadn't eaten or slept for two days, seemed to be working the hardest to move the rocks.

"Alex, you might want to take it easy and save your energy," Wesley said. "You must be really wiped out."

"I know what it's like to spend the night in here," he said. "I don't want to do it again."

Jack posed the question everyone wanted the answer to. "Al, how did you get here? What happened?"

"Well, it's a pretty short story, actually. After I finished my interpreting job, I got into my car, and Peter jumped me. He took me by surprise. He knocked me out, tied me up, and brought me here."

"And worked you over pretty good, it looks like," Jack said.

"Oh, this?" Alex pointed to his shoulder. "Don't worry, it's just a superficial gunshot wound."

"Looks pretty official to me," Jack noted. "So how did you get away?"

"Well, I had a little help from some disgruntled bats who chased Peter off. And then Teddy the wonder dog came and rescued me—" Alex slammed on the brakes in mid-sentence.

Maggie turned around. "I have a dog named Teddy."

"Well, what a coincidence that is," Jack said, covering for Alex.

No one volunteered any more information.

"Is that *my* dog Teddy?" Maggie pressed.

Just then the pile of debris shifted, causing a small landslide, opening up a hole large enough for a person to fit through. The diversion came at a good time, because Jack didn't want to find out how Maggie in her fragile state would respond to the news that her beloved dog had just been blown up.

After Jack and Harlan rolled away the last heavy boulder, the passage was clear, but everyone was beginning to lose what was left of their energy.

"We're getting closer," Harlan assured them, "but we start going up at a pretty rapid pace here, and that's where we might run into some hostiles. That swarm of crickets wasn't a good sign. Whenever you have an imbalance in nature, something eventually comes along to level it out. Everyone stay close to the light."

* * *

After Harlan explained that they might run into some snakes, Wesley thought Imogene was going to have seizure right then. He knew from past experience that she was deathly afraid of snakes, and that's why she moved up to the front and strategically placed herself between Harlan and Jack.

"There goes my view," Jack complained. "Now I've got the backside of Sasquatch starin' me in the face."

Harlan peeked around each corner before pressing forward. "Normally it would be best to go that way, but we'd end up at the north blocked tunnel again. But it's very scenic, and there's a huge cave full of gray bats down there."

Alex could be heard from the back of the line. "I saw it. It was lovely."

Wesley and Amanda turned around and looked quizzically at Alex.

"Well, maybe I didn't *see* a whole lot, but I think that's where I was."

"You were there," Harlan confirmed. "That's where everybody ends up when they don't know where they're going. There are about five different tunnels that lead to that cave. But you must have hooked up with the north canyon pass if you got out. Because the south canyon was sealed up at the time."

Both flashlights were growing dimmer, but at the same time, it appeared to be getting lighter. The cave walls were full of cracks and crevasses. Up ahead, trickles of light filtered into the cave here and there. For the first time, it wasn't totally black. "We're in the twilight zone," Harlan said.

"You mean like, doo doo doo doo?" Jack sang the eerie TV show music.

"No," Harlan said, very serious. "This isn't science fiction. It's a real section of cave where the dark meets light. This is where they used to live."

"Where who used to live?" Jack asked.

"The snakes. But I don't see any yet."

"That's good, right?" Imogene had a tremor in her voice. "That means they found a new place to live."

"Possibly," Harlan said. "But that would be a very dangerous assumption to make. I'm willing to bet that the explosion scared them out of here and into the tunnels."

"Let's pick up the pace," Jack said with agitation. "The only thing worse than running into some of the locals would be running into them in the dark."

"Now remember," Harlan said, "we're treading on their territory. We don't want to harm any snakes. They don't attack unless provoked, so try not to do any provoking."

"I don't plan to," Amanda said to Wesley under her breath. "I get the feeling Harlan is more concerned about the safety of the snakes than he is about us."

"Okay, listen up!" Harlan ordered. "In this next section, we'll have to cross a narrow ledge that slopes to the outside in some spots. Stay as close as you can to the wall, because it has a sheer drop-off on one side. This is the southern section of the canyon pass, and it's deeper and more treacherous than the north canyon pass. We normally don't take visitors this way because of the danger. But you shouldn't have any problems unless you try to look down. Just look straight ahead at the person in front of you, stay next to the rock wall, and don't stop."

Wesley pushed forward without asking questions. Getting information from Harlan was worse than not knowing anything at all. Occasionally, loose rocks fell, and the sound disappeared before they could hear a final resting point.

"You wanna take a gander at how deep this is?" Jack ventured.

"Very deep," Harlan snapped. "Eyes up front, please."

They walked about fifty yards in silence across the canyon and got to the other side, where they entered a winding tunnel once again. After several minutes, Harlan told them, "Everyone link hands. That way we'll all stay together."

Everyone in line extended their arms to the person in front and back of them except Jack.

"No way," he said flatly, refusing to take Imogene's hand. "I'm not touchin' her."

"What is this?" Maggie asked. "Grade school? Why are you being so immature about this?" Maggie reached out and touched the walls on both sides. "Whatever feud you're having with her, just get over it, okay? I'd really like to get out of here."

"Sorry, Mag," Jack said. "I'll do it for you, but I won't get over it." He cringed and offered his hand to Imogene, who took it begrudgingly.

Wesley grabbed Amanda's hand. He noticed his hand was cold and clammy, and he wondered if Amanda was noticing it too.

"So did Alex move up to the front now?" Amanda asked.

"No, he's supposed to be behind you," Wesley answered.

"He's not anymore." Amanda dropped Wesley's hand and turned around. "Alex!" She aimed her flashlight backward, but it couldn't illuminate past the turn in the tunnel.

"Alex is gone!" Amanda was frantic. "He isn't here. I don't know where we lost him. We have to go back. Maybe he fell into the chasm."

Wesley thought this for a moment too, but then he talked himself out of it. "We would have heard him fall. The case is really heavy, and it's slowing him down. We should take turns carrying it for him. He probably just stopped to rest for a few minutes. Alex!"

Amanda took off running in the opposite direction of the group. "He doesn't have a flashlight—maybe he got separated at the turn."

"How could he have disappeared?" Wesley followed her. "He was right behind us!"

13

Over the Edge

Amanda wasn't about to come back without Alex. She and Wesley had risked their lives to save Alex, and she wasn't going to explain to her mom that they somehow lost track of him on the way home. She came back to the narrow ledge and was relieved to see that Alex was still there. But he was frozen in mid stride, staring intently at the rock ledge. He hadn't followed Harlan's advice not to look down, and now he was probably experiencing some vertigo.

Amanda stepped cautiously out onto the ledge and started the hike back to reach Alex, who was about a third of the way back.

"Stay where you are!" Alex ordered.

"It's okay, Alex," Amanda said. "I'm not afraid of heights." She continued to walk toward him.

"No!" Alex told her. "Don't come here!"

Amanda ignored Alex's warning, heading back toward him with speed and agility. She was only a few feet away when her flashlight illuminated a very large diamondback rattler. It was coiled and ready to strike.

Amanda had just foolishly put herself within striking distance.

"Don't move," Alex said calmly. "That's what Jack says to do, right?"

Amanda took one very slow step backward and the snake, sensing her movement, turned its head to face her. It rattled a warning.

Wesley stayed back a safe distance behind Amanda. "Don't run," Wesley warned. "Diamondbacks can strike at one third their body length."

"I've seen a lot of rattlesnakes," Amanda noted, "but never one this big."

"Stay perfectly still," Wesley admonished, "and I'll go back and get my dad."

* * *

It took Jack several minutes to reach the spot where Amanda and Alex were held hostage by the snake. He needed to bring back the entire group, with Maggie and Imogene, since Harlan had the only other flashlight. Maggie was feeling dizzy and queasy and admitted that she had a headache. Imogene complained that her skin was crawling, and she kept scratching her arms and the back of her neck. Jack had to find a secure place to set them down inside one of the tunnels before moving back out onto the ledge.

When he came upon the scene, the snake had moved within a foot of Amanda.

Amanda had been a *Snake Stalker* fan even before she knew Jack in person, so she knew what she was supposed to do. But holding still when a giant snake was in close proximity was harder than it looked. Jack was relieved to see that she was still okay, but when he saw the size of the diamondback, even the Snake Stalker himself was rattled. From the width of its body and size of its head, Jack figured it was probably close to ten feet long. But the last thing Amanda or Alex needed to hear at the moment was that he'd never seen such a big rattlesnake.

"Jack, I'm really scared," Amanda said without taking her eyes off the snake. "I was about to use my pepper spray on it."

"No, no, no! Don't do that!" Harlan limped up next to Jack as fast as he could and shined his brighter light on the snake edging in more closely.

Jack was about to order him to stand back, but Harlan waved him aside as if Jack didn't know what he was doing. In one hand he sported a long, thick stick he had picked up somewhere in the cave.

"I don't believe it!" Harlan said as though he just received the best Christmas present ever. "You found Randy! He walked without trepidation around Jack on the outside of the ledge and went toward the snake until he was standing right next to Amanda, and well within striking distance. "Randy." He leaned over like he was talking to an old friend. "I thought you'd be gone by now. You sure have gotten big."

"You know this snake?" Jack asked in a puzzled tone.

"Do I *know* this snake? He's like kin to me. It's okay, he's pretty docile. I remember when he used to have only one fang, but these guys have the ability to grow a new set of choppers." Harlan reached back and handed the flashlight to Jack, then stretched the stick out. The snake he called Randy slithered onto it, and Harlan raised it off the ground. Randy coiled his extra-large body around it. "You guys don't know how lucky you are to run into this guy. Now Doris, on the other hand, would have been quite a different story. I'm afraid we would have had an incident with her."

Amanda took the opportunity to scoot back, away from both Randy and Harlan. Alex couldn't change positions without getting closer to Randy, so he stayed where he was and smashed himself closer to the rock wall.

"Wait a minute, mate." Jack was completely befuddled. "I know you said we entered the twilight zone. But as far as I know, rattlesnakes aren't tame. You can't train them like some sort of pet."

"I never said Randy was *tame*. I said he was *docile*. He's just not as aggressive as some of the others. Snakes are just like people—they come in all sorts of personalities. We have a mutual respect for one another, Randy and I. He knows I'm not going to hurt him. He must be going on . . . what . . . eighteen years old by now."

"That would explain his large size," Jack commented.

"Harlan," Alex said, "when you mentioned 'some of the others . . .'" He cleared his throat. "How many *others* are there?"

"I don't know. A couple dozen. Maybe more. I haven't been in the south passage for a long time. I brought Randy here when I was eight, but they closed this off when I was twelve. Doris—she's the oldest female—has been around for maybe seventeen years. As for the kids, I'm not sure how many have stayed around."

"The kids?" Jack shook his head. "You said you *brought* Randy here?"

"From the north side of the cave," Harlan explained. "For safety reasons. We didn't want the tourists harassing them."

"And I'm sure the tourists felt the same. I think we better move out of here before the whole family decides to drop in. Sorry to put a damper on this reunion, mate. But maybe you and Randy could catch up on old times a little later, after we're in another zip code."

Harlan walked past Alex to find a safe place to deposit Randy back into the crevices of the rock. Alex took the opportunity to scoot away from both of them. As he did, rattles echoed inside the wall. A triangular head shot out of the cracks and hissed down by Alex's leg.

Jack shined Harlan's flashlight into the yellow-slitted eyes. "Behind you, Al!" he yelled.

Alex turned just in time to see the rattlesnake poised to strike. The diamond case was down on the ground next to his feet. He nudged it with his foot just as the snake lunged for him. The snake's open maw hit the aluminum briefcase instead of Alex's leg. With only a few seconds before the snake would rebound and try another attack, Alex tried to get out of the way. He took a step to the side, knocking the case as he did, and ran back toward Jack and Amanda. The diamond case tipped over, landing precariously close to the edge.

As Harlan had warned, some sections of the ledge sloped toward the chasm, and this happened to be one of those sections. They watched helplessly as the diamonds inside shifted, tipping it off balance. The case slid a few inches and looked like it might stop. But then the momentum pushed it an inch too far, and the laws of motion and gravity took over.

The briefcase teetered and then tumbled off the edge. Everyone heard the sound of the aluminum bouncing off the steep rock once, twice, and then a long time of nothing.

Alex turned around and looked at the vacant spot where the snake must have retreated. It was eerily quiet as Harlan came back and joined the group, without Randy and his twisted stick.

Alex sighed and slid his hand over his face.

"Nice moves," Jack said to Alex. "Way to give 'em the slip."

"Yeah. That little slip only cost two hundred million dollars." Alex looked sick.

"Hey, it's only money," Jack declared. "Can I break the news to Imogene? Oh please, can I tell her you dumped her fortune into a bottomless pit?"

"Oh, it's not bottomless," Harlan said. "There's definitely a bottom—it's just not too easy to get there. But there's nothing we can do about it now. We'll have to send a recovery crew in later."

"Shh!" Jack put his finger up to his lips. "Don't let her know that. Tell her they're gone for good."

While Amanda and Wesley discussed the possibility that the case had broken open and diamonds would be scattered everywhere, the group traversed back to the wider area where Maggie and Imogene were sitting.

Imogene didn't need to wait for Jack to fill her in. "Did I hear you right? You just dropped my diamonds over the cliff?"

"Yep," Jack said happily. "Two hundred mil and some change just went bye-bye. Looks like you'll have to trade in the Maserati. I hear Ford Fiestas are nice."

Imogene started to wail. She scratched at her arms and legs. "I can't stand this anymore!" she cried.

"It's tough to lose your best friends," Jack said, "but we'd appreciate it if you'd suffer in silence."

"No, my skin is itching and burning!" Imogene cried.

"My skin is itchy too," Maggie said.

"I can explain that." Harlan lowered himself into a squat. "Your itchy skin is caused by the acidity of the water in the underground pool. Limestone will do that. You just have more sensitive skin than most people. But scratching it will only make it worse." He stood up, looked around at the group, and clapped his hands once. "We have to change the plan."

"Why?" Jack asked.

"Because one of our flashlights just ran out of batteries, and the one I have isn't going to last very long. That little detour cost us time. According to my watch, it'll be dusk in about thirty minutes. And we're about a mile and a half from the exit. We need to find a safe zone where we're less likely to run into more snakes—if and when our light goes out. And this isn't a safe zone. It looks like we'll have to find a place and hunker down for the night."

"I am *not* spending the night in here!" Imogene ranted. "Not with those horrible crickets and giant rattlesnakes!"

"Hey," Jack interjected. "It's *Randy*."

"Are you sure there are no other options?" Alex prodded. "A mile and a half isn't that far. Isn't there some other way out of here?"

"Not unless we had some special equipment," Harlan answered.

"We can't spend the night in here," Jack said. "It's cold, and we all have wet clothes on. Maggie and Alex both need to get to a doctor."

"I know," Harlan said, "but the question isn't whether we're going to stay in here all night. The question is where we're going to stay. We just saw two snakes, and I think you already know that these rocks are full of them, and they aren't very happy with us. And I don't care how much you know about snakes. It's just not wise to take seven people on an excursion through their recently disturbed territory without the proper equipment. We'll go back to the original plan, and I'll go alone and bring back help."

"No," Alex said sternly. "We only have one working flashlight now. That would leave us all here with no light and no knowledge of how to get out of here if something happened to you. And no one knows where we are. From what you've told us, this whole section of the cave has been inaccessible for years."

"That's what I've been trying to tell you from the beginning. If anyone else has a better idea," Harlan challenged, "I'd like to hear it."

* * *

Alex was suddenly overcome with a feeling of déjà vu. He had never been trapped in a cave before on any of his undercover missions, so he couldn't understand why he felt like he'd been in this situation before. The group was having a heated discussion on what they should do while Alex took a few steps back and tried to focus on the problem. He kept thinking that he already knew the solution because he'd done this before. If only he could remember what it was.

"The elevator isn't an option anymore," Harlan clarified.

A light went on in Alex's head. *The elevators don't open on the first floor.* A flash from his dream came to him. He was in the high-rise building again. *All the exits to the ground floor were blocked.* The only way outside was to go up. It was suddenly clear to him what they had to do.

"Harlan," Alex said, "how do the bats get into that cave you were talking about?"

"There's a small opening at the top of that cavern," Harlan said, "but it would be easier for us to climb up the elevator shaft than scale those rocks. And then I'm not sure most of us could fit through the space even if we did manage to get to the top."

"But if you could climb up there, you would be at ground level, right?"

"Right. *If* you could climb up there, which you couldn't."

"Have you ever tried it?"

Harlan patted his prosthetic leg. "Climbing's not my specialty."

"I'm a good climber," Wesley said, "and so is Amanda."

"Does anyone have a cell phone besides me?" Alex asked.

Wesley and Amanda shook their heads.

"Peter took mine away," Jack said, "and Maggie's is in the car."

"Do you have the car keys?" Alex asked.

Jack checked his pockets and shook his head. "Mag, do you remember—?" He stopped himself. "I don't know what happened to the keys. They probably fell out in the underground pool."

Alex pulled his phone out of his pocket. "I have my phone. I don't know if it was permanently damaged in the blast or if there's any charge left in it, but if someone can give me a boost, I can climb to the top of the cave and try to make a call for help. Maybe I won't even have to fit through the opening. Don't you think that's worth a try?"

"Well, if it doesn't work, at least we'll have a safe place to stay the night," Harlan said. "That's one of the few places we can get to from here without having to cross the canyon again."

"Please, let's try it," Maggie said with desperation in her voice. "I really need to get out of here."

"To the bat cave, Robin!" Jack sounded like he was starting to get giddy. "But Alex is in no condition to do any climbing. I'll do it."

14

Back in Black

Wesley was trying to hold steady while balancing on his dad's shoulders, but it wasn't easy with Amanda sitting on Wesley's shoulders. He braced himself against the smooth rock wall, which had no footholds for eight feet. After that, there was a shallow ledge and jutting, jagged rocks that looked only slightly more negotiable to climb. Above that they could only speculate, because Harlan's one and only flashlight couldn't illuminate that far.

Amanda had convinced everyone that if she had a big enough boost, she was sure she could climb from the shallow ledge to the ceiling. Jack couldn't stand on Alex's shoulders because of Alex's bullet wound, and they needed another several feet of height to be able to reach the ledge, so Wesley volunteered. He had felt pretty confident about it earlier, but now beads of perspiration were dripping from his forehead.

Amanda was the smallest person in the group and would be most likely to fit through the opening at the top of the cave. Normally no responsible adult would ever encourage her to try something so risky. But these weren't normal circumstances. After trying several different combinations of people making pyramids, everyone agreed that Amanda was the only person they could hoist up.

It was dusk and winter, so most of the bats were hibernating inside the cave. Amanda would be getting extremely close to them, and there was a possibility she could set them off in a frenzy like Alex had done earlier. But it was either that or just sit in the cave and wait. If there was just enough charge left in Alex's cell phone to call 911, it was better than nothing.

"I can't reach the ledge yet," Amanda told them. "I'm going to have to stand on Wesley's shoulders. I feel like a cheerleader up here."

"Well, if you fall, the quarterback will catch you," Jack grunted, bracing himself against Harlan and the wall.

Harlan shined his light up so she could see. Even though Amanda was very strong and athletic, the odds of anyone getting to the top of this cave without a rope and almost no light were pretty slim. Wesley felt Amanda's weight shift, and he tried to counterbalance with his own weight, but that made Jack a little wobbly. As Amanda stepped onto Wesley's shoulders, the three-high stunt started to shake. Harlan steadied Jack at the base while Amanda grabbed the top of the rock ledge and pushed off Wesley to get some momentum. That push shoved Wesley off Jack's shoulders. He was quick enough to land on his feet.

Wesley looked up to see Amanda swing one leg up to the ledge. Her safety net was gone, and she strained to pull herself up. Harlan's light was so dim it barely helped her out. After she situated herself on the ledge, she pulled her feet underneath her and stood up. She switched on the mini flashlight around her neck.

"What's it look like up there?" Alex yelled.

"Lots of bat droppings," Amanda answered. "Pretty disgusting."

"Can you get to the top?" Wesley called up to her.

"I don't know yet," Amanda said. "It looks like I'm at least thirty feet from the top. I have to climb higher to get a better look." She disappeared from everyone's view as she went behind another rock.

"I see a way up if I can get across to the other side," Amanda told the group. "If I go up and around and then jump across, I can reach it, I think." She lowered her voice to a near whisper. "I can see the bats, and I don't want to wake them up, so I'm going to stop talking."

"Amanda, don't try anything too dangerous," Alex said like a true parent. It was quiet for several minutes. No one wanted to introduce screaming bats into an already tense situation.

"This isn't good," Alex said. "I'm sorry—it was a bad idea. I don't know why I agreed to send her up there."

They heard a scuffle, and some loose rocks came rolling down.

Amanda screamed. In the distance, a swarm of bats dislodged, and the patter of wings could be heard below.

"Amanda!" Wesley shouted. "What's going on?"

She didn't answer.

More rock and debris rained down from the ceiling. A bat swooped down, setting off screams. It was impossible to see what had happened so high up without a stronger light. Harlan aimed the flashlight at the floor, and everyone gathered around the circle of light to see what had fallen from above.

In the pile of scattered rocks lay Alex's cell phone. The battery had broken, and the screen had cracked.

No words could describe the abject frustration everyone felt. Even if Amanda got out, there wouldn't be any rescue tonight.

* * *

Amanda's hands were scraped, her knees shaking, but she was able to reach the top of the cave and shimmy out of the narrow crevice in the ceiling. After that it was only a few large steps in a hunched position until she was outside breathing the fresh, cold air. She had a feeling of exhilaration. At the very last moment, she had thought she wasn't going to be able to make it to the top. A few bats had flown in her face and had thrown her off balance, but she didn't fall down the rock face. With her heart beating rapidly, she reached into her sweatshirt pocket for Alex's cell phone.

It wasn't there.

In a panic she retraced her steps to the opening at the top of the cave. "Can you hear me?" she yelled. She knew they probably couldn't, but even if they could, she wouldn't be able to hear their response. This was bad. Her exhilaration turned to anger and then disbelief that this had happened. She didn't even know how to get to Jack and Maggie's car. They said it was northeast, but which direction was that? The sun had already set behind her, and in a forest like this with no trail, she would be lost in a few minutes. To start walking in some random direction and hope she got it right would be foolish. Harlan had told her how to explain their location to a 911 rescue team, and she had paid more attention to that, thinking that was the most important thing to remember. She was so eager to be the hero; she hadn't expected to end up without a phone.

She briefly entertained the thought of trying to work her way back inside so she could let them know what had happened but knew that would be way too risky. Once inside, she'd never be able to jump across that ledge again. She had barely made it without falling the first time, and she might not be so lucky a second time. And everyone was counting on her. Alex had trusted her with this mission. She couldn't bear to tell them she had gotten this far only to fail.

If only I had worn my sweatshirt with zippered pockets. If only I hadn't been stupid enough to text Alex and let Peter know we were here. Her eyes filled up and overflowed, spilling down her cheek. It was warm and somewhat comforting to allow the tears to drip freely onto the ground. Dusk was fading quickly into night, and she needed to keep moving, if for no other reason than to stay warm. The car could be a hundred yards or several miles away; she couldn't remember what they said.

You were so right, Wesley, she thought to herself. *This isn't fun.*

* * *

It was dark when Maria pulled into the vacant parking lot of a remote trailhead. Jack's red convertible was parked there, and it looked like they had to leave in a hurry, because one of the doors was still ajar. Maria was both relieved and terrified to find it. She didn't know if she had the guts to look inside and see what she might find. She felt like she was the sole survivor in one of those teenage horror movies. She was the one wandering around recklessly who would run into the bodies of all the victims before she would finally have to face the killer alone.

What she was going to do next was a complete mystery. She didn't have a plan, but she had hoped she could come up with something by the time she drove here. The only thing she had accomplished was biting her fingernails to the quick. It was a habit she had discarded many years ago, but it decided to resurface today.

She pulled up and looked inside Jack's car. From where she was, it appeared to be empty. She couldn't see into the backseat, but to get out of her car didn't seem like a good plan. Her hands were shaking as she turned off the motor and headlights.

Maria still didn't know what to do. Just sitting here inside her car and doing nothing was even more useless than sitting at home. At least she could be giving aid and comfort to Penny and Walter or could be with them when any news came.

She checked the backseat, where she had thrown several blankets, water bottles, and her seventy-two-hour emergency kit. The more she thought about what could have happened or what might still happen to five people she loved dearly, the more distraught she became. She had felt compelled to come here, but why? Should she just blindly walk into the forest and put her own life in danger, only to make a bigger mess out of an already horrendous situation?

"I don't know what I'm supposed to do!" she said aloud as she pounded on the steering wheel. The horn honked accidentally. The sound startled her. She thought of the horror movie again and how she had just done exactly what the careless and stupid victim would do to give away her location. She checked again to make sure the doors and windows were locked. No one was here, and if she had any sense at all, she would leave now.

She should have listened to Penny and Walter, but she was too stubborn and too upset to just sit at home and wait for someone to call. She thought maybe Elliot coming to her home was some sort of sign that she needed to help. But, as usual, she was allowing her emotional state to cloud her judgment. She turned the engine back on, looked in her rearview mirror, and backed up. When she turned forward, a movement in the trees caught her eye. For one frightening moment, she thought Peter might be coming to finish her off too. She pushed the gas pedal and peeled the car out, but a person darted out directly in front of her car.

Maria had to think fast. She could gun the car and try to run the person over, or she could hesitate and risk falling prey to the attacker. She kept her foot on the accelerator for a brief second and then slammed on her brakes, barely missing the figure who seemed to be run-ning straight for her. She turned her headlights on just as the person ran over to the driver's-side window. Maria's heart stopped when she saw who it was.

It was Amanda.

* * *

Six people huddled together on the cave floor in the pitch dark. The flashlight wasn't completely burned out but was dim enough to be useless. Harlan had switched it off and claimed it could only to be used in an emergency. After witnessing the day's events, what might be considered an emergency in Harlan's mind was anybody's guess.

"Harlan," Alex begged, "please let me have the flashlight. I can get out of here—it took me less than an hour to do it this morning. I know where to go. I think I can do it."

"No." Harlan acted like he was a parent and Alex was a teenager asking for the car keys. "Last time, you had a guide dog with you and a flashlight. This time you have neither and a high probability of running into any number of Randy's progeny. And you can't go the same way you went before—you'll run into the blocked north tunnel. We voted, and we're staying here for the night."

"We never took a vote."

"Go ahead, ask them," Harlan retorted.

There was silence to go along with the darkness. Jack couldn't believe he was siding with a tour guide instead of a Navy SEAL. He didn't want to risk getting Harlan angry. "Sorry, Al. I promised Maria I'd bring you back for the wedding. As much as I want to get us all out of here and get Maggie to a doctor, I just don't think any of us can risk leaving without a light."

"But it's going to be just as dark tomorrow!" Alex argued. "Amanda may have gotten out, but we know she doesn't have a phone, and we're miles from any kind of traveled road. Someone needs to get out and find her before she gets picked up by some maniac." He sighed. "What was I thinking?"

"That she'll come through for us," Wesley said. "Because she *will* find a way to bring help. She's very resourceful."

"More like reckless," Imogene said. "That girl never did have any common sense. From what I understand, if she would have stayed at home this morning, none of us would even be here in this miserable hole full of bat waste and vermin—"

"Someone smack her senseless for me," Jack said.

"Wait a minute. I remember now!" Maggie said. "You're that really rich lady—I've seen you from the news. Vandergrift . . . you're Imogene Vandergrift, right?"

"That's great," Jack sighed. "Your memory is coming back, and the first person you remember is her. What else do you remember?"

"That's it," Maggie said. "Why are we trapped in a cave with one of the richest people in America?"

"Correction," Jack said. "One of the *former* richest people in America. And it's really complicated. Just know that Imogene is not your friend, okay? End of story."

"Harlan," Wesley quickly interjected, "Why aren't there any snakes in this section of the cave?"

"For a couple of reasons," Harlan answered. "This area is big, making it colder. Their food source is better in the tunnels, and they can't get up and down the smooth walls. I suppose they could come in here if it suited their needs."

"Oh," Wesley said. "So they *can* get in here."

"Don't worry, Wesley," Jack said. "If there are snakes in here, they aren't going to bother us."

But Wesley did sound worried. "Well then, something else is making sounds over there."

"It's probably the bats," Harlan said.

"I don't think so. Listen."

Everyone stayed quiet, and they could hear a noise coming from some corner of the cave. But in total darkness and an echoing cave, it was difficult to pinpoint exactly where the sound was coming from.

"Harlan, turn the flashlight on for a minute," Alex said.

"No," Harlan answered. "This isn't an emergency. We need to save it for getting out tomorrow."

The noises continued. It sounded like some large animal scraping the sides of the cave wall, not the noise of fluttering bat wings or chirping crickets.

"I spent a lot of time in here yesterday and today and never heard anything like that," Alex stated. "That sounds almost—human."

"I'm with Al," Jack said. "Turn on the light, Harlan."

"Whatever it is, it's still over there, not here," Harlan started to explain.

"Wait a minute, where's Imogene?" Jack said.

"I'm right here, you idiot."

The sound of something large tumbling down the cave walls silenced the group.

"Amanda?" Wesley said, and suddenly it was five against one.

"Harlan," Maggie cried, "you're outnumbered now. Turn the flashlight ON!"

"Give us the flashlight!" Jack lunged to where he thought Harlan was and landed on top of Imogene instead. Alex tried to assist him, but it ended up in a brawl that included every person in the huddle. Everyone started hitting people and blindly grabbing at things like a bunch of football players trying to recover a fumbled football. Manners and decorum were replaced by raw nerves and sheer terror. It was every man for himself.

The skirmish continued, and Jack sensed that Harlan was attempting to stand up and make a break for it. He felt around until he grabbed onto the hard ankle of Harlan's fake leg. He gave it a jerk. Harlan tripped and went thudding to the ground. Jack scrambled for the flashlight; he heard it eject from Harlan's hand and land somewhere on the cave floor.

"He dropped it!" Jack yelled frantically. "Al, help me find it." Jack was beginning to feel dizzy from the darkness. He remembered what it was like to be blind, but this was a totally different feeling. At least then he could still see fuzzy shapes and shadows and could keep his balance. In the cave it felt like he was spinning. He suddenly became totally immobilized.

"I found the flashlight, Dad!" Wesley announced.

"Turn it on, Wes!"

"It won't turn on. The bulb is broken!"

The bad news spawned even more backlash, with every person scolding either Jack or Harlan or both for letting things get out of control. The fight would have continued much longer than it did if a light from above hadn't appeared from out of nowhere. Everyone stopped exactly where they were and looked up. A bright orb appeared near the ceiling, like someone had just turned a switch on.

15

Filling in the Gaps

Jack's senses came flooding back. "What the—?"

"Is anyone having the same hallucination I'm having?" Maggie asked.

"You mean that ball of light floating midair like an alien spaceship?"

"That's the one," Maggie said.

Everyone slowly extricated themselves from the pile of nerve-frayed people. Several of them looked at Harlan, thinking he should have an explanation for the phenomenon. He appeared as dumbstruck as the rest of them.

As the light descended farther, they could see it was a lantern suspended from the ceiling. Alex was the first person to get up and run over to it. The high-powered lantern was attached to a long rope going all the way up to the cave ceiling and disappearing.

As the light continued to travel down to them, it landed near a pile of blankets and a large duffel bag lying on the ground. The items tumbling from the top of the cave would explain the strange noises they heard. The lantern, however, which was too fragile to be dropped, had to be lowered down slowly.

Alex quickly took control of the light before Harlan. A notepad and pencil were tied to the rope right above it.

The rest of the group had made their way over to Alex, who took the notepad and scanned the letter. He closed his eyes and heaved a sigh of relief.

"Well—read it to us!" Jack said.

Alex read the note aloud:

> *Amanda is safe with me. Rescue team will be there in the morning.*
>
> *Have Harlan write down directions to your location.*
>
> *Thought you could use this emergency kit and some food.*
>
> *Is everyone okay?*
>
> *Love,*
> *Maria*
>
> *P.S. Kiss Alex for me.*

Everyone in the group cheered, and Jack grabbed Alex's face with both hands and planted a kiss on his cheek.

"How did Maria get here so fast?" Wesley wondered.

"I don't know, but this couldn't have been better timing. You guys were all losin' it." Jack untied the rope.

"Who's Maria?" Harlan asked.

"Amanda's mother and my fiancée," Alex said proudly. "We're getting married in five days—if she'll still have me."

"I'm pretty sure she will," Wesley said.

"But you might need a shower first," Jack added as he rummaged through the seventy-two-hour kit.

"Do I know Maria?" Maggie asked.

"Yeah, she's your best friend," Jack said.

"I thought my best friend was Sharalee."

"She is too," Jack said, "but she moved away last year."

"Oh." Maggie mulled over the info. "I have another question. Why did Wesley call you *Dad?*"

Jack looked at Alex for permission to open up the discussion. "Because he's my son."

"And who is his mother?" Maggie asked dubiously.

"Should we tell her, Alex?"

"If she's asking you," Alex said, "you should tell her."

"Nicki is his mother," Jack explained. "Do you remember the boat accident?"

"Yes," Maggie said. "But your baby died when he was one, and his name wasn't Wesley."

"Actually, he didn't die," Jack said. "He was rescued from the ocean by a woman who kept him and pretended she was his real mother. She raised him until he was twelve, and that's when you made a house call to see his dog and invited him to your parents' ranch for a day. Penny told him the shipwreck story. He connected the dots and figured out who he was and that his so-called mother had been lying to him all those years."

"Wesley is my nephew? I don't believe it. What kind of horrible woman would steal someone else's baby?"

"That's a very good question." Jack planted his eyes directly on Imogene. "Why don't you ask her?"

Maggie looked at Jack and then at Imogene, who was suspiciously quiet during Jack's rendition of the story.

"It was *you!*" she asked Imogene.

Imogene paused a moment before commenting. "You can disparage me all you want, Jack, but the truth is Wesley wouldn't be here today if it weren't for me. That fact seems to have been omitted from your story."

Maggie shook her head in disbelief. "This is so bizarre."

"Oh, if you think this is strange," Jack said, "just wait until you hear the unabridged edition."

Maggie walked over to Wesley and studied his face. "I can see it now in the light. You look like Nicole and I—and your dad too. So how old are you now?"

"Almost fifteen."

Maggie looked perplexed. "But that's impossible. You can't be that old."

"You're thirty-six, Mag," Jack told her. "But you don't look it."

Maggie was quiet for a moment. "But I still don't understand why we're all here trapped in this cave together."

Wesley decided to take a shot at explaining things to her. "We're here because Amanda and I came to look for Alex, who is engaged to Amanda's mom, Maria. He was kidnapped by this guy named Peter Jaworsky. But Peter caught me and Amanda and made us call you and tell you they would kill us unless you got Imogene out of jail and brought her here to show him where she hid a briefcase full of diamonds."

"Which I *selflessly* did to save Wesley's life," Imogene said.

"Hey, check your halo at the door," Jack interrupted. "Nobody's buyin' it. You were so selfless you locked Maggie inside an airtight vault to protect your assets."

Maggie was horrified at this revelation. "She's a kidnapper, and she tried to kill me, and now she's just sitting here with us? Why isn't this woman in some sort of restraints?"

Jack held up his wrist with the broken handcuff. "My point exactly. I've been tryin' to tell you that, Mag. But it's easier said than done. As soon as we get out of here, she'll be turned over to the authorities."

Imogene laughed. "I don't think so. Have you forgotten that you just bailed me *out* of jail, Jack?"

"And I can unbail you and put you back in."

"Oh no, you can't. I'm free until my hearing. I read the papers before I signed them. So you might want to show me some respect or you could be out of a home."

"Alex?" Jack asked, hoping he could refute what Imogene just said.

"I don't know what kind of deal you made, Jack," Alex said. "It may be awhile before you can get another hearing."

"But she committed another crime!" Jack protested. "She tried to kill Maggie."

"I did not!" Imogene retorted. "My decision to close the vault kept all of us alive, Jack. Besides, no one else was there to verify your story. I believe the other two witnesses are dead. I could just as easily say that *you* locked your wife in that vault and then killed the others."

"You can say whatever you want," Jack scoffed. "But you're the one with the criminal record—not me. No one would believe your story for two seconds."

"Sometimes juries make very surprising decisions."

"You're right. Why don't we just take you back to your own private little section of the cave right now and leave you there? What jury wouldn't believe that you ran away and got 'lost'?"

Alex was busy rummaging through the emergency kit. He found some granola bars and some water bottles and started passing them out. Jack and Imogene took them without missing a beat from their argument.

Jack took a swig of his water and wiped his face. "I can't believe you had this place built, and had that underwater thingamajig, all to hide your stolen diamonds. Whatever happened to good, old-fashioned money laundering? You know, diversified investments, stocks, bonds . . ."

"Jack—not that your ridiculous question even deserves a response—but I did not *steal* the diamonds. I bought them. If you recall, I am and have been a woman of considerable wealth for many years. And that water table regulator and vault were built before I was born."

"Wow!" Jack tore into his granola bar. "I didn't know cavemen were that smart!"

"Hey Alex," Harlan said, "are there any earplugs in that duffel bag?"

"Seriously, could you stop fighting?" Maggie asked. "I can understand now why you don't like her, but this isn't helping my headache. Besides that, we're going to have to be in here all night with her."

Jack shook his head. "Oh, no we're not. Now that we have flashlights, we can hike out on our own. Why wait for people to come and get us?"

"Maybe because we don't want to disturb the ferocious snakes in here," Imogene reminded him.

Jack spread his hand out in a fan as if setting up a newspaper headline. "Former billionaire found dead from ferocious snake bite. I like it."

"I'm not the only one who'd be in danger, you moron," Imogene shot back. "Obviously, you don't seem too worried about anyone else in your family."

"Harlan, do we still have to wait until morning?" Alex asked. "It looks like we have this lantern and three other flashlights, and we've got food and water to give us some energy."

"Are we going to have to listen to these two go at it all night?"

"Most likely," Alex conceded.

Harlan rolled his eyes. "That's what I needed to know," Harlan said. "Let's get out of here."

* * *

The backseat of the Subaru wasn't the best place for sleeping, but Amanda had curled up into a fetal position and was breathing the slow, rhythmic breaths of a very sound sleep. Maria, on the other hand, wasn't going to close her eyes until the rescue team arrived early in the morning. She checked her watch. That wouldn't be for several more hours.

Two police cars and a fire truck had come already. The ambulance would come later, when they were closer to getting everyone out. Another car, whose occupant Maria assumed must be the mother or close relative of Harlan and his brother, was also waiting in the parking lot. The woman appeared to be in a great deal of distress, but Maria didn't know how she could help her. She thought how it just as easily could have been her who had lost someone, and she realized just how fortunate she was that things had turned out as they did. She said a silent a prayer for everyone inside the cave to get out safely and for the woman who had just lost a son.

* * *

Wesley dragged his feet as he walked through the never-ending maze of tunnels. He couldn't remember a time when he'd ever been this tired. He shined his flashlight on his watch. It was still 2:45 A.M. He could have sworn it was 2:40 an hour ago. He shook his watch to make sure it was still working. Everyone had their own flash-light or lantern now except Maggie and Imogene. Maggie had a blanket slung around her neck, and Jack and Harlan carried small packs with some first aid essentials inside, including several flares, which they could use to scare off the snakes if they ran into any. So far so good. They hadn't run into Randy, Doris, or any new swarms of crickets.

When they came upon a wide area, Harlan told them they needed to take a little break, and then they would have a short way left before getting out of the cave. Everyone had learned by now that Harlan was the boss, and it was best not to argue with him—most of the time. Besides, there wasn't a single person who couldn't use a break, so they all sat down on the hard ground.

Imogene sat down right next to Wesley, as if that were the most natural thing in the world. It was so uncomfortable that Wesley didn't know how long he could stand it. He wondered what she wanted him to say to her. She didn't think like a normal person, and he didn't have the energy to have a conversation with her.

"You should eat your PowerBar, Wesley," Imogene said. "You need some calories."

Wesley was glad it was dark so that he didn't need to make eye contact with her. "No, thanks. I'm not hungry," he said. But what he wanted to say was she wasn't his mother anymore, and he didn't need her or anyone else to tell him when he needed to eat. He looked over at Maggie and Jack. Maggie was very weak, and Jack was trying to convince her to let him carry her.

Imogene twisted the metal handcuff still attached to her right wrist. Her skin was red and swollen. "I was going to open the vault," she said to Wesley.

"Then why didn't you?" Wesley turned to her angrily.

"I had to do it to buy us some more time—Peter would have killed all of us if I opened it for him. And then I got knocked out from the blast."

"Yeah, well, Maggie would have died if we hadn't figured out that I could open it. Why didn't you tell me? And how did you get my voice programmed into that computer anyway?"

"You mean you don't remember?" Imogene acted surprised.

"No. I don't remember."

Imogene scooted closer to Wesley, and he resisted the urge to move away from her.

"That night when I brought you to the cabin, I gave you some binoculars to look through. That was a retinal scanner. Then I asked you if you still remembered your Japanese. It was easy to get a recording of your voice."

"I don't remember any of that."

"That's because you were very tired that night."

"Or because you drugged me."

"Wesley," Imogene said firmly. "Everything I've done, I've done for you." She made a swooping motion with her hand. "I've spent the past eight months in jail because I wanted us to be together. I could have bought my way out or found some other way to escape, but that would have meant I could never see you again. And you are the most important thing in the world to me. Why can't you trust me?" She picked up his hand tenderly, and Wesley felt his stomach turn.

Because you're never honest, Wesley thought. He jerked his hand away and stood up. *And I'll never trust you.*

* * *

A loud tapping on the car window woke Maria with a start. She jumped and hit her knee on the steering wheel. Where was she? It was still dark, and she couldn't remember what had happened. A bright light shined through the fogged-up car window, and she saw the outline of a person. She hit the button to make sure the car was locked and unlocked it by accident.

A man opened the door, grabbed her by the arm, and pulled her out of the car. When she was fully awake, she realized who it was.

"Alex!" Maria threw her arms around him.

He winced in pain. "Go a little easy on the shoulder there," he said. "And the ribs." He gave her a kiss. "But the lips are fine."

"Are you okay?" Maria was afraid she might burst into tears.

"I don't know," Alex said. "Do you still want to marry me?"

"Of course I do."

"Then I'm good."

"Amanda said you'd been shot." Maria saw the blood on his shoulder.

"Yeah, well, lucky for me the bullet missed the important stuff. But I'm afraid my career as an NFL quarterback is over now."

"Maybe we can find you a desk job somewhere."

Amanda sat up in the backseat and rubbed her eyes. "Am I dreaming, or are you two kissing in front of me again? Wait a minute. You're here! You guys got out!"

"Thanks to both of you," Alex said. "Can we head home now? I'm pretty beat."

Amanda opened her car door and went out to receive a hero's welcome from the rest of the group.

16

Unfamiliar Territory

Jack sat in Dr. Coleman's office nervously tapping his foot on the carpet. Penny sat across from him, strumming her fingers on her purse, while Walter thumbed through a golf magazine. He got bored and traded it for a diet magazine.

A skeleton head and full torso hung on a hook next to Jack. He stood up and stuck his hand into the back of its hinged jaw; then he moved it up and down like a puppet.

"Hey, Penelope," he said, making the skeleton talk, "you want to throw me a piece of candy, love? I think my blood sugar's gettin' low."

Penny smiled as she reached into the candy dish on the doctor's desk and threw Jack a piece of taffy. He unwrapped it and popped it into his mouth. Seconds later he made a face, spit it into his hand, and headed for the trash. The doctor came in at that moment, as Jack wiped the gooey residue on his pants.

"Hello Jack, Penny, Walter." The doctor nodded at each person like they were at a social gathering and shook their hands. "Sit down please, Jack." He motioned to the empty chair.

"If you don't mind, I'd rather stand," Jack said nervously. "Don't beat around the bush. Just give it to us straight."

"Well, I wish I could just tell you straight out what's causing Maggie's amnesia and how long we can expect it to last, but the truth is the brain is a very complicated instrument, and we just don't know if or when she'll regain her memory."

"But when we take her home," Jack insisted, "you said familiar surroundings might trigger something. It's been two days, and the girls really miss her."

"Yes, she's physically well enough to leave the hospital, but mentally you'll have to take it slow. She only seems to be missing the past three years of her life, which is right before Wesley and Jack came into her life. She has no recollection of ever getting married or having children. But she does want to go home. Penny and Walter, you seem to have a calming effect on her. She knows you and feels like you accept her for who she is."

"I accept her for who she is." Jack sounded insulted.

Dr. Coleman shook his head. "That's not what I meant. Maggie isn't the same person she was two days ago. All your shared memories are gone. She might know who you are, Jack, but she doesn't know you as her husband. At least Penny and Walter are still her parents, and she's still their daughter. She feels comfortable with them because in the past three years that relationship hasn't changed."

Dr. Coleman pulled some charts off his desk and thumbed through them. "Maggie is basically in emotional shock, and this is going to be a difficult time for you and for your children too. You'll have to start over and give her some time to get to know you again. You can't assume she will react the way she always has with you. Her likes and dislikes may be totally different, and she'll make new connections as she gains more experience. Amnesia cases like this are rare, and sometimes the victims recover some or all of their memories. We would like to hope for that. But unfortunately, sometimes they never do, and they learn to start living again from that point in time. You have to prepare yourself for that situation. If her memory loss was completely psychological, we would have a better chance of getting her back. But in this case, the oxygen deprivation caused a blood flow restriction to her brain, which means that those connections may be permanently wiped out."

"You mean she has brain damage?" Jack asked.

"Yes, actually she does. But not in the sense you might normally think of brain damage. Her cognitive skills are still intact and much of her memory. Only her most recent memories are gone. You're very fortunate that she came out of this as well as she did. She's a completely functioning individual. It could have been much worse."

"What can we do?" Penny asked.

"Take her home and let her tell you how much she wants to know and how fast. Don't expect her to remember all the things she used to do. She'll need some help taking care of the kids, but don't treat her like she's helpless, because she's not. It's very important to give her space. Don't try to inundate her with too many stories and overwhelm her with how much she doesn't remember. I'll recommend a very good psychiatrist. She'll need to come in once a week for several months for some counseling, and we'll just take it one day at a time."

"Isn't there some kind of drug she can take?" Walter asked.

"Like some sort of memory pill?" the doctor asked. "Walter, if I had that, I'd be the richest man alive. The best medicine right now is patience."

* * *

Wesley sat in his math class trying to avoid eye contact with Tiffany Banks, the girl who sat next to him. She was the school information source and was trying to get his attention, and he was trying to not to give it to her. Some people had lives full of adventure, and other people had to live through other people's adventures. He remembered back to a few years ago when he was the kid with the boring life, a kid who fit into the latter group. Now that he was in the first group, he was big-time entertainment for people like Tiffany, who was at this moment passing a note to him, asking him if he was going to die from the fallout of the nuclear bomb explosion. He shook his head.

The first day back at school hadn't been quite what he expected. The news media had already sensationalized the story considerably, but some of the stories that were going around school bore only a slight resemblance to the truth. According to some of the urban legends, Wesley was attacked by a twenty-foot-long rattlesnake after he had launched a grenade and single-handedly killed three people. Then someone set off a bomb—nuclear, no less—that blew up a passage that led to a diamond mine, and he was led by a paraplegic tour guide, a hermit living in the caves all his life. Then Amanda scaled a hundred vertical feet to reach civilization, in the process getting bitten by rabid bats.

For obvious reasons, the police press release had left out the part about the lost diamond case. If mass numbers of people were aware that a case full of diamonds was lost inside the cave, treasure hunters and cavers from all over the world would be crawling all over the area within days, and that would prevent the recovery crew from doing their job. Everyone involved in the cave incident was under strict orders to keep the diamond information confidential, and Wesley was wondering how long that would last with Amanda's track record for keeping secrets.

It was hard to concentrate on boring school stuff when his life was so complicated. The bell rang, and Wesley tried to jump up and get a head start in front of Tiffany. Unfortunately, Tiffany was on the track team.

"So Wesley," she said after she easily caught up to him, "are you going to be on the news again tonight?"

"I hope not." Wesley shrugged. "It's an old story now."

"But I guess you and Amanda are the new story, huh?"

"What do you mean?" Wesley blushed.

"Well, I don't kiss and tell, but some people do. I hear you're no longer available. Too bad for us, right?"

"Uh . . ." Wesley was at a loss for words. He hadn't been expecting this information to leak out.

"I guess you two have hooked up."

"I don't know about that. Amanda's not really my girlfriend."

"Oh really? That's not what I hear. You two are locked in a room, tied up together with thirty seconds to live, and nothing happened?"

"We weren't tied up, and we've been friends for a long time. Um, I have to go to my locker—back in the other hall—I'll see you later, Tiffany."

Wesley sprinted away from Tiffany and the crowd of people that was starting to gather. After he celebrated escaping Tiffany, he saw another person coming at him in the hallway. He thought of turning around, but it was too late. This person looked at him directly and stared him down. If news about him and Amanda was getting passed around school, this person was not going to be pleased with him.

"Hey, Elliot," Wesley said casually.

"Excuse me?" Elliot said bitterly. "I don't think I know you. Oh wait. I remember now. You're the *backstabber*, right?"

"Elliot," Wesley started to explain, "this is really a big misunderstanding . . ."

"Hey, no problem." Elliot threw his hands in the air and walked past Wesley. "I do you a really big favor by missing a whole day of school to drive you out to the middle of nowhere, and you repay me by stealing my girl. Some friend you are."

"First of all, Amanda isn't your girl." Wesley decided to defend himself. "And even if she was, I didn't steal her from you. It was just something that happened—it wasn't a big deal."

"It wasn't a big deal?" Elliot looked like he might punch Wesley in the face. He shook his head solemnly. "That's the really sad thing, you know. You kiss the girl of my dreams—the most beautiful girl in the world— and you think it's *no big deal*. Thanks. Am I supposed to feel better now?"

Wesley looked at his watch. "That's not what I meant. I meant it wasn't planned. It just sort of happened. I have to go, or I'll be late for English. I already have three tardies." Wesley sprinted away and walked into English just as the bell rang. He may as well have missed the class completely for all that he got out of it. Why did people have to talk about him like his life was their business anyway? Who was Elliot to call dibs on Amanda like she was his personal property and tell him what he could or couldn't do?

When school got out, he waited for the class to empty before venturing out into the hall and then making his way to the bus. The bus didn't wait for stragglers, and Wesley was half hoping he would miss it and have to hitch a ride with some serial killer to get home.

The bus was just pulling away, but the bus driver saw Wesley coming and stopped for him. He climbed on the bus, and as soon as he saw Amanda, he quickly looked away to avoid eye contact with her. Her seat was already full of chatty girls who became totally quiet as he walked by them. He took a seat in the far back next to someone he didn't know very well. Thank goodness for people like Bartly Whats-his-name, who didn't follow the local gossip.

"Hey, you're Wesley, right?" Bartly asked, scooting over to make room for him on the seat. "The guy who blew up those dudes in the mine."

Wesley sighed and looked out the window. "Not really. I didn't blow anyone up, and it wasn't a mine."

"Why is everyone talking about it, then?"

"Because people have to talk about something!" Wesley snapped. "If you don't mind, I really don't want to talk about it."

"Sorry." Bartly looked at his hands.

Wesley felt bad for losing his temper, but he just really didn't want to get into this with Bartly. He looked up to the front of the bus at Amanda, and at that same moment she looked back at him. He quickly averted his eyes, but it was too late. She caught him looking at her. But then, he caught her looking at him too. That made them both guilty. He wished he could talk to someone about his situation, but he and Amanda had a lot of shared friends, and he didn't know whom he could confide in. Maggie would normally be the person he could go to, but she didn't even know him anymore. And he definitely couldn't tell his dad, because this would seem so trivial compared to all the other stuff he was dealing with.

Wesley stared out the bus window, wondering how two and a half days could change all of their lives so drastically. He nearly missed his stop because his mind had drifted, and he didn't even notice that the bus had stopped. When he stepped off the bus, Amanda was already several paces in front of him. He ran to catch up to her.

"Amanda, wait up!" he called out.

Amanda picked up her pace and then turned around. "If you didn't notice, I'm not talking to you." She slung her backpack over her shoulder.

"I did notice." Wesley caught up to her. "But you could at least tell me why."

Amanda shook her head. "Oh, I don't know. Maybe it's because you *dumped* me."

"I didn't dump you!" Wesley protested. "How can I dump you when you're not even my girlfriend?"

Amanda stopped walking and faced Wesley. "Exactly. I'm *not* your girlfriend. Thank you for making that perfectly clear to everyone at school today."

"Wait a minute," Wesley shot back. "Who went around telling the whole school we're going out now?"

"I don't know," Amanda said angrily. "I told Samantha—about the kissing part—and that's all."

"Well, you might as well have told the whole school!"

"Well, you didn't have to deny it and make me look like an idiot!"

"I didn't deny it—I just—" Wesley knew he was in deep trouble, and he searched frantically for the right words. "I didn't want to talk about it."

Amanda's eyes flashed with even more anger, showing Wesley that he had not been successful in his word search. "That's not what I meant. What I meant was . . ." He trailed off not knowing what he meant, or how he would explain it if he did.

"That you don't want to talk about it. That's good, because neither do I." She turned away and took a shortcut through a field to get home.

Wesley decided not to follow her and took the long way home.

* * *

Maggie was stunned when Jack pulled up in front of their two-year-old home with the expansive, lush landscape complete with a waterfall and a pond full of swimming ducks. Since the house was next door to the house she grew up in, the land was familiar, but it looked so different with the house there.

"This is our home?" Maggie asked.

"Do you like it?" Jack asked.

"It's beautiful," Maggie said. She bit her lip nervously. "But this is pretty scary. What if I don't recognize my own children?"

"It's okay, Mag. They'll recognize you. Just remember, C.J. is mini-me, and Emily is mini-you."

Maggie studied the twins' snapshots her mother had brought to her in the hospital. When they pulled into the garage, Maggie didn't want to go inside. This was a totally foreign world to her. She had a handsome husband who seemed to adore her, so why was she not thrilled that she was married to him with two kids? Out of all the men in the world she could have chosen to marry, why would she choose the one who used to be married to her sister?

Jack opened the door for her and she stepped inside the house cautiously. This didn't seem like her home. It didn't look or smell familiar. At the hospital, she had held onto the hope that the moment she set foot inside her house, she would feel like she was home. Everything would come back to her, and she would feel like herself again. Instead, she felt like an alien there.

The woman named Maria, whom she had met at the caves, was sitting cross-legged on the floor of the family room playing with two toddlers. Maggie observed them quietly. These were *her* children. Jack was right. They looked nothing like each other.

Emily was the first to notice her. "Mommy!" She hopped up from her playthings and ran toward Maggie and reached her arms up to her. Maggie picked her up and kissed the top of her soft head. It seemed like the appropriate thing to do. Emily put her arms around her neck and snuggled up to her, and Maggie felt tears well up in her eyes.

C.J. was too busy to notice them, so Maggie called her name to get her attention. She looked up and darted straight for Jack.

"She's obviously Daddy's girl," Maggie said.

"Depends on the day," Jack said, as he lifted C.J. up and put her on his shoulders. "You remember Maria. You met her at the caves."

"Yes, I know we're friends," Maggie said. "I'm at such a disadvantage here, not knowing what we normally talk about."

"It's okay, Maggie," Maria said. "I can do enough talking for the both of us. It's good to see you home. Thank you for your part in bringing everyone home safe."

"You're welcome, but I'm not sure what I did. You're the one who deserves the thanks."

"Well, I'm just glad everyone is here," Maria said.

Emily had scampered down out of Maggie's arms, and Maggie drew her gaze up to a large framed picture on the wall. It was of her and Jack on their wedding day. The wedding dress she had bought was for her never-to-be wedding to Brian Edwards. But she couldn't remember picking it out or marrying the man standing next to her in the picture. The room suddenly went out of focus, and she started to feel light-headed.

"What's the matter, Mag?" Jack asked. "You look really pale." He put C.J. down.

"I don't know," she said. "I think I'm a little dizzy. Maybe I need to lie down for a minute. Which way is the bedroom?"

Jack directed her to their bedroom down the hall. She went over to the left side of the king-size bed and sat down.

"Uh, actually the right side of the bed is yours," Jack said.

"The right?" Maggie said. "But I always sleep on the left."

"It's okay, I can switch."

Maggie suddenly felt very awkward. She couldn't sleep in the same bed as this man she hardly knew. Even though she was married, she felt very self-conscious about it.

Jack must have sensed her uneasiness. "Mag, I'll sleep in the guest room if it makes you uncomfortable."

"No, you take this bed. I'll sleep in the guest room. Just until I get used to this. I'm the one who feels like a guest in this house anyway."

Jack was still looking at her like he was searching for a missing person. Maggie's discomfort intensified.

"Um, the girls are very pretty," Maggie said. "It seems strange that they're really mine—I mean, ours. But I think I love them already."

"Yep, they take after their mum. Except in personality. C.J.'s a pretty wild one, you know."

"Yeah. Everyone keeps telling me. But she seems to favor you. I saw the dog food bowl in the kitchen. Where's Teddy?"

"Well, Mag," Jack stalled, "that's part of the story that we haven't really gone into yet. Teddy isn't exactly with us anymore."

"You made me give up my dog?"

"No. Teddy was the best dog in the world—I mean that."

"*Was?*"

"Yeah, he was. He was killed a few days ago in the caves. He saved all of our lives by intercepting a grenade that Peter threw at me and Alex. We would have been killed for sure if it weren't for him. Instead, he took out the criminals."

"Teddy's dead?" Maggie confirmed.

Jack nodded. "I'm sorry, Mag. We didn't want to tell you sooner, because you already had a lot to deal with. I know how much he meant to you."

Maggie's eyes filled with tears. "He was my best friend."

"I know." Jack leaned in to give her a hug, and Maggie cried into his shoulder.

"I rescued him from the animal shelter when he was a puppy."

"He returned the favor in a big way," Jack said.

"There's so much I don't know." Maggie wiped the tears from her face. "I really want to remember us, Jack."

"You will. Just give it some time."

Maggie wanted to believe that time would fix everything, but right then it didn't seem like things could ever be right again.

17

Strained Relationships

Jack woke up to the sound of someone rummaging through the kitchen banging pots and pans and slamming the cupboard doors. He looked over at the undisturbed side of the bed where Maggie usually slept. The covers were still tucked in. The sun wasn't up yet, and it felt like the middle of the night. He plodded into the kitchen to find that C.J. was awake and sitting at the breakfast table without a booster seat eating a chocolate doughnut. Maggie appeared to be the cause of all the noise. Distressed and irritated, she was looking intently for something.

"And a good mornin' to you!" Jack said jovially.

"Not yet, it isn't!" Maggie snapped. "Where is it?"

"Where's what?"

"The coffeepot! If we've been living together for almost three years, you should know I don't function until I've had my coffee in the morning."

"Mag," Jack shook his head, "you quit drinkin' coffee two years ago. When you got pregnant with the girls.

And just as a side note—we aren't livin' together. We actually did get married. I have a license to prove it."

"And I suppose you don't drink coffee?"

"Never touch the stuff."

"Great." Maggie threw her hands up. "I'll go over and get some from my dad, then." She headed toward the back door.

"Stop!" Jack held up his hand. "Mag, I can't let you do that. You don't need any coffee, and you'll be mad at me if I let you start drinkin' it again. You feel a lot better since you quit."

"Thank you for telling me how I feel and what I need." Right now I *feel* like a nice hot cup of coffee. And I *need* a coffee pot to make it. I think I can make that decision without your help."

Jack shrugged. "I'm tellin' you, you'll be sorry."

C.J. offered Jack a gooey fistful of her breakfast. "Doh nah," she said happily.

"No, thanks. Daddy doesn't want a doughnut right now. That's not usually what she has for breakfast, Mag."

"I didn't give it to her—she must have gotten it out of the pantry herself."

"While you were trashin' the place lookin' for the coffeepot," Jack said a little too hastily.

"And *you* were asleep in bed."

Jack checked the kitchen clock. "It's only 6:15. We don't usually get up this early."

Maggie sighed. "Well, tell that to your daughter because I'm not familiar with the routine."

Jack saw that this was going to escalate into a full-blown fight if he didn't do something to stop it. "You're right, Mag. I'm sorry. Why don't I fix us all some breakfast while you run next door and get some coffee from Walter."

Maggie's tone softened. "I'm sorry. I don't mean to be difficult. You're probably right. I don't really need any coffee. It's just that this is all brand new to me. I don't know how this is supposed to work. I don't know what I normally do."

"It's okay, Mag. You're fine." Jack went over and gave Maggie a hug, but her body stiffened under his embrace.

"I'm sorry for being so cranky. I guess I'm still not a morning person. I'll just jump in the shower, and I promise I'll do better when I'm out."

Later, while Jack was making some French toast, Maggie finished her shower and came into the kitchen holding the pair of hot pink high heels with rhinestones and ankle straps. She looked mortified.

"Do I also have some crazy aunt I don't know about who would give me these shoes?"

"Actually, you bought those yourself." Jack flipped over a piece of toast.

"I did not! There is no way I've changed *that* much. I'd need two weeks of practice just to walk in these death traps. Not that I'd even try—they're hideous."

"Well, you picked them out yourself to wear at Maria's wedding," Jack assured her. "You thought they were a pretty hot little number a few days ago and couldn't wait to wear them."

"Really?" Maggie stared at Jack, as though he were making it all up.

"Cross my heart. You've become a fashion maven, Mag."

"Or the queen of tacky." Maggie opened up the kitchen trash compactor and threw the shoes inside. "I am not wearing those." She dusted off her hands as though she had just rid herself of some toxic waste.

"The next thing I'll probably find out is that I gave up flossing."

"Don't worry," Jack said, "you're still the floss police." He looked forlornly at the shoes in the trash and resisted the urge to dive in and rescue them. For some reason he couldn't explain, it felt like Maggie had thrown her wedding ring in there instead.

* * *

Maria was doing everything humanly possible to try and force Amanda to hurry up and get out the door before she missed the bus, but Amanda was intentionally stalling. "I'm not going to drive you when you're perfectly capable of making it on time," Maria scolded her. "And where's Wesley? He's going to miss the bus too."

"He didn't come to pick me up," Amanda said flatly.

"Why not?" Maria asked.

"Because he hates me."

Maria stopped what she was doing. "Why would you say that?"

"Because he does. But it doesn't matter, because I hate him back, so I'm fine with it."

"What?" Maria was shocked. "You two have had disagreements in the past, but it doesn't mean you hate each other." Maria shook her head. "Wesley is your best friend."

"Not anymore. It's not like Wesley is my only friend, Mom. Just because we've known each other since we were babies doesn't mean we have to hang out together for the rest of our lives. But I'm not taking the same bus as him, so you can either give me a ride to school or I'll call Alex and ask him to take me. Or I have an even better idea—I'll just stay home from school today."

Maria sighed. "When did you suddenly become a difficult child?"

There was a quick knock on the door, and Amanda opened it and let Alex in. "Hola, Padre," Amanda said cheerfully. "You're just in time to give me a ride to school."

Alex looked quizzically at Maria.

"Amanda is claiming that as of today she and Wesley hate each other, and she is refusing to take the bus to school because she doesn't want to talk to him. But I was about to remind her it's only two days before the wedding, and we are both very busy."

Alex made eye contact with Amanda. "No problem. I'll drive you to school. It's on my way."

Amanda could have sworn Alex gave her mother some sort of secret-code look or she wouldn't have agreed so quickly. She grabbed her backpack and followed Alex out the door.

When they got in the car, Alex got straight to the point. "You want to tell me about it?"

"Not really."

Alex smiled. "Well, does it have something to do with what happened when you and Wesley were locked in the ticket office?"

Amanda blushed. "How did you know?"

"I used to be a spy."

"And you still are. You saw us, didn't you?"

"Maybe I did."

"It's not what you think," Amanda tried to explain. "We thought we were going to die. It was just one kiss, and now everything is messed up. You didn't tell my mom, did you?"

"Of course not. Why would I tell her?"

"Don't you tell her everything?"

"No, I don't. I'm specially trained to withhold information."

"Okay, well, file this information in the same place as all that other top-security clearance stuff."

"Sure." Alex left it at that. He turned on his blinker and shifted lanes.

Amanda switched the station on the radio, even though it was barely audible. "So that's it? You don't want to know why we're mad at each other?"

"Not unless you want to tell me. I'm not one to poke around in other people's business."

Amanda sighed like somehow Alex was forcing the information out of her. "Oh, all right. Wesley got mad because everyone at school was talking about us like we were boyfriend and girlfriend, and Wesley said we weren't, and I got mad because he said I wasn't his girl-friend—and even though I'm not, I wanted to be the one who said we weren't, but I wasn't sure I wasn't—so that's what happened."

Alex smiled. "Thanks for clearing that up."

"So it's really dumb for us to be fighting, isn't it?"

"I don't know. Sometimes fighting is the only way to address the problem when there are no other options. Especially if the other person is being totally unreason-able."

"You think Wesley is being unreasonable?"

"Do you think he is?"

Amanda thought for a moment. "I don't know. Maybe he's having a rough time because of what hap-pened to Maggie and everything. He's really stressed out about this, and he probably just said the first thing that came into his head."

Alex nodded and didn't say anything.

"You're right, Alex. I guess I'm being pretty tough on him. So you really think I should talk to him, huh?"

Alex shrugged his shoulders. "If you think so."

"Well, if I have to. Thanks, Alex," she said as she opened the car door to step out onto the curb. "You really gave me some good advice."

Alex waved good-bye to her. "Glad I could be of assistance."

* * *

For the second day in a row, Penny had flatly refused to let Maggie use their coffeepot. "You're going to have to get your dad to give you some of his bootleg coffee. I'm not going to be a co-conspirator in getting you back on the stuff."

"Co-conspirator?" Maggie huffed. "Why does everyone treat me like I'm some sort of felon? Since when did coffee become an illegal substance in the U.S.?" Maggie paced the floor of her mother's kitchen. "Never mind. I'll drive all the way out to Starbucks— like I have anything better to do."

"Now that you mention it," Penny looked at Maggie directly, "what *are* you doing?"

"What's that supposed to mean?"

"Exactly what it means. What do you do all day?"

"I have seventeen-month-old twins, and you have to ask me what I do all day?"

"What are you doing to get your life back on track? You've been home two days and you're avoiding every-one. You can't get through this challenge on your own, Maggie. You need to ask for help."

"Mom, the doctor said I don't have a lot of control over that. I'm trying to look through pictures. I'm doing everything I can to remember."

"Are you talking to your husband?"

"Sure. Well, not a lot. Just sort of the basic stuff, like where the pot holders are."

"Riveting," Penny said in a scolding tone. "Y'all need a special date or something; I mean, really get to know each other. Has he told you the story about how you fell in love?"

Maggie suddenly understood where her mother was going with this conversation. "Maybe I'm not ready for that yet."

"And when will you be ready for it?"

"Mom, listen to me a minute, will you? This whole memory loss thing seems so simple to everyone else because they've never experienced it. They think all I have to do is try hard enough and somehow all the missing memories are going to magically appear. But it doesn't work that way. You think that Jack and I can just have a few dates and everything is going to go back to normal again?"

"No," Penny furrowed her brow, "but you can't just treat Jack like he's the family pet or something. At least act like you have some interest in why you married him. He's suffering too because he's wondering if he's lost you."

"He *has* lost me! *I've* lost me!" She was angry but she didn't know why. She sat down at the kitchen table, picked up a napkin, and folded it into squares. She didn't want to have to look straight into her mother's eyes.

"Mom, I only know Jack as my brother-in-law. Even if someone could tell me all the events that transpired leading up to our marriage, they wouldn't be able to tell me how I felt at each moment. Because I'm the only person who felt it. I mean, what makes a person fall in love with another person anyway? Is it just the person, or is it what the person does that makes it all happen? Or is it all chemistry?"

"I guess it's some complicated mix of all those things."

"Right. So if all those things come into play, what if some of the very big things are missing? Like shared experiences. I know that I married Jack of my own volition, but I don't know why. It would be like you waking up one morning and finding yourself married to Uncle Artie."

"Now that's a disturbing thought," Penny said with revulsion. "You can't possibly compare Jack to Uncle Artie. Uncle Artie is a con man with a comb-over. And he picks his teeth with a letter opener."

"Okay, it might not be exactly the same, but it's just as shocking. I don't know how to just pretend to be me, because I don't know who I am. I used to live alone, and now I have a husband who is also my brother-in-law, a teenage son who is also my nephew, and two toddlers who are both smarter than me already. It might be a wonderful life, but it's not my life. It's some other woman's life who experienced it all instead of me." Maggie sighed. "Never mind. I can't explain to you how I feel."

"You feel like something very precious has been taken from you."

"Yes, but that's not all. Sometimes I wonder what I've done to myself. How could I have married someone so different from me? What made me change so drastically that I would give up my career as a vet to stay home full-time and change diapers?"

"Because you chose something better. You wanted to stay home and raise your kids. You've always wanted children."

"I know I have. And I love the girls—and Wesley too. I guess I love Jack, too, but it's different. I don't think I can be the person he loves."

"You already are. And trust me, he does."

"So what is my problem then? I hear everyone telling me things, but I can't believe them. I found this awful pair of pink shoes in my closet, and Jack said I picked them out myself. They're ridiculous! Why am I so different now?"

"We all change, Maggie. It's a necessary part of life. And some changes are good—like quitting coffee. And you're a wonderful mother."

"Maybe I *was* a good mother, but I'm not anymore. I let C.J. have a doughnut for breakfast yesterday."

"We'll, get child services over here."

"I'm serious, Mom. I'm failing at everything."

"You're not failing. You're learning. Maybe I don't know what you're going through, but I'm here to help you through it. I want you to know that Jack adores you, and you used to be head over heels for him. No matter what your feelings are right now, please be kind to him. I know women who would give their eyeteeth to get a man to treat them as well as Jack treats you. And besides that, he's a good provider, he's got a sense of humor, and he's pretty good-looking to boot."

Maggie couldn't disagree with that. "I know, I know— he's always been your favorite. Are you sure you didn't bribe me into marrying him?"

"Maggie—that doesn't even deserve an answer!"

"I'm kidding. I promise I'll be nice to him."

* * *

It smelled like rain, and the wind picked up a few smoky gray clouds to block out whatever small warmth the sun was providing. Wesley was a little cold because he had left his jacket at home, but he wasn't going to go back and get it. He had ridden his horse, Rocky, out to the lake on his grandparents' property. Normally he would go out with Grandpa Walter, but today everyone was busy getting things ready for the reception the next day. He knew he should be back there helping, but he was in a lousy mood and didn't feel like putting up a front for his dad and Maggie. His fight with Amanda might seem trite compared to all the other things his family was dealing with at the moment, but he couldn't just shrug it off.

Within the past few days, his stepmother had forgotten who he was, his dog had died, and his best friend had stopped speaking to him. He deserved to feel sorry for himself. After all, no one else was going to. Everyone at school thought he led a charmed life. He was a smart kid who got easy A's, he was the son of the famous Snake Stalker, his family was rich, and he had his own horse to ride whenever he wanted. He shouldn't complain, but he was going to anyway.

He only had a few minutes to wallow in self-pity before he saw another horse in the distance. No doubt Grandpa Walter or someone else had the same idea and was trying to evade some assigned chore. He really didn't feel like any company, but if he rode away now, it would be obvious he was deliberately avoiding them. When the rider got closer, he could see it was Amanda.

Great, the very worst person possible. His luck was so bad, it was starting to get comical. He considered jumping on Rocky and riding away really fast, just to make her angry. She was a big part of his present state of despair— and he selfishly hoped that she was suffering just as much as he was. But in some twisted way he was glad to see her. Things couldn't get any worse than they already were. *Bring it on*, he thought.

In a few minutes, Amanda had pulled the tan palomino horse up next to Wesley. She didn't get off, and she wasn't smiling. "Everyone's looking for you, you know."

"So?" Wesley said defiantly.

"So, I'm supposed to come get you."

"So, pretend you didn't find me," Wesley shot back.

"No way; then I'll have to do both of our jobs. The wedding is day after tomorrow." Amanda decided to dismount.

"Thanks, I didn't know that."

"Are you going to be this grumpy for the next few weeks?"

"I was planning on it. It's not like you're Miss Cheerful."

"Whatever." Amanda shrugged as she picked up a smooth, round stone off the ground and threw it into the lake with a flick of her wrist. The stone skipped seven times before it sank in the water.

"Double or nothing," Amanda said.

Wesley didn't need to ask what she was talking about. They had an ongoing rock-skipping wager that was up to about twenty million dollars by now, and whoever could skip their stone the most times was the current winner of the bet. Amanda was usually ahead because she had the most throwing skills, but every once in a while, if Wesley could find the right stone, he could come up with a six or a seven. With his current luck, he would have no chance of beating her, but he took the wager anyway.

He scoured around for a decent rock and threw it into the lake. It dropped after five, but that was still respectable.

"That's forty million dollars you owe me." Amanda stuck out her palm.

"Okay," Wesley agreed. "I'm good for it. I just need to haul it out from the bottom of a cave."

Amanda laughed. Wesley didn't want to give up on feeling sorry for himself just yet, so he didn't laugh with her.

"I was thinking . . ." Amanda said, "that instead of paying me, maybe we could make a truce and be friends again. Just for a few days anyway. I think it would be the mature thing to do."

"So now you think I'm immature?" Wesley demanded.

"Yes, you are. And so am I. If we stay angry at each other, it will totally ruin their wedding day. Let's just try to get along for their sake. And Jack and Maggie's too. This whole thing is starting to make me feel depressed."

"So what are you saying?"

"That we should stop fighting and be friends again."

Wesley couldn't believe that she had just said it so plainly, but he was glad she had. "Okay. I think we should too."

"But it's not like we're girlfriend and boyfriend."

"Right." Wesley nodded.

"That means no kissing—at least until we're eighteen."

Wesley thought a minute. "Not even for practice?"

"No, not even for practice. Because even if we did get married someday—like in eight years or something—it would be stupid for us to only date each other now, right?"

"Really stupid. Moronically stupid."

"Okay, I get the point. So we're friends again?" Amanda asked.

"Yeah, we're friends again." Wesley wanted to hug her, but he wasn't sure if that would be breaking the rules.

Evidently it wasn't, because Amanda reached out and hugged him. "Best friends?" she asked.

"Yes, *best* friends."

"Good." Amanda picked up a rock and threw it at a tree about thirty yards away. It hit the trunk and bounced off. "I feel a lot better now."

"Now that we're speaking again, could you do me a favor?"

"What's that?"

"Call Elliot and ask him to call off his henchmen. I haven't been able to sit down in the lunchroom for three days."

Amanda thought for a minute. "I'll give it a try."

18

Unwelcome Guest

Baskets of flowers hung from the freshly painted gazebo, and tropical plants bloomed next to the electric
warming torches. The sky had threatened rain earlier,
but the sun came out and drove off most of the clouds
just in time for the long-anticipated wedding day.

Maria was wearing a stunning, tea-length wedding
dress with a pink sash that would have matched the
shoes Maggie had thrown in the trash. Alex didn't
look quite as stunning, since his tuxedo pants were
about two inches too short. With all of the events of
the week, he had missed his tailoring appointment and
didn't even try on his tux until the night before the
wedding. Maria said she didn't mind and that it
reminded her of the Harrison Landry days, and she
thought he looked adorable. She was grateful that
Alex was still around, and that put everything else into
perspective.

The bride and groom were beaming after the wedding ceremony had taken place earlier that morning.
Alex's parents stood next to them in the reception line

in the brick area in the front yard by the pond, shaking hands and hugging all the visitors. Maria hadn't had any contact with her family in Mexico for about ten years, so Jack and Maggie stood in for the bride's parents.

Jack's tuxedo may have fit better than the groom's, but he was pretty uncomfortable anyway. He kept tugging on his collar and twisting his cufflinks. He was getting stressed out from standing in the receiving line next to Maggie and trying to second-guess whether he needed to introduce her to whoever was coming through. He couldn't remember half the people's names he knew he was supposed to, and the pressure was starting to get to him.

Wesley and Amanda were busy rounding up C.J. and Emily in their pink floral dresses. C.J. had spilled red punch down the front of her dress before it was time for pictures, and Emily had pulled the bow out of her hair and tried to put it on Wesley's Chihuahua, Hercules.

Maggie pasted on a smile and recited her fabricated speech to minimize explanations. "Thank you so much for coming. I'm fine, thank you. And I'm already starting to remember things. I'll be back to myself in a few weeks."

Jack nodded and went along with Maggie's short story. Maggie wasn't fine, and she wasn't starting to remember anything. But they needed to keep the line moving and get through this day. No one was in the mood to rehearse the doctor's ambiguous prognosis eight dozen times. And then there were the people who didn't even know Maggie had lost her memory. It took even more skill to avoid bringing up the subject.

Jack kept watching Maggie for signs that she'd had enough. "Mag, I think they can finish up without us now. Why don't you go inside and take a break?"

"Because I don't want to ruin my best friend's wedding," Maggie said through her clenched-teeth smile. She waved at Mrs. Crowley from up the street.

"Maria and Alex aren't even aware that anyone else is here," Jack noted. "Look at them gazing into each other's eyes. The sooner we break this thing up, the sooner they can head out for their honeymoon."

Maggie suddenly looked at Jack with a pained expression. Her face scrunched up, and she started to cry. Without an explanation, she bolted out of the line, through the sliding glass door, and into the house.

This was exactly the situation Jack had been trying to prevent. He excused himself and followed her.

When he found her, she was in the guest bedroom, sobbing into a pillow.

"Mag, what is it?"

"Just go away, please."

Jack started to leave and then turned around. "If you really want me to leave, I'll go, but if you'd like to talk, I would like some excuse to stay here."

Maggie's chest heaved, and she wiped her eyes with her hands. "I never had a wedding or a honeymoon."

"Yes, we did—we went to Charleston."

"Maybe *you* did, but I don't remember a thing. So as far as I'm concerned, it never happened."

"We'll have another honeymoon."

"It's not possible!" Maggie cried. "We have kids and jobs, and I've been thrown into the middle of this life, and I don't know how I got here!"

Jack threw his hands up in the air. "You're not the only person who's been thrown into this, Mag! It's pretty tough for all of us. What do you want me to do about it?"

Maggie shook her head.

Jack knew what *he* wanted to do. This was all Imogene's fault. He wanted to make her suffer, to pay for the pain she had caused Maggie and his whole family. He wanted more than anything to send her to a place where it would be impossible to ever hurt the people he loved again.

Jack's hands curled into fists, and his neck seemed to have grown two sizes, because his collar felt even tighter and stiffer than it had earlier. He was ready to leave Maggie alone in her tantrum when there was a knock on the bedroom door.

"Dad, it's me," Wesley called through the door. "I need to tell you something."

"This is a bad time, Wes. Can it wait?"

"No. It's important."

"Okay." Jack opened the door, and Maggie turned her face away from Wesley. "She'll be all right, mate. She's just havin' a tough go of it today. What is it?"

"Uh, we have a situation. Guess who just showed up at the wedding?"

"Aunt Sylvia's first husband? We'll get Jamal to kick him out."

"No. Someone much worse."

* * *

When Jack saw her, Imogene was placing a professionally wrapped present on the gift table. She was dressed in a pink tailored skirt and jacket that looked very expensive, with a matching hat tilted at an angle and secured onto her coiffed hair. Maria and Alex were surrounded by a mob of people and hadn't noticed she was there yet.

Imogene bent down and picked up Hercules. The dog wagged his tail, remembering his former owner. Imogene stroked him affectionately.

Wesley started to run toward her, but Jack put his arm up. "Stay back, Wes." Jack marched up behind Imogene and tapped her on the shoulder with two fingers.

She slowly turned around and looked at Jack as if she might ask him to get her some punch.

"What are you doing here? I'm sure you weren't invited."

"Well this is awkward, isn't it, Herkie?" Imogene said to the dog instead of Jack. "I just assumed it was an oversight. Since I am Maria's dearest friend, I think it was rather rude of her not to invite me, wouldn't you say?" Imogene continued to pet Hercules and looked past Jack, connecting eyes with Wesley. "But under the circumstances, I'm willing to let bygones be bygones. I came here to wish the new couple well. Bury the hatchet if you will."

"I'd like the bury the hatchet too. Just not in the ground."

"Jack, you have such a clever sense of humor. It's no wonder your wife finds you so charming."

Jack looked around for anyone who could restrain him from strangling Imogene at that very moment. Wesley had brought in the reinforcements in the form of Jamal Hoskins, a six-foot-four former linebacker who was a close friend of the family.

"The Mackeys would like you to leave, Mrs. Vandergrift," Jamal commanded.

Imogene didn't flinch. "How are things in the ghetto, Jamal? Or haven't you been home lately?"

"Do you need some help getting to your car?" Jamal persisted.

"I'll leave just as soon as I speak to Maria," Imogene said.

"You won't go anywhere near Maria," Jack said angrily. "I'm calling the police."

"That would make a lovely scene, now wouldn't it?" Imogene smiled and set Hercules back down on the ground. "Just what are you going to tell them I'm doing here? I've come to make a peace offering—that isn't against the law. I think the police might end up questioning you, Jack. Like why *did* you have me released from prison? I don't believe that information has been released to the public yet. Do you know it's illegal to negotiate with kidnappers?" Imogene touched her four-carat diamond necklace, as if daring him to call her bluff. "First you bribed a judge to keep me in prison, and then you bribed a judge to let me out. Now you're ordering me off your property simply because I showed up to my very best friend's wedding to try and make amends. Do you see me making a scene here? The only person I see who is out of control is you, Jack."

"No, out of control would be me attacking you with the cake knife. You're leavin' right now. And take your present with you. G'day." Jack picked up a random gift off the table and shoved it into Imogene's stomach.

"You know, Jack, you're very ungrateful for someone who got his entire family back safe and sound from a very perilous situation. You've already forgotten that if it weren't for me, you and your wife would both be dead."

Jack knew he should let it go, that reasoning with a lunatic like Imogene was impossible. But he couldn't allow her to give herself credit for saving him and Maggie. He couldn't let her lies stand unchallenged and give her the satisfaction of having the last word. He shouldn't make a scene at Alex and Maria's wedding, but he was so angry he couldn't hold back. The words came out of his mouth like molten lava.

"Get off my property! You would have let Maggie *die* in the vault! You didn't *save* her! You didn't save anyone. You're the one who nearly got us all killed. And you better hope and pray that at your trial next month the jury finds you guilty, because if they don't lock you up for good—I promise you—I'll come after you myself and kill you."

Imogene looked around smugly. At least a dozen people had stopped what they were doing and focused on Jack's outburst. Maggie was one of them. She had come back outside and onto the scene just in time to hear Jack threatening Imogene.

Imogene directed her comments to Maggie. "I hope, for your sake, Maggie, that your memory never returns. Besides your husband having a very bad temper, he has a few more secrets he'd rather you didn't know." Imogene raised her eyebrows as if she were privy to those secrets. She put the present back on the table and gave the onlookers a nod before turning around in her Italian leather pumps and walking unescorted off the Mackey property.

* * *

Wesley watched Imogene leave their yard and went directly to the gift table. He picked up a medium-sized gift wrapped in white embossed paper and a satin ribbon.

"Dad, this is the gift she brought. I think we'd better open it and see what it is before it gets mixed up with all the others."

Jack seemed to be in another world, not listening to anyone around him. "C.J. and Emily—where are they?" He spun around trying to find his daughters.

"They were with Grandpa," Wesley answered.

Maggie looked around. "She couldn't kidnap our girls in front of all these people, could she?"

"Oh, yes, she could!" Jack was still fuming. "Find them right now. Imogene doesn't ever just show up for a friendly chat. She doesn't operate that way."

Wesley spied a pair of pink dresses over by the pond. "They're both over there with Grandma and Grandpa."

Jack spun around again in a panic. "The present!" Jack said. "Get the present she brought!"

Wesley didn't want to repeat that he just mentioned that. He handed Jack the gift Imogene had brought. She had actually written congratulations on the card and signed her name.

Jack snatched up the gift and put his ear to it. "It's ticking. I can hear it." He didn't need to say anything more.

"It's a bomb!" someone in the crowd yelled. "Run!" Guests in the immediate vicinity started to flee. Wesley, Maggie, and Jamal stayed put.

"Jamal," Jack ordered. "Get Chief Hicks—he's around here somewhere. I'll get this away from all the traffic."

"Someone call 911!" a voice from the crowd yelled.

Jack took off running through the crowd holding the present out in front of him, as if an extra foot of distance would make a difference if it exploded. By now most of the wedding guests had heard the word *bomb*. Wesley tried to run after his dad, but hordes of frantic people blocked his way. He pushed through them and saw Alex running after Jack.

"Jack, stop!" Alex grabbed onto the tails of his tuxedo, and it ripped before Jack could slow down, tripping him and nearly causing him to fall.

"Put the package down!" Alex yelled. "If it is a bomb, the first rule is don't move it!"

An older woman with a chocolate éclair in one hand backed away from Jack into the wedding cake table and knocked the cake with her arm, taking a bulldozer-sized chunk out of the delicate piece of art.

"I have to get it away from all the people!" Jack argued.

"No." Alex took the package away from Jack, handling it as if it were a brimming bowl of acid, and set it on the ground. "It might contain an unstable explosive. We need to move the people out of here now. I'll handle this." The sound-system speakers were only a few yards from where he was, but the romantic music was getting buried by the sounds of screaming guests. Alex grabbed the microphone and turned it on. "Attention everyone!" He raised one arm, as if he were ready to offer a toast.

The frantic crowd stopped and looked at him. "Thank you for coming to our wedding reception. We have a slight problem here, and we need you to vacate the premises immediately. There's no reason to panic. If you would kindly move in a quick and orderly fashion as far away from where I am standing as you possibly can, that would be appreciated. Thank you again for coming."

The stunned audience didn't need any extra prodding to exit the reception. Hysterical mothers grabbed their small children by the hands and dragged them away from the scene. Maggie had gone to get the girls inside the house.

Wesley boldly walked up to Alex and his dad. "I don't think that's a real bomb, Dad. It's not her style."

"Wes," Jack ordered, "get away from here!"

"But she wouldn't want to kill me," Wesley tried to explain. "Not after what she did to save my life."

"We have no idea what goes on in that twisted mind of hers," Jack reminded him. "Get inside the house, now!"

Wesley reluctantly went over to the house but didn't go inside. He watched as three police vehicles pulled up with their sirens on and lights blinking. Several cars blocked their entrance, so one vehicle drove across the beautifully manicured front lawn to get closer to the reception area. An officer with a bullhorn jumped out of his car and tried to regain control of the panicked crowd. It was too late for that. People were already dispersing like ants from a disturbed anthill.

Cars roared out while others screeched onto the property. Within minutes, men with bioterrorism masks and gloves entered the scene, and Jack directed them to the suspect package. They apprehended the box, deposited it inside a black bag, and then ran with it out toward a less crowded area to examine it.

Maria was trying to get over to where Jack and Alex were, but the police promptly ordered her to stand back behind some imaginary line they had drawn. The entire wedding party had erupted into mass hysteria. The photographers were dismantling their tripods, and people were trying to move their cars off the property all at once.

Some people ran into the Mackeys' house for cover and crouched under the dining-room table or stuffed themselves into the interior rooms. Wesley stood outside, away from the traffic, and soaked it all in. He didn't know how he knew it, but he was sure that the package didn't contain a bomb.

* * *

Thirty minutes later, Jack sat inside his kitchen staring at the refrigerator. Any minute he expected an explosion to rock the property. Maria and Alex were in the kitchen too, snacking on pieces of fruit and wedding cake like there was nothing wrong. Chief Hicks came inside looking rather frazzled. The three of them looked at him.

"There's no danger." Chief Hicks pulled up a barstool, sat down, and helped himself to a piece of cake.

"They dismantled the bomb?" Jack asked.

"No," Hicks answered. "But they did dismantle a lovely clock from Pottery Barn."

"What?" Jack threw his hands in the air.

Chief Hicks gave him a sympathetic smile. "You were right about one thing, Jack. It *was* ticking."

Maria and Alex looked at Jack but didn't say anything.

"Hey, how could I have known that?"

"It's all right, Jack," Alex said. "You couldn't have known."

Jack got up from the table and paced the floor. This ruse made him almost angrier than if it had been a real bomb. "She did that on purpose!"

"Of course she did," Alex agreed.

"Sorry to ruin the reception, mates."

"This is not your fault," Maria consoled. "And you weren't the only target. I'm sure she wanted to leave her mark on the most important day of my life. If you haven't noticed, nothing makes Imogene more angry than the happiness of those she dislikes. I'm not even mad at her, because that would be admitting she ruined my perfect day. And I won't give her the pleasure of doing that. The only way she could have ruined this day would be if she stopped us from getting married, and, thankfully, she didn't manage to do that."

"You're absolutely right," Alex said. "We had a wonderful day."

"Okay, that's enough of the positive attitude!" Jack made a slicing motion with his hand. "I'm about to be sick. I guess I'm not as forgiving as the two of you. I just added this to a long list of stuff I'll never forgive her for."

Alex put his arm around Maria. "Well, as long as things are under control, and if no one needs us for anything, I think we'll just exit quietly without any more fanfare."

"Tell Maggie how much we appreciate everything," Maria said. "I don't want to stress her out any more. We'll see you next week."

Alex waved at Chief Hicks. "See you later, Chief. Try not to call me."

"Will do, mates." Jack gave Maria a hug and slapped Alex on the back.

"Don't get into trouble while we're gone," Alex said to Jack.

19

Survival Mode

The fifteen candles on his birthday cake looked more like two dozen. Wesley felt like he was much older, and yet he still had another year before he could legally drive. The party guests had to sing fast, because C.J. was already crawling onto the table and blowing out the candles. Maggie was trying to restrain her, but C.J. wasn't happy about it, and it wasn't going to last long. Wesley made a wish before he blew out the candles. If he could have one wish, he didn't need to think about what it would be. He wished for Maggie to get her memory back.

It had been two months since Alex and Maria's wedding reception debacle and a little more than that since the incident in the caves. Wesley was ready to wave the white flag. Things were supposed to have gotten better by now. Maggie should have been remembering things, Imogene should have been put back in jail, and his dad should have been acting like his cheerful, carefree self again.

None of those things had happened. In fact, Maggie's memory loss was almost certainly going to be permanent. The doctors could offer no solutions. They thought she might have suffered such a severe psychological trauma that she was actually suppressing her memory as some sort of protection mechanism. Everyone in the family had tried to find some trigger that would make her memories start coming back, but nothing seemed to work. They had spent hours gathered together as a family, relaying stories and catching her up on the last three years. They watched home videos and dug out recent pictures and stuck them into photo albums. At first Maggie seemed to enjoy the stories, but after a few weeks it only made things worse. She felt bad for having lost those precious moments and had started feeling like she would never be able to meet everyone's expectations.

Slowly Maggie had withdrawn from the family. She didn't talk much, made excuses to be away from the home, and hired babysitters frequently when she couldn't cope with everyone and everything.

Jack responded to her sullenness by working more and staying away from home, too. He agreed to do a two-part *Snake Stalker* special on the Great Barrier Reef, which meant he had to fly back and forth to Australia more than usual. That kept him conveniently away from Maggie and her frustration. Wesley didn't really blame him. He looked at the two of them now, standing on opposite sides of the room. The space between them seemed devoid of energy. They used to be such a fun-loving couple, and now they were like two college roommates who got thrown together by chance and simply tolerated each other for the semester because they didn't have any other choice. They didn't fight—at least not in front of him—but he would have almost preferred that to the silence.

Wesley knew Maggie was making a concerted effort to talk to him and was trying to get caught up on things in his life, but there was just no way that his stories could replace all the real experiences they'd had together. It was like there was another person living inside the shell of Maggie. Even C.J. and Emily seemed to notice something different about their mother, but they were much too young to understand. The family had tried group counseling for a few weeks, but then Jack was always gone and Maggie didn't think it was doing any good, so they stopped.

Then Imogene managed to get her trial postponed for several more months. Supposedly trial extensions were very common, but Wesley couldn't understand how she could get away with it. When he asked for an explanation, everyone just told him the legal stuff was too complicated for him to understand. All he knew was that the judge wouldn't rescind the bail hearing decision, and that meant Imogene was currently roaming around a free person.

Every day Wesley was afraid that she might show up unannounced, and every day he wondered if she would find a way to skip the country and disappear until the next time she felt like she needed a son again. Wesley figured the only reason she hadn't left the country was because the diamond case hadn't been recovered yet. Search teams had been looking for it, but because an underground river ran through the bottom of the canyon, it wasn't an easy task. It could have been buried or even washed away. Chances were slim that they would ever be able to find it.

In addition to that, Amanda was moving in a few weeks. She, Maria, and Alex were busy packing up the guesthouse next door. They made an appearance at his birthday party to cut the cake. Even though he and Amanda were friends again, Wesley felt like they were growing more distant, too. Amanda was all excited to move into her new house now. Wesley was glad she was able to get over her earlier reluctance, but it only validated his feeling that everyone in his life was abandoning him.

While his sisters sat in their high chairs smashing cake onto their faces, Wesley picked at his piece.

"What's wrong, Wesley?" Maggie asked. "Don't you like your cake?"

Wesley had never been too fond of chocolate cake with chocolate frosting, but that wasn't what he was moping about. Maggie would normally have known that his favorite was cherry chip with cream cheese frosting. It was pretty much a tradition, but then she didn't know about any of their traditions, and he missed that. But he had hoped that there might have been a chance that he would get a new puppy for his birthday. He had already opened all his presents, and that wasn't going to happen either.

"The cake is great," he lied. "I'm just full from dinner."

Hercules scampered in, reminding Wesley of a birthday party three years ago. He liked Hercules, but he was such a small dog that he couldn't do the same types of things that Teddy could. Even though Teddy wasn't Wesley's own dog, he still missed having him around.

"Okay, Wes," Jack announced. "In case you didn't notice, there wasn't a present in there from your dear old dad."

Wesley's hopes soared. There was still a chance for a puppy. He sat up straighter in his chair. "So what is it?"

"How would you like to miss the next ten days of school?" Jack asked.

It wasn't a puppy, but missing school was good, too. "Keep talking."

Jack went over to Wesley and handed him an envelope. He opened it up and pulled out an itinerary.

"A plane ticket to Australia?"

"Lucky!" Amanda crooned.

Jack nodded. "Yep. To help me finish up the Barrier Reef special. That is, if you want to go."

Wesley smiled. "Hmm, I don't know." He pretended like this was a difficult decision. "I told Grandma I'd help her weed the garden, and then I have a quiz in biology."

"Maybe some other time then," Jack said.

"When do we leave?" Wesley asked.

"At the end of the week. Just the two of us."

"But what about Maggie?" Wesley didn't want her to think they were abandoning her.

"Don't worry about me, Wesley," Maggie said, "Sharalee is coming for a visit while you're gone."

Wesley let out a sigh of relief. "Lucky for me I won't be here."

Everyone laughed because even though they all dearly loved Maggie's high-energy friend Sharalee, she was a talker and left most people exhausted after twenty minutes with her.

Wesley guessed that his dad had some ulterior motives about the timing of the Australia trip. Maggie had always been against Jack doing anything in the shark-infested waters of the Great Barrier Reef. She said the kids needed a father and made Jack promise to stay away from the deep oceans. She would have forgotten all about that, so Jack wouldn't have to make any promises this time. She would also worry incessantly about Wesley going in the water. He wasn't the best swimmer, and even though Maggie didn't tend to be overprotective about most things, she was just that when it came to him and the ocean.

"So am I going to get to scuba dive?" Wesley asked.

"You're not exactly certified," Jack said. "How about a snorkel?"

"Okay then." Wesley was secretly relieved. Scuba diving wasn't on his list of things he wanted to do. He wouldn't admit it, but he wasn't all that comfortable in anything deeper than his grandparents' pool. But for the first time in months, he had something to get excited about. He ripped the new iPod out of the box. "I better start loading this baby up. It's a long plane ride, and tunes will definitely be necessary."

* * *

Maggie searched through the photo albums and loose pictures scattered all over the bedroom floor. She had never been into scrapbooking, but she did like to collect pictures. Knowing her organized nature, Maggie would have wondered why she hadn't had all her pictures neatly and chronologically filed in books by now. But she had just spent the past two months trying to get used to being a mother of three and she knew the answer.

She had a good life, she decided, for anyone who had the chance to do things one step at a time. But to be a single veterinarian one day and then wake up the next morning to a life so completely different was no easy task. Nothing was quick and simple anymore. She couldn't just go to the mall and buy something. She had to plan everything in advance: get someone to take the girls or try and strap them into the double stroller and bring them along—and remember to give them wide enough berth so that they couldn't grab things off the shelves. She had already been embarrassed when the security buzzer went off in Target and Emily was caught absconding with a Black Sabbath CD.

C.J. was like a miniature Houdini, and no car seat or stroller could keep her restrained for more than five minutes. Jack told her that they sometimes put C.J. on a leash when they had to take her places and Maggie couldn't believe she would do something so humiliating to her child—until C.J. escaped in the mall and mall security found her thirty minutes later in the food court eating a corn dog she had commandeered from some kid twice her size. After that Maggie started carrying the kid leash with her at all times.

Still, Maggie adored her girls and never once wished that she didn't have them in her life. Getting used to being married, for some reason, was much harder. Without any real memories of how they fell in love, Maggie couldn't shake the idea that Jack was her brother-in-law. She enjoyed his company, but at the same time she felt uncomfortable around him. He knew all about her, but she didn't know him, and that made their relationship very one-sided. But at some point, she decided to take her mother's advice and do something about it. That's why she had the pictures strewn all over the floor. The current project was to use them to fill in some gaps. She studied each picture of her and Jack and tried as hard as she could to remember.

She picked up one that seemed to be dripping with laughter. This was obviously a happy event for her. She was wearing shorts and a T-shirt, and she and Jack were standing out in front of her parents' house, both sudsy and soaking wet. It looked like Teddy's bath day had turned into a water fight. Or maybe they were washing the car. Whatever they were doing, she was having a good time. The next picture from the same event showed Jack lifting her up with her arms pinned to her side. She looked like she was protesting and laughing at the same time. She wondered who had taken the picture. Was it her dad? Or Wesley, maybe?

Maggie sighed and slid the pictures into a photo album. These two people were obviously crazy about each other. Could it ever be that way again? The phone rang, and she let it ring a few times before she picked it up.

"Hello?"

"Hey, Mag. It's me."

"Hi, Jack."

"You know how we've been meanin' to have Harlan over for dinner?"

"Yeah. Did he agree to come?"

"Well, he says he's free tonight, and he's in the area and wants us to meet his new girlfriend. So I said I'd check with you and see if we could go out to a nice dinner on the town—just the four of us."

"Sounds great." Maggie wished she could put some more enthusiasm into her voice. "I'll see if Wesley's up to tending the girls tonight."

"Tell him I'll make it worth his time. Oh, and Harlan sounded pretty love struck on the phone. I don't know why, but for some reason he's afraid we won't approve of his girlfriend."

"That's ridiculous. Why would he think that?"

"I don't know. But he sounded nervous, like he really wanted to impress her."

"Well, you're a big TV star, and his girlfriend is

probably from a small town like he is, so she might be a little shy."

"Yeah, and I think Harlan probably doesn't have too much experience with women. We'll have to really build up his self-esteem, you know. Make him look like a rock star."

"As far as I'm concerned, he's Superman. He saved my life."

"Yes, he did. Okay then. How about six? We'll make it a date."

"It's a date." Maggie hung up and looked at the pictures again. Jack was really a sweet and caring person. She had tried to act more like the adoring wife she thought he deserved, but he could tell when she was pretending, so she needed to really feel it. She looked at the dog-washing pictures again and thought maybe she was starting to figure out why she had fallen in love with Jack. Maybe all she needed was some more time. For the first time in two months, she was actually looking forward to a date with her husband.

20

The Girlfriend

At the restaurant, Jack noticed that Maggie seemed to be a lot more talkative than usual, and she sidled up close to him in the booth while they waited for Harlan and his girlfriend to show up. Maggie reached over and grabbed Jack's hand. This was a new development.

"So tell me, what's my favorite Chinese food?" Maggie quizzed him.

"Mu shu pork," Jack answered with certainty.

"I guess you're right. How did you know that?" Maggie asked.

"I've known that since our first date."

"That's kind of personal information for a first date."

"Yeah. Well, you moved in on me fast. So what's my favorite dish?"

"Hmm, this isn't fair, you know. I'll say that it's sesame beef."

"Close," Jack said, "but it's actually General Tso's chicken."

Maggie nodded. "Of course. The General."

"Not to be confused with the Colonel," Jack added.

Maggie laughed, something she rarely did nowadays, and Jack remembered how much he missed that. For a moment it seemed like Maggie was becoming her old self again, and Jack wished that he could have this evening alone with her, but it was too late to cancel on Harlan. In fact Harlan was walking over to their table at that very moment with his familiar gait. Jack looked for his date, but he appeared to be alone.

Harlan greeted Jack with a handshake and sat down in the booth across from Maggie.

"Katrina is on her way," Harlan explained. "She had to take a phone call."

"No problem," Jack said. "We're anxious to meet her."

"I have to warn you. She's the most beautiful girl in the world," Harlan said. "No offense, Maggie."

"That's okay, Harlan. I'm not offended. Jack and I are so glad you found someone."

"Yeah, she is *some*one," Harlan said. "I think she might even be *the* one."

"Wow." Jack opened up his chopsticks and attempted to pick up an ice cube out of his water with them. "Sounds terminal, mate. I didn't know you had been dating for that long."

"Well, we haven't. I met her at my brother's funeral. That sounds a little strange, but we just had this connection. We hit it off right away. We're really different—she's from the city, and I'm just a country boy, but it was love at first sight. For me, anyway." Harlan beamed as he raised his arm to motion for someone to come and sit down. "Here she is now."

Jack was in the process of taking a drink of his water when he looked up and saw the woman heading for their table. The shock was immediate. He choked on his water and involuntarily spit it onto the table. He covered his mouth and started coughing convulsively.

Harlan wasn't kidding when he said his girlfriend was beautiful. She was a gorgeous blonde with a model's figure. But this wasn't the first time Jack had seen her.

Maggie thumped Jack on the back to try and curb his coughing spasm while Harlan introduced Katrina to them. It was fortunate that Jack had been rendered speechless, because he didn't know what he would have said to Whitney Ray as she slid into the seat next to Harlan. She glanced at Jack and tossed her long locks over her shoulder.

For Maggie, there was no history to deal with, so she was completely composed. "It's so nice to meet you, Katrina. Harlan has been telling us wonderful things about you."

"Emmett is just the sweetest thing." Whitney fawned all over Harlan. She avoided looking directly at Jack, who had finally recovered enough to breathe.

Jack couldn't believe this was happening. Whitney Ray was Imogene's niece and had been responsible for starting tabloid rumors that she and Jack were having an affair. Then she had given him drugs while he was in the hospital and had been part of a scheme to make them think his first wife, Nicole, was still alive. Maggie had none of these memories, and Jack didn't wish to explain any of it to her right now. He didn't know whether to excuse himself or just play along with the charade. But he knew he didn't want to upset either Maggie or Harlan, so he simply put out his hand cordially. "Katrina—nice to meet you. Jack Mackey."

"Yes, I know," Whitney said.

For a minute Jack thought she was going to explain just exactly how she knew him, but instead she continued.

"I've been watching *The Snake Stalker* ever since I was a little girl. Everyone knows who you are."

"Yeah, Trina's a real snake lover herself," Harlan said. "She wants me to take her into the caves to meet Randy."

Sure she does, Jack thought. It was clear what was going on here. Whitney wanted the diamonds, and she was using Harlan to get them. He had to give her credit; she was going about it very skillfully. Harlan was eating out of the palm of her hand. Whether she was working for Imogene or against her, he didn't know, but he couldn't just sit there and let it happen. He tried to think of what to say as the waiter came to take their order, but he couldn't piece together a coherent sentence.

Jack's appetite had completely disappeared. He was stating to feel warm and very uncomfortable. "So, *Katrina,*" Jack said in a stiff voice, "tell us about yourself. Where are you from?"

"I'm from California," she answered as she kicked Jack's leg under the table. "Near Beverly Hills."

Jack didn't know what that kick was supposed to mean.

"Katrina is a model," Harlan filled in.

"Imagine that," Jack said.

"I'm not surprised," Maggie said. "You're very beautiful."

"Thank you," Whitney said. "Oh! I forgot to wash my hands. If you'll excuse me, I just need to make a quick trip to the ladies' room." She darted out of the booth.

In less than a minute, Jack's cell phone vibrated. Jack covered the screen with his hand and read the caller ID. It said *Harlan* but obviously he wasn't the caller.

"Uh, I better take this out in the lobby," Jack said. When Maggie looked at him quizzically, he added, "It's Wes, but it's a little noisy in here."

Whitney was waiting for Jack in the lobby of the restaurant. "You want to tell me what's goin' on here, *Katrina?*"

"Hey, it's my real middle name—I'm not lying."

"Oh no, you would never lie—not even to get your greedy paws on a certain briefcase full of diamonds."

Whitney opened her mouth to say something and then changed her mind. "Jack, if you tell Harlan who I am, I'll tell your wife we had an affair."

"Sure—why not recycle that old story? The one we both know isn't true."

"Maybe you know it and I know it, but Maggie doesn't know it. You really want to try and explain that to her?"

"You don't care how many lives you ruin, do you?" Jack shot back. "You're going to break Harlan's heart. He thinks he's in love with you! But that's your plan, isn't it?"

"You don't know me, Jack. Maybe I like Harlan. He treats me good, and he's funny too."

"Give me a break! And you just happen to run into him at his brother's funeral? You never knew Harlan's brother."

"Yes, I did. His name was Eddie," Whitney replied. "And I just lost someone very close to me, so I know what he's going through."

"So do I." Jack grabbed her by the arm just as Maggie walked into the lobby behind them. Jack let go quickly and tried to act natural.

"Jack, is something wrong at home?" Maggie asked.

Jack noticed his phone was clenched in his fist. "Uh, no. Wes just wanted to know what time he should put the girls down for bed."

"I told him eight thirty," Maggie said.

"Yeah. He must have forgotten."

"Yeah, well it runs in the family," Maggie said with a hint of suspicion. The three of them headed back to the table.

"I'm so sorry, honey," Whitney said to Harlan. "We left you here all by your lonesome."

"That's okay," Harlan said. "As long as you didn't run off for good."

"Well if I did, you'd have to catch me." Whitney giggled.

Jack thought he was going to be sick. As much as he wanted to warn Harlan what he was getting into, this wasn't going to be the right time to say anything. He took his seat next to Maggie, dumped his egg roll into some sweet and sour sauce, and stuffed it into his mouth.

* * *

"What was with you tonight?" Maggie asked Jack as he was driving them home from the restaurant. "You were acting strange."

"That's because strange things were happening."

"You don't like Katrina, do you?"

"No, I don't," Jack said bluntly. "And her name isn't Katrina."

"What do you mean? Do you know her?"

"We've met. And I'm not going to let her get away with this."

"Get away with what?"

"She's using Harlan."

"How would you know that?"

"Because her name is Whitney Ray, and she's Imogene's niece, that's why."

"She's Imogene's niece?" Maggie was shocked. "She doesn't look like Imogene."

"That's because Imogene is the ugly sister," Jack explained. "And her niece, just like Imogene's sister, is a gold digger who sees an opportunity."

"But why would she want to go after Harlan? He doesn't have any money."

"Or does he?" Jack asked. "A certain briefcase full of diamonds has yet to be located by the police. Harlan just so happened to grow up in the caves where it was lost, and he's on a first-name basis with a pack of giant diamondback rattlers that guard the place. He also told us it would be nearly impossible to find. Maybe that's because he already found it. His alibi is covered."

"Now you're telling me Harlan is a criminal and you think he's in on some secret plot to steal the diamonds."

Jack thought for a moment. "Yeah. That's what I'm sayin'."

"Harlan isn't that type of person. If he was going to steal them, he would have had a better chance when we were in the caves."

"Well, maybe he didn't care about the diamonds then. But now if it means keeping a beautiful blonde hanging on his arm, he might be persuaded."

"Are you sure about this? She seemed to genuinely like Harlan."

"I'm sure," Jack reassured her. "Women like her don't go for guys like him."

"Wait a minute." Maggie sounded offended. "What do you mean by 'guys like him'?"

"What I mean is he isn't rich, he isn't famous, and he has one leg."

"So what? It's the person inside that counts. That type of thing doesn't matter to some women."

"She isn't *some* woman. She's a rich, spoiled brat. And I can guarantee it matters to her."

"If you're right, then that's very sad. Harlan's obviously crazy about her."

"I know that. What I don't know is how I'm going to break it to him."

"You're not going to tell him, are you?"

"Of course I am. I owe it to him."

"Maybe you owe it to him to keep quiet. This isn't really your business."

"Mag, are you serious?"

"Yes, I'm serious! Just let it play out, and maybe he'll figure it out for himself. If you say something to him, he's only going to get defensive and angry with you. And I think you may be wrong. Maybe Katrina really likes Harlan."

"It's all an act. Did I mention she's an actress? And it's *Whitney*. Although Katrina is a more accurate name—a hurricane is exactly what she is. She moves in quickly and leaves a wake of destruction in her path."

Maggie studied Jack's face for a moment. Jack turned to look at her. "What?" he asked defensively.

"You're really worked up about this, aren't you? There's something more going on here than just trying to protect Harlan. What aren't you telling me?"

"Like I said, if you knew what I knew . . . this woman is *trouble* with a capital T."

Maggie's eyes flashed with anger. "Obviously I don't know what you know. So why don't you fill me in?"

Jack thought for a minute and wondered if he should risk going into more detail. Maggie was just starting to warm up to him. He didn't want to ruin it all by bringing up sordid details from the past. This story in particular was one he hoped would stay forgotten.

"There's nothing more to tell. She's Imogene's niece, that's all."

"And that alone means she's a bad person."

"Yes—I mean no. It just means she can't be trusted." Jack knew he was digging a hole for himself, and it was time to stop. "You're right, Mag. Harlan's a big boy and can take care of himself. It's not our business."

* * *

It was half-past midnight when Jack pulled his car into the parking lot in front of the carcass of an abandoned strip mall. Out of habit, he parked between the lines, even though it seemed pretty ridiculous when the area was completely deserted. In a few minutes, a bright yellow Corvette pulled up next to him. This was going to turn out badly, and he knew it. In fact, he should have refused to meet with her after she called him yesterday, but either way, he was going to be in a heap of trouble, and he thought this way at least he would be able to figure out what he was up against.

Whitney waited for him in her car. Jack got out of his car and walked over to her with his hands up, to show her that he wasn't packing a weapon.

She opened the passenger-side door for him. "Get in, Jack," she said as if they were old friends. "I know that you're not going to try and shoot me."

"Well, now that that's out of the way," Jack said as he ducked inside and shut his door, "you can tell me why you called this little meeting. But first let me tell you that I've already sealed up in an envelope a note to my lawyer saying that you arranged this. It has a postmark on it from today before five. So in case you want to get some more front page pictures, I'm covered."

"Jack, I told you. Those days are gone. I'm a new person. And I called this meeting because I like you, and I want you to like me too."

Jack started to open his door. "This is where I leave . . ."

"No!" Whitney stopped him. "I don't mean I like you *that* way. What I mean is we should be friends. I think we should work together on this. I want Imogene out of the way just as much as you do."

"That much I believe is true. Which is why you're using Harlan to get the diamonds before she does. Yeah, yeah, I know all that."

"You don't know anything, Jack. This wasn't my idea. My mother is making me do this. Peter was supposed to get the diamonds. But as you know, he was killed."

"Yeah, so was my dog," Jack said.

Whitney stopped for a moment, and Jack could hear something change in her voice. "My mother is forcing me to get close to Harlan so he can show us where the diamonds are."

"And now you would like me to get out of the way so that you can make sure it happens. You're still not tellin' me anything I don't already know. I figured that much out the minute you sat down at the restaurant."

"What you don't know is that I'm not after the diamonds. I want out. I'm through with my mother, Aunt Genie, and especially Peter."

"That's convenient, since Peter is dead, Imogene is going to jail, and your mother is a *lunatic*. So you're tired of being in the gang, huh? Or did they just kick you out? What brought on this sudden change of heart?"

Whitney looked at Jack and took a deep breath. She averted her eyes and then said hesitantly, "I've fallen in love with Harlan."

Jack broke out into raucous laughter. "Somehow, I highly doubt that. Sorry, Whitney, but you're just not that good of an actress."

"Jack, it's true. At first I was just pretending to like him, but after two months of being around him, I realize he's the sweetest person I've ever known. He treats me nice, and he doesn't think I'm stupid."

"Just because he doesn't *say* you're stupid doesn't mean he doesn't *think* it." Jack continued to laugh. "Don't kid yourself."

Whitney suddenly became angry. "That's exactly what I'm talking about! You and Peter—and every man I've ever met! You're all alike!"

Jack was taken aback by her sudden outburst, but he did get a piece of new information. "Wait a minute . . . Peter Jaworsky was your . . . boyfriend?"

"You didn't know that?" Whitney put her hand to her mouth like she had accidentally blurted out a secret.

"Peter didn't happen to mention it in our conversation that day." Jack shook his head. "Wasn't he a little old for you?"

"He's only twelve years older." Whiney shrugged as if there were nothing unusual about that. "I'm very mature for my age. But now that I look back on it, I consider myself lucky that he died before he could completely ruin my life. Do you know what it's like to be around someone who doesn't respect you? Someone who treats you like you're not good enough, and no matter what you do, or how hard you try, it's never right?"

"More than you know."

"You know what Peter's pet name for me was? He called me Dim-Whit. That's the real reason I changed my name to Katrina. I'm sick of everyone running my life thinking I don't have the brains to make my own decisions. Maybe I'm not as smart as Peter, but you know what? *I'm* still alive!"

"You have a point there."

"It may seem like Harlan and I don't really go together. But he never makes me feel worthless. And I think he's adorable. He has the most handsome brown eyes, and when he smiles, he has the cutest dimples."

"The dimples are what really do it for me." Jack couldn't believe he was having this conversation.

"I know you think that just because he has one leg he's somehow less of a man, but I don't care about that. It's the person inside that matters."

"So why are you telling me all this?" he asked.

"Because I want to make a fresh start. I don't want Harlan to know who I am."

"He's going to find out sooner or later. You're wanted by the police."

"Well, maybe I wouldn't be if I could get those diamonds back and turn them in."

"Can't help you there, mate."

"Yes, you can. Harlan thinks he knows where they are, but he can't climb down there—at least not by himself. You could go with him. That way we can make sure Imogene doesn't get them."

"Why not cut out the middleman and just go directly to the police?"

"Because that would ruin everything."

"Ruin what 'everything'?"

"Okay, I'll be honest. There is something in that case that belongs to me, and the police aren't going to give it to me."

"Just what is this item? Let me guess: a diamond?"

"Not just any diamond. It's pink—and very rare. It's a princess cut that Peter promised to me."

"But it wasn't Peter's to give you. It's a stolen gem. You're right. The police aren't going to give it to you. And you just admitted to me that you're still in it for the money."

"It's one diamond out of a thousand. I wouldn't care about it, but I need to sell it so I'll have something to live on. That's why I can't get away from my mom—I don't have my own money. Whenever I try to break away from her, I run out of money and have to come back."

"What about your modeling career?"

"I've spent all that—and if I want to stay in Georgia, there aren't many opportunities out here."

"You're going to give up your former life and modeling career in California just to stay here with Harlan?"

"Yes! Jack, I've already burned out on that life. Seriously, I just want something else. Why can't anyone believe that?"

"Because you have a track record of lying to get what you want. It goes with the territory. And what about your mother?"

"She thinks she controls me. But I told you, I'm not working for her anymore."

"But you're still her daughter."

"So?" Whitney rummaged through her purse for a stick of gum.

Jack studied Whitney's face. She was a stunning beauty. It was difficult for anyone to believe she would really be interested in an average guy like Harlan. But then Harlan wasn't exactly average once you got to know him, and he was sure Whitney wasn't lying about Harlan treating her well. Why was he starting to believe her?

"So what are you thinking?" Whitney asked.

"I'm thinking someone's going to jump out of those bushes any minute and tell me I've just won the 'dupe of the year' award."

"How do you get that?" Whitney asked as if it were a real award.

Jack shook his head. "Tell you what. I have no idea why, but for some reason I believe you. I know that I shouldn't, but my mother-in-law is starting to rub off on me. Everyone deserves a fresh start, and I'm going to let you have it."

"You're not going to tell Harlan?" Whitney couldn't have looked more thrilled than if he had handed her a million bucks.

"I'm not going to tell him, but you are. Harlan is a good person, and if you really are in love with him, he'll understand."

"Really?" Whitney looked as though she might embrace Jack.

Jack threw up his arms. "Don't touch me, okay? I think we may be able to work together on this if you really want to break away from your mum and aunt permanently. And if you keep your word about everything you just said, you can have your cake and eat it too."

"No thanks. It goes straight to my thighs."

"No, I don't mean real cake. That's just an expression that means you get everything you want."

"You mean I can have Harlan and my diamond too? Why didn't you just say that?"

"I can't promise anything about the diamond, but we may be able to get your criminal record expunged— uh erased," Jack clarified. "Just don't try to put one over on me, because you won't get another chance."

21

Incriminating Evidence

Wesley and Amanda were throwing a baseball back and forth on the front lawn after school. He was supposed to be packing for his trip tomorrow, but he didn't want to be inside on this seventy-degree afternoon.

Alex pulled his car into the driveway at the same time Walter came running over from next door. Walter was moving pretty fast for a sixty-two-year-old.

"Hey, y'all!" Walter motioned for them to stop what they were doing. "Get inside and turn on the TV! Jack's on the news!"

"I know. I just heard it on the radio," Alex confirmed.

Wesley didn't understand what everyone was getting all excited about. Being on the news was no big deal for any of the Mackey family members. In fact, Wesley would be glad if he never had to be on the news again. If Walter and Alex thought it was important, it must be something big. Wesley didn't ask questions and hurried inside the house to find out what everyone was so riled up about.

Maggie already had the TV on and was recording the news story.

"This is absolutely unbelievable!" she said as Walter came in and sat down next to her on the couch. "Here, I'll start it from the beginning." She pressed the rewind button on the DVR and went back to the beginning of the news story.

An anchor duo with smug grins promised the audience this breaking news story would be worth listening to. "As you know, a little over two months ago we brought you coverage of a cave explosion involving indicted billionaire Imogene Vandergrift and the Snake Stalker, Jack Mackey. A recent twist has been added to this already bizarre story. We'll go live to Rebecca Robbins at the state courthouse for the details. Rebecca?"

The shot went to a woman in a red suit jacket holding a stick mic. "Thanks, Keith and Brenda. Eyewitness News has uncovered some startling information about the motives behind the recent bombings in the Walker County caves. Until recently, it was unclear how and why Imogene Vandergrift had been able to get released on bail so quickly. According to court documents, Jack Mackey is the person who secured her release. But the question is why would he want to release the woman who allegedly took his son away and raised him for eleven years?"

"Just wait," Maggie said. "It gets worse."

The reporter continued. "According to Vandergrift's newly appointed attorney, Joey Ferraro, Mackey wants to makes sure Vandergrift never goes to trial. Mackey has made numerous death threats against Vandergrift, and one of those was caught on videotape two months ago at the wedding reception of Maria Perry—a mutual friend of Vandergrift and Mackey."

"Mutual *friend?*" Alex said incredulously. "I don't think so."

The video cut to a professional-grade video clip of Jack in a tuxedo, standing face to face with Imogene. The audio portion of Jack's threat couldn't have been any clearer. "You better hope and pray that at your trial next month the jury finds you guilty, because if they don't lock you up for good—I promise you—I'll come after you myself and kill you." The sound bite cut back to the reporter, who checked the notepad in her hand.

"Now the source for this video has asked not to be identified, but we do know that Vandergrift's lawyer has obtained a restraining order against Mackey. Ferraro says that Vandergrift is fearful that Mackey may make an attempt on her life before she has a chance to plead her case in court in three months. I have Mr. Ferraro here with me now." The shot opened up to include a powerfully built, dark-haired man with a neatly trimmed beard and wearing an expensive pinstriped suit.

"What can you tell us, Mr. Ferraro, about your request to file a restraining order against Jack Mackey?" The reporter shoved a microphone in Ferraro's face.

"Well, Rebecca, obviously—as you can see from this tape—Jack Mackey is a very dangerous man and poses a viable threat to my client. I think the judge saw what we all saw, and that's why he granted us the restraining order. This isn't the first time Mr. Mackey has made this type of threat, and it's my job to make sure my client remains safe while our defense team gathers new evidence for this case."

"Any information you can give us on this new evidence?" the reporter asked.

"I'm sure you understand, I'm not at liberty to discuss any of this information before it goes to trial, but I can say that we are very confident that once a jury hears the circumstances surrounding this case, Imogene Vandergrift is going to be cleared of all charges. Thank you." Joey Ferraro was whisked off the scene by two men in sunglasses who looked like Secret Service agents.

"How can Imogene serve *Jack* with a restraining order?" Walter exploded. "It should be the other way around!"

"What's a restraining order?" Amanda asked.

"It means if Jack comes within a certain distance of Imogene, he'll be arrested," Alex said.

The reporter recapped the story and then finished with "Jack Mackey has been unavailable for comment. He said he cannot discuss the details of the transpired events until after the trial. Keith and Brenda, back to you."

"What kind of a judge allows this information to get out?" Maggie asked. "This could taint the whole trial."

"That's exactly what she wants to do," Alex explained. "Imogene wants to make it look like she's the victim here—like Jack has been threatening her—so she can gain some sympathy from the jury."

"And did you see that sleazebag lawyer? Joey Ferraro. Where have I heard that name before?"

"He's the guy who got Timothy Sharp off for murdering his wife," Alex said. "He's one of best of the worst defense attorneys in the nation. He's young and has an attitude, but unfortunately he's very good at what he does. He doesn't care if you're guilty or innocent—only how deep your pockets are. He loves high-profile cases like this. I swear he could have found a way to get Adolf Hitler off on a technicality."

"Great." Walter slapped his thigh. "Well, we can get some bigwig lawyer too, can't we?"

"Barry Simms is a great lawyer," Alex said. "I wouldn't advise Jack to replace him with someone he doesn't don't know and trust. Besides, Imogene wants to get Jack all riled up. That way she can make a case to the jury that he's harassing her. She wanted Jack to lose his temper in front of witnesses at our wedding so she would have grounds to file a restraining order. She's trying to make him as angry as possible."

Walter thumped his fist on the table. "Well she's doing a good job of that! What if the jury gets her off? What if the judge feels sorry for her?"

"Let's just hope that doesn't happen," Alex said. "But let's not make things any worse by trying to get even. Imogene is like snake venom. The more you get agitated, the faster it spreads, and the more damage it does."

* * *

Jack and Wesley had left for Australia a few days earlier, and Maggie had mixed feelings about them being gone. For sure, things were quieter, but she also missed their company. The pressure of having to try and remember everything was gone, and she could relax and spend some one-on-one time with her girls without feeling like someone was looking over her shoulder to make sure she was doing everything in proper order. But at the same time she realized how empty everything seemed without them. She stretched her legs in the warm May sun next to Sharalee and sipped her soda by the calming waters of the waterfall.

Having her best friend come and visit for a few days was the best medicine she could have asked for. Maggie and Nicole had hung out with Sharalee since grade school, and they had always lived near each other until last year, when Sharalee and her husband, Earl, moved to Virginia. Maggie had enjoyed having her visit for the past few days, but she was starting to get worn out from her high-energy friend and was glad Sharalee would be flying home that night. Sharalee had a southern accent as thick and sweet as honey and could ramble on for hours if you couldn't find a way to stop her.

"You know," Sharalee said, "sometimes I wish me and Earl could start over like you and Jack. I think it would be kind of fun getting to know each other all over again."

"You're always the optimist, Shara," Maggie said. "It's not as fun as you might think."

"Yeah, I don't think I'd want to have to train him to put his socks in the hamper all over again. I'm too old for that. I know that forgetting the past can have its drawbacks, but at the same time—it's kind of adventurous and romantic too. You and Jack are just the perfect couple."

"That's what everyone keeps telling me."

"Because it's true. So why don't you just make the best of it and start making new memories? Consider yourself lucky that you don't have to remember any of the bad stuff."

"What exactly do you mean by the *bad stuff*?"

"I didn't mean bad stuff like anything really bad, just those nasty rumors that were going around in the tabloids."

"Jack and I were in the tabloids?"

"Of course you were! Well, Jack mostly. Maggie, I hate to break this to you, but your husband is a famous TV star. It's required by law to have at least three mean and untrue stories written about him every month."

"Yeah, I sort of noticed that. So, did I used to get upset about these stories?"

"No, of course not." Sharalee flipped her wrist and picked up a bottle of fingernail polish and shook it up. "You never even read them."

"If I didn't read them, then why would they be bad memories?"

Sharalee unscrewed the nail polish bottle and tried to gloss over what she had just said. "Oops!" Sharalee tipped over the nail polish, dripping it onto the plastic lawn chair. "Oh, sorry. I'll clean it up."

Maggie handed her some napkins, and Sharalee added to the mess by sticking them to the chair.

"We should go out for Italian food and then watch your favorite movie, which just so happens to be a romantic comedy," Sharalee suggested.

"My favorite movie is a *romantic comedy*? You can't pull that on me. I like action shows. *You* like the romantic stuff."

"Well, watch it first and then call me a liar."

"Okay, I'll just have to trust you. We'll go to Giovanni's and then watch some sappy chick flick."

"We will . . . after you call your adorable husband and tell him you can't wait for him to come home because you miss him terribly."

"That actually sounds like a good idea," Maggie agreed.

"Which part?" Sharalee asked hopefully. "The food, the movie, or the adorable husband?"

"All of it. But I can't call Jack right now because they're fourteen hours ahead of us in Australia.

"So wake him up in the middle of the night! I promise you he won't mind."

"I'll be sure to tell him that. Have you always been this nosy about my love life?"

"Yes, and it's a good thing too. I was the one who told you to dump that awful Mitch Yeager. And I was so right about him. Lucky for you, I saved you from *that* disaster."

"Thanks, Sharalee. You're a true friend."

* * *

The phone rang at six A.M., at exactly the same time that Jack's alarm went off. Wesley was asleep in another room at Jack's brother Tommy's house. They weren't going to get too much time to recover from jet lag before they needed to head out to the islands for the shoot. Jack saw that the call came from home, or he would have ignored it and gone back to sleep. He was pleasantly surprised to hear Maggie's voice.

"Hi, Jack. Did I wake you up?"

"Hi, Mag." Jack rubbed his eyes and tried to sound coherent. "Nah, I just got through with my early-morning 5K."

"Sorry, I know it's early, but I just wanted to call you."

"You can call me anytime. How are my girls?"

"Good. Everything is great. Sharalee and I are having fun." There was a short pause. "I just wanted to tell you that I miss you."

Jack was suddenly wide awake. Did he really hear her right? "Uh, I miss you too, Mag," he stuttered, as if he were a teenager trying to impress a new girl.

"It's just not the same around here with the two of you gone."

"Is that good or bad?" Jack knew he was fishing for compliments.

"I just wish you were coming home sooner. A week is a long time."

"Get Penny and Walter to take the girls, and you can fly out here and meet us."

"No, I know you're working, and it's a long flight. By the time I got there, it would be time to come home. You and Wesley have fun. Shara and I are getting ready to go to dinner, so I need to go. Promise me you won't do anything too risky, okay?"

"Who, me?"

"Yes, you. And Wesley too. I worry about both of you being safe."

"Mag, I promise you we'll both be very cautious."

"Good. You'll call me later, then?"

"Sure. But I'll be on the bottom of the ocean most of the day so I might not be able to call you until tonight—morning for you. Kiss the girls for me." He said good-bye and hung up the phone.

She can't stand me when I'm home, and suddenly when I'm nine thousand miles away, she decides she misses me? Jack thought as he instantly lost his enthusiasm for filming his next show. He wished more than anything he could get on a plane right then and head home.

* * *

After dinner, Maggie and Sharalee returned home to two sleeping girls, but told the babysitter to stay there, because they would be leaving again for the airport in an hour. Sharalee insisted there was time to watch the first half of their movie.

The TV room looked neat and tidy at first glance, but as soon as Maggie opened the video cupboard, an army of DVDs and videos came spilling out onto the floor.

"So tell me what we're looking for," Maggie said.

"I don't know. I think there's a guy and a girl on the front."

"Great." Maggie sighed. "That really narrows it down. Would you settle for *Shrek 2* instead?" She threw a CD case out onto the floor. "Obviously I've turned into a complete slob since I've been married."

"You're not a slob. You just have a family. This is great compared to my house." Sharalee pulled out a rancid juice cup and some squeaky toys and threw them in a pile.

Maggie started throwing things out. "Okay, we've got soda cans, comic books, an empty vodka bottle . . ." She stopped. She held up the alcohol container and showed it to Sharalee in horror. "What's this?" Maggie asked.

Sharalee looked stunned.

"We don't drink, and we definitely don't keep alcohol in the house," Maggie stated.

"It's just a bottle," Sharalee explained. "It could be something Wesley uses for bottle rockets."

"I know Jack used to have a drinking problem," Maggie said, "right after Nicole died."

"But he doesn't drink now. Do you think it's Wesley?"

"If it were Wesley, don't you think he'd be smart enough not to leave something like that around where you could find it?"

"You would think," Sharalee agreed. "But he's a teenager. They aren't that smart sometimes."

Maggie dug deeper into the back of the video cabinet and gasped. "Shara—there's a rum bottle back here too! And this one is half full."

Sharalee shook her head. "This is awful, Maggie."

"How would Wesley get hard liquor? It has to belong to Jack. Maria and Alex are nondrinkers too."

"Maybe because he's been so depressed lately," Sharalee started to explain.

"That's no excuse!"

"You don't know for sure that these belong to Jack, Maggie."

"I know he's never home. How do I know what he does when he's gone on weeklong trips?"

"It just doesn't seem like he has a problem anymore."

"Alcoholics know how to hide their addiction very well, but in this case, he didn't do a very good job of it."

"Maggie, I'm so sorry. I don't know what to say."

Maggie set the bottles down on the coffee table and rubbed her face with her hands. She had tried so hard to remember everything, but now she wondered if there were some things she really didn't want to know.

It took a while for Maggie to convince Sharalee that she was fine, but she finally agreed to let Maggie take her to the airport. After Maggie got back and sent the babysitter home, she went looking for more evidence, hoping somehow that she would find an explanation for the bottles. Instead, she found one more bottle stashed away in the back of Jack's side of the closet. There was no question who they belonged to anymore. Jack had a serious problem and was keeping it from her.

Maggie tried to figure out how to confront Jack about it. She would call him just as soon as she took care of her splitting headache. She went to her nightstand drawer where she always used to keep some ibuprofen. The drawer was crammed with junk, and she ripped it out and emptied the contents onto her bed. Miscellaneous jewelry, pill bottles, magazines, photos, newspaper articles, and scribbled pictures littered the bedspread. She found what she was looking for and emptied two pills into her hand. She was going to get some water when a tabloid newspaper article caught her attention.

The magazine was folded in half, and when she opened it up, the blood immediately rushed to her head, causing her headache to intensify. She thumbed through the rest of the paper to make sure she wasn't imagining what she just saw. It was a photo of Jack kissing another woman. When she looked closely, she realized it wasn't just any other woman—it was Harlan's girlfriend.

Maggie's mind started to race. She remembered Jack's discomfort at the Chinese restaurant when Katrina—or Whitney or whatever her name—was came in. Soon after that, Whitney excused herself and Jack did too, and then they both seemed to be in some sort of heated discussion when Maggie walked up on them. And Jack had admitted that he knew her and seemed genuinely distressed about the whole thing. She knew there was something more going on than Jack trying to protect Harlan. It all made sense now.

But why was this tabloid in her nightstand drawer? Was this the traumatic event that her memory was trying to suppress? Maybe this was the event that was so painful it was keeping her from remembering the recent past. Added to the alcohol bottle stashed in the closet, it was definitely causing her stress at the moment.

Then again, maybe this was all a mistake. Sharalee had said Jack was in the tabloids all the time. This might have been one they laughed at—but then why would she keep it? And if he had nothing to hide, then why wouldn't Jack have told her about it that night after they left the restaurant?

She picked up the phone and called Jack's cell. He was probably unreachable right now, but she needed to try. She listened to the phone ring six times, and then Jack's voice message came on. "This is Jack. Call you when I get back."

"Jack, I have to talk to you now. Call me as soon as you get this message." She threw the phone down on the bed and slammed her fist into the pillow.

22

Down Under

This was the third time Wesley had been to Australia, but it was the first time he had gotten to see Great Barrier Reef up close, and it was even more magnificent than he could have imagined. His uncle Tommy had flown them all out in his helicopter to a remote side of the Keppel Islands while his dad went several miles out into the ocean with Zeke and Steve and the rest of the diving crew to shoot an underwater adventure. Wesley and his cousin Josh got dropped off at the beach with their snorkel and fins, while Uncle Tommy and another flight crew guy went to refuel the chopper.

Wesley was a little disappointed he couldn't go along with his dad, but they were shooting all the video underwater today, and he would be stuck out on the boat by himself the whole time. But snorkeling with his cousin was a pretty good consolation, especially because Josh, who was sixteen, was about the coolest person he'd ever met next to his dad. He was glad Amanda hadn't been invited on this trip, because she would have been fawning all over Josh, and even though he shouldn't be, Wesley knew that would have made him jealous.

Josh had white-blond hair, ocean-blue eyes, and that Aussie accent girls went crazy over. Add to that how he was obviously Grandpa C.J.'s favorite grand-kid, and he was pretty tough competition. He was Uncle Tommy's only son and was interested in becoming a doctor just like Grandpa C.J.

"Hey, Wesley!" Josh splashed out of the shallow water in his swim fins. He was wearing bright orange floral swim trunks, with a mask and snorkel slung around his neck. "Come over here!"

Wesley knew it must be something really interesting from the sound of Josh's voice. He was pretty unco-ordinated walking in his swim fins, but his dad made him promise to keep his shoes or fins on at all times. Not only could the coral be very sharp, but there were all kinds of poisonous creatures, including the deadly box jellyfish, that you could easily step on. So far, he had been obedient to his dad's wishes, but it was becoming increasingly inconvenient. Every time he took a step, he had to lift his foot up high and force it through the water. It took a lot of muscle. He lurched awkwardly behind Josh until the water was deep enough to swim in. His dad also told him to stay right next to the shore. "Next to" was a pretty broad term, so he didn't think he had violated that yet.

He put on his mask and snorkel and followed Josh into the area he was pointing out. About fifty yards from the shore, the white sandy bottom dropped out beneath him, and he put his face in the water. A few years ago, he would have started to panic at the thought that he was in water over his head without a life jacket on, but now he was pretty comfortable.

Below the surface it was like a giant undersea village with beautiful white-bleached coral. His dad told him that the coral turned white when it was dead. An orange-and-white striped clown fish zipped in and out of the cauliflower-like formations. Josh was motioning for him to take a look at something, and Wesley kicked his fins and followed him to an outcropping of rocks and seaweed.

A large sea turtle was hovering just above the bottom, barely twirling its arms and legs. Sea turtles were fairly numerous, but this was an especially big one, and it was the first one Wesley had ever seen in person. Josh dove about fifteen feet down and tried to touch the turtle, but it skirted away. He rose to the surface and took a breath of air. Wesley did the same.

"You want to catch it?" Josh asked.

"I don't think I can swim that fast," Wesley said. "You try."

"Nah. It's actually illegal to catch them. Not that anyone would know. We're the only people within miles."

Wesley tried to tread water as smoothly as Josh, but he was already starting to get tired.

"Crikey!" Josh shouted. "Jellyfish at three o'clock!"

Wesley looked around, startled. He wasn't sure which way to swim. This was exactly what his dad had warned him about, and he started to panic. He couldn't see the jellyfish and was afraid he would swim right into its tentacles.

"Just kiddin', mate." Josh laughed at him. "Made you look!"

Wesley splashed him in the face, and Josh splashed back.

"Hey, I'm starvin'. How about you?"

"Yeah. What's for lunch anyway?"

"Whatever the Mackey boys want to fix," Josh said. "My dad left a cooler full of sandwich stuff on the beach."

"As long as it's not Vegemite. That stuff is nasty!"

"Yeah it is, isn't it?" Josh agreed. "Don't worry, my mom is into real food. I'll race you back to the beach, and whoever gets there first has to fix both sandwiches."

"No way," Wesley argued. "I already know you can swim faster than me."

"Okay, then. How about this to make it fair? We'll stand up and walk as soon as we can touch bottom."

"In swim fins? That's no help," Wesley said.

"Then you can take yours off, but I'll have to leave mine on."

"But what about the jellyfish?"

"There aren't any jellyfish. Your dad just said that because he wants you to be careful. Besides, it's fall. This isn't the right time of year for them. And I haven't seen one all day," Josh said.

"Neither have I." Wesley had forgotten that everything was backwards in Australia. Fall was in the spring, and winter was in the summer.

"Okay, so are you going to race or not?" Josh asked.

"Go!" Wesley shouted as he tried to get a head start on Josh, but Josh was a lot faster and took the lead right away. With Josh, everything was a competition. Amanda was the same way, but at least Wesley could beat her at some things. He wished there were something he could do better than Josh. As soon as he saw the sandy bottom, Wesley checked all around him for jellyfish before shucking his swim fins. He stood up and started walking in the waist-deep water. Without his cumbersome fins, he only had to go about twenty yards before he nearly caught up to Josh.

Wesley started to pass Josh and yelled, "I'll have my turkey sandwich with cheese and extra mustard and a—" Wesley let out a shrill scream when something sharp ripped into his foot. He took another step and felt a painful sting. His first thought was that his dad was going to be really angry at him for not wearing shoes. "Josh," Wesley shouted, "I think I stepped on a jellyfish!"

"Yeah, right!" Josh plodded ahead in his swim fins. "Good try, mate." He pushed through the tide and regained his lead.

The pain in Wesley's foot was excruciating, and he dropped his swim fins in the water and tried to see exactly what his attacker was. There was something spiny sticking out from the sand, and Wesley knew he had to get to shore as quickly as possible. It wasn't a jellyfish that had stung him after all. It was something much, much worse.

* * *

One hundred thirty feet below the surface of the ocean in the hull of a sunken ship isn't the best time to get a really bad feeling, but that's exactly what came over Jack. He knew there were sharks in the area, and he had seen more than a few great whites in the waters off the shores of Queensland. Maggie had made him promise a few years ago not to do shark shows anymore, and even though she didn't remember that, he had kept that promise.

He wasn't there for sharks anyway. He was looking for something much smaller but far more deadly. The blue-ringed octopus was only four inches in diameter but packed enough venom to kill a person forty times over if they were unlucky enough to get bitten. Jack wasn't planning on getting bitten, but so far he hadn't had any luck locating one. The theme for their Barrier Reef special was "The Good, the Bad, and the Deadly," and it would add a lot if they could find one of the deadliest creatures alive.

Zeke, Jack's Aborigine friend and show producer, was up on the boat waiting, and he had given Jack specific orders to stay down by the coral-encrusted ship hull until he came back with some good footage. He punctuated that by saying that so far, this Barrier Reef special was going to be about as interesting as C-Span.

Jack agreed with Zeke, but the truth was, he didn't really care. He had a lot of other things on his mind. After talking to Maggie this morning, he just wanted to get this shoot over with as quickly as possible and go home. He couldn't focus on what was going on. He kept thinking about her and how she had called that morning to tell him she missed him.

Jack didn't let on to anyone just how strained things had become between the two of them lately. It was obvious Maggie didn't feel the way she used to about him, and he didn't know what he could do about it. She couldn't remember all the experiences they shared, and his marriage had turned into an endless blind date. He didn't know how to move forward from here, so he went back instead. He kept replaying the day at the caves, wishing he had done it all differently. If only he had listened to Wesley and Amanda when they told him Alex had been kidnapped. And he should have never thrown away that handcuff key. If he had been able to swim over himself and open the vault just a minute sooner, it might have made all the difference. But all that was 20/20 hindsight. He made poor choices, and now he would have to live with the consequences of those choices for the rest of his life.

Steve, his underwater cameraman, was motioning for him to do something. He pointed to a school of bluefish, and Jack wondered why. There was nothing interesting about a bluefish. He looked to see if the blue-ringed octopus might be nestled in there, but he could see it wasn't. He still had a really bad feeling. Why shouldn't he have a bad feeling? Imogene had caused so much pain and trauma to his family, and now she was not only walking around a free woman, but she was also trying to paint *him* as the bad person. Jack dutifully swam into the rotting wooden hull of the ship, barely noticing the interesting coral formations. What was Steve trying to show him?

And then that new lawyer Joey Ferrari—or whatever his name was. He had scumbag written all over his pinstriped suit. How much money did he and Imogene have to pay that wedding photographer for the video? The more he thought about it, the more he was certain that Imogene had staged the whole event from the beginning. She had dangled the bait, and like a fool he had taken it.

A small tiger shark swam by. It was pretty but not too exciting. The restraining order was the last straw. The next thing Imogene would probably try to do is claim that he was an unfit parent. And then she'd get her sleazy lawyer to try to get Wesley put in foster care and—

Suddenly something shot out right in front of his face. Jack saw sharp teeth and one steely eye. He recoiled and pushed against the water with his hands, his heart pounding rapidly. He was under attack.

It was fight or flight, and Jack chose the latter. He backed out of the hull and kicked his way to the surface.

He looked back only long enough to see if Steve was following him. He forced himself to slow down and breathe normally so he wouldn't get the bends from coming up too fast.

After several minutes, he surfaced, and Zeke pulled him out and helped him into the boat. Steve came up several minutes behind him. After they had taken off their scuba masks, Steve proceeded to give Jack a thorough reprimand.

"What was that all about!?" he asked. "Why didn't you stay down there?"

"What do you mean?" Jack asked. "I barely miss gettin' bit by a moray eel, and you want me to stick around and give him a second chance?"

"Yes!" Steve answered. "That's what Jack Mackey usually does! You may have heard of him. He has this TV show that's full of *dangerous* animals and *exciting* video."

"You ran away from an eel, boss?" Zeke was perplexed. "What's wrong with you?"

Jack didn't know what to say. They were right. It was out of character for him to back off of a challenge, especially if it was good for the show. Normally he would have stuck around, waited for the eel to return, and played a little cat and mouse with it for a while. He didn't want to admit he was so preoccupied he didn't even see what attacked him at first.

"I thought we were lookin' for the octopus."

"Yeah, mate," Steve said, "but we'll take whatever comes along—and this was good stuff. You should have seen it, Zeke—a giant moray about took Jack's face off. The audience would have loved it! But now we have nice footage of Jack runnin' out of there like a little girly man."

Jack tried to downplay the event. "Hey, enough already. It's an *eel*," he said as if he had been attacked by a housefly. "What's to like about it? It's mean, it's ugly, and it's slimy. Not to mention one of the nastiest creatures that roam the planet. And talk about unattractive! With that mouthful of teeth, the red hair and bulgy eyes . . ."

"What?" Zeke looked at Jack and then Steve.

Jack stopped talking and noticed Zeke and Steve were staring at him like he was a lunatic. "What?" He threw up his hands.

"You're losin' it, boss. You just said that the eel had *red hair*."

"I did not say that."

"You said it." Steve nodded.

Jack hung his head. "Okay, maybe I'm thinkin' about other things right now," Jack admitted. "It's been a rough day—week—year for me. Can we just get out of here? I don't know what it is, but something isn't right."

Steve shrugged. "I know somethin's not right. It's *you*. But either we haul you back ourselves, or we call the men in white coats to come and get you."

23

Deadly Poison

Somehow key events in Wesley's life always seemed to involve helicopters, and this was one of them. After Josh realized that Wesley wasn't kidding, he called Uncle Tommy and told him what happened. Luckily he had already gassed up the chopper and was headed back. Now Wesley was being transported to a hospital out in the middle of who knows where. Josh and some other unidentified person were fixing a bandage that looked suspiciously like a tourniquet around his ankle. He looked down and saw that his foot looked like a rubber glove that someone had blown up. It felt even worse than it looked.

"On a scale of one to ten, how bad does it hurt?" Josh asked, as if he were a medical doctor.

It was an easy question. "Ten," Wesley answered.

"Sorry, mate. I didn't believe you at first. I still can't believe you stepped on a stonefish. I mean, what are the chances?"

When it came to beating the odds, this wasn't the first time Wesley happened to be the one in a million.

Wesley was trying to slow down his breathing so he wouldn't start to hyperventilate. "I just stepped on the most venomous fish in the world," he said. "My dad is going to kill me."

"Uncle Jack is going to kill me first. I told you to take your fins off. I'm supposed to watch out for you, and I really messed up."

Wesley shook his head. "It's not your fault," he said as he winced in pain. Wesley was already mad enough at himself for what he did. "Am I going to die?" he asked in all seriousness.

"No way, dude! They have antivenin for a stone-fish, and we'll get you there fast. My dad's had a few speeding tickets in his day. You know you got three stingers in your foot. I pulled them all out, but one of them was pretty deep. I wish I would have had some boiling water with me—that takes out the poison you know."

And gives me third-degree burns instead. The pain had blended into a throbbing ache. He really should have listened to his dad. Was there no end to the calamity his family had to go through?

"Grandpa is going to meet us at the hospital," Josh explained.

Grandpa C.J. was probably going to give him a bigger lecture than his dad. He wished Grandpa Walter would be there instead. But that wasn't the foremost thought in his mind right then. He just wanted the unbearable pain in his foot to go away. He didn't know whether he was hot or cold, but he suddenly started to shiver. Josh started to panic and shouted something to Uncle Tommy, who was busy flying the helicopter.

Wesley was beginning to feel strange. He couldn't understand what Josh was saying because his words got chopped up in the helicopter blades like that machine Grandma Penny used to cut up vegetables. He thought of sliced carrots and how his toes looked like those little sliced hot dogs his sisters ate for lunch. He tried to speak, but his mouth was dry and wouldn't make the sounds. His thoughts became fuzzy and disjointed, and his tongue felt fat. Even though he was breathing, he wasn't getting enough air.

His dad wasn't going to kill him. He was going to die first.

* * *

It was 3:49 A.M. when the phone by Maggie's nightstand rang, startling her out of a dreamless sleep. It took a moment for her to realize it was probably Jack, and it was the middle of the day for him. Her anger from earlier that day resurfaced as soon as she remembered why she had asked him to call. She fumbled for the receiver and dropped it on the table with a loud clatter.

She cleared her throat. "Hello?"

"Maggie, this is Tom Mackey. I don't know if you remember me—I'm Jack's brother." He sounded very serious.

Maggie suddenly took a deep breath. There would be no reason for Tom to be calling her in the middle of the night unless something bad had happened to Jack. She braced herself for the news.

"Tom, is something wrong?" she asked as she sat up on the edge of the bed. The blood rushed to her head, and she decided to sit there until she could stand.

"Are you alone or is there someone at the house with you?"

That's not what Maggie wanted to hear. "I'm alone." Maggie's heart was racing. "Don't tell me; Jack was bitten by a shark." As angry as she was at Jack, she was suddenly very afraid.

"Jack is fine. We're trying to reach him, but in the meantime, I think you need to know about this."

"Know about what?"

"Wesley has been stung by a stonefish." There was a slight pause. "Do you know what that is?"

From her medical training, Maggie knew what a stonefish was and how quickly the deadly poison could kill someone. She tried to stop herself from trembling. "Is he alive?"

"Yeah, he's alive." There were a few seconds of silence on the other end. "Up until awhile ago he was conscious, but he is in respiratory distress right now. If we can't find Jack, we'll need your permission to treat him. I think we should transfer him over to the mainland, where they have antiserum, and they're more equipped to handle this type of injury, but the doctors here are saying not to move him."

"He's in respiratory distress?" Maggie felt dizzy. "Don't move him. He could have a heart attack."

"We know that, Maggie. There are risks both ways. If he were my son I'd—wait a minute—Jack just got here."

"Let me talk to him please," Maggie said sternly. This couldn't really be happening. Not on top of everything else. How could Jack have been so careless with Wesley? Didn't he just promise her that he would be careful? He had always been a risk-taker himself, and now his actions were endangering their child. She heard muffled voices, and thought Tom must have put his hand over the speaker for a moment. There was a scuffle, and then Jack's voice came on the line.

"He's going to pull through, Mag. But we need to get him out of here fast."

"Jack, don't risk it. What are the doctors telling you?"

"Doctors don't know everything."

"Doctors know more than you!" Maggie cried. "You have to do what's best for Wesley."

"I am, Mag; trust me."

"Trust you?" Maggie was suddenly angry again. "I trusted you to keep him safe! Obviously I *can't* trust you!"

There was a brief silence. "Can we discuss my shortcomings later? The important thing is, Josh and Tommy knew what to do, and they got him to the hospital in less than an hour. They don't have the antiserum here, and I don't want to wait for them to send it. Mag, I don't want to risk him gettin' an infection. If that happens, they'll have to amputate. I'm not going to take any unnecessary risks that would leave Wesley a cripple for the rest of his life."

Maggie's experience as a vet told her that the first few hours are the most critical, and moving a patient usually causes the most injury. "Jack, what if this is the rest of his life? I don't think you should move him unless you have to."

"I'm sorry, Mag, I have to go—you're going to have to let me handle this. I'll call you right back as soon as I know more."

Maggie could hear the beeping of the heart monitor and the voices of hospital personnel in the background. "Don't hang up on me, Jack!" she screamed just as the line disconnected.

* * *

Thirty minutes later, Penny and Walter were sitting in the family room in their pajamas trying to calm down their daughter. Maggie was distraught and angry, and Jack refused to talk with her while he was tending to Wesley. Walter managed to get Tom back on the phone and was talking to him about Wesley's condition.

Maggie was pacing around in her bathrobe. She was on emotional overload and it was making her sick to her stomach.

"He hung up on me, Mom!" she ranted. "I get news from my brother-in-law that Wesley is dying, and then my husband hangs up on me when I suggest he might not be doing the right thing. I've only been through eight years of vet school—and he thinks I don't know anything!"

"You don't know that he's doing the wrong thing, Maggie," Penny said. "Jack's there, and you aren't. You don't know what the hospital is like. It might not be equipped to handle this sort of thing. Jack would never do anything that wouldn't be in Wesley's best interest."

Maggie wanted to believe that about Jack, but the items she had found yesterday were tainting her view. "I'm not so sure of that."

"What's that supposed to mean?" Penny was aghast.

"It means exactly that. Jack doesn't always make good decisions. He's a human being, just like all of us. Why does everyone around here always take his side and just assume he's doing the right thing?"

"Wait a minute! No one else is taking sides here, but evidently you are. You blame him for this?"

"Yes, I blame him for this. He took Wesley to Australia—he's supposed to be watching him to make sure he's safe. I told him yesterday to be careful, and he promised me he would. And then he wasn't even there when it happened!"

"Maybe he thought it was safer to leave Wesley behind. He's fifteen years old. He doesn't need a babysitter."

"No, but maybe he needs a father who has some sense of responsibility."

"Maggie, you're not being fair. Things like this just happen. It's nobody's fault."

"No, Mom. Things like this happen to other people once in a while. Things like this happen to people in our family on a daily basis, and somebody needs to hold Jack accountable for it!"

Walter got off the phone, and Maggie and Penny both looked at him for the latest information. "While you two hash things out, I think I'll make myself useful and say a prayer for Wesley."

* * *

Wesley woke up in the hospital with an IV stuck in one arm and a breathing tube in his nose, feeling like he had just been bludgeoned with a blunt instrument. He had a slight throbbing in his left leg, but it was more of a dull ache than a severe pain. He looked down at his legs, and the left one looked oddly misshapen under a mound of gauze. There was a call button close by his hand, but he didn't know if he wanted to call anyone just yet. He was afraid of what they might tell him, and he wasn't sure he wanted to know about it.

Several minutes later, his dad came in the room. "Wes, you're awake. How do you feel?"

"Okay for stepping on a stonefish. I guess I'm grounded, huh?"

"You got that right. You gotta stay in this hospital bed for another few days. But the reason you're really in trouble is that you found a stonefish and didn't tell me. Do you know how hard they are to find? They look just like a rock or a piece of coral. I've been lookin' for one of these bad boys for my show for years. You come here like some bigshot and upstage me by findin' one without any effort."

"Guess I have the magic touch." His dad was a little too talkative and seemed to be trying to avoid an unpleasant issue. Wesley was afraid to ask straight out, but he had to know. "What did they do to my foot?"

Jack walked over to the side of the bed and studied his bandaged leg. "It was touch and go for a minute there, Wes. But don't worry, you still have a foot—or two feet I should say. But you won't be walkin' on it anytime soon."

Wesley sighed with relief. "How long?"

"A few weeks maybe."

"When can we go home?"

"As soon as you're ready to spend thirty hours on a plane."

"Sorry about that. I guess I could stay here until you finish your show."

"Nah. I was gettin' a little homesick anyway," Jack said. "Who can get to sleep without one of the munchkins poking you in the eye every time you lay down?"

"Yeah," Wesley agreed. "And who can eat a pretzel that hasn't been slobbered on first?"

Just as he said that, Josh came into Wesley's hospital room with a stack of Sudoku puzzles and bags full of junk food. "I'm not going to comment on that, but you Americans are pretty weird." He set his load on a tray and wheeled it over to Wesley. "Hey cuz'—how's it goin'?"

"Pretty good." Wesley smiled.

Josh looked at Wesley's foot, shook his head, and clicked his tongue. "See, you should have listened to me when I told you to keep your swim fins on."

"Yeah, next time I'll listen to you, Josh."

"Okay, I know you're a chess whiz, and I didn't feel like getting my butt kicked, so I didn't bring the chess board. So how about some Chinese checkers?"

"Chinese checkers? That sounds like a fun game. Can you teach me how to play?" He didn't mention that he was even better at Chinese checkers than he was at chess.

"A rookie, huh?" Josh pulled out the game board, set it on Wesley's food tray table, and wheeled it over.

"I don't know if Wes is feelin' up to that already, Josh," Jack said.

"He looks bright eyed to me."

"It's okay, Dad. I think I can handle the physical exertion."

24

The Confrontation

Jack brought Wesley home at the end of the week, as soon as he was stable enough to handle the thirty-hour plane trip. Wesley's foot was tender, and he had to walk on crutches. There was still a chance of infection, but they loaded him up on antibiotics and came back on a chartered plane. Jack called the TV executives and asked for an extension for his Barrier Reef show. They said they needed the edited tape by the middle of June. That was only a month away, and it wouldn't be possible for him to go back to the Barrier Reef in that short of a time, so he cancelled the show.

Jack had been pretty worried about what the situation at home might be like when he got back, but it turned out to be even worse than he expected. Maggie was happy to see Wesley but was about as happy to see him as the moray eel and even less friendly. Jack hoped that once she saw that Wesley was okay, she would lighten up a bit, but now she was even more sullen than before he left. She avoided all conversation with him except when it was completely necessary, and after a day and a half of trying to get her to talk to him, he persuaded her to go horseback riding with him over by the river.

The day was warm, bordering on hot, but Jack felt the temperature drop when they both parked their horses and dismounted in a spot near a large oak tree. He was back at the bottom of the ocean again, with that sinking feeling that something terrible had already happened, and he just didn't know about it yet. Jack sat on one of the raised, gnarled roots that stuck out of the ground and snapped open a soda can. "Want to split a cherry Coke?"

"No, thanks," Maggie said as she sat down a comfortable distance away from Jack.

"So how was your visit with Sharalee?" Jack asked. "Has she changed since you last saw her?"

"I told you already. It was fine. And she's pretty much the same."

"So you two had a good time, then?"

Maggie waited before answering. "Let's just say it was eye opening."

"Really? How so?"

"I learned some things that I really wish I hadn't."

Jack set his soda down and scooted closer to Maggie. "Okay, Mag, I think it's time we just got this out in the open. Other than the normal stuff, like the fact that I'm irresponsible, and you don't like me in general, what's going on?"

Maggie turned her head away and avoided Jack's gaze. "I never said that I didn't like you."

"Well, I can't imagine where I got that idea, then."

"I was hoping you could tell me what's going on. I tried to call you, but then Wesley had the accident, and I never got a chance to talk to you."

"So talk to me now."

"Jack, whatever you do, don't lie to me."

"Mag. I don't have any reason to lie to you. Whatever it is that's bothering you, just tell me, and I'll be honest."

"Well, when you were in Australia, I stumbled onto some 'things.' And I think now I know why I can't get my memory back."

"Really?" Jack flicked a dragonfly off his sleeve. He was afraid that if he looked Maggie directly in the eye, she might stop talking. "What is it?"

"Dr. Schroeder said I was subconsciously or even deliberately repressing some really horrible memory because it was too much for me to deal with."

"I know. So do you think you know what that memory is?"

"Memo*ries*." Maggie pulled the folded tabloid magazine out of her pocket. "I discovered this stashed in my nightstand drawer. You sort of neglected to tell me the reason you were so upset about Harlan's girlfriend was because she used to be your girlfriend."

Jack was relieved that it was finally out in the open. He involuntarily started to laugh. "Mag—you can't be serious!" He grabbed the paper and waved it around. "I promise you Whitney was *never* my girlfriend. This is just a gossip paper. This story—those pictures are all part of a scheme that Imogene staged to try and ruin my life—our lives. You knew all about it at the time. And so did everyone else in the family. You can ask them."

"If I knew all about it, why didn't you tell me about it that night at the Chinese restaurant?"

"Because I didn't want to get into it then. Not with Harlan there. It was a long and complicated story. And I was afraid that . . . I didn't want you to go through any more than you had to. I was just tryin' to protect you."

Maggie pulled her knees up to her chest and stared straight ahead. "And were you also trying to protect me from your drinking problem?"

"What?"

"I found empty and full bottles of hard liquor in your closet and in the video cabinet."

Jack looked at her directly now. "Mag, I swear to you I haven't had a drink in thirteen years."

"Then how do you explain the bottles?"

"I have no idea."

"So do you think Wesley has a problem, then?"

"No, I don't think so. I sure hope not. This is really strange."

"Yeah, it is, isn't it?"

Jack shook his head. "For all I know, Imogene hid those bottles in our house too." He took a sip of his soda. "Wait a minute! The wedding bomb. That's it! I couldn't figure out what Imogene was doing here at the time, but now I know. She wanted us to think she brought a bomb so that in all the chaos she'd have the opportunity to slip inside and plant stuff in our house. The bottles, the magazine—that explains it all!"

Maggie didn't look convinced. "Well, that's convenient, isn't it? Why don't you own up to your own problem? Why can't you just be honest and forthright? I know Imogene Vandergrift is a very bad person, but you can't blame every mistake in your life on her."

"It's not a mistake—it was a setup! She wants to frame me! She knows you can't remember anything, and that's why she put this tabloid in your drawer and the bottles—wherever you found them."

"I never saw her come inside the house."

"So she sent someone else in. We didn't know everyone at the reception, so it's the perfect cover. You have to admit she had the opportunity." Jack looked at Maggie. "Mag, you have to believe me. I don't drink, and I've never been unfaithful."

"I don't know what to believe, Jack."

"I'm tellin' you the truth."

"Just like you told me the truth that night at the restaurant?" Maggie said bitterly. "I may have lost my memory, Jack, but I still have half a brain. I saw the way you reacted when Whitney sat down at our table. I know there was no phone call from home—it was all a cover-up."

Jack searched Maggie's eyes for some glimmer of hope. Her eyes were full of hurt and resentment. "You're right. I shouldn't have lied about the phone call, but the rest of what I'm sayin' is true," he started to explain, but the look on her face made him stop.

"That's not even all of it, Jack. I got another phone call while you were away. It was from a jeweler. He was trying to get a hold of you to tell you that he had the appraisal for the diamond—the one you wanted to get for your 'wife.' It was a pink princess cut of considerable value. Even though I don't really care for huge diamonds—especially in pink—I was willing to give you the benefit of the doubt because I don't remember things. But he supposedly talked to me on the phone about the diamond a few days ago."

Jack ran his hand through his hair and sighed. "Mag, I never told him I was buying a diamond for my wife. It's just an appraisal. But there is an explanation for that. Just hear me out on this."

"You can save your explanation for someone who is gullible enough to believe you. Let me guess. That was another one of Imogene's plots to destroy you too. I really don't want to hear any more of your excuses, Jack. I'm not the same person you married. I won't pretend to look the other way just to keep the peace. Maybe that's what I used to do, but not anymore. You really can't expect me to tolerate this kind of behavior from the person who has sworn to honor and cherish me."

Jack looked at Maggie in disbelief. This situation was unthinkable. He had no idea what to say to her, and his frustration quickly turned to anger. "No, I can't expect that," he said, not holding back his resentment. He got to his feet and dusted off his hands. Without another word, he climbed on his horse and rode away.

25

Moving On

Alex admired the brick house with the steep shake roof and manicured lawn shaded by several large maple trees. For the first time since he'd left home for college, he was living in something other than a barracks or hotel. It was the perfect home for the three of them, even though it had a few more bedrooms than they needed, but Alex was hoping that wouldn't be the case for long. He was busy unloading boxes from the backseat of his car when Jack drove up and parked on the street. He looked like a movie star in his convertible with his sunglasses on and the radio turned up to rock-concert volume. Jack turned off the car engine and jumped out.

"I like your place, Al. It looks like you."

"You mean old?" Alex said. "I think my house has a few years on your car."

"That's what gives it personality."

"Well, as luck would have it, you're just in time to bring in a load with me."

Jack took of his glasses and threw them in the backseat. He went over to Alex's car and pulled a large box from the trunk. He grunted as he picked it up. "What's in here, your bowling ball collection?"

"Just books. Maria packed it. I find it flattering that she thinks I'm the Incredible Hulk."

"Yeah, that's one way of lookin' at it." Jack rolled his eyes as he took a deep breath and heaved the box up.

"So what brings you here?" Alex asked as he picked up another slightly lighter box and headed through the open front door. Jack wasn't the type who just turned up for a social visit.

"Nothin' really. I just thought I'd come here and help you move instead of going to the gym today and liftin' weights."

"I appreciate it." The two of them walked up the steps onto the front porch. "But you have a workout room in your house."

"Well, it's always nice to have a change. Amazing how much stuff we really own. You could probably throw half of it away and never miss it. Over here?" Jack motioned to a spot on the living room floor.

"That's good. You're right. I wouldn't miss half of this stuff." Alex let his box down with a thud. "But Maria would, and I would really like to stay married."

Jack rubbed his hands together and looked at the floor. "This is some pretty nice carpet you put in here. It's a good color."

"Thanks. It's taupe." Alex felt pretty awkward, but he knew Jack hadn't come over just to admire the carpet. "So, how's Maggie doing?"

"Good." Jack nodded and looked around the room for something to do.

Alex waited for Jack to elaborate. He hoped he wouldn't have to force it out of him. He knew Jack needed to talk, but he wasn't going to fall for the same ploy that had worked so well with Amanda. Alex thought of all the interrogation techniques he knew and decided to use the wait-in-uncomfortable-silence method.

After a full minute, Jack finally said, "She basically hates me." He sat down on top of the box he had just deposited on the floor. "I need your advice, Al."

"Jack, I'm honored that you would think I had any advice to give you, but I've only been at this marriage thing for a few months. I don't know what to tell you."

"Well then, I need you to answer a question for me. And I want you to be honest."

"Sure. I'll be honest with you."

"When you first met me, in person, what did you think?"

Alex was ready with an answer. "I thought you didn't like me, you didn't trust me. And you were afraid that I was some demented criminal."

"Okay, that's pretty perceptive," Jack said. "But besides what you thought I thought about you, what did you think of *me*? Did you think I was a jerk? Like the type of person who was out for himself all the time?"

"No, I didn't think that at all. You had good reason to be suspicious of me, because I *was* an undercover agent. You were only trying to protect your family—and your family was very important to you. So I thought you were basically a good guy." Alex hesitated before asking the next question. "Why do you want to know that?"

"Evidently I have some pretty major character flaws. And I need to find out what they are before I can fix them."

"Is that what Maggie says?" Alex asked.

"Not in so many words. She doesn't really talk to me anymore. She just gives me disappointed looks."

"Maggie's still pretty confused, Jack. I think she needs some professional help."

"Yeah, well, that's another thing. She's gettin' help, and her psychiatrist isn't helpin' my cause. He thinks that I'm a big part of the problem."

"Sorry to hear that. Maybe it's time for a new doctor. I don't know if you want me to get involved, but I can talk to her. I know Maria has already tried."

"So have Penny and Walter. It doesn't matter. She doesn't trust anyone who already likes me. She thinks her parents are snowed over by my charm."

"Well, you *are* pretty charming."

"You think?" Jack brightened.

"Okay, Jack. You want my advice. I'll give it to you. But I'm warning you now—you might not like it."

"I'll take my chances."

Alex looked Jack in the eye. "Stop running away from your problems, and start confronting them."

"You think I'm not confronting my problems?"

"Whether you realize it or not, you're becoming a victim. You're blaming Imogene for everything that's happening, and you're letting her control your thoughts and feelings. Your anger keeps building, and it feeds on itself and keeps you from feeling happy about what is good in your life. In a sense, Imogene is winning because you're letting her."

Jack mulled that over for a moment. "Ouch. So how do I stop lettin' her control me?"

"Get her out of your head. She's occupying way too much space in there. Let go of your anger and resentment."

"Like you and Maria let go on your wedding day?"

"Yeah, like that. Just tell yourself that you are the master of your thoughts. And make her disappear."

"That's easy," Jack said sarcastically. "And while I'm at it I can I build a rocket and send her to the moon."

"That's another option."

"Now that we have that solved, what do I do about Maggie? I can't just erase her from my life. You think I'm lettin' her control me too?"

"Yes, but in a different way. When Maggie says things to hurt you, instead of dealing with it, you just avoid her. You're running away from your problem instead of facing it."

Jack threw up his hands. "But I thought I was supposed to give her space."

"There's a difference between giving someone space and being proactive about changing things."

Jack nodded as he sliced open a box of books with his pocketknife. "Funny, last week Zeke told me I was a wimp when I ran away from an eel. And now you're tellin' me the same thing."

"I don't recall using the word *wimp* in our conversation."

"But that's basically what you're sayin' here."

Alex shrugged. "I said you might not want to hear it."

"Maybe I didn't, but I *needed* to hear it. I think you're right. It's time for me to take control of my life."

* * *

Wesley hobbled into Amanda's house next door on his crutches. Most of the house was packed up, and Amanda was busily sealing the boxes with tape and labeling them with a marker.

"Don't come near me with your gangrene foot," she warned him.

"It's not gangrene. It's just some dead tissue. I promise not to take the bandage off this time."

"Better not. It's really gross. That picture you sent me on your phone about made me throw up. Too bad you're handicapped and can't help us move any of these boxes."

"Yeah, too bad," Wesley said with relief. He read the label Amanda had written on the box. "Um, maybe it's not the best idea to pack the computer monitor with kitchen glasses and the power drill."

"Why not?" Amanda asked. "Everything fit."

Wesley started to explain it to her and then just said, "Never mind. So guess who's moving into your house after you leave?"

"Let me guess. Katie MacKenzie?"

Wesley scrunched up his face. "No. She was so *last year* anyway."

"Anyone I know?"

"Yeah. Me."

"Right," Amanda said sarcastically. "You're moving out of your house, and you're going to live here all by yourself."

"I thought it was about time I got my own place." Wesley hopped over on his crutches and stretched out on the couch.

"So are things really that bad at home?"

"Even worse than my foot. They don't know I know it, but Maggie has gone to DEFCON one, my sisters have turned into beasts that get into everything, and my dad is going to abandon us all by taking off to shoot another show. Tomorrow he's leaving again."

"Sorry to hear that. He's going back to Australia?"

"No, he doesn't have time to go back to Australia. I pretty much blew that one for him. Get this—he's going back to Diamondback Cave."

"Seriously? He really wants to go back to that cave? I'm still have nightmares from when we were there."

"But at least you weren't left home twiddling your thumbs," Wesley reminded her.

Amanda smiled. "That's true. And it wasn't *all* bad."

"No, I guess not all of it," Wesley agreed. "But I feel like it's my fault that Teddy is dead."

"I know, I think about that too, but Alex told me if you want to take responsibility for Teddy's death, then you also have to take credit for saving his life—and Jack's and Maggie's too."

"Yeah, I guess so. I wish I could do something to help Maggie remember things. I'd give my left foot if I could make things the way they used to be."

"My mom tried to talk with her the other day, but I don't think she helped at all. It's like they aren't really friends anymore."

"Maggie's not even friends with my dad anymore."

"It makes me sad. But maybe there's one good thing to come out of all this."

"What's that?"

"My mom says in our new house I can have a dog."

"Really?" Wesley was shocked. He was glad Amanda was finally going to have a pet. "What kind are you going to get?"

"I don't know yet. But it won't be as big as Teddy and definitely not as small as Hercules. I don't really care as long as it's a dog. This is a really big breakthrough. My mom has never liked dogs, and Alex has never had any pets, so I thought I was doomed.

But because Teddy saved everyone, now they both want one."

"That's great. I was hoping to get a new puppy for my birthday, but I got this instead." Wesley stuck out his foot. "But I don't think Maggie would go for a new puppy right now. She's still trying to get used to the girls, and lately Hercules is really annoying everyone. He barks all the time and fights with Bob the cat. Bob is running out of places to live, so he'll have to move in here with me."

"Now that Teddy's gone, Hercules doesn't have his bodyguard anymore. He's just grumpy because he misses his best friend."

"Yeah, he and my dad have something in common."

26

A Rock and a Hard Place

The trail to Diamondback Cave looked completely different now that summer had turned everything green, and wildflowers sprouted out from between the carpet of wild ferns and phlox. The entrance to the cave was sealed off with yellow crime-scene tape, and a plywood barrier had been placed in front warning people not to cross the line. Jack checked his backpack for the pick-axe he had brought with him in case he needed to bust down the barricade. He had arranged for Harlan to meet him here to help him plan out his next *Snake Stalker* adventure. Harlan had been almost as excited about the show as he had been about his girlfriend.

Harlan laughed when he saw the entrance. "Talk about lame!" he said. "If the cops don't want any treasure hunters coming in here, they might want to put up a little more substantial barricade. Like someone can't just walk through this tape and go around the plywood." He squeezed through the opening. Jack followed him but had a little more difficult time fitting through the narrow slit than Harlan did. Harlan was wearing a hard hat with a light on top and was dressed in appropriate hiking attire. Jack wore his climbing shoes, a pack full of rappelling equipment, and had brought at least four flashlights and extra batteries with him.

"So, Jack. Where's the camera crew?"

"We're it, mate. I got a camera in the bag."

"It's just the two of us, then?"

"Yeah, for now. Once we plot out where we're going, we'll get Chad to come back tomorrow with the rest of the crew. That way, when we get arrested for crossing a crime scene without permission, it won't cost as much to bail us out."

"Where do you want to start?" Harlan seemed unconcerned about the trespassing issue.

"In the place where we saw Randy."

* * *

At the dressing table in the suite of the five-star hotel, Whitney ran a straightening iron through her long blonde hair while her mother checked the mirror to see how her skintight jeans looked on her forty-something figure.

"You think it's time for some more lipo?" Delphina asked. "I dread the day I start looking my age." She looked at Whitney like a drill sergeant inspecting one of her soldiers. "You really should curl your hair to give it more body. Straight hair pulls your face down. And I think you'd better spend some time in the tanning beds today. You're looking a little pasty."

"I hate tanning," Whitney said. "It makes you wrinkled, and Harlan could care less if I'm tan or not."

"Well Harlan is in seventh heaven that you would even look twice at him. And he should be. But you'll be done with him very soon, and then you can start dating whoever you want. So think ahead."

"And what if I want to stay with Harlan?" Whitney asked.

Delphina looked mortified. "Why on earth would you want to do that?"

"Because maybe I like him."

Delphina started to laugh. "Don't scare me like that!" She threw her hand to her chest like she was having a heart attack. "For a minute I almost thought you were serious."

"Well of course I'm not serious. He's getting the diamonds for me today. What reason is there to stick around?"

"I can't think of one!" Delphina hooked a chandelier earring in her earlobe. It dangled to her shoulder. "I only wish my dear sister was going to be just as easy to ditch."

Whitney doused her cheeks with rouge. "Aunt Genie isn't going to go away. Maybe we should just split it with her three ways. And then she'll leave us alone. We were going to do that with Peter anyway. We'll still have a lot of money."

"Absolutely not. She had her chance to work with us and she refused. She's the one the Feds will be watching. We'll only draw attention to ourselves by including her. And as much as I like attention, that isn't the right kind."

"But how are we going to sell the diamonds without her or Peter?"

"Whitney, honey, I don't know why you haven't realized this, but when you're young, rich, and beautiful, you don't need to worry about how to get things done." Delphina outlined her lips with lipstick, smacking them together. "There are plenty of men who will stand in line for the chance to do it for you."

* * *

When they reached the south canyon passage, Jack shined his flashlight into the deep cavern below them. "I'm kind of glad we couldn't see that well the first time we were here. I'm not so sure I would have made the trip back."

"It's a beautiful place though, isn't it?" Harlan seemed to belong here, just as much as any of the creatures that called this place home.

"Yeah . . ." Jack agreed with some hesitation. "Especially if you like sheer drop-off cliffs in a pitch-black cave teeming with giant diamondbacks."

"I thought you loved snakes."

"I do, when I can see them. But I haven't seen one yet. These guys are just like the highway patrol."

"Come again?" Harlan said.

"Snakes—they're like cops. They're always hangin' around when you want to avoid them and nowhere to be found when you really need them."

"I told you they aren't hibernating anymore. It's late spring. And it's warm enough to spend the day outside."

"I know that. So maybe we'll have to wait for night." Jack slipped past Harlan to the place on the rock ledge where the group had been trapped several months earlier. "This looks like a good place to attach a climbing rope."

"Jack, you're not really going to climb down there, are you?" Harlan asked.

"Unless there's another elevator you didn't tell me about."

"There won't be any snakes down there."

"I know."

"So you really aren't after the snakes, are you?"

"What else would I be after?" Jack said, knowing that Harlan already knew the answer.

"The diamond case."

Jack strapped a harness around his waist and chuckled. Harlan wasn't one to beat around the bush. "And if I am? Let's just be honest here. You came to get it too."

"Why would you accuse me of that?" Harlan asked.

"Oh, I have my reason—a gorgeous blonde reason."

"You think I want to get them for my girlfriend?"

"It's okay." Jack shrugged. "I don't care. I want to find them for another reason. An ugly redhead reason."

Harlan didn't respond.

Jack finished buckling his harness. "So let's just get this over with and you show me where to look. I'll climb down there, pick it up, and when I bring it back we can fight over what to do with it."

Harlan looked at the ground. "It's not that easy, Jack."

"I never claimed it would be easy, mate. I just said I was going to do it."

Harlan narrowed his eyes and studied Jack. "Why didn't you tell me who she was?"

"Who?"

"Whitney."

"So she told you, huh?"

"She did. But I already knew who she was before I met her. Peter showed us a picture of his girlfriend and I knew she was Imogene Vandergrift's niece. What I didn't know is that you knew that too. So why didn't you tell me?"

K.L. Fogg

"I don't know." Jack threw up his hands. "Didn't want to spoil your fun, I guess. I knew if I waited long enough, I wouldn't have to. I mean, admit it. She may be nice to look at, but she's as dumb as a stick. You're a smart guy, and I thought you'd figure it out sooner rather than later. Then there's the fact that she and I were plastered all over the tabloids last summer, and I was trying to avoid explaining that little piece of information to my wife."

"So Maggie doesn't know who she is either?"

"She does," Jack said with obvious regret. "And things aren't going too well at home because of it. But I don't want to get into that right now."

"Jack, you may not believe this, but Whitney and I have a lot in common."

"Let me guess. You're missin' a leg, and she's missin' a brain. Harlan—you don't have to explain anything to me, really."

Harlan plowed through his explanation anyway. "We've both been judged all of our lives on our outward appearance. She has the appearance of perfection—and I have the appearance of imperfection. In both cases, people have always judged us by who they think we are or what they think we can or can't do. I have one leg—that makes me slow, or handicapped at most everything. She's blonde and beautiful—so that makes her dumb or shallow or spoiled or all of the above. After hearing it all the time, you start believing it. And then you start to become the person others expect you to be. Maybe we both want people to stop telling us who we are and give us a chance to be who we want to be."

"Sorry, mate." Jack hammered one of the pylons into the rock face. "I'll just remove my foot from my mouth now."

304

"It's okay. I'm used to it. I'd rather have people joke about my leg than act all uncomfortable about it. I'm just curious. If you really think I'm here to get the diamonds for Whitney, why would you trust me to come with you alone into the caves? How do you know that I won't pull a gun on you or something?"

Jack turned around and looked Harlan straight in the face. "Because you're a good man, Harlan. You saved the lives of three people who are very important to me. If I can't trust you with my life, then I can't trust anyone."

Harlan scratched his cheek.

Jack continued. "For whatever its worth, Whitney told me she's in love with you. Thought I'd pass it along."

"She told you that?" Harlan broke into a grin. "Really? She said she loves me?"

"Yeah, you really got her with those dimples. But you might as well get over it. Women will break your heart every time. The prettier they are, the harder you fall. Speakin' of falling, didn't we lose the case right around here somewhere?"

"No, this is where we saw Randy. The case fell over there." Harlan was suddenly energized. He pointed to the narrowest part of the ledge.

Jack pulled a rope out and tied it securely to his harness.

Harlan helped him tighten the rope. "But that's not where you're going to find it. Teams have scoured this place, and if it was down there, they would have found it by now."

"Okay." Jack looked around. "Any ideas on where we might look then?"

"I have one." Harlan took the lead, and Jack followed him over to a crevice in the rock wall.

"In here?" Jack was perplexed. He shined his light down a crevice two feet wide in the rock. It went down for an eternity until he couldn't see anything but inky blackness. "Holy bottomless pit. If you were under the impression I was insane enough to go down there, you were sorely mistaken. There are plenty of horrible ways to die, but slowly rotting at the bottom of that hole is definitely up in the top three. Nobody in their right mind would climb down that."

"Well, if you want to recover the diamond case, you'll have to find someone crazy enough to try. Because that's where it is."

"How do you know?"

Harlan pulled an old, wrinkled map out of his pocket and showed it to Jack. "Remember how I told you about the underground rivers that run in this cave?"

"Yeah, I remember you telling me that before Peter put the kibosh on the guided tour."

"Well, there was this kid who drowned in the underground pool about sixteen years ago. I think he got sucked under when he discovered the vault and tried to open it. Anyway, they looked for his body everywhere, but they never found it. The reason they never found it is because the underground river carried his body to a place where nobody could get to."

"And you think the river washed the diamond case into the same place where the kid's body is."

"I'm pretty sure. Look at this map." Harlan took out a folded the piece of paper from his shirt pocket. "It's the only thing that makes any sense. This part of the cave is like a cracked molar. Picture a tooth that has an opening to the root—that's this crevice right here. Now at the base of the tooth there's a cavity, a small opening where the water can wash things in pretty easily, but it's hard to wash out. That's what the river does. When it rises, it carries things into that pocket and deposits them there, but a lot of things get stuck in the hole because they get hung up on all the debris and can't get out."

Jack though for a moment. "Okay, sounds reasonable. But isn't there an easier way to get there other than straight down?"

"Well, you could climb around this way, but you'll end up over here. And then you wouldn't be able to access this cavity unless the water was high enough— but you wouldn't really know until you got down there. Of course you could just go to the underground pool and swim there. It looks like it connects."

"Yeah, but what if it flushed you down some tunnel with no air in it?"

"Exactly. This is the shortest, safest route to the backflow area."

"I like adventure, but this is above and beyond risky."

"Hey, I'd do it myself if I had two good legs."

"What happens if I get stuck?"

"Well, that would be bad, but getting stuck isn't what I'd be worried about."

"What would you be worried about?"

"Once you're down there, who knows what might live in that backflow area.

"Psh! Couldn't be any worse than an average day at work for me."

"I don't think this is the kind of stuff you run into every day. It was enough to scare off the recovery squad."

"Some creepy-crawly cave dwellers were enough to persuade a professional recovery team to give up on two hundred million? Is there something you're neglecting to tell me?"

Harlan turned away and ignored Jack's question.

"Harlan. Why won't anyone go down there?"

"The locals all think it's haunted."

"Haunted by what?"

"Well this cave has a reputation for not returning people to the world of the living. It's not haunted; things just happen to people who don't respect the cave, and that's exactly what happened to Joey Ferraro. People think that his bones are in there, and that he haunts the cave.

Jack did a double-take. "Wait a minute! *Whose* bones are in that crevice?"

"Joey Ferraro. He's the kid who drowned sixteen years ago. They never found his body. They say his spirit roams around down there, and that's part of the folklore that scares everybody away."

Jack grabbed him by the shoulders and shook him. "Harlan, this is unbelievable."

"Well, I didn't say I believed it."

"How old was this kid when he drowned?"

"He was a little older than me and Eddie. Maybe fifteen or sixteen."

"And they never found his body?"

"That's right. Haven't we been through this discussion a few times already?"

"Yes, but not with the name Joey Ferraro attached to it. Here's a spooky coincidence. Joey Ferraro is the name of Imogene Vandergrift's lawyer."

"Joey's dad is her lawyer?" Harlan was stunned. "Joe Ferraro single-handedly ruined our family. We used to be pretty well-off with our tourist attraction. After his son died, he sued the county and our family for everything we were worth. Took everything he could get his hands on and then moved away—to New York City, I think. Our family lost everything. The bank foreclosed on us, and we were forced to sell the cave for practically nothing. I never knew who bought it until I met Imogene. So now the same guy is Imogene's lawyer. Doesn't surprise me."

"No, I've seen Joey Ferraro," Jack explained. "He's a young guy—about thirty-two."

"Then it can't be him. He was about forty years old sixteen years ago."

"You're right. It can't be Joe Ferraro Senior, but it could be Joey Junior who *supposedly* died in the cave." He paused to let that sink in. "Maybe they never found his body because it was walkin' around in broad daylight."

Harlan looked like a lightbulb went off inside his head. "You think they planned a fake drowning so that they could set up a lawsuit to shut us down and get access to these caves?"

Jack threw up his hands, his expression saying everything. "Harlan, between the two of us, we're a genius."

"This is unbelievable," Harlan said. "All those years we thought it was a tragic accident . . . it was just a scam to take away our property. But if all this is true, then we're in a lot more trouble than you think. The Ferraro family has mob connections and people to take care of people they don't like. You don't want to mess with any of them. I say we walk out of this cave right now and forget what we know. Diamonds aren't worth much when you're dead."

"Sorry, mate, but I don't run away from a challenge. Call me crazy, but that little discovery just gave me the incentive I need to climb down into the pit of despair and collect those diamonds pronto. Now, you can leave and pretend we never had this conversation, or you can secure this rope and hand me that waterproof flashlight. Better yet, hand me the video camera. Because I'm goin' down."

27

Separate Ways

Maggie returned from her interview with mixed emotions. She had gone to talk to a friend about working part-time in a local veterinary office, and they were interested in hiring her. But now she was afraid that everyone was going to disapprove of her going back to work. She knew Wesley and the girls needed her as a full-time mom, but she just had to get out of the house before she went crazy. Why should Jack get to be gone all the time without being harassed about being a full-time dad? She felt guilty about wanting to work again, but Dr. Schroeder told her that she needed to start doing things that made her happy and not worry about what her family said. The problem was, she didn't know what would make her happy until she gave it a try.

She had left the girls over at her parents' and had told them she needed to run some errands, but she didn't feel like going over to pick them up just yet. Penny and Walter would start their summer horseback riding camp next week, and she wouldn't be able to leave the girls with them after that, so she thought she'd take advantage of them now. Besides, Jack's car was here, and she hadn't talked with him since he got back from his most recent trip. It seemed like they were never home at the same time, and if they were, they didn't say much to each other. She looked around and found him in the bedroom. She said hello to him and he barely acknowledged her. He had been this way ever since he'd come back from the caves, but she thought he would come out of it if she just left him alone.

He was obviously not in a good mood, so it probably wasn't a good time to bring up the vet job. Maggie watched as Jack threw his suitcase on the bed and emptied his entire drawer into it. He didn't bother to fold anything or even check to see if he had matching outfits.

"You just barely got home a few days ago," Maggie said. "Now you're leaving again?"

"Yeah, I'm leavin'." The way he said it, it sounded permanent.

"Where are you going this time?"

"Does it matter?" Jack asked.

"Yes, it matters. You can't just take off without telling anyone where you're going or when you'll be back."

"Or can I?" Jack said.

Jack wasn't the type to brood about things, and Maggie knew that something bad must have happened. She noticed a black metal handle sticking out of the debris in Jack's suitcase. She pulled out a .38 handgun. "And why are you taking this?"

He grabbed the gun away from her and threw it back inside his suitcase. "I have some important business to take care of."

"Important business that involves a gun?"

"It's just a precaution."

"And you won't even tell me how long you're going to be gone?"

"As long as it takes." Jack pulled a blanket off the unmade bed and added it to the overflowing suitcase.

"As long as it takes to do what?"

"To make things right."

"Make things right?" It was like she and Jack suddenly spoke different languages. "What are you talking about?"

Jack went over to his nightstand, opened the drawer, and pulled out a nine-by-twelve envelope with a stack of papers inside.

"Jack, why are you acting so strange?"

"You think I'm acting *strange*?" He laughed. "How would you know? You think I drink when I'm alone and cheat on you when I'm not. Now I'm just packin' my suitcase and minding my own business, and you think that's strange."

"You're not giving me a straight answer."

"Why should I bother? It doesn't matter what I say. You already have the answers." Jack opened up the envelope and pulled out some legal documents. "The good news is you don't have to deal with my bizarre behavior anymore. Here you go. I talked with Barry, and he wrote this up yesterday." He set the papers down on the bed.

Maggie picked up the papers and looked at them. At first she didn't know what they were, and then her heart rose into her throat. "You're divorcing me?"

Jack nodded. "I can't live like this anymore. It's tearin' me apart, Mag. You don't trust me, and I can't stand lookin' at you every day, knowing that you think I've betrayed you and been dishonest with you. A friend of mine told me that people sometimes become the person others expect them to be. I don't want to be the person you think I am."

Maggie was silent and continued to read down the page, but her eyes started to blur, and she put it down.

"I gave everything to you," Jack explained. "You can have the house, and whatever else you want is yours. I want joint custody of the kids, but the girls can live with you most of the time. I'll come by as often as I can to visit them. Wesley is old enough to choose for himself. I don't know where we'll live yet. That's it. It's not ideal, but then this sort of thing never is."

Maggie was reeling from the initial shock. She was so overcome that she had a hard time choosing the right words to form a coherent sentence. "You've obviously given this a lot of thought." Her voice cracked. Any minute she was going to break down and lose control. "So this is what you want, then?"

"No," Jack said bluntly. "It's not what I want." He paused and took a deep breath. "But it's what you need. I want you to love me again, but as much as I've tried, I can't make that happen. I want everything to be how it used to be—for you to trust me. But I can't make that happen either. I don't want you to think you're stuck with being married to some jerk for the rest of your life."

Maggie held back tears and fought to keep herself from begging Jack not to do this. This was some horrible mistake. He couldn't be serious. Jack was hurt, so he was trying to hurt her too. She looked into his eyes. "I—I don't know what to say."

"You don't have to say anything, Mag. Your face says it all. You're relieved, because whether you realize it or not, this is what you want."

"This isn't what I want."

"Yes, it is. You didn't want to suggest it first, because that would make you the bad person. Penny and Walter would be disappointed with you and try to talk you out of it. But this way you don't have to carry that load. I'm the one who filed for divorce. It was my idea. You have absolution."

Maggie could no longer hold back the tears. Her eyes filled up and spilled over onto the documents and smeared the ink.

"You don't have to sign it right away," Jack said. "You can think about it for awhile. My copy is already signed and locked in the safe, along with my new will. But the sooner you let me go, the sooner you can move on and start livin' your life again. I really do want you to be happy." He smashed his suitcase shut, zipped it, and yanked it up. He headed through the house and opened the door to the garage.

"Jack, wait!" Maggie cried.

Jack stopped at the door and waited for her to say something.

"Please don't go," she begged.

Jack shook his head and turned around without speaking. He walked through the door and shut it.

* * *

Wesley was coming in from the barn to get a drink when he saw his dad back the Camaro out of the garage. The top was down. He half limped, half ran over to see where he was going.

Jack slowed down to let him catch up. "Hey, you remind me of Harlan with that limp," he said, but he didn't sound like himself.

"Hopefully mine won't be permanent," Wesley said and noticed his dad's eyes were red. "What's the matter? Is something wrong?"

Jack waited before answering. "Yeah, something is wrong. But I don't want you to worry, because I'm going to make it right, okay?" He ruffled Wesley's hair.

"Where are you going?" Wesley motioned to the suitcase Jack had thrown in the backseat. "You have a big enough suitcase packed."

"You never know what the weather's going to do in June." He suddenly became very serious. "Wes, sometimes we have to do things we don't want to do, but we do them because we have to."

"What are you going to do?"

"I can't tell you that, because it's not your problem to deal with. And I'm not so sure I can go through with it, but I know I have to try. So I just want you to know that you are the best son in the whole world. And I'm so sorry that you've had to deal with so many things at your young age. Just remember that I love you, okay?"

"I love you too, Dad." There was something foreboding in his dad's tone, and it made him uncomfortable. It was like he was saying his final farewell. Wesley looked into the back of the car and saw a dented briefcase sitting on the seat next to the suitcase. It was partially covered by a blanket, but Wesley recognized the handle and the five-digit combination lock. He reached over and pulled the blanket off.

"Dad, is that the diamond case?" Wesley asked.

Jack glanced behind him and tilted his head. "Oh, that. Don't tell anybody. This may look like a piece, but I'm pretty sure I'm drivin' the most expensive car on the road."

"Dad! Are you serious? What are you doing with them?"

"It's all right. I'm not going to keep them."

Wesley was suddenly very afraid of what his dad might use the diamonds for. "Then why haven't you turned them over to the cops?"

Jack looked at his watch. "I'm going to, Wes. Just as soon as I'm finished with them."

"Are you going to find Imogene?"

Jack's failure to answer was Wesley's answer. "Dad, you can't do this alone!"

"Don't worry, Wes. It'll be okay. I have to do this." He smiled earnestly. "You are the greatest son I could have ever hoped for. Have I told you that?"

Wesley nodded. "Dad, you're scaring me. I don't want anything to happen to you."

"What could possibly happen to me that hasn't already? I'll be fine. You're the man, Wes. Take care of Maggie and your sisters for me." Jack eased the car back, forcing Wesley to move away from the door. He put his sunglasses on and sped down the long driveway.

28

Lockdown

Maggie sat on the edge of the bed, frozen in stunned disbelief. This was the real deal. Jack was asking her for a divorce. It was true that she had been distant and aloof lately, but she had never even considered divorcing him. She figured she just needed some more time to sort out her feelings for him, and she didn't like pulling her family into the fray, so she had been trying to work things out alone. But she never expected this.

If Jack was completely innocent of all the things she was accusing him of doing, then he had every right to be angry with her, and she had brought this on herself. But then again, maybe the divorce was just his way of getting out now. She couldn't deny that she had treated him terribly. But this hurt her even more than she could have imagined.

If he was right and this was what she wanted, why should it be so hard for her? Like he said, she didn't have to look like the bad person. He was setting her free. But she didn't want her freedom. She wanted her husband, but for some reason she hadn't been able to say the words out loud when she had needed to. Her world was spiraling out of control.

Suddenly she picked up the divorce papers and ripped them in half and then again and again until they were tiny little pieces scattered all over the bed and floor. The very act of doing that fueled her resolve. She wasn't going to let him divorce her without a fight. She realized that she still loved him, and she wasn't going to give up until they worked things out.

Maggie wiped her eyes and remembered Jack telling her there was another copy in the safe. The safe was in the office. She rushed through the house, nearly tripping over Hercules and Bob, who were in the middle of one of their usual skirmishes, growling and hissing at each other.

She didn't know what the combination to the safe was, because she hadn't opened it since she had lost her memory. She tried several usual combinations that she was familiar with, and none of them worked. She tried the twins' birthday, and that didn't work. She tried to remember when her anniversary was. When she dialed that combo, the safe clicked. She pulled the handle and opened the door as wide as it would go. The safe had a few rifles standing vertically in the very back, but it was almost completely empty. *Why in the world would we need such a large safe?* she wondered. There were several stacks of papers and two more handguns on the top shelf. She pulled the papers down and was rummaging around for the divorce papers when she came across Jack's will. There was a recent date on it. Maggie had started to read it when Hercules darted into the office with Bob close on his heels.

"I've had it with the two of you! Stop fighting!"

Hercules took advantage of the open safe as a retreat. He scampered inside and cowered in the back.

Bob started to go in after him, but then Maggie shooed him away with her foot. She found the copy of the divorce papers under the will, just like Jack had said. She had hoped somehow that he really wasn't serious, but he was. They were already signed and dated. She threw them down on the desk and called Hercules out of the safe.

"Come on, boy. Get out of there."

Hercules didn't budge.

"Hercules, I'm not in the mood for this. Get out now!" Maggie got on her knees and reached into the back to pull him out, but Hercules had squished himself into the corner, and she couldn't reach him without climbing all the way inside. "Hercules, you poor excuse for a dog! Why do you let Bob control you like this?" She crawled in on her hands and knees, ducking her head under the middle shelf. Just as she was about to grab him, Hercules slipped through her hands and jumped out of the safe. On the way out, he knocked the door and tripped the broken hinge.

There wasn't time to react. Maggie sensed that the room was going dark only a split second before the heavy iron door slammed into the back of her feet, sealing her inside the safe.

Maggie screamed. She bumped her head against the guns in the back and attempted to turn around and face forward. It was pitch black inside, and she immediately started to hyperventilate. She knew this was a genuine antique safe, and they didn't used to make them with safety mechanisms to open from the inside. How in the world was she going to get out?

Suddenly a light flashed on in her head. A feeling of déjà vu accompanied the realization that this had happened before. She was gasping for air, only it wasn't in a gun safe. It was inside a vault. For the first time, she remembered that horrible feeling of being locked inside the vault with the diamond case.

She banged on the door. It was hot, and she could feel herself sweating. She thought she heard the sound of rushing water, or was it just the blood rushing to her head?

Another scene flashed in front of her, so vivid and clear it was like a movie playing on a big screen. Jack was with her, and he was blind. They were looking for wedding rings, but they were only pretending to be engaged. Then they were in a garden outside of a bed-and-breakfast inn. She could smell the honeysuckle in bloom as he was asking her to marry him. She tried to slow her breathing and shouted for someone. But she knew no one was home. It was getting hotter and stuffier inside the safe.

Another flash, and she was in Imogene Vandergrift's mansion treating a tiny puppy that belonged to a charming boy with a familiar face, but she couldn't place where she knew him. There was an instant connection between them.

A second later she was in a hurricane, jumping off a sinking boat with Wesley. She felt the cold water slap her in the face.

Then it was her wedding day, and she was flooded with feelings of how much she wanted to spend the rest of her life with Jack. She could feel Jack's arm around her waist, and she felt beautiful in her dress even though it was uncomfortably tight.

In another instant she was in the hospital giving birth to twins. She felt the labor pains for just an instant, and then looked into the faces of her baby daughters.

Maggie gasped for air. *I remember everything. Please don't let me die now.*

* * *

Wesley rushed into the family room. He didn't know if Maggie was home, but he had to tell someone about the conversation he just had with his dad. She would be the only one who might be able to talk some sense into him.

"Maggie!" he called. Then he remembered he wasn't supposed to shout in the house. He didn't want to get a lecture for that, so he went to look for her. Her car was in the garage, but that didn't mean anything. She could be next door or riding her horse somewhere.

Hercules ran past him, barking and agitated as usual. "Hercules, go find Maggie!" Hercules sat down and wagged his tail. "You're useless."

As if insulted, Hercules darted off toward the office. Wesley decided to follow him. When he got inside and saw that Maggie wasn't in there, he picked up Hercules and was going to shut the door, but Hercules jumped out of his arms and ran toward the safe and scratched it, and then barked in his annoying, high-pitched bark.

"Stop that!" Wesley scolded. "If you just put scratch marks on the safe, you're toast!"

Wesley turned to go when he heard a pounding from inside the safe. He ran over to it when he heard the muffled screams and knew it had to be Maggie.

"Maggie, I'll get you out! What's the combination?" Only the adults were allowed to open the safe, so Wesley had never been given the combination. It was also used for hiding Christmas presents, so there was no reason for him to have access.

Maggie tried to yell the numbers to Wesley, but it was hard to hear through the heavy metal door. It sounded like she was saying "line many way hive." Wesley couldn't translate that into numbers. He shouted for her to repeat it.

"Our anniversary!" she yelled.

Wesley got it this time. He thought for a moment and then tried 9-28-05. The combination clicked on the first try, and he opened the door. Maggie was crouched in the bottom of the safe. He reached down and helped her out.

Maggie stood up and gave Wesley a giant bear hug. She appeared to be okay, other than her flushed face and rapid heartbeat.

"Wesley! Thank you! I thought I was going to die for sure this time."

"How in the world did you get locked in there?" Wesley asked.

"I was trying to get Hercules out, and the door slammed on me. But it doesn't matter. Wesley, I remember everything! Getting locked in there triggered everything. I remembered getting shut inside the vault and running out of air, and then it was like a flood—it all came back to me."

"Really?" Wesley couldn't believe the good news. Even with the recent trauma, Maggie looked more like herself again. "Are you okay? Do we need to get a doctor?" Wesley asked.

"No, I'll be fine. I don't think I ever ran out of air. I just panicked in there. It's a good thing you came along when you did, or I would have really been in trouble."

"I guess Hercules isn't worthless after all. You got your memory back. This is the greatest news in the world!"

"This is wonderful." Maggie collapsed into the office chair. "But this is terrible." She dropped her head into her hands. "I've been an absolute beast to your father."

"It's okay. He'll forgive you," Wesley assured her. "You can call him and tell him right now. He's going to be so thrilled that he'll come right home!"

Maggie picked up the desk phone and hit Jack's number. Wesley could hear that it went straight to his voice mail. "He's either on the phone, or he turned it off. Do you have any idea where he went?"

"No. I was hoping you did. That's why I came looking for you. When he left the house a little while ago, I'd never seen him so upset. He looked like he'd been crying. He's not himself, and I think he's going to do something crazy."

"He already did." Maggie pointed to the papers on the desk. "He filed for divorce."

"What?" Wesley sat down in the leather armchair. "He would never do that! He worships the ground you walk on."

"Maybe he used to before I started accusing him of doing terrible things and treating him like dirt. The sad thing is, I didn't realize how awful I'd been until now. I thought maybe the divorce papers were just a test to see how I'd react. But he was serious. He already signed them and everything. Did he say anything to you about it before he left?"

"Not exactly. But he admitted that something was wrong. He was talking about making things right and doing what he had to do."

"He said that to me too."

"But that's not what made me really worried." Wesley paused. "He had the diamond case in his car."

"The diamond case?" Maggie's eyes got wide. "The same one we lost in the caves?"

"Yes, I'm positive it's the same one. And he even admitted the diamonds are still in it. I asked him what he was going to do with it, and all he said was that he wasn't going to keep it. Then I asked him if he was going to find Imogene, and he didn't answer me."

Maggie gasped, and her hand flew to her mouth. She stood up abruptly. "This is even worse than I thought."

"What?"

Maggie picked the divorce papers and the will off the desk and scanned through them, furiously turning the pages. She shook her head as if trying to convince herself that what she read couldn't possibly be true. "This isn't good."

"What does it say?" Wesley asked.

"He had a new will drawn up—and he left every-thing to *me*."

"So why is that bad?"

"It's bad because I can only think of one reason why he would do that."

Wesley waited for Maggie to explain.

"If a person commits a crime and either gets killed or ends up in prison, the insurance company won't pay their family any benefits. And whatever money or assets the family is supposed to receive can get taken away in lawsuits. That is, unless the money already belongs to them. It looks like your dad is planning to do something risky, and he's trying to protect us finan-cially."

"But you haven't signed the papers."

"No, and I hope I don't have to. But if your dad did something illegal and ended up in jail, I *could* sign these divorce papers and then the house and every-thing would belong to me, and they wouldn't be able to take it from us. I didn't want to tell you this before, but he had the .38 packed in his suitcase. He doesn't ever take that with him."

"He packed his gun? Do you think—?" Wesley didn't want to finish the sentence.

"This is all my fault." Maggie wrung her hands. "He tried to tell me, but I wouldn't listen. I wouldn't have thought it was possible earlier, but now that I have my memory back and I realize what I've done to him . . . I think right now he's capable of anything."

There was silence for a moment. Wesley didn't want to say it, but he had to make sure he knew what Maggie was talking about. "Even murder?"

Maggie looked at him soberly and nodded.

29

The Hunt

It took about forty-five minutes to gather the extended family into the Mackeys' kitchen for a meeting. Maggie and Wesley called Maria, Amanda, Penny, and Walter over to the house and briefed them on the situation. Everyone was excited to learn that Maggie had regained her memory, but in light of the recent information about Jack, there was no time for a celebration. With six people piecing together all the clues, they hoped to be able to figure out where Jack might have gone. Everyone had called Jack from their different phones, hoping he might pick up, but he didn't answer.

Walter led the discussion. "I think we can assume from the information so far that Jack went to try and find Imogene, but we don't know what he's going to do when he finds her. I think no matter how upset he is right now, he won't do anything that drastic."

Maggie shook her head. "Dad, you didn't see him today. Would you have thought yesterday he would file for divorce?"

"No. You got a point there." Walter scratched his head. "So did he take the hollow-tip bullets?"

Maggie blanched at the question. She was already disheartened to know that no one seemed as surprised as she was about the divorce papers. That she had mistreated Jack wasn't news to anyone.

"I wish I could get a hold of Alex," Maria said. "Maybe he knows something. He might even be with Jack now. He said he was going on some undercover operation yesterday."

"My dad said he was going alone. If he had government agents working with him, I don't think they would let him carry two hundred million dollars around in the backseat of his car."

Maria shuffled some maps around on the table. "Too bad his car doesn't have that tracking system that can find your car if it gets stolen."

"I know," Maggie said. "He has that in his truck but not in his old Camaro."

"That's it!" Wesley brightened. "Why don't we report Dad's car as stolen? We give the police the license number, and if he's out on the highway or parked somewhere, the police can pull him over and arrest him. It's not a very common car."

"Great idea, Wesley," Amanda said sarcastically. "We're trying to *prevent* Jack from getting arrested, not cause it."

"No, wait," Penny said. "Wesley has a point. Better to stop him now than to let him go ahead with something he'll regret later. He's not in his right mind. He'll thank us eventually."

"I doubt he'll be thankful for prison life," Walter said. "Because that's what he'll get when they find stolen diamonds on him. You guys are way off track.

Do you know how many stolen cars are reported every hour? Cops don't even pay any attention to that stuff. They might find him in two or three weeks, but we don't have that kind of time."

"Then what do we have time for?" Maggie asked. "We have nothing else to go on. Unless he turns his phone on or comes back home, we're helpless here."

"Why not try to call that one-legged guy that helped you out at the caves?" Walter suggested.

"Harlan?" Maggie asked. "What would he know?"

"I don't know." Walter shrugged. "He was with Jack in the past few days. But don't listen to me, I'm just a senile old man . . ."

"Enough, Dad," Maggie said. "It's an option. But how do I get his number? He doesn't have a home phone, and Jack is the only one who has his cell number."

"No, I have it," Amanda volunteered. "He said his dog just had puppies, so I was going to call him about it later. Amanda pulled out her cell phone and called. She handed her phone to Maggie.

Maggie was startled that Harlan answered right away. "Hello, um, Harlan? This is Maggie Mackey."

"Hi, Maggie, how are you?" Harlan answered.

She dispensed with the formalities. "I'm okay, but a little stressed out at the moment, and I was wondering if you could help me out."

"Sure—what is it?"

"Okay, this may sound strange, but I'm calling to see if you know where Jack is. I'm a little worried about him, and I can't seem to get him on his phone. I know he spent some time with you a couple of days ago. Did he happen to mention that he was going somewhere?"

There was a suspicious pause. "I don't know if I'm at liberty to discuss that with you, Maggie."

"Harlan, please. I need to get in touch with Jack as soon as I can. I know who he is going to see, and I also know what he has with him. What I don't is where. Harlan, I know you don't owe me anything, but if you consider Jack your friend, you need to tell me where he is so I can stop him before it's too late."

"I'd like to help you, Maggie, but I honestly don't know where he went. All I know is this is something he's going to do no matter what you say. So if I were you, I'd stay out of his way and let things be."

"I can't do that. He's doing this based on information that isn't correct anymore. Can you tell me anything at all about where he might have gone?"

Harlan sighed. "Just a minute."

Maggie could hear Harlan's hand cover the speaker and that he was talking to another person, but she couldn't understand what he was saying. She could tell that Harlan probably knew a lot more than he was letting on.

A woman's voice came on the line. "Hello, Maggie? This is Whitney—you know me as Katrina. Harlan wants me to tell you that he doesn't know where Jack is and that you should just stay out of it."

"Whitney—do you know where Jack is?"

"I might. But if I did, why should I tell you?"

"Because—" Maggie thought for a minute. "Because I need to talk to him."

Whitney laughed at her. "That's not a reason. From what I understand, you haven't been very nice to Jack. I don't think he likes you anymore."

"No, I haven't, and yes, I'm aware of that. But that's not really your business, now is it?"

"Well maybe it is my business what Jack does today."

"What is he planning to do?"

"He's meeting with Imogene. He didn't tell you that?"

Maggie didn't want to admit that Jack didn't tell her that. "Please, Whitney, I'm begging you to tell me where he's meeting her. What do you want? I'll pay you."

"You can't blackmail me. I promised not to tell, and I'm going to keep that promise."

Maggie decided not to explain to Whitney that she was actually trying to bribe her, not blackmail her. "Whitney, I promise you Jack would want you to tell me. He doesn't know I got my memory back." Maggie felt a catch in her throat. "But I need to tell him right now before he does something he'll regret."

Whitney gasped. "You got your memory back? And he doesn't know?"

"That's right. That's why this is so important."

"Well, this changes everything."

"It does? So you'll tell me where he is then?"

"Well, he did me a favor, so I guess I'll have to return it. But even if I tell you where he is, you won't be able to get there in time. He went to Coral Cove. I set up a meeting with Imogene to give her the briefcase. She thinks I'm coming to meet her to divide up the diamonds. I made her promise to go there alone, and she couldn't send anyone in her place."

"Where exactly is Coral Cove?"

"Some cliff. The one right above the spot where she found Wesley. Actually, I don't even know where that is. When she explained it, I wasn't listening, since I knew I wasn't going to be there. We agreed to meet there at 7:30 tonight."

"And she doesn't suspect a trap?"

"She always suspects a trap. But she thinks I'm not smart enough to double-cross her on my own. Even if my mother were in on this, she thinks she can take us both out with one hand tied behind her back. She doesn't think I have any reason to be working with Jack."

"You're right. I never suspected that you would be working with Jack either. Thank you for telling me," Maggie said. "You've done the right thing. I really appreciate it." Maggie said good-bye and shut Amanda's phone. She checked her watch.

"Unless Whitney is lying to me, we know for sure now he's meeting Imogene," Maggie told the family. "But there's nothing we can do about it. It's 5:30 now. Whitney said he's meeting Imogene on the Coral Cove cliffs at 7:30. I've driven from here to there enough to know it's two and a half hours minimum. Unless you know someone with a helicopter, we can't get there in time."

"I can drive it!" Wesley yelled. "We can take the back roads and just speed the whole way there."

"The back roads are even longer than the freeway, and it's rush hour right now," Maggie said.

"You know," Walter said, "that road construction on the double-lane highway has blocked off everything through the Old Mill Bridge. If you went through the detour signs, you wouldn't run into any traffic at all for about fifty miles."

"And no road, either," Maggie noted.

"Well, maybe in some spots." Walter shrugged. "That's what four-wheel drive is for."

"You're right, Dad." Maggie nodded. "If I leave now, I just might be able to get there in time."

"That's not safe!" Penny warned.

"I can't sit here and do nothing!" Maggie said. "I've got to stop Jack before it's too late."

"Can I come with you?" Wesley asked.

"No, Wesley. I'm going alone," Maggie said. "This is my mess, and I need to clean it up without putting anyone else in danger."

"I don't understand why we can't just call the police," Penny stated.

"Because if they catch Jack with those stolen diamonds, he'll get life in prison!" Maggie reiterated. "I won't do that to him. I just want to talk to him."

"But Maggie, you won't know which cliff they're meeting on," Wesley said. "There's more than one."

"Do you know which one it is?" Maggie asked. "The place where Imogene pulled you out of the ocean?"

"I think so. Imogene used to take me there when I was little. She never told me why, but now I know it has to be the place. You won't have time to search for it."

Maggie was ready to refuse again, but Penny stopped her. "There's no time to argue, Maggie. Just take Wesley with you and get on your way!" She pushed her in the direction of the garage.

A scene from the past flashed into Maggie's head of a windy dirt road and a raging forest fire. She was in the backseat of a jeep, and Jack and Alex were both unconscious, while fourteen-year-old Wesley drove them in a high-speed chase.

"Okay, let's go!" Maggie conceded. "Get in the car, Wesley, but you're *not* driving."

* * *

An hour and a half later, Maggie was speeding on the back country roads while Wesley navigated with the map. The gas light had been on for a long time, but there were no gas stations in sight.

"Maybe we should have taken the freeway," Wesley said.

"And maybe we should have stopped and filled up at that gas station thirty miles back, too," Maggie said. "But neither of those are options anymore. I just wish Jack would pick up the phone. We just have to get there in time, or I'm going to regret this for the rest of my life." She pushed the accelerator, and the car sped up to almost one hundred again. There were a few other cars on the road, and she had just passed a truck like it was standing still.

"I am really not comfortable at this speed," Maggie said. "But I don't want to slow down. Just remember when you get your license that it is not okay to go this fast. These are extenuating circumstances."

Wesley nodded. "I'll remember, but I think that car behind you is a cop."

Maggie knew her luck would run out eventually, but she told herself she would deal with that when the time came. She checked her rearview mirror just as a light and siren came on. It was time to deal with it.

Maggie sighed. "Once again, Wesley, don't you ever try this," she said. "But I'm going to try and outrun him. Hold on." She pressed the gas pedal to the floor.

"Just stop now and explain this is an emergency," Wesley said. "Maybe he'll let you go."

"I wish that were possible, but that's not how cops do things. I'm already going almost twice the speed limit. He won't just give me a ticket. He'll impound my car."

At that moment, the car started to sputter, and Maggie realized that she was out of gas. The power steering went out, and the brakes were hard to push, but she guided the car over to the edge and stopped.

She pounded on the steering wheel and screamed, "Please not now!"

In an instant, a police officer wearing dark sunglasses was at her window. She rolled it down.

"Do you know how fast you were going, ma'am?" he said sternly.

"Evidently not fast enough," Maggie said under her breath.

"I clocked you at one hundred and six miles an hour. This here is a fifty-five-mile zone. Any reason you seemed to be in a such a hurry?"

Maggie shook her head.

"Can I see some ID, ma'am?"

Maggie pulled her purse out and showed the officer her license.

"Step out of the car, please."

Maggie complied.

The highway patrolman looked at her license. "Margaret Suzanne Mackey. Don't suppose you're any relation to the famous Jack Mackey," he said jokingly.

"Yes," she said. "He's my husband."

"Well, I'll be!" The officer was both shocked and pleased. "I got five kids, and we had to get a satellite dish installed just so they can watch *The Snake Stalker*. It's our favorite show."

"That's wonderful," Maggie said, forcing a smile, and at the same time trying to get the officer to hurry up. Then she remembered it didn't really matter, because she wasn't going to be able to go anywhere.

"It's so hard to find good entertainment for the family nowadays, I reckon. *The Snake Stalker* is about the best thing on TV. Your husband is a hoot. Is he that funny in real life?"

Maggie nodded. "Even more so."

"Wow. The kids aren't going to believe me when I tell them this. Is that your son in the car, too?"

Maggie nodded and decided to go for broke. "Officer, I know I was going way over the speed limit, and you may not believe this, but the reason I'm speeding is I'm on my way to find my husband right now. There's been a—um—family emergency, but I can't get him to answer his phone. And I need to reach him right away."

The officer pulled off his sunglasses and looked into Maggie's eyes. "What kind of emergency?"

"Well, it's personal, and I don't have time to go into it right now, but you are like an angel sent from heaven, because you may be able to help me prevent a serious tragedy from happening." Maggie didn't know if she sounded more like Sharalee or her mother with that "angel sent from heaven" comment, but it didn't matter. At this point she was willing to try anything.

"How is that?"

"I promise you," Maggie said emphatically. "I'm normally not a lawbreaker, but to be totally frank with you, if I don't get to my husband right away, there might not ever be another episode of *The Snake Stalker*."

"That sounds serious." The policeman was checking her license plate and writing it down. "I'll need to run these plates." He didn't seem to be buying her story.

"Officer, please." Maggie was running out of time and was actually considering just jumping into the police car and driving off when she suddenly got an idea. "Can I ask you a question?"

"What is it?"

She pointed to his police car. "How much do you think your car is worth?"

He gave her a confused look. "Not much, but it runs, and that's all that matters."

"I couldn't agree more. See my car here?" She pointed to her vehicle. "My husband paid cash for it brand new less than a year ago. It's a Lexus 470 four-wheel-drive, and I'll trade you my car right now if you'll let me borrow yours for a few hours. I understand that you need to write me a ticket—and I don't deny that I was doing 106. But these are extenuating circumstances, and I really do need to get to my husband as quickly as possible."

"If you tell me where he is, I can radio ahead—"

"No, this is something Jack needs to hear from me. If I could tell you, I would."

The officer shook his head. "I'm off duty now, and as much as I would like to take your vehicle, Mrs. Mackey, I've been sworn to uphold the law . . ."

"It's not illegal if you give me permission. My car is out of gas." Maggie couldn't think of what else to say. "You can phone someone to bring you some gas. I'll pay for it. Take my car to your home and give the whole family a ride. After I handle the emergency, I can bring Jack back with me in person to exchange cars with you. I'm sure he'd love to meet your kids. There's no risk to you. If you never see me again, you definitely have the better end of the deal. The title's in the glovebox."

The policeman eyed her skeptically. "You know I could haul you down to the station right now and charge you with bribing a police officer," he said.

"I know," she said, her hopes deflated. "But I had to try."

"Now I need you to answer one more question for me." The officer gave her a stern look. "Does it have a sunroof?"

30

Taking Control

Warm wind whipped up the cold ocean waters. Frothy waves crashed against the sharp rocks. The cliff dropped three hundred feet from the top of the outermost part of the jagged cliff to the ocean below. If anyone were to slip off and manage to land in the deep part of the water, they would be crushed into the coral and rocks by the next giant wave. The only other way down was a steep and arduous climb about a quarter of a mile away from the spot.

Jack stood on top of the cliff and examined the surroundings. It was hard to believe Imogene had been able to negotiate these cliffs. He tried to picture Imogene fourteen years ago climbing down to rescue Wesley from the rough and angry water. Not many people would even attempt it.

This was a good place for them to meet. The swirling pool of water covered a beautiful coral reef. But the small beach below wasn't frequented by tourists, because of the limited access. Once in a while a person who was familiar with the area might come here to the cliff for some solitude. There wasn't any place to park, and nothing marked the highway a half mile back to give a person any reason to stop. The cliff was also visible from many other areas, so although there were plenty of hiding places farther back, it wasn't possible to get to the outer cliff without being noticed.

Jack looked out at the blue ocean as the early evening sun from the west reflected a silver gleam on the water. His brief second of admiration for Imogene's daring rescue dissipated into a long list of unforgivable sins. Was he going to be able to go through with it after all? He couldn't believe that he'd handed Maggie divorce papers a few hours ago. He didn't know how he expected her to react, but he had to admit that she handled it much better than he did. He had held out the hope that if he gave Maggie an out, and she didn't feel trapped, she might stop trying to run away from him, but instead she only ran away faster. But he had to let her go. He loved her too much to watch her slowly crumbling away each day. He had already endured the death of his first wife, and he didn't want to go through the emotional death of his second wife.

Jack packed away his thoughts for another time and place. Right then he needed to focus on what he had to do.

Imogene would be there any minute now. He would be ready for her.

* * *

Imogene reached the spot where the rendezvous would happen. There was only one thing left to do, and then there would be nothing standing in the way of her freedom. Her idiot niece would have no idea which diamonds were the most valuable, and she didn't plan on giving her any of the extremely rare ones. It was like taking candy from a baby. But just in case Whitney tried to pull something over on her, she had a second line of defense waiting on the bench.

After she had the precious stones in her possession, she had two options. Hopefully, her lawyer could stack the jury and pay them a tidy sum to acquit her. She had enough money to be as persuasive as she needed to be. If that couldn't be arranged, then she would simply disappear before she went to trial. Disappearing was something she was very good at. She had access to private jets and yachts that could ferry her to the Bermuda islands, where she could lie low for several months before heading on to Europe. Unfortunately she wasn't going to be able to take Wesley with her now. But she was confident that someday he would realize that she had been a good mother to him, and he would want to be her son again.

A warm sea breeze was blowing as she reached the top of the rocky cliff that she remembered so well from fourteen years ago. She could almost envision the little yellow life raft floating in the ocean, carrying its precious cargo. How was it possible that it was mere coincidence? She was meant to find Wesley that day and save his life. How could he not see that? How could he not appreciate that she had given him life?

The noise of the surf crashing against the rocks and the smell of the ocean melted together to add flavor to her memory.

Imogene checked her watch. 7:33. Whitney never had been the punctual type, and she was going to get an earful if she didn't show up soon. Angrily she turned her back to the ocean side of the cliff to see if she was coming. A noise behind her caused her to spin around. It sounded like someone was singing. As the melody carried over the din of the ocean, the Australian accent was eminently clear.

Imogene flinched and pulled a small gun out of her handbag. She walked over to the edge of the cliff, toward the direction of the voice. She could see that there was a small ledge that jutted out about six feet down from the top. It was extremely narrow, and it had never occurred to her that it was possible to hide out in such a precarious spot, but Jack Mackey was there. She had never thought Jack was terribly bright, but even for him, this was beyond stupid.

Jack didn't seem too concerned that Imogene was standing above him with a gun in her hand. "Lookin' for this?" He pointed to a briefcase tucked neatly under his arm, like a kid taunting another kid with an ice cream cone.

Imogene cocked her gun, but Jack was unfazed, as if he were expecting that.

"I wouldn't be so hasty if I were you," he said.

Imogene didn't move.

"Guess what?" Jack said. "This diamond case is attached to me." He showed her the rope that was wrapped around his wrist and tied to the handle. "You can shoot me—that's true. But I will definitely fall off this cliff when you do. And when I do, this briefcase and its contents come with me. That means a whole bunch of valuable merchandise would go straight to the bottom. So if and when they ever do recover my dead and rotting body, I don't think they'll be returning these to you. But you'll definitely be number one on the list of suspects for my murder."

Imogene kept her gun aimed at Jack.

"So let me outline the choices for you. You can throw your gun in the ocean right now, or you can kill me and spend the rest of your life in prison without your money."

"And if I do throw my gun away, I suppose you want me to believe you're going to let me have the diamonds?" Imogene laughed.

Jack held onto the ledge with his left hand and pulled his gun out from his pocket with his right. "No. I'm not planning to give them to you no matter what. But there is option three. I can just shoot you now."

Imogene hesitated, and Jack fired a warning shot. She threw her gun into the ocean.

"That was easy," Jack said. "Now, hands in the air where I can see them."

Imogene's hands flew into the air.

Jack holstered his gun, and in one fluid motion he threw the diamond case up over the edge of the cliff, pulled himself up onto the top, and stood up in front of her. "Didn't obey the rules, I see," he said as he pulled his gun back out. "You brought a weapon."

"You didn't obey the rules either," Imogene shot back. "Did you really expect *me* to? How do you know I don't have backup waiting nearby to take you out when I give them the signal?"

"How do you know I don't have backup that already took care of your backup an hour ago?" Jack asked. "Let's be honest. I'm a little smarter than Whitney. But then again, maybe gettin' out of here alive isn't all that important to me. Maybe I have a higher purpose."

Imogene swallowed. "What's that supposed to mean?"

"I'm a man on a mission, and I'm not going to leave until it's finished."

"So what is this mission?"

"I'm going put an end to all the pain and misery your wretched life has caused me," Jack said. "You know, normally I'm not a violent person. I don't take pleasure in other people's suffering. But thanks to you, I'm a new man!" He cocked his gun and aimed it at her head. "Kneel down and put your hands on your head!"

Imogene looked around. Jack could be bluffing, but then again, she didn't think he was. She put one knee down slowly and then the other and placed her hands on her head. "Let's talk this through, Jack. You're not going to kill me, because you're not that type of person, and we both know it. You don't want to do this to your family. There's nothing to be gained and everything to be lost."

"You sure about that?" Jack dangled the diamond case in front of her face like a hypnotist with a shiny watch. "You want to know somethin'? I already lost it. Today I left my wife, whom I love more than life itself. And you can't even imagine what I went through to pick up this case full of diamonds. Do I seem like a man who has his wits about him? Do I seem *rational* to you?"

"No," Imogene said stiffly. "As a matter of fact, you don't."

Jack paced in a circle around Imogene. "Since when have you cared about my family, other than to make it your life's work to tear it apart? You won! You finally found a way to take away the most precious thing to me in the world. And you did it on purpose. Why? That's all I want to know. Why did you have to do it?"

"You know the answer to that as well as I do. This is all a game, and you have to admit I am the better player."

"At this very moment, I don't think so."

"You took Wesley away from me, and I'll do whatever it takes to get him back. You can't blame me for trying. And you can't blame me for your marital problems. It's not my fault your wife hates you."

"I think it is. It's your fault you locked her in an airtight safe that left her with brain damage."

"I told you; Peter would have killed us all—"

"And it was your fault you planted liquor bottles and that old tabloid inside my house that you knew she would eventually find."

"You can't prove that was me," Imogene defended.

"I don't need proof, and I don't really care anymore. There's nothing left for you to do to us. So this is where I make things right."

Imogene cringed. "Just let me go," she pleaded, "and I promise to leave you and Wesley alone. I'll never bother you again."

"I know you won't. I'm going to make sure of it. But first, I want you to know what it feels like to have the most important thing in the world taken from you. I want you to see what you could have had and watch helplessly while someone takes it away from you—just because he could." He lifted up the case to show her and then set it on the ground and untied it from his wrist. "Go ahead. Open it."

Imogene's hands were shaking as she lowered them from her head slowly. She turned the numbers in the combination and clicked open the briefcase. She carefully raised the lid as Jack held the gun to her head. She pulled out one of the pouches and poured them into her hands. This was the product of her life's work. The sparkling white diamonds caught the sunlight and splashed her face with a prism of color. She let out a remorseful sigh.

"They're so precious to you, aren't they?" Jack tempted her. "You'd like nothing more than to just take these and run."

"Jack, you're not so different from me. I'm sure these gems make your heart beat a little bit faster too."

"Wrong." Jack tossed the loose stones back into the case. He kicked it shut with his foot, locked it tight, and picked it up. "Watch this." He took several steps over to the edge of the cliff. His feet were only inches from the sheer drop-off. He kept his left hand on the trigger of his gun and pulled back his right arm, heaving the case forward, letting go at just the right moment. The case went sailing out over the ocean.

Imogene winced as she watched the case disappear. Jack was out of his mind. For the first time she believed that he had the capacity to kill her.

"Why would you do that?" Imogene bellowed. "Do you have any idea what you just threw away?"

"Oh yeah. I know exactly what I just threw away." Jack gave her a satisfied smile. "I liked that. It was actually quite cathartic. I'd have to say fun, even. See, you and I are nothing alike. Now this next part is going to be much more difficult—and a bit messy, I'm afraid."

"You kill me and you'll get the death penalty. You've already gotten your revenge. Why do you need to do this?"

"Why indeed?" Jack pretended to think. "Is that a rhetorical question, or would you really like an answer?" Jack moved in closer to her. "I have to do it. There's too much pain and anger, and I need to make it all go away. Otherwise it'll keep eatin' at me until there's nothin' left. Today I'm takin' control. So let's get this over with."

* * *

Maggie abruptly turned the police car light off and pulled off to the side of the coastal highway. She noticed the tire marks in the dirt off to the side but didn't see any place to park. She rolled down the window and could hear the ocean surf crashing in the distance.

"Are you sure this is the place, Wesley?" Maggie asked. "I don't see any cars."

"Yeah this is it. I'm sure."

"Do you see anything?" Maggie asked as she scanned the rugged cliffs for signs of life.

Wesley looked through the binoculars. "I can see two people way out there. It's hard to tell who it is, but one person is standing, and the other one is kneeling. What color shirt is my dad wearing?"

"I don't know, red maybe?" Maggie said.

"Then it's him," Wesley said. "It has to be Dad and Imogene."

"What are they doing?"

"I can't tell. Maybe you should honk the horn or something to get his attention."

"He can't hear us from here—they're too close to the ocean. I'm going to have to run out there. Wesley, listen to me. I want you to take this car and drive back out to the last turnout on the main highway and wait for me. If I don't call you in fifteen minutes, use the police radio and tell them what's going on."

"No, I can't leave you here," Wesley said.

"Wesley, please!"

Maggie jumped out, and Wesley crawled over to the driver's seat and pulled the car away.

Maggie couldn't believe that she just talked a cop into loaning her his car, and that she just ordered her fifteen year old to drive it all by himself. But there wasn't any time to do anything else. She took off running as fast as she could. Nothing mattered except getting to Jack before he did something terrible.

As she got closer, the ground became gravelly and then sandy. She could see that the person standing on the cliff was definitely Jack. He was holding a gun to Imogene's head. She knew that Jack didn't have great vision, and he probably couldn't see her. She waved her hands in the air and screamed his name, hoping he would notice her, but she still wasn't close enough to be heard. She kept running toward him. She screamed Jack's name again, but the sound was cut off when she was suddenly hit by a painful electric shock that took her breath away. She fell to the ground with a thud.

It was as if someone had pulled her feet out from beneath her and she was completely paralyzed. She probably would have broken both arms if she hadn't fallen in a patch of soft sand. At first she thought she must have been shot, but she couldn't feel the bullet wound. For ten seconds she lay motionless, gradually regaining control of her muscles.

Before she had time to get to her knees, a man came out from a rock outcropping, covered her mouth with his hand, and dragged her off behind some large boulders into a shallow ravine. She struggled to get free, but he held a knife to her throat.

The man had a familiar voice, but she couldn't place it. "Just sit tight. You're not going anywhere until the fat lady sings."

From where she was, the view of the cliff was blocked. She wanted to scream and break away, but she was stunned from her fall and wasn't in full possession of her faculties yet.

"So you're Jack Mackey's wife," the man said. "Wow. He did pretty well for himself." He took his hand off her mouth but kept the knife close by.

Maggie turned and got a look at her attacker's face. He was a large man with jet black hair and a neatly trimmed beard. He wasn't wearing a three-piece suit, but she knew who he was.

"And you're Joey Ferraro. Please let me go. Believe it or not, I'm trying to stop my husband from killing your client."

"Exactly." Joey smiled. "That's why you're staying right here with me."

"You want Imogene to die?" Maggie gasped.

"Either way works for me," Joey admitted. "If Jack takes her out, this will be a win-win situation for both of us. You split the contents of that case with me right down the middle, and I'll make sure your hubby doesn't go to jail. If he doesn't kill her, then I'll just have to fix the trial outcome for the highest bidder."

Maggie had no doubt that he could do what he said. She couldn't believe she had come this far only to be stopped a few yards from reaching Jack. She was about to plead with Joey when suddenly a gunshot ripped through the air. It echoed several times.

"No!" she screamed.

Joey clamped his hand over her mouth and muffled her cries. "Keep it down!"

Maggie's heart rose into her throat. She couldn't see what had just happened, but she knew either Jack had fired the shot or someone else had fired at Jack. Either way, it wasn't going to be good.

Joey kept his knife close to Maggie's neck as he shifted to lift his head above the rocks to see what had happened. He was in good physical condition, and Maggie knew that he would naturally assume that she was a frightened and defenseless woman and it wouldn't take much to restrain her. He was about to find out otherwise.

Maggie grabbed his wrist and bent it down hard, using a technique Alex had taught her. While forcing him to drop the knife, she ducked underneath his arm and twisted it back behind his back. She slammed his body up against the big boulder and put him in a choke hold.

The element of surprise had given Maggie a definite advantage. Now she was in a position where she had all the leverage, and even though he attempted to fight against her, in under a minute he had passed out cold. Maggie let him drop to the ground. She couldn't risk looking to see what had happened to Jack without making sure Joey was properly restrained. She picked up the knife and used it to cut off his shirt, which she tore into strips and then used to tie his hands behind his back and bind his feet together. It wouldn't keep him under control indefinitely, but it would certainly slow him down after he regained consciousness.

Maggie also found a taser gun in his pocket and realized that was what he had stunned her with earlier. She quickly pocketed the gun and the knife and climbed out of the ravine.

She took a large gulp of air and looked around. There was no one out on the cliff anymore. She kept moving forward, wondering how Jack and Imogene could have evaporated so quickly. Maybe the two of them had fought and tumbled off the cliff. Maybe Imogene had shot Jack and was hiding now. Her adrenaline was so high she was beginning to feel sick.

Then she saw him. Jack was sitting all alone on the edge of the cliff with his legs dangling over the edge. He was still alive. She ran with a renewed burst of energy to within a few yards of him. His back was to her, and she didn't want to startle him when he was so close to the edge.

She walked up to him cautiously. "Jack?"

He turned around slowly to look at her. He seemed not to recognize her at first. The expression on his face was deep and methodical. She was afraid to ask him what just happened.

"Where's Imogene?"

"She's gone."

Maggie tried not to lose composure. She was too late. "So you killed her?"

Jack stood up. "Kill her?" He shook his head. "That would have been too easy. I did something that I never thought I was capable of."

Maggie didn't want to think of what could be more horrible than murder, so she looked out at the ocean, trying to keep herself steady. "And what was that?"

"I forgave her."

She wasn't sure she understood what he just said. "You *forgave* her?"

"I had to." Jack looked as though something had changed in his face. "I didn't really want to, but there was no other way to let go of all that anger inside of me. It's no wonder you couldn't trust me, Mag. I haven't thought of anything but getting revenge ever since the day you lost your memory."

A rush of relief flooded over Maggie. "So Imogene is alive?" Maggie wanted to make sure she heard him right.

"Kickin' and screamin'."

"And where did she go?"

"The cops took her away."

"The police are here?"

"Yeah, right over there." Jack pointed behind her.

Maggie turned around for the first time and saw two police cars parked over by the road, where several officers were getting Imogene settled in the backseat of one of the patrol cars.

"And who fired the shot?" She asked.

"I don't know. You'll have to ask them." Jack still didn't look all that happy to see her. "Why are you here, Mag?"

Maggie bit her lip. "Jack, I have something very important to tell you."

Jack's demeanor sagged. "If it's about the divorce papers, I'd rather not go into it right now."

"It is. I mean that's part of it." Maggie could only hope that she wasn't too late again. "I ripped them up. And I don't want a divorce." She paused to see if his expression changed. "I remember everything, Jack. I got my memory back."

"You got your memory back, and you remember *everything*?" Jack repeated.

"Everything. You know how I asked you fix the gun safe, and you never did? Well, the door slammed shut on me, and I got locked inside the safe, and I thought I was going to die. Then I remembered that day I was locked inside the vault. And all my memories just came back to me in flashes, like they'd never left.

"I remembered the day you asked me to marry you. I remember our wedding day and our honeymoon, when the girls were born, the pink shoes . . ." She trailed off. "And how much I love you, and I always have. I don't know how I could have forgotten that. Jack, I'm so, so sorry for how I've treated you. I know how much it must have taken for you to forgive Imogene, but do you think maybe you could forgive me, too?"

Jack's jaw dropped, and he looked as though he might fall over. He took a few steps away from the edge of the cliff, just in case he did. "I don't know, Mag. You only ripped my heart out, threw it on the ground, and stomped on it. And now you're askin' me to forgive you?"

Maggie looked into Jack's blue eyes and tried to read his expression. As she did, she saw the hint of a smile steal over his face. She ran over to him and threw her arms around him. Jack returned her embrace and kissed her passionately.

After a moment, Jack looked at her and pushed the blowing strands of hair out of her face. Maggie asked him again. "So does this mean you forgive me?"

"I'm thinkin' about it. But I might need some more persuasion."

Maggie pulled his face to hers and kissed him.

* * *

Unnoticed by Maggie and Jack, Wesley walked onto the scene flanked by two police officers. Wesley was still limping on his injured foot, but he didn't notice the pain. With a huge grin on his face, he pulled his cell phone out of his pocket, held it up, and took a picture of Jack and Maggie kissing on the cliff and sent it to Amanda's phone.

One of the officers named Fernandez cleared his throat, but Jack and Maggie didn't acknowledge him. Finally he stated loudly, "Jack, we have some questions for you. You have a very valuable briefcase that needs to be turned over to the authorities."

Jack turned his attention away from Maggie and said to the policeman in an irritated voice, "Do you mind, officer? My wife and I are havin' a private discussion here."

Fernandez turned to his partner and said, "Funny, that's not what a 'discussion' looks like with my wife." He directed his comments to Jack. "I'm afraid we're going to have to place you under arrest, Jack, unless you can tell us where the diamond case is."

"Okay." Jack threw up his hands and turned to the officers. "Since you so obviously can't take a hint, let's get this over with. I admit it. I threw the case in the ocean."

Maggie was aghast. "You threw the case in the ocean—full of diamonds?"

"You *what*?" Fernandez roared.

"Of course it was full of diamonds," Jack said. "If it was empty, that would have been no fun at all."

"Jack," Maggie started, "that was two hundred million dollars—"

"Probably closer to two twenty," Jack interrupted. "But don't worry. I have it all under control."

"You have it under control?" Fernandez bellowed. "Until you produce that diamond case and we can check the contents, we're going to have to take you into custody."

"Officers," Maggie interjected, "if you need someone to arrest, Joey Ferraro is knocked out and tied up in that ravine over there. But the choke hold I put on him is definitely going to wear off in a few minutes, so I'd take care of that right away if I were you."

"Ferraro is here?" Fernandez looked at his partner. "How did you miss him, Wilson?"

"How did *I* miss him? The same way *you* did, I suppose." Wilson pulled his gun out of his holster. "Don't you go anywhere," he said to Jack. "We'll be right back." The two officers jogged over to the place Maggie had pointed out to them.

Jack looked at Maggie with admiration. "You took out Joey Ferraro with a choke hold?"

"After he shot me with a taser gun. It made me mad."

"He's a powerful guy," Jack noted. "I hate to tell you, Mag, but you're in trouble now."

"So maybe I took out a powerful guy, and maybe I commandeered a police car to get here, but at least I didn't throw two hundred million dollars off a cliff."

Jack threw his hands out. "Hey, I might be crazy, but I'm not *stupid*. Wes, come over here."

Wesley marched over so that he was next to his dad and Maggie. He still had the binoculars draped around his neck. "Can I borrow those for a minute?" Jack asked.

"Sure." Wesley handed the specs to his dad.

Jack walked over to the edge of the cliff and put the binoculars up to his face. He waved his hand above his head like he was motioning to some invisible person out in the ocean.

"It's all good," Jack said and handed the binoculars back to Wesley. "Here, Wes. Take a look and see for yourself."

Wesley was a little more timid approaching the edge of the cliff, but he put the binoculars up to his face and searched for the mystery person down below. "There's someone down in the water. He's in a raft, and he's holding up a briefcase. Who is that?"

"Oh, just some guy who works for the government," Jack said. "Special Agent Harris I think was his name."

"You had Alex here with you the whole time?" Maggie inquired. "That would have been nice to know."

"Yeah, but he wasn't *with* me," Jack corrected. "I was up here, and he was down there."

"Jack." Maggie sighed. "That makes four times today that I've almost had a heart attack. Everyone thought you were coming here alone to kill Imogene."

"It might have crossed my mind. But you know, forgiveness is a pretty powerful thing. For the first time in three years, I feel like she's gone. She's finally out of my head."

"Dad, do you think when you hand that case over, they'll make us stay here for questioning, or will they let us go home now?"

"Hey, I'm not lettin' anyone spoil the celebration. If the cops want to ask us any more questions tonight, they're gonna have to catch us. Race you home!"

Maggie exchanged glances with Wesley. "We'd love to do that, but we don't exactly have a car anymore."

Jack looked back toward the road. "What happened to it?"

"We had to bribe a cop not to arrest us for going a hundred miles an hour," Wesley said. "But don't worry—we've got it all under control."

31

A Big Surprise

Jack and Maggie sat next to each other in the chair swing outside on the back patio. Emily was sitting next to both of them and trying to make the swing go higher by pumping her legs, but all her efforts couldn't override Jack, who was gently rocking the trio with one of his legs. C.J. was headed straight for Jack with a plastic cup full of ice-cold lemonade, and she was spilling most of it on the way. Wesley was sprawled out on a lounge chair, fanning himself with a magazine.

"When are they going to get here with the really big surprise?" Wesley asked. "I'm hot." C.J. changed her mind and brought Wesley the lemonade instead. "Thank you, C.J." As he reached out to take the cup she offered, she poured it on his shirt instead.

Maggie laughed. "You asked for it. You said you were hot."

Wesley took a piece of ice and rubbed it on his face.

"They should be here any minute now." Jack looked at his watch.

A brand-new, white 4-Runner came tooling up the driveway. "A new car!" Wesley sat up straight in his chair. "Is that my surprise?"

"Don't think so, mate. That's Alex and Maria's new car," Jack said as he watched them drive up the long, front driveway. "Looks like he got a little kickback from the diamond deal."

Alex parked the car, and the three occupants filed out. Amanda had a silver blue-eyed puppy cradled in her arms. She beamed at Wesley like a proud parent. "Look at my new baby," she said. "Her name is Sophie."

"Can I hold her?" Wesley asked. "Even though it's not really a surprise," he complained to his dad. "I knew Amanda was going to get a puppy all week."

While everyone gathered around to gawk at Amanda's new puppy, a truck pulled up behind the 4-Runner. Jack stole away from the group and came back moments later with Harlan in tow.

Jack pulled out a nearly identical puppy from behind his back and showed it to everyone. "And this is Sophie's brother," he announced.

"Is he mine?" Wesley asked excitedly.

"If your mum agrees to it," Jack said, looking at Maggie. "He's a purebred Weimaraner."

"Are they from your dog, Harlan?" Maggie asked.

"Yeah, my dog had six puppies, and this is the pick of the litter."

"And if I said no?" Maggie said as she reached her hands out to hold the puppy. "What would we do with him?"

Emily reached over and grabbed a chunk of skin and fur in her chubby hand. "Look at that face, Mag. Only a coldhearted soul could say no to that."

"Then you already know what my answer is," Maggie responded as she petted the puppy. "This guy does have a cute face."

"See, I told you that one had the cutest face," Harlan said.

"So what are you going to name him?" Amanda asked.

Wesley wanted to pick a name in honor of Teddy, but then he thought it would be better to retire Teddy's name like a number on a sports jersey. "How about Harlan?"

"That's a good name," Maggie said. "I'll second it. As long as it's okay with the original Harlan."

"I'd be honored. No one's ever named their dog after me before."

"But I did name a wombat after my mother-in-law once," Jack said.

"Can I hold Harlan?" Wesley asked. "You're right, Dad. This was a really big surprise. But the 4-Runner would have been nice too."

"Maybe when you're sixteen," Jack said. "But the puppy is only part of the surprise."

"Really? There's more?" Maggie asked.

Jack gave Harlan a nod. "I thought the whole gang could stay here for dinner. We'll order Chinese take-out, get Penny and Walter over here, and watch some TV tonight."

"Sounds fun." Maggie gave him a questioning look. Normally she liked to have advance notice on a party. "We can rent a video."

"Nah, who needs a video?" Jack responded. "There's a program I want to watch at eight. It's supposed to be really good."

"What is it?" Wesley asked.

"I don't know. You'll have to wait and see," Jack said with a smirk. "But I hear the two guys that do the show are really good."

"Wait a minute!" Maggie said dubiously. "You and Harlan did a show? Why didn't you tell me?"

"About a month ago we weren't really talkin' much," Jack said. "Besides, then it wouldn't be a surprise, would it?"

"I didn't know about it either," Wesley said. "Did you know?" he asked Amanda.

Amanda shrugged and shook her head.

"Well, lucky for me, you guys don't watch a lot of TV or read the entertainment magazines," Jack said. "You know how hard it was tryin' to make sure nobody caught the preview commercials?"

"So that's why you were always grabbing the remote away from me," Maggie chided.

"No, that has nothin' to do with it," Jack said. "Real men never let their wives get control of the remote."

"Now you're asking for it. You seemed to have forgotten that I can take you down."

Jack smiled. "And you seemed to have forgotten that I've got some pretty good countermoves myself. Never underestimate what fast reflexes can do." Wesley saw Jack nod at Harlan, like they were involved in a secret plot.

"Don't forget, your wife took out Joey Ferraro," Alex warned Jack, "and he was armed."

Maggie gave Jack a self-satisfied smile.

"Speaking of Joey Ferraro," Wesley said, "what I don't understand is why he didn't change his name. No one would have ever figured out he was the same person as the kid who drowned if he had gotten a different name."

"I think I know why," Alex said. "First of all, these people are arrogant. He didn't want to give up his name because of the prestige and power attached to it. I think he thought that small-town folks wouldn't be smart enough to figure it out."

"But he was wrong," Harlan said.

"He also thought his mob connections would scare everyone away," Alex said.

"That did scare me," Harlan admitted.

"Well, we haven't gotten any death threats yet," Maggie said. "Should we be worried?"

"I don't think so," Alex said. "The talk on the street is that one of the big bosses is going to write us a thank-you note for helping them out. Evidently there was no love lost between them and the Ferraros. Little Joey was getting pretty cocky and starting to move in on their turf. If anything, you just helped them out by getting him out of the way."

"Too bad," Jack quipped. "I was sort of lookin' forward to the witness protection program."

"So what does this mean for Imogene's trial?" Maria asked.

"It means she'll get a new lawyer who's probably just as bad as the last one," Alex said. "But I don't think she has much of a chance of getting off, now that she's a bit short on funds. And believe it or not, Whitney has been a big help providing us with additional information."

"Harlan," Maggie said, "you should invite Whitney to our party. Does she know about the show tonight?"

Jack furtively nudged Maggie's arm and made an X with his two index fingers.

Harlan cleared his throat. "She had to go back to California for a few weeks—to settle some stuff with her mom, but she's coming back. I can watch it with her then."

"Oh," Maggie said, with a tinge of embarrassment. "Do you know when?"

"Last time I spoke with her, she said she wanted to surprise me." Harlan seemed completely oblivious to his being dumped.

Wesley felt bad for him. He knew the chances that Whitney would ever come back to Harlan were slim to none.

"Yeah, that Whitney," Jack said. "She's full of surprises."

"So, Harlan, now that the Ferraros have been indicted for that fraudulent lawsuit they brought against your family sixteen years ago, it looks like your family will have an opportunity to buy the caves back. You think you'll start up with the cave tours again?"

"I was planning on it. My dad died a few years ago, so it's just me, my mom, and my older sister. My sister lives in Virginia, but now she and her husband are talking about moving back and helping me get the business up and running. And if our show gets good ratings tonight, that'll give us some good advertising."

"What do you mean *if* it gets good ratings, mate? This is a worldwide premiere. You better start hiring hordes of people to take care of things already."

* * *

Whitney sat outside under the canopy at the sidewalk café, sipping a frothy iced mug of root beer. She had a few bites of a hamburger and fries left on her plate.

Delphina marched up to Whitney's table, wearing a scowl on her face, along with a halter top, rhinestone-embellished sunglasses, and a zebra-print headband.

"Get up right now. You're coming with me," she said to Whitney.

"Mother! How did you find me here?"

"I've had enough of your little independence tantrum. Now it's time for you to listen to me."

"I don't care what you say. I'm twenty-two years old, and you aren't the boss of me. I'm moving to Georgia."

Several looks and angry stares from surrounding tables forced Delphina to pull up a chair and sit down across from her daughter.

"I cannot believe what I'm hearing. First you hand our diamonds over to Jack Mackey, and now you're planning on running off with some one-legged freak to live in a trailer park in Hicksville. What in the world is wrong with you? I did not raise you throw away your future like this."

"Don't you dare call Harlan a freak. You don't even know him. He doesn't live in a trailer park, and he has a good job. And for your information, marrying the richest man in the world isn't my goal in life."

"So what is your goal in life?"

"To not end up with six ex-husbands like you."

"That's five. You always count Desmond twice."

"Whatever!" Whitney railed. "All I know is that I don't want your life. I want my own life. I'm going to college. And that may not be what you want, but that's how it's going to be."

Delphina took a deep breath and fanned her face with her hand. She then put both hands out in a calming gesture to show that she was under control. "I know I've put a lot of pressure on you, Whitney. But it's only because I want what's best for you. Sometimes it isn't easy to do the things necessary to reach your full potential, dear."

"What *potential*? To be the richest, thinnest, tannest person around?"

"Well certainly not the thinnest if you insist on eating that junk." Delphina motioned to the remains on Whitney's plate. "Is that a *non-diet* soda?"

Whitney nodded.

"Let's be perfectly honest, dear," Delphina said patronizingly. "You just don't have the amplitude for college."

"Thanks, Mom, for letting me know once again that I'm not smart enough. For your information, the correct word isn't *amplitude*—it's *ineptitude*."

"So, you think you're so smart? Just wait until that eighty thousand dollars runs out, and you have no place to turn and no one to take care of you."

"I don't have eighty thousand dollars."

"What? You've spent it already?"

"No, Mom. You know that pink diamond Peter promised me? It was a fake."

Delphina looked like she might pass out.

"Don't look so surprised. I'm not. That's what happens when you hang around with selfish people who only care about money. And that is exactly why I'm moving as far away from you as possible. If you try to stop me, I have several pieces of indiscriminating evidence against you that I can give to the police that will put you jail for at least thirty years."

Delphina opened her mouth and attempted to speak, but no words came out.

"So, that's all I have to say, except that Dad already sent me some money from England. He agreed to pay my tuition, and I've enrolled in some college classes for this fall. I might give you a call when I graduate. I need to go now, because I'm late for something very important." She sipped the last of her root beer very loudly with her straw. She got up from the table and wiped her hands on her napkin, then tossed it onto her plate.

Delphina was completely speechless.

"Oh, just one more thing," Whitney gloated as she slung her purse over her shoulder. "I gained two pounds last week."

32

Diamondback Cave

Everyone gathered in front of the big-screen TV in anticipation of the upcoming Diamondback Cave special when the doorbell rang.

Wesley didn't want any more company right now. He'd been waiting all afternoon to see the show. "Don't get that—it's starting!"

"It might be important," Maggie said.

"Or it's the Girl Scouts," Jack said with annoyance. "Tell 'em to take a hike. We have a two-year supply of cookies."

"It's okay; we're recording it," Maggie said. "I better get it before Emily does." Maggie disappeared down the hall and returned shortly. Bob darted into the room and ran over to the sleeping puppies, checking out the new arrivals.

"Who was it?" Jack asked.

"Just a Girl Scout," Maggie said as Whitney strolled into the room behind her and gave everyone a shy little wave.

Harlan jumped up to make a place for her on the love seat.

"Hey, look what the cat dragged in," Jack said. "I thought you were in California."

"I was, but I'm back," she said. "I hope it's okay to crash your party. I saw the previews on TV yesterday." She squeezed into the seat next to Harlan, who looked elated but not all that surprised to see her. He quickly introduced her to Penny, Walter, Amanda, and Maria.

"We're glad you came," Maggie said. "We've got plenty of food. How about some moo goo gai pan?"

"No, thanks. I already ate."

Wesley felt a bit awkward seeing Whitney after all this time. He had known her for a long time, since she was supposedly his cousin, but he wasn't all that comfortable talking to her now that she was Harlan's girlfriend. She smiled at him, and he felt his face get hot. Luckily the show was starting, so he wouldn't have to think of something to say.

In the first segment of the show, Jack introduced Harlan and showed them the outside of Diamondback Cave. They traveled through the lighted tunnels to the bridge at the north canyon pass and hiked over the bridge and through the tunnel that had been cleared of the blockage from the explosion.

Harlan was a natural on camera and gave some interesting history about the cave. He told them how many hundreds and thousands of years it took to cut out the canyon and form a stalactite. After checking out some millipedes and zooming up on a cave cricket, they headed over to the south canyon pass. Wesley recognized it immediately as the place where they saw Randy. Jack lowered himself down into a deep crevice to explore, leaving Harlan at the top.

"I'm getting claustrophobia just watching this," Maggie said.

"Did you find anything good at the bottom?" Amanda asked.

"Just keep watchin'. You'll see."

Since Jack was alone in the crevice, he was the sole cameraman, and the video got a little shaky. The crevice opened up into a wide cavern tall enough to stand up in. Jack searched through the debris scattered inside.

"This looks like a great place to meet up with some troglodytes," Jack narrated as he waded through two feet of stagnant water at the bottom. "Troglodytes are permanent cave residents that have adapted to the dark cave conditions." He had reached down into the water and scooped up something with his free hand.

"Here we go." Jack showed off a seven-inch pinkish-white salamander with brown spots. "If I'm not mistaken, this little beauty is the Tennessee cave salamander. Look at those lidless eyes. He's nearly blind. But he makes up for it by playin' a mean acoustic guitar. These guys are perfectly adapted to livin' in the dark, damp cave. And right now he probably isn't enjoyin' my visit down here with my bright light." Jack put the salamander back down in the water, and it skirted away.

Jack continued to explore the fissure, telling his audience how this area was like a cracked molar with a cavity at the bottom, where debris could wash in easily but often ended up getting stuck. "So there's no tellin' what I might find down here." Just then he turned around and let out an ear-piercing scream. He dropped the camera in the water, and the picture went black. The show went to a commercial.

"What was that?" Penny shrieked. "What did you see?"

"Not tellin'." Jack smiled. "It's too hideous to describe."

"Come on, tell us," Wesley said.

"Shh!" Jack kept his eyes on the television and told them to be quiet. "This is my favorite used-car commercial." Multiple people bombarded him with couch pillows and threw popcorn at him.

After the group took bets on what was down inside the crevice, ranging from a swarm of vampire bats to the Loch Ness monster, the show came back on. Jack had recovered his camera and illuminated the object of terror.

It was Harlan.

"You won the bet, Walter," Jack said. "It was the Loch Ness monster."

"How did you get down there so fast?" Whitney asked.

While Harlan explained to her that the film had been taken and edited in a three-day span, Jack warned him not to spoil the surprise.

Jack and Harlan continued exploring the depths of the cavity together. Somehow a third member of the party must have joined them, because Jack and Harlan were both in the shot at the same time. It turned out Harlan hadn't hiked down to the bottom of the crevice, but he had swum—or rather slid—through a tunnel connected to the underground pool. He left his artificial leg on, so he'd be able to walk when he got down there. The cameraman had attached a camera to himself and had gone down the same way Harlan had.

"A nature-mode waterslide!" Wesley said. "It looks fun!"

"That is the scariest thing I've ever seen in my life!" Whitney exclaimed.

At the next commercial everyone couldn't wait for more information. "But Harlan," Amanda said. "How did you know that there would be air in that tunnel or where it would even lead?"

"I guess I took a pretty big chance," Harlan said. "But I got to thinking. Joey Ferraro supposedly drowned in the underground pool. There were five other kids with him when it happened, and they never saw him resurface. Unless he got them all to go along with his phony story, it would have had to look like he really drowned. The water starts to get low in June, and that's when he supposedly died. So I figured if there was any chance it could be done, it would have to be in the summer. I jumped in and took a chance."

"You could have been killed!" Whitney scolded, as she put her arms around him protectively.

Harlan seemed to revel in the attention. "Yeah, but even if I had to hold my breath for a minute or two, the underwater current would have spit me out eventually, because it doesn't run into a dead end. I checked the maps and everything before trying it."

"Yeah," Jack said sardonically, "he checked the maps."

"See what I have to live with?" Maggie said to everyone. "This is great. The show's not even over yet, and he always saves the most daring shot for last."

"You think we have something that can top that?" Jack asked. "Wow. This is a tough crowd." He gave Harlan a knowing look.

In the final segment, Jack and Harlan discovered a way to get back to the top without climbing the rope inside the crevice. They ended up back on the ledge at the south canyon passage. It looked very different now that it was completely lit up.

"That's where we were," Wesley proudly told his grandparents.

"Yeah, and that's where Alex and I almost stepped on an eight-foot rattlesnake," Amanda told her mom.

"He wasn't eight feet long," Jack corrected.

"Well, close to it," Amanda assured them.

"Actually, he's closer to twelve," Jack said, just as Randy took the spotlight.

"That's him!" Wesley pointed to the TV. "You got Randy in your show! How did you convince him to come out?"

"We had to cut a deal with the snake union," Jack said, "but Randy eventually agreed to do it for time and a half."

Harlan took over as narrator again on this particular part of the show and used a pole to show off Randy and give the history of how he came to live there. He also warned people to be cautious when exploring any caves or hiking in areas where rattlesnakes live.

Jack added, "Randy may very well be one of the largest diamondback rattlesnakes that have been discovered in the U.S., and Harlan claims there are a few dozen more almost as old. So we might just have to change the stats on how big these rattlers can get." Just then, another snake came out of the rocks behind Jack. Harlan was handling Randy, so Jack had to deal with this one on his own.

As usual, the Snake Stalker kept his cool. The cameraman was shooting from a safe distance, so he zoomed in. "You might think there's no way out of this mess without resorting to violence," Jack said. "But we've got it under control. Right, Harlan?"

"Right," Harlan said as he was busy trying to expel Randy from the pole. "We're guests in their home, so we need to respect their privacy. He shimmied away from Jack. Jack backed up a few inches and then dug

his climbing shoes into a shallow foothold in the nearly vertical rock wall and climbed for a few feet to try
and go around. He couldn't hold onto the rock very
well and started to slip.

Wesley knew his dad would be okay, but he still
held his breath as Jack slid down the rock face and
nearly landed on top of the snake. The snake rattled a
warning and moved into striking position, and Wesley
thought it was inevitable that Jack would take a hit.
But Harlan leaped in between the snake and Jack. The
snake struck Harlan on his lower left leg, and Wesley
knew that's exactly what Harlan had intended.

On television Harlan yelled to Jack, "It's Doris!
Get out of here!"

Jack was in a position where he could have taken
the less dangerous route and headed out on the ledge
toward Randy. He looked at Harlan but seemed reluc-
tant to bail on a friend. Doris reared back, ready for
another attack. She struck at Harlan's right leg this
time, and Harlan quickly dodged out of the way, but
because he was so close to the edge of the cliff, he lost
his balance and fell on top of the ledge. Jack was close
enough on the inside of the ledge to reach over and grab
Harlan's arm to prevent him from rolling off the cliff. As
he did, Doris prepared herself for another attack.

With Jack stooped over and Harlan sprawled out
on the ground, both of their faces were only a few feet
away from Doris. With the two of them well within her
strike zone, the only question now was which one of
them she would try for this time.

Maggie was holding a pillow up to her face. "I can't
stand it!" she wailed.

Jack pulled the pillow away. "You might want to
watch to see if we live or die."

The camera zoomed in so close that Wesley could see Jack and Harlan's reflection in the snake's eyes.

In the next second, Doris struck again. This time she aimed directly at Jack's face. The video went to slow motion, and you could see Doris's inch-long fangs as she prepared to sink them into Jack's cheek. With lightning speed he extended his right hand and caught her around the neck. If the snake could have closed its mouth, it would have bitten him. The video went to freeze-frame, the music started to play, and the credits rolled.

ABOUT THE AUTHOR

K.L. Fogg is a former television news anchor, reporter, and talk show host. She received her bachelor's degree in communications from Brigham Young University and studied for her master's in journalism at the University of Missouri, where she worked for NBC 8. She and her husband, Doug, have three children.